DARKEST PLACE

ALSO BY JAYE FORD

Beyond Fear

Scared Yet?

Blood Secret

Worldwide release soon:

Already Dead

*All titles available now in Aust/NZ

For dates and news on the international release of Jaye Ford thrillers, sign up
for her newsletter on her website www.jayefordauthor.com

DARKEST PLACE

JAYE FORD

Copyright © 2021 by Jaye Ford

ISBN 978-0-6487532-7-8 (paperback)

All rights reserved.

No part of this book may be reproduced in any form or by any electronic or mechanical means, including information storage and retrieval systems, without written permission from the author, except for the use of brief quotations in a book review.

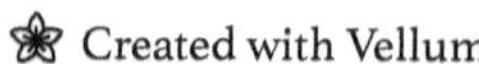 Created with Vellum

Dedicated to perseverance

1

————

Carly scrambled from bed, stumbling and snatching at the darkness, caught between fight and flight.

Where? Where was he?

Listening, straining for sounds, she heard the thump of her heart, the dry gasp of her breath. No taps, no knocks, no bumps. That didn't mean a fucking thing.

Her mobile was in her hand. She didn't remember picking it up. It took three tries to dial the numbers. Forever for a voice to answer. She wanted to shout, managed to pull it back to a hiss. 'There's someone in my apartment.'

'NEWCASTLE POLICE. We received a call about an intruder at this apartment.'

Carly pressed her mouth to the intercom. 'Me. From me. I don't know where he is.'

She hit the release for the security entrance. Finally heard deep, hushed voices in the corridor outside. A thump on the door. She cracked it open and saw two uniforms. Men, waists bulky with equipment, chests heaving from the run up the stairs. Both swept their eyes over her – bare feet, flannel pyjamas, clutching a hair dryer.

'Are you hurt?' one asked.

Stiff shake of her head.

'Is there someone in the apartment with you?'

'I . . . don't know.'

He shot a look over Carly's shoulder into her hallway. His partner checked back the way they had come. A radio crackled with static and Carly's stomach clenched.

'Can we come in?' he asked.

Please. She pulled the door wide, saw guns and handcuffs on their belts. The one who'd spoken found the panel of switches on the wall and flicked on the hall lights. Carly squinted in the sudden glare, her feet itching to run.

'I want you to wait here while we check the apartment,' he said.

Close to the exit, behind cops with guns. 'Okay.'

His partner unclipped a radio mic from his jacket, speaking into it quietly as he passed. Carly stayed by the door as the single bulb in the living room came on. Two more officers appeared in the corridor, a man and a woman, barely acknowledging Carly as they hustled in.

She edged along the wall behind them. There were no drawn guns, no hand signals. One took the stairs to the loft, another turned the key in the handle of the French windows and stepped out. The others shoved at the panes on either side. Had he come in there?

'How long since you saw him?' It was the first guy, back from the loft.

'I . . .' Carly cleared her throat. 'What time is it now?'

'Three twenty-two.'

'It was three something when I looked at my mobile. And that was . . . a minute, I guess, since he'd . . . since he'd been . . .' She touched her throat.

'Okay. Wait there.'

He turned away, speaking fast, indistinct words into his radio. There was a brief conference with the other officers, nods and exchanges and pointing.

Carly pulled her pyjama top tight around her chest and listened to the words they threw around: perimeter search, a car, acronyms she couldn't catch, something about a slow night and more officers turning up for a search of the other floors. She turned her face to the dim night-time lighting beyond her front door, the black void on the other side of the railing. Five stories of old warehouse covering an entire block. There were a thousand places to hide.

'You can come in now,' the first cop said. 'There's no one here.'

Carly walked to the kitchen on shaky legs, turned on the tap and gulped straight from the faucet. The wetness barely touched the dust-dry lining of her mouth. She scrubbed at her cheeks, her neck, snatched up a tea towel, buried her face in it and burst into tears.

'Are you cold?' First Cop asked.

She was shaking all over. It wasn't from the chill in the air but she nodded.

'Can I get an officer to find you some warm clothes? A dressing gown? Socks?'

She saw the motley purple of her feet before registering that they were almost numb. 'There's a dressing gown on a hook upstairs. Uggs near the bed.'

'What's your name?' He was in front of her now, arms slightly raised as though he might need to catch her.

'Charlotte Townsend.' No, she didn't want to be Charlotte tonight. Charlotte was pathetic. 'Carly. Call me Carly.'

'Carly, I'm Dean, okay?' Dark hair little more than stubble, eyes like black coffee. Not a young hotdog: mid-thirties, something kind in his straightforwardness.

'Okay.'

'You want to put down that hair dryer now?'

She was holding it like a huge red handgun, muzzle up, power cord trailing on the floor. It felt stupid now but she couldn't let it go. 'It was all I could find for a weapon.'

'Sure.'

'If I had to hit someone.'

'You could do some damage with that thing.' He took it by the muzzle end, slipped it from her trembling fingers as though he was disarming her and laid it on the kitchen counter where it couldn't hurt anyone. 'Why don't we sit down?'

She walked through the sea of dark uniforms to the single small sofa, feeling anxious and wobbly and pathetic in her green pyjamas with their fat white sheep – thirty-three- year-old woman living alone and wearing a flock of sheep to bed. Dean spoke quietly to the other officers and they dispersed. He produced a notebook and pen and sat knee-to- knee with her.

'Can you tell me what happened, Carly?'

She rubbed at her thighs. 'I woke up and . . . and . . . I . . .' Her brain was buzzing with words, her mouth struggling to let them out. Fast forward and slow motion at the same time. 'He, uh, . . .' A hand fluttered around her neck and cheek. 'Touched me and . . .' She twisted her fingers into a knot. 'He left.'

'You were in your bedroom?'

'Yes.' The hand fluttered above her head in the direction of the loft room.

'He was touching you when you woke up?'

The memory of it – the pressure, the caress – made her shudder. 'He was standing beside the bed.'

'And then he touched you?'

She pressed the tea towel to her lips, trying to force down the pulsing and scrambling inside her. The memory was fuzzy and disorganised, but her throat and cheek burned as though she'd been scorched.

A soft touch at her shoulder made her jump. The female officer was back with Carly's dressing gown and slippers. Wrapped inside them, Carly was warmer but still shaking. She clamped her hands between her knees to contain it.

'I'm going to ask some more about all of that in a minute,' Dean said. 'But first, I want to get some information out to our other patrols. Can you describe the man?'

Carly shook her head.

'I know it's hard, but a description is important.'

'No, I mean I can't. I couldn't see anything.'

'Take a second to think about it, Carly.'

'I don't need to *think* about it. It was *dark*.'

He nodded as though her anger made sense. 'You said he was standing beside the bed. How did you know that?'

'I saw him,' she snapped, then realised that was stupid. 'The shadow of him.'

'Can you tell me what the shadow looked like?'

She scratched the backs of her hands. Tucked them away in the pockets of her dressing gown. 'It was a shadow. It looked like a *shadow*.'

'It's okay, Carly. Relax.' He waited a beat. 'There are patrols driving around. If the intruder is on foot, there's a chance he could be spotted if I can get a description out. Okay?'

She nodded.

'So let's try this. Was the shadow tall?'

'It was . . .' *Think*. 'Tall enough to –' she held hands in front of her face, like she wished she'd done when he was there '– bend over me. And . . . and . . .' He'd breathed on her. 'Man-shaped and thin-ish. Not fat, anyway.'

'What about clothes? What was he wearing?'

'Everything was black. He was a black shape in a black room.'

'Do you think his clothes might have been black?'

She lifted her eyes. 'Yes. That makes sense.'

'What about his head? Was he wearing a cap? Or a hood?'

'It was . . .' Carly used two cupped hands to make an arch over her head. 'A smooth outline. It must have been a hood.'

'What about his face?'

Blinking, trying to see it again, she got . . . nothing. Come on. The warm staleness of his breath had whispered across her face, he must have been close. Really close. She scrunched up her face. 'I don't . . . I just remember black.'

'Could there have been something on his face, like a balaclava?'

'Maybe.' That would explain it. 'I didn't think of that. Yeah, it must have been that.' She smiled a little with relief, until she remembered a man had been in her bedroom with a balaclava and a hood and his hand on her throat. 'Shit.'

'And you thought it was a man?'

'Yes.' Her voice was firm on that one.

'Okay. Wait here a moment.' Dean spoke to the guy he'd arrived with, the only other officer left in the room. He pulled the radio mic from his jacket, turning away as he spoke.

'We're getting a description out,' Dean explained, sitting again. 'How are you doing, Carly? Can you answer some more questions?'

She tugged the lapels of her dressing gown closer, ran a hand through her hair. The limb-jerking had eased up, something shivery taking its place. If answering more questions meant two burly officers would stay for a while longer . . . 'Yes.'

'Is there anything missing from your apartment? Something he might be carrying?'

Her eyes scanned the room: slim pickings if he'd wanted to rob her. 'I don't know, I don't have much.'

'When he was touching you, did you try to push him away?'

Her hands curled into fists.

'Do you think you might've scratched him? Caused some damage we could use for identification?'

She pushed to her feet, arms tight around her waist, stumbling as she got away from the confined space of the sofa and coffee table.

'Carly?' Dean joined her, something gentler in his words. 'I know it's difficult but I have to ask this, for your own sake.' He waited until she'd lifted her gaze. 'Did he hurt you, Carly? Maybe touch you somewhere else?'

She pressed fingers to her lips, her stomach wanting to rise.

He spoke before she could answer. 'I can request a female officer to be here, if you'd prefer.'

'No, it's all right. He didn't rape me, if that's what you're asking. I told you everything, it's just . . . I didn't . . . *do* anything.' She touched the hollow of her throat below the hinge of her jaw. Her fingertips were icy; his had been hard and rough and eager. 'Nothing. I just lay there and let him put his hands on me.'

'Fighting back isn't always the best thing, Carly. You might have saved yourself by keeping still.'

Doing nothing to help herself – she was an expert at that. A tear trickled from the corner of her eye. Dean cocked his head at the sofa, a suggestion she might be more comfortable there. She shook her head, couldn't sit.

'So he stopped touching you and left?' he asked.

'It didn't happen like that. He took his hand away and just . . . stayed there. Bent over me. Watching, I think.'

'You could see him?'

'Not after I closed my eyes.'

'Did he say anything?'

'No.'

'Make a noise?'

'No.'

'And then he left?'

She nodded. 'When I opened my eyes, he was gone.'

2

———————

'Tell me about your doors,' Dean said.

They were standing at the French windows, Carly peering cautiously beyond the balcony into the early morning. There was only one police car in the street now. The neighbourhood was asleep, the unrenovated warehouses hulking and dark.

'Do you usually leave the key in this door?' he asked, pointing at it.

'I've been leaving it there,' Carly told him, 'so I don't have to go searching for it every time I want to open up.'

'Do you usually lock it before you go to bed?'

'I've only been here three nights.'

He raised his eyebrows in a question.

'I've just moved in.' Two whole days, three nights; not long enough to be home, just the promise of somewhere better.

'Where were you before?'

'Out west. North-west really. Past Tamworth.' Eight hours' drive. Another life away.

He glanced around the apartment. 'Is it just you?'

There was one sofa, a coffee table and a small wrought iron table with two matching chairs, meant for outdoors but arranged in her dining space. Maybe he thought there was a partner coming with the rest of the furniture. 'Just me, no baggage.' It was a lie; her baggage was itching under her skin like mites.

'Did you go out last night?'

'I walked around the corner to the supermarket in the afternoon. Cooked dinner, watched a DVD and went to bed.' She'd stood on the balcony, too, and toasted her new life. Maybe a little hasty. 'I locked this door earlier in the night.'

He tried the handle. It was secure but he gave it a shove, testing how hard it might be to force. It didn't budge. 'Did you check it before we got here?'

'Was it unlocked?'

'No. Do you think you might've come over here first? Made sure you were locked in before you called us?'

She hesitated, trying to catch the hazy memory. Remembered she'd thought about the doors when she was staggering on the stairs but her feet had gone the other way. 'I went straight down the hallway. To wait for you.'

'Do you leave a key in the front door too?'

'No, they're in a bowl on the kitchen counter.'

'Are they still there?'

Had he taken her keys? Carly stumbled in her hurry to find them, clutched the bunch in her palm with relief. Talked as she led the cop down the hall to the door. 'I didn't turn the deadlock. I thought it was dangerous to lock yourself in, you know, in case there's a fire and you can't find your keys. Besides, there's no handle on the outside, you need the key to get in.'

'Have you given a key to anyone else?'

'No.'

'Is there a chance the door might not have closed properly? Maybe you just swung it and it didn't catch when you came back from the supermarket.'

Did she have her hands full, or …? She couldn't think that far back now. 'I don't remember. It's not something that's happened before.'

'You've only been here three days.' Dean opened the door a little and gave it a light push towards the jamb. There was a soft metal clack as the bolt met the strike plate but when he pulled on the knob, the latch slipped out of the lock again.

Carly sucked in a breath. 'Shit.' She stared at Dean, then the lock, then back at the cop. 'I *let* him in?' She reeled away. She was a fucking idiot.

'Sometimes it happens like that. Offenders buzz random apartments from the security entrance until someone lets them in, then they wander around until they find a door they can open. You're not far from the stairs, maybe he didn't wander too far.'

Carly rubbed hands over her face. She'd let him in and she'd let him touch her.

'You're okay, Carly. That's the main thing.' Dean signalled his partner. 'And someone in your home is a serious matter, whether you locked your doors or not. I'm going to log your details now and organise fingerprinting and a check of CCTV before my shift ends.' He paused to glance at the dark expanse of the warehouse beyond her door. 'Maybe a canvass of your neighbours. And I'll be recommending your case gets handed over to detectives. You should expect a call later today.'

Carly copied his glimpse at the corridor. 'What if he's still in the building?'

'The building has been searched and there's been a troop of cops through here tonight. That kind of thing usually scares an offender off.' Dean's partner moved between them into the quiet gloom.

Carly lowered her voice. 'What if he lives here?'

Dean made a doubtful face. 'Is there someone you can call?'

'No.'

'A family member? A friend?'

'I don't know anyone in Newcastle.'

'What about your neighbours?'

She hadn't met them yet. She'd barely spoken to anyone since she'd moved in – and she wasn't about to introduce herself at four o'clock in the morning and ask if she could camp on their sofa. 'No, there's no need to wake anyone.'

Dean produced a business card. 'This is my mobile number. Call if you're worried. I'm working until nine but I keep my phone on during the day.' He was through the door by the time he'd finished, held out a hand to shake. It was warm and firm and calm, everything Carly wasn't. 'Lock your doors and try to relax, okay?'

CARLY TOGGLED the deadlock back and forth, gave it a firm tug and pressed her back to it. Held up her hands, eyeing the twitching and jerking of her fingers: her baggage was trembling and breathless inside her.

She didn't need to hide it now, so she let it carry her away, long strides down the hallway and through the living room, unlocking and re-locking the balcony door, keeping the keys in her fist as she moved about. Restless, fearful, searching. She didn't know what she what she was looking for, only that a man had made his way through the apartment to her bedside without waking her. He could have been here for hours.

Wishing she had more lights to switch on, she lifted the cushions on the sofa, looked in the kitchen cupboards, the half bathroom. Then up in the loft: under the bed, in the ensuite, inside the wardrobe. There was nothing except the anxious apprehension crawling under her skin.

She couldn't go back to bed. She was repulsed by the thought of him in her loft, and couldn't risk lying still when she was like this. Hauling at the sheets as though they were infested, she tossed them over the rail for washing later. She wanted a shower to scrub off the memory of him but was scared he'd come back when she was wet and naked so she stalked the apartment instead. Tired but wakeful, drained but hyper, turning on the telly, flicking aimlessly through the channels, shifting from the sofa to the kitchen counter to the wall of checkerboard glass that looked out onto the balcony.

A cup of tea kept her still for fifteen minutes. Another one made her doze fitfully for ten. At six forty, she stood at the windows and watched the sun lighten the sky, her body telling her she needed to be outside, pounding a path. Walking had been her physical and mental therapy for so long it was the first thing her body craved when the agitation started.

She zipped her mobile and keys into the pockets of a jacket and ran the four flights of zigzag stairs to the foyer, her breath steaming in the frosty air when she hit the street. She followed the route she'd taken both previous mornings, a flat, five-minute walk through the old industrial neighbourhood – long strides, arms pumping, focusing on walking, not thinking, like she'd done for years. But by the time she saw the harbour, she was puffing hard. When she reached the restaurants on the boardwalk her legs felt like lead weights and her bones were aching. Not from exertion, not in twenty minutes, but from the effort to keep the itching, scrabbling anxiety at bay. Freaking out could be exhausting, she reminded herself. She was only halfway to the headland but gave up punishing herself and ordered a cappuccino at the last cafe in the row.

She'd been there twice, it had gas heaters out front and a brew that made her blood flow. Today, she sat at a table with a warm cup between her palms, watching a tugboat rock and roll in the wake of a container ship and trying to talk herself to calmness.

It wasn't about her, she told herself. She'd paid for her sins. She couldn't change the past but she could begin again. It was why she was here. Why she'd walked away from everything she knew, the small town where her guilt and pain were a part of the collective memory. Where every day was a reminder of what she'd done and who she'd been.

'Perfect morning for soaking up C's and D's,' a waiter said as he collected her cup.

'C's and D's?'

'Caffeine and vitamin D, essential for good winter health. I'm Reuben, by the way. I'm here every morning.' He dropped the newspaper from under his arm onto Carly's table. 'Stay as long as you like, we're having a quiet one today.'

'Thanks.'

'Another coffee?'

Carly glanced at the path back, not ready to return. 'Yes, please.' Her lovely apartment in the renovated warehouse was meant to be inspirational, a metaphor for her own renewal. But the image wasn't so appealing now. Yes, it was her fault the door was unlocked, but that didn't change the fact that someone had pushed it open and walked in. All the way to her bedside. A man who had snuck past the security entrance, or a neighbour. Not your average *Oh look, that door's not closed properly* neighbour but someone who saw it and took advantage. A creepy guy she lived with.

3

───────

The warehouse looked like a warehouse on the outside: red brick, flat facade, the peaks and troughs of a sawtooth roof. Old, industrial, ugly. It was the inside that had sold itself to Carly.

Walking through the hush of the foyer, her runners making soft squelching sounds on the polished floors, she stopped in a warm pool of sunlight and tipped her face to the ceiling. *This* was what had sold her before she'd even seen the apartment.

Five storeys of eighty-year-old warehouse: original timbers, the floors stacked like the layers of an enormous cake around a huge square of open space. It'd been a bond store, holding goods for import and export, anything from mine machinery to packaged food, the stuff shuffled around by cranes, up and down through the centre of the building. Now, with the machinery gone, the hollow middle became a massive atrium that looked straight up to vast sheets of glass in the sawtooth ceiling – and the sky looked back, filling the shaft with a cascade of natural light. Staircases zigzagged upwards, suspended walkways connected the landings, and a forest of old timber columns supported the first floor. Standing at the bottom, Carly felt like she was at the base of a labyrinth.

'The light is fascinating, isn't it?'

The voice came from behind her, and as Carly turned, pushing the lethargy and headache to one side, she reminded herself she had no past here, she could be who she wanted. An older woman was sitting on a bench near the lift. She'd been there yesterday, back straight, well dressed, observing the comings and goings like a gate-keeper. Carly wondered if she was the first branch in the warehouse grapevine – and whether she'd heard about the police arrival during the night.

'Yes, beautiful,' Carly said.

'I had to argue for this seat to be installed, but it was worth it, and not just for old ladies like me to rest.' She shuffled awkwardly to the edge of the seat, placing her feet carefully, knocking a lumpy grocery bag to the floor. Carly skipped a few steps through the shadows to help, then stopped, warned off by the determined hand the woman held up. 'Thank you, but while I can still manage my shopping without assistance, I intend to do so.'

Carly watched the woman's painstaking progress, noticing sensible walking shoes under nice trousers, the white blouse and red blazer, a chunk of dark blue rock at her throat. When she was on her feet, Carly skirted around her and pressed the button for the lift.

'Are you waiting for the elevator?' the woman asked. 'Or assuming I can't press the button myself?'

It was headmistress condescension mixed with old lady uppity, and Carly couldn't tell if the woman was actually incensed or it was her usual manner of speech. But she saw the wince on her lined face as she leaned on a walking stick and figured she deserved some leeway.

'I'll ride with you, if that's okay,' Carly said.

The woman took a moment to assess her before hobbling into the cab, claiming a place at the control panel as though making a point. She lit up the button for the second level then looked at Carly.

'Four, please.'

'So you're our new resident.'

She'd been discussed already? 'Yes. I moved in on Monday.'

'The east wall, I believe.'

'That's right.'

'You have a harbour view.'

Maybe she hadn't heard about the police. 'A slice of it. And I can see the tops of some yachts.'

'The marina. I don't have that pleasure. I'm on the north wall, where we enjoy the sunshine through winter.' The woman tipped her head back and looked at Carly through the bottom of her glasses. 'And where have you come from?'

'Out west.'

'Do you have family here?'

'No. I don't know anyone.'

'Are you here for work?'

Was she writing a report? 'No, I'm enrolled at the TAFE campus. I start next week.'

'I see.' The lift jolted to a stop. 'Do you read?'

Carly figured she wasn't asking if she was literate. 'Fiction, yes.'

As she stepped out, the woman held a gnarly hand to one door to keep it open. 'I host a small book club for residents. Members are usually required to read the selected title but for July we are celebrating the life of Charles Dickens. Our next meeting is on Tuesday evening. If you've read Dickens, you're welcome to join us.'

A part of Carly wanted to break out a goofy smile but she kept it cautious and polite. 'Thank you. I'd like to.' She hadn't read Dickens since school but she had a week to rectify that.

'Apartment 109. I'll expect you at seven fifteen sharp. I'm Elizabeth Jennings.' She held her bony hand out to shake.

'Lovely to meet you, Elizabeth. I'm Carly Townsend, apartment 419.' Yes, she'd be Carly here.

When the doors had closed and all Carly could see was her own reflection in the stainless steel, she said, 'Day Three of her new life and Charlotte decides to be Carly, who meets a neighbour and receives an invitation.' She grinned then. 'And Carly laughs to herself as she rides the lift to her new apartment.'

·   ·   ·

Her moment of joy slipped away as the elevator opened on the fourth floor. On the other side of the atrium, a man was at her front door. Palm on the wall, head lowered like he was listening.

She hesitated outside the cab, a twinge of agitation in her belly. He must have heard the lift because he turned, and she realised it was her neighbour. They hadn't met, but Carly had seen him leaving his apartment once and yesterday he'd passed her at the top of the stairs with a tight-lipped nod. Last night, as she stood on her balcony with her glass of red, she'd spotted his battered leather jacket rounding the corner at the end of the street. Hands jammed into the pockets, slight limp, a tense stalk.

Now, as he started across the suspended walkway towards her, his forceful stride made her want to call the lift back. She held her ground as he got closer, measuring him up against the shape beside her bed. *Tall enough, not fat, man-shaped*. He was all of those things. So was a quarter of the population.

His first words: 'I saw cops at your place during the night.'

Was it a complaint? Maybe it'd been him and he wasn't happy.

'You all right?' he asked.

It was concern? 'I had a break-in. I'm fine, thanks.'

His eyes flicked over her as though he was making sure, then he seemed to relax. He wasn't so scary, then. He was wiry and tanned. If he'd been thirty years older, she might have called him grizzled.

'We're neighbours, right?' Carly asked.

'Yeah, sorry. I'm Nate,' he said, as though he'd just realised the rush across the walkway was a little weird. He held out a hand.

She felt the rasp of tough, work-roughened skin. 'Carly.'

'A break-in? And it took them until after three to get here?'

'Oh, no, it was during the night. They were here in a few minutes.'

He frowned. 'Someone broke in while you were there?'

'Yes.'

'You sure you're all right?'

Tired and freaked out, but she gave him her standard answer. 'Yeah, sure.' She'd spent thirteen years enduring in silence whatever was thrown at her. She had no right to complain – she was alive, her friends were dead.

'How did he get in?'

'I might've left the front door open.' A shrug, making light of her mistake. 'Not wide open. Just not closed properly. The police thought someone might've been buzzed in downstairs and wandered around until they found an open door.'

Dark blue eyes watched her a moment. 'Are your locks okay? I could take a look at them.'

A prickle at the back of her neck: she didn't know him, she didn't want him in her apartment. 'They're fine. It was user error.'

A nod, a pause, like maybe there was more, then he was walking away, heading for the stairs.

THE POLICE CAME in the afternoon. A forensics officer first, who Carly watched from across the living room as he bent over the doorknob on the balcony, wondering if someone else had done the same thing twelve hours earlier.

Two detectives arrived as Carly was seeing him out. A tall, broad-shouldered woman called Anne Long and a shorter, younger man introduced as Elliot. Carly offered to make coffee, needing something to cut through the lingering fuzziness in her head before they started asking questions.

She showed them the locks and the loft while the kettle was boiling, climbing the stairs to her bedroom like she weighed three tonnes. The energy low that had hit on the walk had hung around, making her listless and dozy. She'd had things to do – sorting cupboards, unpacking boxes – and had ended up doing none of them. At other times, when the agitation had been bad, she'd gone for days before exhaustion wore it out.

Carly swallowed a couple of painkillers while she waited for the cafetiere to brew.

'What's that you're taking?' Anne asked.

The tone was polite but Carly had heard it before. 'Paracetamol.' She said it slowly, clearly, an edge to her voice. 'I've got a *headache*.'

The woman lifted a hand. 'Just making sure you're okay.'

There was just enough furniture for them all to sit, Carly and Anne on the sofa, Elliot on a chair from the wrought iron outdoor setting.

'Nice place.' Anne glanced around, getting settled.

Nice? It looked like something from a glossy magazine with Paris or New York in the captions. Exposed brick, soaring ceilings, timber floors, stainless steel kitchen, industrial staircase. Even today it could start a smile at the corner of Carly's mouth. She owned it, she lived here, she'd done it. 'Thanks.'

With Anne asking questions and Elliot taking notes, Carly talked them through the events of the early morning. When she was done, Anne took a moment to flip through the pages of a notebook she took from her bag.

'Constable Quentin said you were unable to give a detailed description of your intruder.' She read from handwritten notes. 'You said he was tall enough to bend over the bed, thin-ish, not fat. Possibly wearing black clothes, possibly a hoodie and balaclava.' She looked up. 'I imagine you were pretty shaken up last night. Would you like to add anything to that now?'

'I wish I could but like I told Dean – Constable Quentin – it was dark. Really dark.'

Anne's lips tightened briefly. It made heat rise to Carly's cheeks.

'I think the clothes and the mask are more than a possible,' Carly added, wanting to do better. 'I mean, I've been thinking about what I saw and there was definitely something over his head.' She made the arch shape over her own head with cupped hands again. 'I don't know it if was a *hoodie*, like on a sweatshirt. It might've been a jacket or a coat, but there was a hood.'

'You saw the hood?'

'I saw the *shape* of a hood. Also his face was black, solid like the hood. A balaclava is the only explanation for that. So I'd definitely say a hood and balaclava.'

The detective said nothing for a moment, taking her time to finish the remains of her coffee. 'And you're certain it was a man?'

'Yes. Absolutely.'

'I'm wondering about that, Carly. The intruder was close enough to breathe on you but you didn't actually see the hood and mask. Yet you're sure it was a man.'

'Yes.' It was the only thing she was sure of.

'There's no chance it *might* have been a woman?'

'No.'

'Can you tell me why you think that?'

Carly folded her arms, irritated at the scepticism in the detective's voice.

'See, it's just' – Anne held up a palm – 'I've got big hands and I'm tall. I've been mistaken for a man once or twice.'

The detective beside her spoke for the first time since they'd sat down. 'She's being modest. She's mistaken for a man all the time.'

The two cops exchanged a chuckle. 'He's just jealous.' She rolled her eyes at Carly. 'So do you think there's any chance it might've been a woman?'

If the joking was a tactic to make Carly reconsider, it worked. Her mind rewound, remembering the heart pounding, the ragged breathing and the shadow looming over her face. She pressed her spine into the sofa as though he was there now and she was cowering. 'The smell of him, his breath . . .' She shook her head, rubbed her arms. 'The hand, it was big, yes, but the way he touched me – it was rough and it was a caress. My ex-husband used to do that.' She glanced away, annoyed she'd thought of Adrian. Annoyed her conviction was wavering. 'I suppose it could've been a woman but I thought it was a man.'

'Okay. Thanks, Carly.'

She saw the *Let's go* look Anne shot at her partner and spoke up before either of them could move. 'Should I be worried about my neighbours?'

'Do you think it was a neighbour?'

'If he pushed open my front door, he was already in the building. That could mean a neighbour.'

'Okay, look.' Anne reached to the coffee table, laid her notebook across the top of her handbag. 'I will tell you there have been other break-ins here.'

'In my apartment?' Carly glanced at the French windows. Why hadn't anyone told her? *Before* she bought it?

Anne held up a palm like a stop sign. 'I meant at the warehouse, not *your* apartment. And not recently. The last incidents were almost twelve months ago.'

Okay. Right. 'Incidents? Plural? Was anyone hurt?'

'No. No assault involved. There were some items listed as stolen. A couple of residents reported seeing the intruder.'

'In their bedrooms?'

Anne answered slowly, as though Carly might startle. 'Yes, there were some reports of a person in the bedroom.'

Oh geez. She interlaced her fingers, clasped her hands tight together. 'Did he . . . *touch* them?'

'There were no reports of that.'

'What did he do?'

A small hesitation. 'He probably searched for money and jewellery.'

Probably? 'And what? He got away with it so now he's getting gamer?'

'No, look – ' another stop sign ' – it's sporadic incidents. Eight or nine over the six years there've been apartments here. Which suggests, firstly, it's not one of your neighbours. And secondly, some of the victims described the intruder as a woman, which suggests it's not the same person. It's more likely different offenders getting access to the building. They're nice apartments, they probably think there's something worth stealing.' She shifted to the edge of the sofa, picked up her handbag.

'He didn't take anything last night,' Carly said.

'No.'

'He leaned over my bed and touched my face.'

'Yes.' Anne stood .

That can't be it. Carly got to her feet too, speaking quickly. 'Detective Quentin said something about CCTV and a canvass of my neighbours.'

Hoisting her bag to her shoulder as she spoke, Anne said, 'As it turns out, there is no CCTV for the building and nothing nearby that's useful. And a door knock for information about someone who might have been buzzed in isn't practical for an apartment complex of this size.'

Carly nodded reluctantly – it made sense, it just didn't make her feel any better.

'All sorts of people get into the abandoned warehouses around here,' Anne continued. 'Sometimes they break into people's homes. The best thing you can do, Carly, is keep your door locked.'

She didn't say the rest but Carly heard it anyway: *Like you should have done last night.*

On the way out, Anne took another glance around the high ceilings. 'Is there a building supervisor here?'

'Yes.' Though Carly hadn't met him yet.

'You could have a chat to him about making sure the residents only let in people they know.'

'Okay, I will.' Carly shook their hands like they'd been doing business. Had one last question. 'In those other break-ins, did the intruder ever go back to the same apartment?'

'Several victims did report repeat break-ins.' Anne held up a hand like a pre-emptory warning. 'It's not clear if it was the same intruder.'

'Several victims?' The detective could pat the air all she liked, the information had landed like a bomb in Carly's chest. 'The ones who saw someone in their *bedroom*?'

'There are discrepancies between your account and the old ones. I don't think it's something you need to worry about.'

'What did the other people report?'

'My advice, Carly, is to keep your doors locked and have a chat to your building supervisor.'

Carly watched their departing backs, wishing she knew more.

Wishing she'd done a better job of the description. Wishing she'd shut the damn door in the first place.

A soft laugh travelled across the atrium as the two detectives waited for the lift. Possibly they were reliving Elliot's *mistaken for a man crack*. And possibly they were saying *Crap witness, stupid woman, deserves to have someone walk in.*

4

___

'Yo.'

It was the first time Carly had heard anything but a voicemail message on the building supervisor's phone. 'Howard Helyer?' she asked.

'You got him.'

She'd imagined an old guy getting a few bucks off his rent to act as live-in supervisor. But Yo? 'It's Charlotte Townsend. I moved into 419 on Monday.'

'Yeah.'

'I've been trying to get in touch with you.'

'Yeah.'

She frowned. 'About my garage pass not working properly?' That was three days ago. Then more messages, that she needed light bulbs replaced and a key for her mailbox and the garage pass still didn't work.

A pause. 'Ah . . .'

'Yeah,' she threw right back at him.

'That. Right. Come see me and I'll sort it.'

'And light bulbs?'

'Hardware store in Baxter Street.'

'That's not part of the service?'

'What service?'

Yeah, exactly. 'Replacing bulbs. Is that your job?' *Ten metre ceilings? Broken necks? Building supervisor?*

'You can do it if you want.'

'I'd need a ladder.'

'Hardware store in Baxter Street.'

Amusement edged its way into her irritation. 'I don't want to *buy* one.'

'Right, right. There's a couple in the storage room.'

She held her breath, afraid to ask. 'Where is the storeroom?'

Another round of absurd Q&A got her directions to a door on the ground floor. She wondered if it was pointless to talk to him about anything else, but . . . 'About building security – I had a break-in the other night, and the police thought someone might have been buzzed in through the front door.'

There was some throat-clearing and phone-bumping. She hoped he was shaking off whatever his problem was, not falling over. 'You okay?' he asked.

'Fine. You didn't notice the sirens and flashing lights?'

'I'm on the west wall, the east wall could be falling down and I wouldn't know. Wouldn't have checked anyway. The police are always dropping by the empty warehouses. People get in and make a mess and the cops like to make their presence felt. Most of us are pretty happy about that.'

Message received: don't expect the building supervisor to rush to your aid. 'Glad my drama didn't wake the whole building,' Carly said. Actually, more than glad. No need for it to be the topic of discussion in the corridors. She hadn't come here to attract attention.

'Was anything taken?'

Carly gave him a potted version: intruder comes in, she calls triple-O, no sign of the bad guy. And the police theory – he buzzes apartments, someone lets him in, he finds her door. Howard was the building supervisor, he should probably know it all. 'I, ah, might not have shut my door properly.'

'Easy done,' he said. 'I've gotten up in the morning once or twice and found mine wide open.'

No surprise in that, if this conversation was anything to go by. 'Is there some way you can contact the residents? I thought maybe you could send a reminder not to buzz in strangers.'

'Yeah, yeah, good idea. There's an email list. I haven't used it in a while, I don't know how up to date it is but I can get something out.'

How long would that take? 'Can you put me on it too?'

HOWARD HELYER'S directions were as bad as his supervision skills. The storeroom wasn't where he'd said it was and Carly walked around the shadows and hush of the ground floor, trying her key at any door that didn't look like an apartment.

The storeroom was in the corner of the east and south walls, crammed with hand tools and cleaning products and, well, a lot of stuff, including several ladders. Carly half-dragged one across the foyer to the lift, had several goes at getting it into the cab before deciding it was never going to fit. Looked up at the stacked levels above her and groaned.

Her heart was pounding by the time she reached the first floor. At the turn on the way on the second, she had to stop for a breather. Halfway to the third she put the ladder down and leaned on the railing, sucking at the air in the atrium.

A door opened and closed somewhere above. The echo of heavy footfalls rolled down through the great hollow space beside her. Then they were vibrating around her, coming down the stairs – and the ladder took up all the space on the landing. She wiped sweat from her lip, tried to shove the unwieldy hunk of metal to one side and prepared to apologise.

Nate, her neighbour, swung around the end of the staircase and pulled up short. The grim, tight mood she'd seen on him before seemed to shimmer around him for half a second before he reined it in.

Carly smiled cautiously. 'Sorry, just taking a breather. I hope you can get around.'

He started towards her, stopping a couple of stairs from the landing. 'Need a hand?'

God, yes, but she saw the taut set of his face. This guy didn't need the hassle of someone else's ladder in his day. 'I'm almost there. And you sound like you're in a hurry.'

'I've got time.'

And it'd take her twenty minutes to drag it up there. 'The feminist in me wants to tell you I've got it all under control but that would be a lie,' she laughed, trying to inject a little neighbourly humour into it.

'You going up or down?'

Right, no humour. 'Up.' She shuffled backwards, picked up the legs. 'Ready when you are.'

Nate hesitated a second before taking up the other end. It was a bit clumsy but they manoeuvred it around the turn and bumped unevenly to the third floor corridor. He lowered his section and waited for her to follow suit. He must have thought she needed a rest.

'I'm fine,' she told him.

Something stirred behind his eyes. 'I think I can manage on my own.'

'You sure? It's pretty unwieldy.'

'How about I give it a go?'

She stepped out of the way and Nate picked it up. The whole thing, with one hand. Oh, right. Tucking it under an arm like it was made of cardboard, he made the turn on the landing as though he negotiated it every day and leaned the ladder against the wall outside Carly's apartment.

'Changing light bulbs?' he asked as she unlocked the door.

'Yes. I guess it's why most people need a ladder around here.'

'The building supervisor usually helps out with that.'

'I wondered about that.'

She pushed the door, turned to get the ladder, but he did it for her, under the arm and down the hallway. Uneasiness beat in her chest as he disappeared into her living room. She left the door open, hoping he'd set the steps down and leave, wondering if he'd invited himself in to take a look around – or if he'd been there before, in the dark. When she got there, he had set the ladder under the empty socket by the French windows.

'You want to do the climbing or passing?' he asked.

He wanted to change the bulbs too? 'Thanks, but I can do that bit myself.'

'Never thought you couldn't but if we get it done now, I can take the ladder back on my way out.'

Oh.

'Or you can take it down later when you're done. Up to you.'

'Gee, it's a tough call,' she gave an uncertain laugh. *Not one of your neighbours*, Anne Long said. And that ladder was heavy. 'Okay, I'll do the passing. Thanks.' He couldn't do anything too daunting up a ladder.

He was at the top and waiting by the time she'd fetched the bag of replacements. 'I was planning to change them all,' she said.

'Okay.' He reached down for a bulb.

Carly stretched up with a new one. 'If you've got the time.'

'Uh-huh.' Arms overhead, then pointing at the wall. 'Flick the switch.' He paused long enough for the globe to light up then moved the ladder and started climbing again.

'Only two worked when I moved in,' Carly said as she passed up another one. 'I was starting to feel nocturnal.'

'Uh-huh.' He pointed at the switch.

She skipped across the room, amused now by his sign language. He shifted to the next light fitting without a word. Not a weird, tense silence, he just seemed short on words. And more at ease now he was working. She didn't mind his brevity, no room for bullshit in brevity.

'Any suggestions for a good pub?' she asked, interested in the kind of answer she'd get.

He reached down with a dusty bulb. 'Beer's cold at the one around the corner. That's about all I can say for it.'

Two sentences, not bad. 'Where do you drink?'

'Pub round the corner.'

Wasn't after company then. 'Restaurants?'

'Couldn't answer that.'

'Library? I need a book.'

'Nah, sorry.' He started down again. 'I haven't spent much time here.'

'You're new, too?'

'No.' He picked up the ladder, talked as he walked with it. 'Had the apartment four years but I work offshore. Don't get back too often.'

'Offshore as in overseas?'

'As in an oil rig. Technically it's still in the country.'

Carly raised her eyebrows as he resettled the ladder, adding the information to the sun-bleached hair and the lines in his tanned face. The furthest she'd been on the ocean was a ferry ride across Sydney Harbour as a kid. She'd heaved over the side. 'Sounds . . .' she had no idea '. . . amazing.'

His eyes caught hers through the metalwork. 'Long hours, hard work and cramped quarters. Not that amazing.'

Right. 'How long are you here this time?'

'Not sure. A while. Maybe permanently. I'm waiting on a medical.' There was a little more force in his steps as he went up, a muscle at the side of his jaw pumping as he reached for the next bulb.

Carly couldn't tell if going back or staying was the problem, wondered if that's what his limp and grimness were about. 'I hope it's good news.'

He didn't answer, clearly finished talking about it.

'What's the story with the building supervisor?' she asked.

'Howard Helyer?' His voice was muffled behind outstretched arms.

'Yeah. What does he actually do here?'

'Supervise stuff.'

Not that she'd seen. 'Is he . . . the full quid?'

Nate paused, one foot on the floor. 'Howard?'

'Yes.'

'His IQ wouldn't fit in my head.'

'Howard? The supervisor?'

'He's been at uni for about ten years.'

Carly had done three semesters at uni, had met professional students. 'Doing a PhD in partying?'

Nate huffed a quiet chuckle as he picked up the ladder again. 'No. He's already got a PhD in physics, now he's finishing a double degree in engineering and biomedical science.'

Huh. 'Well, I had a really weird conversation with him just now. He sounded . . . hung-over.'

'He doesn't drink. Must have exams.'

Out of questions for the moment, Carly just watched. She had no idea what someone might do on an oil rig but she pictured him with a hard hat, under a burning sun, buffeted by stiff wind off the ocean. Maybe his curtness was the result – or maybe his disposition suited the lifestyle.

'Loft?' he asked.

Carly glanced at the stairs, remembering her blind panic, unsure about Nate going up there. He stood at the bottom, waiting for her decision. Don't be neurotic. There was only one working globe in the bedroom.

'Yeah, sure.'

She went up ahead of him, hoping she hadn't left underwear lying about, chucking her pyjamas into the ensuite as he appeared at the top of the stairs. Another man might have made a joke, some kind of *Well, here we are then*, but Nate avoided her eyes, opened out the ladder beside the bed and climbed. Maybe he was as happy to ignore the loaded bedroom moment as she was.

'At least it'll be a soft landing if you fall,' Carly said when he leaned out over the mattress.

'I don't plan to fall.'

It was meant to be banter but his words felt like a swift slap, the thought making her heart pound. *No one does.*

Maybe Nate had noticed the way she'd grabbed for the handrail at the top of the stairs as though she was the one at risk, because he changed the subject this time. 'Got any more of those questions I can't answer?'

She smiled, glad to be moved on. 'See if you can't answer this. Do you know where the cinema is?'

'Nope.'

'Fresh fish?' Out west, fresh meant eight hours in a refrigerated truck.

'Co-op near the marina.'

Ten minutes' walk. 'Excellent. Nearest takeaway?'

'Indian, around the corner in Baxter Street. Butter chicken is good, vindaloo will burn your throat out.'

'Good to know. Do you know who my neighbour on the other side is?'

'Big guy, walking stick. District court judge, only here three nights a week.' Then he was back on the floor beside her, no bulbs left.

'We done?' he asked.

'I think that's it.' She followed him down the stairs. 'What have I made you late for?'

'Not late. The pub.'

'The one with cold beer and nothing else to recommend it?'

'That's it.'

'Then I hope the fridges aren't broken.'

He stopped at the door and huffed a quiet laugh. He looked better for it, his face a little less rigid.

'Have a good afternoon, Nate,' she said.

'You too, Carly.'

5

―――――

It was late in the day when Carly crossed the foyer carrying her dinner – fish from the co-op and locally made sorbet from the little supermarket in Baxter Street. Elizabeth Jennings was sitting on her bench.

'And this is the young person I was telling you about.' The words were meant for the woman beside her but carried around the foyer like an announcement.

Elizabeth's companion smoothed her sensible grey hair and straightened her jumper. 'Hello, hello there.'

'Carly,' Elizabeth said in her schoolmarm voice. 'May I introduce you to Christina Matheson, a stalwart of our book club. Christina, this is Carly Townsend, our newest resident.'

Age might be troubling Elizabeth's joints but it hadn't affected her memory, Carly thought. 'Hello again, Elizabeth. Nice to meet you, Christina.'

'Welcome to the warehouse.' Christina said it with a chortle, all rather amusing. 'Elizabeth has been telling me you're joining us for our Dickens night.' She was short and wide, wore joggers and ribbed tights with a denim skirt, her voice fast and breathy as though she'd been running.

'Yes, I'm looking forward to it.'

'Christina is a book reviewer,' Elizabeth said.

A serious book club, Carly thought. 'Really?' She smiled, hoping neither of them asked her about Dickens now. Like a test. 'Oh look, here's the lift.'

'It's been and gone three times since I got talking,' Christina laughed. 'I really must get in this time.'

'Elizabeth, do you . . .' Carly almost said *need a hand* before remembering the woman's reaction last time. 'Are you going up?'

'Thank you, Carly, but I'll enjoy the light for a few moments more.'

As the doors closed, Christina hit the buttons for the fourth and fifth floors – she must live in one of the big apartments at the top of the warehouse. 'I've got multiple copies of Dickens,' she said. 'I can drop a couple off to you.'

'That's not necessary . . .'

'Which one would you like? Or I can give you a selection. Yes, I think that's best. Too hard to decide on the fly, don't you think?'

'Yes, but . . .'

'Are you enjoying the apartment?'

'Yes, it's . . .'

'Lovely to have someone in Talia's apartment. A dear, dear girl, such a dreadful way to leave, and not getting to say goodbye. We all wished we could have, signing the card Brooke sent around just wasn't the same thing. I could hear little Talia playing up on the fifth floor corridor, you know. Sometimes I'd take the long way to the lift just to listen. She was a member of our book club, too, and we miss her contribution. Oh, it's been hard on Brooke. Have you met Brooke yet?'

'No, I . . .'

'She'll be glad someone has moved in. I think knowing the place was still empty made it harder for her. She's about your age. You'll know her when you see her. She's the one with the crutches. She'll be at the Dickens night too. Here's your floor.'

Carly stepped out, turned to say goodbye.

'Lovely to meet you, Carly. I'll get those books to you quick smart. Should be a lively discussion on . . .'

The doors closed. Carly grinned. 'Wow, speed talking.' Maybe Christina was the reason Elizabeth had decided to enjoy the light for a while longer.

Christina obviously thought Carly knew more than she did about the woman who'd lived in her apartment. It was the first time Carly had heard the name Talia. All the real estate agent had said was that she'd studied at the Conservatorium, went back to Perth unexpectedly and the property had sat empty for six months – a shame because the single-bedroom lofts were always snapped up.

Opening her apartment, the soft clack of the lock, the deep gloom beyond the door made her scalp tingle with wariness. She pushed the door wide, reached in and flicked the light switches, all of them, a bold glare filling the long hallway, thanks to Nate. The dimness at the other end held her gaze for a moment. Her doors had been locked, she told herself. No one could get in with the doors locked . . . unless they'd copied her key or . . . *Don't start, Carly.* She locked the door, walked the hallway feeling like there were eyes on her back, lit the apartment up like a showroom. *Empty, see?* Still, she turned on the lights over the stairs and in the loft, tipping her head back to look into the bedroom. *Happy now?*

When the fish was in the oven, Carly pulled on a jacket, poured a glass of wine and stepped onto the balcony for the first time since the police had been there. It was cold and breezy, a salty tang from the harbour in the air.

The phone in her pocket buzzed an incoming text. She took a large, bracing mouthful of wine before she pulled it from her pocket.

Are you okay? Have you found a doctor? You can come back, you know. Selina and the kids send their love. Call me, I'm your mother.

Carly closed her eyes, clenched her teeth. She was never going back. She shouldn't have gone back the last time. A long weekend had turned into thirteen years of pain and tragedy and punishment. Everything she'd wanted for herself had been ruined by her own bloodied hands, the proof of it in the lives of the people she'd seen every day.

She took another sip, not managing to swallow down the irritation. Her mother had never understood why Carly couldn't just get over it. *You didn't do it on purpose*, she'd say. Then, *You can't have everything you want, no one can.* Then she didn't trust Carly to get over anything.

Her mother would keep texting until she got a reply so Carly finished her wine and stabbed out a message: *I'm fine. The apartment is fine. I'll call when I'm ready.* Carly fixed her eyes to the view, battling the temptation to think about it, to feel the familiar cold sweat of guilt. Recrimination was a habit; it was easier than being kind to herself. But it was time now, she reminded herself. She'd endured her punishment and she'd left that version of herself behind in Burden.

Turning, she let her gaze rest on the apartment glowing under its new lights and thought of Talia, the woman who'd played music here. Carly imagined something classical and soulful filling the air, wondered what disastrous event had sent her back to Perth. She felt sorry for Talia that she'd had to leave this – and grateful she had. Lifting her glass in a toast, Carly said, 'Have a good life, Talia. I owe you one.'

A MAN and a little girl were at the warehouse security entrance when Carly reached it, out of breath from the fast walk back from the harbour. The pair had matching blond curls. The man was buzzing an apartment, plastic shopping bags and a pink teddy bear in his hand. The little girl was pulling faces in the glass door.

'I forgot my key,' he announced into the intercom.

'Again?' a woman replied and the entry door clicked open.

Was that all it took to get someone to release the lock? A friendly voice and an excuse? There'd been no email from Howard this morning and he hadn't answered his door when Carly had knocked on her way out. It was sloppy. Her neighbours should be warned.

'I'm going to be a tiger today,' the little girl said, tipping her head back to tell Carly.

'Lucky you.' Carly pulled the security door closed, checked it had engaged, and crossed the foyer behind them. The girl skipped through the shadows, holding the man's hand, all skinny legs and bouncing curls. The sight made Carly's palms prickle with heat, the familiar yearning for small fingers to hold. She'd wanted to leave that in Burden, too.

'Last time I was a clown,' the girl said as Carly waited for the lift with them. 'And the time before that I was a pirate.'

'Wow, you get to be lots of things.' Carly returned the man's amused smile.

'I've been practising my growl.' The girl clawed the air, making a sound that was halfway between a gurgle and a cough.

Carly jumped, hands to her mouth in horror. 'Gosh, you scared me.'

'It's okay. I'm not a tiger yet. I have to get the goo first.'

'Of course you do.'

'Face paint.' The father said, tapping the button for the second floor. 'At the markets.'

'There are markets?'

'In the primary school.' He hitched a thumb over his shoulder. 'Every Saturday.'

'I'm going to school there next year,' the girl chipped in. 'We live on the second floor. Where do you live?'

'I'm on the fourth floor.'

'My name's Alice. What's yours?'

'Hi, Alice. I'm Carly.'

'Oh, *you're* Carly,' the man said, his tone more like finger-pointing than identification.

She hesitated. 'Yes.'

'We got the email last night. I didn't know anyone had moved into that apartment.'

'Email?' Last night?

'The group one from Howard.' He reached for Alice's hand as the doors started their opening slide. 'We get a bit lax with security around here. It's not like we're in Sydney. Best to keep yourself locked in if you're nervous.' He shrugged as he stepped out, dismissive, not apologetic. Alice took a standing jump over the door tracks. 'It wasn't us, by the way,' he said.

Carly kept a smile on her face until they were out of sight. 'What the hell?' Why hadn't she got the email? And what had Howard told everyone?

There was still no email five minutes later when she checked her laptop. Had he written about her, not to her? She headed back to the lift, planning another discussion with Howard. But as she stepped out on the ground floor, she passed the noticeboard and stopped. Glass-fronted, with notices about garbage collections and a bridge club, the community gardens and a couple of newspaper articles. She'd been talking to Alice when she came in and hadn't even glanced this way. Surprising, really, considering the poster-sized notice with her name on it.

SECURITY ALERT was written in large, black capitals at the top, then: *Apartment 419 (CARLY TOWNSEND, our newest resident) was BROKEN INTO early Thursday. Carly believes the intruder was BUZZED IN by a resident. She is upset building security is being breached and is worried about her safety. The entry doors and intercom are for the safety of EVERYONE! DO NOT let in anyone you don't know.*

Carly's face flushed as she read it. She'd asked Howard to remind people to be mindful of security, not provide her name and apartment number – and it read like she thought everyone else was to blame. No wonder Alice's father had sounded defensive. *Carly Townsend: here a week and pointing the finger.* Like she had a right.

She slid open the glass and tore the poster from its thumbtacks, wondering what Howard had put in the email. Juicy e-gossip about the new resident? Something for them to think about when they passed her in the foyer, to discuss among themselves in the lift and garage? She was only glad she hadn't gone back to her maiden name; no one would find headlines about Carly Townsend on the internet.

Carly knocked on Howard's door but either he wasn't home or he wasn't answering. She found his number in her mobile and texted: *I did not give permission for my name & apartment number to be made public. Have removed your poster from the foyer. Why have I not received the email? Pls forward asap.*

Then she left the building, walking fast down the street, trying to shut out the memories that were pushing and shoving at her. The furtive glances, the backs that turned, the conversations that stopped when she passed. A decade after the deaths and the police investigation, after the accusations and shunning, people still remembered; it was in their eyes, their reservation, the distance they kept. Even when they didn't, she saw it in the face of the little boy who would never know his father, just a young man when Carly had last seen him, when she'd held his hand through a long cold night he'd never woken from.

Carly swiped at the tears on her lashes. Don't do it, she told herself. She was *here* and her neighbours couldn't know any of it. Howard had made her the demanding new resident, possibly the stupid new resident who'd left her door open. It didn't make her the anxiety-ridden, twice-divorced, childless woman who'd thrust an entire town into mourning.

6

—————

The markets in the school grounds were busy and bright with fruit and veg stalls, plants and T-shirts, food cooking on hotplates and in woks, a jazz band and a woman in a tutu painting children's faces. It smelled and sounded great.

Carly wandered around, bought a bunch of basil and a bag of mandarins, searched for Dickens on a table of second-hand books. She watched a woman turn pretty green beads into drop earrings then handed over five dollars for them.

Someone backed into her as she moved away, a brief tangle of their bags before she looked up and recognised a man from the warehouse. He'd only ever nodded and kept walking, so she copied his example, not wanting to make friends with residents this morning.

'Hello.' He stepped into her path. 'You're new at the warehouse.'

'Yes.' That's me, the one in the email.

'We've passed in the lift.'

'Several times actually.'

'That's right.' He pointed a finger, *Well done* in his tone. 'It took me a second to place you. I tend to be distracted when I come and go. Lots to think about.' He tapped his temple as though there was a party in there keeping him occupied.

'Sure.'

'I work at the university and I'm always overseeing several projects at a time,' he said, a tilt to his head as though it was complicated but he managed.

'Oh.' Carly wondered if she was meant to be impressed. She was just pleased he hadn't connected her to the email. 'I'm Carly.'

'I'm Stuart.' Mid to late twenties, she guessed. Thin, a little stooped, pale and, well, nerdy-looking.

'Nice to put a name to your face.'

'Likewise. I apologise in advance if I forget.' He tapped his temple again, waited as though she'd just have to ask.

Possibly it was fascinating, possibly so interesting she'd be jealous she wasn't at uni again. 'Well, see you in the lift.'

She bought a coffee and was looking at vegetables growing in pots when she noticed a man edging towards her. 'Interested in getting your hands dirty?' His face and shoulders were in the shade of the oversized canopy of a straw hat.

She backed off a step. 'Sorry?'

'The community gardens. We sell these to help fund ourselves.'

Carly glanced around, hadn't realised she'd been standing at the community garden stall.

'Ever done any gardening?' he asked. 'We can always do with extra hands.'

He was thirty-ish, she saw now, lean, wearing old jeans and grinning with horticultural enthusiasm - and she'd spent most of her life in a small country town where backyards were the size of a paddock and everyone had a vegetable patch. She didn't need a reminder.

'I only moved here a few days ago. I'm enrolled in a course, not sure I'll have much time.'

He shrugged. 'If you change your mind . . .' He handed her a flyer. 'Was that you moving into the warehouse last weekend? I'm Damien. South wall, third floor.'

Carly hesitated. She'd come here to meet people who knew nothing about her, now she didn't know what her neighbours knew. 'I'm Carly. East wall, fourth floor.'

He clicked his fingers. 'You're the one who had the break-in.'

'Yeah. That's me.'

'Oh, hey. Sorry about the security doors.'

'*You* buzzed someone in?'

'No, no, I just feel bad it happened. Guess there's no point asking how you're enjoying the place.'

'Actually, the apartment is great, it's just the uninvited company that's off-putting.'

'Understandable. You could come over to the gardens and work out the stress with a little digging and hoeing.'

'Or I could have a stiff drink.'

'That's an option too. Let me know if you're looking for company for that.' He took back the flyer he'd given her and turned it over. 'My mobile number is at the bottom.'

Forgot to add you to the list. Have sent you the email. Feel free to put your own notice on the board. Howard.

Carly read the email on her phone as she waited for the lift. It was the same message with embellishment: Carly's door not latched properly, Carly in bed when someone broke in, Carly attracted to the building because of the security, disappointed it let her down. Subtext: *Carly not taking responsibility for her own mistake.* What the hell did he know?

A voice sailed across the foyer. 'Hold the lift!'

Carly kept it open as Christina hurried through the light and shadows of the atrium. 'Thank you, thank you. I had two cups of that delicious coffee at the markets and the bathroom is on notice.' She stepped past Carly, hand to her chest and puffing.

'Did you run?' Carly asked.

'No, no. I got a ride. Just unfit.' She pointed at Carly's bag. 'So you found our little gem.'

'The markets? Yes. They're terrific. What did you buy?' she asked, hoping to keep the conversation away from Howard's email.

Christina sucked in a breath as though suddenly reminded. 'Oh Carly, I read about your little run-in.'

Excellent.

'Terrible thing. Terrible,' Christina said. 'It happened to me once, back when we were on the farm. These two cretins robbed the house. Just walked right in and, oh . . .' She huffed an exclamation, something between anger and horror. 'They hit me over the head with a roof tile and tied me up. Poor Bernard came back for dinner and found me covered in blood and his good wine gone. Ridiculous, the whole thing, of course. There was nothing valuable in the house, it was all in the paddocks.' She paused, shook her head. 'Oh, but you. Howard said you weren't hurt. It's not all about stitches and broken bones, though, is it?'

No, it wasn't, Carly knew. She took a second to let the image of Christina covered in blood fade. 'That must've been awful. Were you badly injured?'

'Just a few stitches. Bernard always said I had a thick head. It upset me for a while, though. A nasty business.' She gave Carly's arm a firm pat. 'Best not to let that go on if you start feeling that way.'

Carly had always thought feeling that way was part of her punishment. 'Thank you.'

'Oh, and Carly,' Christina called, moving into the centre of the cab, talking as the lift started to close. 'I wasn't sure if I had the number right but I left you a . . .' The last word was cut off. It probably happened a lot with Christina.

There was a package by Carly's door. Three books tied together with string, a brown paper bag on top. *A Tale of Two Cities, Oliver Twist* and *Great Expectations*. An appropriate selection, Carly thought. There was a muffin in the bag and a note scrawled on the side. *White chocolate and raspberry. Happy reading. Christina.*

Carly glanced back at the lift. Christina wasn't all talk.

· · ·

IT WAS a long time since Carly had sat in a classroom. This one wasn't a lecture hall, there were no professors and no one was talking social theory, but three days in it felt full of promise.

Almost fifteen years ago she'd started a university degree in Sydney. She'd planned to forget small-town New South Wales, get educated, explore the world, have a career, live a big life. Halfway through she went home on a cold June long weekend and never left.

Back then she'd been studying social science with a major in anthropology. Unendingly fascinating and totally pointless in the job market, which was why she'd spent a decade yearning to finish and now she had a chance to study again, she'd enrolled in a twelve-month small business certificate at TAFE.

The house she'd owned with Adrian had been sold before they'd even spoken to a divorce lawyer. Carly had used most of her share on the warehouse apartment, which left enough to support herself for six months, if she was frugal. She'd need a part-time job after that but for now she was a full-time student.

She was one of twenty-four students – the oldest was a fifty-something bloke who'd left a desk job to open a cafe, the youngest a pimply plumber. Carly was the only student with no plan for a business. She'd worked in her parents' post office most of her life, figured all that experience would point her somewhere by the time she'd finished. The teacher warned that having no concept might make some of the assignments more difficult. *So what?* Carly had thought. She'd be doing assignments and being someone new.

She spent the afternoon sitting next to a guy in a high-vis shirt who smelled like he'd been digging sewers before he came to class.

'It's Carly, right?' the girl on her other side asked as the class broke up. She had blue streaks in jet black hair and a dad who was funding her mobile hair salon on the proviso she did the course.

'Yes. Sorry, I've forgotten your name,' Carly said.

'Dakota. Never been there, snows a lot.' She grinned, making the stud in her nose move about. 'God, I'm starving.' She yanked opened a packet of biscuits, held it out to Carly. 'Pizza flavour. You want one?'

'No, thanks.'

'Do you drive in?'

'Yes.' Carly smiled cautiously. Was she asking for a lift?

'Great. Company to the car park. I hate walking in the dark.' Dakota leaned closer and lowered her voice. 'I was worried stinky guy might offer.'

Carly glanced around, checked he'd gone. 'You could smell him where you sat?'

'Smell him? I'm going home for a shower.'

Carly had been aiming for serious-older-student but it was too late, she was already laughing behind her hand.

It was after five when they started the ten-minute walk to the car park. Carly gave Dakota only the basics: she'd just moved to Newcastle, had an apartment a couple of Ks away. Dakota said she lived with her dad, broke up with a boyfriend three months ago and needed something new in her life. And her streaks had been pink until last weekend. As they stopped under the floodlights in the parking lot, Dakota offered to do Carly's hair when she next needed a cut, 'mate's rates'. Carly glanced at the blue and said, 'Thanks, I'll keep it in mind.'

'Have you found the campus cafe yet?' Dakota asked.

'No, have you?'

'I scouted it out on my way to class this afternoon. We should check it out tomorrow, do a taste test on the coffee.'

Carly played it cool, like she got invitations to coffee all the time. 'Sure.'

Dakota grinned. 'Great. A class buddy already.'

Carly's smile was wary. She'd come here to make friends but now the opportunity had arrived, it made her anxious. The last friends she'd had, she'd killed.

7

———————

The mattress lurches like a dinghy in rough water.

Harsh, fast gasps fill Carly's head. They are sharp in her chest.

She is afraid. It's not the sound or the lurching. It is what is above her. Large and silent.

On the bed with her.

Carly wants to scream. It's building in her chest. Trapped there, scratching at her lungs as though her ribs are the bars holding it back.

She hears breathing. Not her own. Deep and unhurried. It whispers across her face like a warm cloth. It turns her skin to ice.

She lashes out. Hits, twists, kicks. She sees it in her mind, feels it in her muscles. But it doesn't happen. She doesn't move.

Neither does he.

She sees him now. A shape in the darkness. Above her, black and motionless. He is watching. She watches back. Fear roaring through her bones, pulse thumping in her ears. Her voice wedged in her throat now and choking her.

No. Something else is squeezing, pushing down, making blood thump in her face. Warm hand, hard fingers.

She doesn't want to see. Doesn't want to feel. She shuts her eyes. Waits.

SHIVERING BY THE FRONT DOOR, Carly held tight to the hair dryer, adrenaline prickling across her scalp as she listened to the footfalls in the corridor outside. The knock made her jump.

Different officers: a woman asking the questions, a man keeping an eye on the corridor.

'In my room,' Carly told them, mouth so dry she could barely get the words out. 'He . . . he was . . . *on the bed.*'

Same procedure – lights glaring and a brief, alert search. Carly watched from the hall, saw for herself the apartment was empty. She hugged the hair dryer to her chest as more officers arrived, grateful for their bulk.

'Carly.'

She blinked at the uniform in front of her.

'Dean. I was here last week. We talked, remember?'

Dark hair, dark eyes, kind voice. She grabbed his forearm like it would stop her from slipping to the floor. 'He came back.'

'Did he hurt you?'

She shook her head. 'He . . . was . . . *on* the bed. On the *bed.*'

He steered her to the kitchen. She gulped water from the tap, coughing and gagging in her hurry to slake the dryness, then leaned against the pantry, arms tight across her chest. 'I locked the doors. The doors were *locked.*'

He pulled a notebook from his jacket. 'Let's start with what happened.'

Carly went through it – waking up, someone on the bed, silent except for the breathing, still except for the hand at her throat. Her voice trembled through the retelling but her eyes, when she was done, were hot and dry, the tears waiting like steam behind her lids.

'Did you get a better look at him?'

'It was dark and . . . he was a shape.' She used shaky hands to draw a hood in the air around her head. 'Like before. A balaclava and hood.'

'You saw that?'

'Not the detail. The *shape*.'

He left her to speak to the female cop who'd been at the door. A low-voiced conference, nods and references to his notebook, fingers pointed at the doors and the loft. Carly assumed he was telling her about last time. Twice, two visits. Not someone letting a prowler in, not her stupid enough to leave her door unlocked. He'd come back. Fuck. The realisation made the hairs on the back of her neck stand up and the fists tucked into her armpits to tremble. He returned with the dressing gown another officer had fetched from the loft.

'The doors were locked.' She said again. 'I made sure.'

'What time was that?'

'I checked them both before I went to bed around ten.'

'Have you given anyone else a key?'

'No.'

'A neighbour, maybe? You know, in case you lock yourself out.'

'*No*.' She pushed a hand through her hair. 'I've only been here a week and a half, I don't know my neighbours like that.'

'That's right, you've just moved in.' He replaced the notebook in his pocket. 'I'd like to look at the points of entry with you again.'

She felt like she was walking on puppet legs, jerky and uncoordinated as she went back to the front door. 'I make sure I shut it properly every time I come in.' It was open now so she pushed it to the jamb, checked the deadlock like she'd been doing. 'No way it can be pushed open.'

Dean gave it a tug. 'And the balcony?'

It was the same lock he'd inspected last week, but she wanted to show him again, make sure he didn't mix it up with another break-in with a flimsy back door. As they passed the three other officers standing in a huddle by the sofa, the woman broke away and joined them.

'Carly, hi, Jacinda. How are you feeling?' she said.

Jumpy, fuzzy, thirsty. 'Fabulous.'

'Yeah, I'm sure. Dean told me you had a break-in last week.' The tone of her voice said *I'm asking the questions now*. 'You thought the offender was still here when we arrived?'

'I didn't know. I didn't see him leave. I thought he might've . . .' She glanced around the furniture that had cast shadows in the gloom from the street. 'I don't know.'

'Did you hear anything down here?'

'No, but . . .' She knotted fingers together. 'I was scared.'

'Sure.' Jacinda nodded. 'Can you show us the locks here?'

Carly turned the key, pushed, and a gust of cold air hit them.

Jacinda rattled the right-side door, tried the top fastener. 'Can you step out with us?'

Carly stood on the balcony, something trembling inside her, and not just because of the bitter early-morning breeze. The two cops inspected the drop over the edge and the apartments either side, their equipment belts clunking on the railing, passing each other wordlessly as they swapped sides. Voices inside made Carly turn. A cop crossing the floor, heading into the hallway.

He opened the front door and a voice carried to the balcony. 'What are you doing here?' It was the practised flat tone of a police officer but something in it made Carly pay attention.

'I live in the warehouse.' Male voice, muffled from the distance.

The door swung wider and her eyebrows rose. It was Nate. Up and dressed. At four o'clock in the morning.

                                  8
                         ———————

'Is Carly all right?' Nate was trying to look past the cop and down
the hall.
        'You know the owner of the apartment?'
    'We're *neighbours*. Is she all right?' There was a slight tussle of
bodies as Nate tried to come in, the cop blocking the doorway with
his body.
    'The situation is under control,' the cop said. 'You're not . . .' An
exchange of low, harsh words, the cop's stance turning stiff and broad,
edging Nate back into the corridor.
    'I didn't realise you could see the harbour from here.'
    Carly turned back to Jacinda, who was talking to Dean as though
she was a potential buyer and he was the agent.
    'I wouldn't climb up there,' Jacinda said.
    Dean tipped his head side to side. 'Not impossible, though.'
    'No.'
    Was that what they were thinking? Someone had climbed the
outside of the building to get in?
    Jacinda turned to Carly. 'When was the last time the windows
were cleaned?'
    'Last week. After the fingerprinting was done.'

'Makes sense. Leaves a mess, doesn't it?' She turned to Dean, lowered her voice. 'I'll get fingerprinting back.' Raised it again for Carly. 'Okay, we're done. Sorry to keep you out in the cold.'

There was only one cop left in the apartment, tapping on his phone. Jacinda called to him as she stepped through the door. 'Hey, Flinto, put the kettle on for Carly. It's freezing out there.' Then she headed for the front entrance, looking both ways before disappearing into the corridor. The purpose in her stride made Carly wonder if Nate was still out there.

'Carly?' Dean's hand closed around her elbow.

Carly pulled away, goosebumps rising on her arm. 'What happened with the fingerprints they took last week?' she asked.

'I haven't seen a report.'

'How long does it take?'

'It can be a while. I'll follow it up.'

He flicked a look at the front door, made no attempt to move – she wondered if he was waiting for his colleagues to deal with her neighbour or deciding to stay for a chat.

'Have a cup of tea,' he said. 'Better than coffee for the shakes.'

They weren't going anytime soon. 'Okay.'

'Take care, Carly.'

She followed Dean and his partner to the corridor, wondering what had happened out there, wondering if Nate was in handcuffs being read his rights, then feeling bad when the floor was deserted. At the lift, Dean waved a *Goodbye/Go back inside*, and as she turned back she saw a stripe of brightness under Nate's door. Whatever had been said out of Carly's sight, it hadn't sent him back to bed.

She shut the door, checked the lock. Twice. Hurried through to the French windows. Dean had fastened them but she needed to do it herself to try to calm the agitation. She made tea with trembling hands, scalded her lips as she drank, impatient for it to cool. It was itching inside her now – under her skin, in her legs, her lungs. She wanted to walk but it was dark outside. She flicked on the telly to hear real voices, filled the sink and found things to wash, to keep her hands busy.

It. Her psychologist called it anxiety. That was the clinical explanation.

It was her cross to bear, the memento of what she'd done, her penance.

It was the face of guilt and grief, reproach and fear. The agitation that lay on the surface above it all, making sure she remembered.

Carly picked up a tea towel and started on the small mound of dishes. A long time ago, she'd accepted the anxiety as a passenger on board her life – fighting it had always felt like denying responsibility. Staying busy, giving the restless energy an outlet, helped to keep the images turned down so they didn't make her crazy, so the people she'd hurt wouldn't have to be reminded that the sole survivor was the weak one. Thirteen years on, *it* was a low hum most days. Times like this, though, when fate seemed to be trying to even the score, it grew loud and strong inside her, trying to make her relive the night that had almost killed her too.

She squeezed her eyes, felt glass snap inside the tea towel. Blood oozed from her middle finger, the sight of it felt like an explosion in her head. She climbed the stairs, held her finger under water in the ensuite, telling herself tonight wasn't about that, she'd paid her price for the blood she'd spilled. She taped her finger, cleaned the basin and the mirror and the loo while she was there, gritting her teeth on the memories that were clamouring to be heard.

She finished in the kitchen and started on the downstairs half bath but *it* was too loud tonight and the effort to contain the agitated, anxious jittering in her bones finally exhausted her, finally made the idea of just letting it out feel like comfort. A cigarette when you were fighting the addiction. The touch of a man's body when loneliness was overwhelming.

And there it was.

Did you guys turn into wusses while I was gone?

The challenging laughter of her own voice brought a cold sweat to Carly's face.

Come on, one more time before you all become boring old farts.

She sat on the floor at the edge of the French windows, fists clenched as she waited for the show.

They'd started late, all four of them slow with hangovers and tiredness. Debs complained of a headache, Jenna wondered if they were going to have enough time, Adam stopped once to heave. *Wusses*, Carly teased. She and Debs had been joined at the hip since preschool. They'd met Adam and Jenna on the first day of high school. Together they'd been the quartet, a royal flush, an Awesome Foursome. The canyon was an hour and a half out of town, an overnight excursion: waterproof gear, helmets, harnesses and ropes. They'd done it half a dozen times before, abseiling the falls, sleeping under the stars at the base of the cliff, hiking out in the morning.

It's fucking freezing up here, Carl, Adam said as they walked the ridge, the valley hundreds of metres below them. *Crybaby*, Carly called back. He was silent for a while, she figured he was battling his hangover or ticked off with her smug Sydney attitude again. Then his voice lifted: *Emma's pregnant.* Their shock echoed off the high, sheer cliffs of the chasm. *What? Bullshit! Pregnant?* They stopped for details, Carly wasted more time leading a toast with energy drinks. It was late when they started the abseil.

There were twelve sections, each dropping to a narrow ledge that stepped out to the next descent. Debs and Adam hadn't been canyoning since Carly had left town, Jenna was working in an office and had lost her old fitness – and all three were slow. At the fourth shelf, they needed head-mounted torches in the dusk. Resting on the fifth, close enough to the waterfall for its icy spray to dampen their clothes, their spirits had waned to anxiety about how far they still had to go.

I think the next couple of shelves are wider, Debs said. *We should spend the night on one, tie ourselves on.*

I'm not sleeping on the cliff, Jenna said.

We'll be doing most of it in the dark, Adam warned.

Not if we stop pissing around talking, Carly said.

She led the way, faster and fitter from the rock wall at uni. Teasing and cajoling, she egged them on, thinking about the relative comfort at the bottom versus a cold, exposed night lashed to a tree. The next ledge was wide but with an incline sloping towards the sharp edge of the shelf.

Here, Debs said.

Jenna was sitting against the rock wall. *I wouldn't have bloody come if I knew we were going to sleep here.*

She was always first to complain. Carly and Debs looked to Adam for another opinion.

I don't know. He dropped his pack from his shoulders, rubbed at his arms. *I'm not feeling so great.*

What's wrong?

Tired, hungover. I had that flu last week, it feels like it's freshening up. He shrugged. *What do you think, Carl?*

She was the game one, the scout, the one who mapped their routes – and it was only now she wondered if they were up to this canyon. She'd glanced around as though she was the expert, arrogant even then. They were halfway down, Jenna and Adam were slow but managing, the incline made it feel like they were slipping when they were standing still, so she made the decision. *We keep going.*

Debs wasn't happy but a brief argument decided they'd reassess fitness and conditions at the next ledge.

It had suffered a rock fall since the last time they were there, the widest part reduced to standing-room only. It was almost eight thirty and would have been pitch-dark except for a full moon. Their torches jerked and slid around what remained of the crumbling ledge.

Fuck, Debs said for all of them.

Christ, I need to lie down, Jenna groaned.

Don't. The ground's not stable. Adam scuffed a shoe and pebbles tumbled over the ledge.

He was shivering, Carly saw. *We keep moving.*

Where, for fuck's sake? Deb's voice was sharp with anger and alarm. *We can't fucking see.*

There, Carly aimed her light. *We can anchor on that tree. We used it once before.*

Silence as four torch beams settled on the craggy, stunted trunk that clung to the rock shelf. The path to it was a narrow ledge, only wide enough for single file, sloping steeply towards the drop into the valley, the rubble underfoot slippery. She took the lead, faking confidence, hoping the darkness hid the trembling in her legs. *Come on, it's fine.*

Carly kept her light on them as they moved slowly towards her, keeping distance between them like they'd been taught, so one falling person didn't take everyone with them. It didn't matter. There was a skittering of stones, a snap-crack under Carly's feet. Jenna gasped. Adam swore. Debs' head lifted, fear in her eyes as they met Carly's. Then the whoosh, as though the canyon had taken a great gulp of air. The night filled with screaming. Carly's body tumbled and twisted, suspended and pelted by the darkness . . . all the way to the agonising, bone-breaking thump to the shelf below.

9

———

Carly sat at an outdoor table with her coffee, a scarf and gloves doing little to protect her from the chill.

'You sure you're okay out here?' Reuben asked, rubbing his hands together in the doorway of the cafe. 'It's not like you'll be fighting for space in here. Only the brave are out this morning.'

'I'm fine, thanks.' She needed the touch of ice to numb her and the solitude of the empty tables around her. An edgy, anxious fuel was still running through her veins, exhaustion was weighing down her limbs and she wanted to keep it to herself. This wasn't the person she came here to be.

'Another coffee then?' Reuben asked. 'Can't have our regulars dying of pneumonia.'

'I'm a regular?'

'I put your name on the barista's board. *Carly, skim cap, one sugar, on the hot side.*'

She smiled. Probably wasn't good to drink coffee all morning but the process – stirring, drinking, behaving like a normal person – was dulling the need to wring her hands. 'Then I will have another.'

Detective Anne Long rang as Carly took her first sip.

'Where are you?' the detective asked.

Carly glanced around, suddenly wary of the table in the open air, where anyone could see her. 'I'm by the harbour. I needed a walk.' Should she have stayed out of sight?

'Right. About last night, I'd like to go over it with you. Can you come to the station?'

'When?' The sooner the better. She needed to offload the fear.

'I'm here until ten, then back again at three.'

Carly checked her watch - it was just after eight. Her first class started at eleven, the last finished at five. 'I'll be there in an hour.'

'I'VE READ the report from the officer in charge last night.' Anne Long spread a hand over the manila folder on the table between them. 'How are you doing now?'

They were in a small room with a large window that looked into an open-plan office. Anne and Elliot on one side of a table, Carly on the other, her head thumping and her bones aching. 'Not bad.'

'Do you think you can manage to go over it again?' The reservation in Detective Long's voice made it sound like she expected Carly to be a blubbering mess any second.

Carly preferred to keep that to herself. 'Of course.'

Anne nodded an *Off you go*. Beside her, Elliot wrote as Carly went through it, clearing her throat when her voice found a tremble, blinking back tears. 'And that's it,' she finished, fingers interlocked to hide the shakes.

'And you're confident it was a man?'

'Yes.' Firm, sure. 'Is this what happened to the other people at the warehouse?'

'Still some discrepancies there,' Anne said. 'How do you feel about your description now?'

Carly wanted to know what the discrepancies were, but the thumping in her head left only enough space for one thought at a time. 'I saw the shape of a hood. His face . . . it's like he hasn't got one.'

Elliot lifted his eyes.

'It makes sense, though,' Carly said. 'If the guy is climbing over balconies to get into my loft, he's not going to let me see his face. It has to be a balaclava, right?'

Anne ignored her question. 'Why do you think he's climbing over balconies?'

'That's what the officers at my apartment thought last night.' She flicked her eyes to Elliot and back. 'At least, that's what I thought they thought. Isn't that why they wanted the fingerprinting done again?'

Anne dipped her head, noncommittal. 'There are probably easier ways to get into your apartment. Who has keys?'

'Just me.'

'Did you change the locks when you moved in?'

'No.'

'Who was your real estate agent?'

Something squirmed in Carly's stomach. She found the business card, which was still in her wallet, and passed it to Elliot, remembering the man, Vincent, who'd shown her through the apartment two months ago. Early twenties, bad skin, fake smile, surprised when she made an offer on the spot. Had he climbed onto her bed last night?

'You've got a building supervisor, haven't you?' Anne asked.

'Yes.'

'Has he got a set?'

'Not from me.'

'Did he ever let prospective buyers into the apartment?'

'I've no idea.' Howard Helyer? Who still had her garage pass, who she hadn't laid eyes on yet.

'I'll make some phone calls. See where that gets us,' Anne said.

'Should I change my locks?' How much would that cost?

Anne dipped her head again, slower this time, doubtful. 'At this stage, it's not clear that's how the offender is getting in.'

Carly looked back and forth between the two detectives again, wanting more. Advice, assurance, instruction.

Elliot spoke for the first time. 'You could install a safety chain. Not as expensive as new locks, and if he's trying to be quiet that should put a stop to it.'

Carly looked back at Anne, expecting another head dip, confirmation or otherwise, but the detective simply stood. 'Okay. Thanks for coming in, Carly.'

'So you don't think it's the same guy who broke into the warehouse twelve months ago?'

Anne picked up her folder, tucked it under her arm. 'Personally, no. Like I said, there are discrepancies.'

'One of my neighbours turned up while the police were there last night,' Carly said. 'He was asked to leave. Is there a problem with him?'

'What's his name?' Anne asked.

'Nate. I don't know his surname.'

'Nathan? Nathaniel?'

'I don't know.'

Anne turned to Elliot. 'Have we got a Nate in the notes?' Elliot shook his head. 'Can't help you with that,' Anne said. 'Perhaps the officer knew him.'

Carly remembered the tone of the conversation. If that had been recognition, it wasn't a good recommendation.

10

———

It was almost eleven when Carly left the police station, her first lesson about to start. She watched the traffic heading in the direction of the campus, then turned her head and looked towards the warehouse - and her anxiety flipped to indecision. Eyes right then left, foot hovering between accelerator and brake: she needed to get to class, she needed a security chain. She had to make this life work; the man on her bed might have a key to her apartment.

Come on, Charlotte, pull yourself together.

She took a breath. Okay: leave the security chain until later and she might not get it installed by tonight. Skip the first class, be back at the campus after lunch. She dropped her foot on the accelerator and steered towards the warehouse, told herself she needed to feel safe, promised herself she'd make it to class later. Then she found something else to focus on – Anne Long and her questions.

Who had keys?

The real estate agency had sent them to Carly in Burden. Had someone kept a copy? Possibly it was standard procedure. Which meant any number of people had access to it: staff, clients, cleaners. She pictured it, her key in an envelope, a drawer, on a board, with other keys for other properties. Why take hers? Because he knew the warehouse? She flicked the indicator, waited for a right-hand turn. Maybe some guy was breaking into apartments and houses all around the city and . . . wouldn't the police have a list of similar break-ins? Not just old reports with 'discrepancies'.

Leaving the main road, she thought of Talia, the former owner. Had she given a key to someone? A house-sitter or boyfriend? Girl-friend? The only thing Carly knew about her was that she played music. She might've left a key with a neighbour, like Dean suggested. Nate, perhaps, or the man on the other side who Carly hadn't seen yet. Or with Howard Helyer? Maybe storing keys was part of his job. And so far he'd been bad at his job.

What about Talia's friend, Brooke? Carly hadn't seen her, either, but she was a woman on crutches, it wasn't her in the loft last night. Maybe Brooke had a key and gave it to someone. To break into her friend's apartment and scare the new owner? Carly shook her head; that made no sense. Maybe someone *stole* it from Brooke.

Carly stopped at the kerb opposite the warehouse and eyed the east wall. There was nothing fancy about the facade; it had been a storage facility, built for function, not charm. The brickwork was a flat face, no ledges, no cornices, no architectural features that could be used for a foothold. Not even the balconies protruded, their metal railings strung across openings that had once held windows and delivery doors. There were pipes running down from the roof but they were positioned at the corners, well clear of the nearest balconies. The apartments inside ranged from one- to four-bedrooms and were configured like Lego bricks, mix-and-match sizes that fitted together to make the most of the shape and space. It took Carly a moment to find her own: second storey down from the top, three rail-ings in from the corner.

A long time ago Carly had climbed up and abseiled down sheer faces with Debs, Jenna and Adam, and in training for the Rural Fire Service. For thirteen years she'd barely let herself think about it or the person she was then - her stomach was churning now as she looked the wall over again with a climber's eye. She wouldn't trust her own body to do it, but it was doable. With ropes. Possibly without, if you were good. And confident.

She steered the car back into the road and kept going to the hardware store on Baxter Street. A shop assistant took twenty minutes to talk her through the options and sizes. The one she chose, he told her, wouldn't stop a determined intruder but they'd need boltcutters or brute strength. In other words, a large tool or a lot of noise, which was very different to creeping around with a key.

THE FIRST SHRIEK from the drill Carly had found in the storeroom ricocheted around the atrium like a primal scream. She released the trigger, opened the door and glanced warily around the corridor, worried about complaints - then decided letting her neighbours know she was installing some security wasn't a bad thing.

She drilled until her ears rang and her head felt like it was about to explode, then inspected the doorjamb. Barely a dent in the timber. She tried again, same result. Ten minutes later she still didn't have a hole deep enough for a screw. 'Shit!' She stalked the hallway and back, hands shaking from the force of the vibration. She'd used a drill before, what the hell was she doing wrong? She gave the door a thwack with her hand.

It knocked back ... and Carly jerked away, the shadow of a man flickering through her mind, the lurch of the mattress rocking through her body. Lifting the drill, she held it like the hair dryer, wishing the security chain was already in place.

'It's Nate,' came the voice through the door.

He'd been awake and dressed at four in the morning. The police had asked him to leave and . . . Carly glanced at the drill. The screeching must have filled his apartment too.

She opened the door enough to flick eyes over him. Jeans, long-sleeved T-shirt, possibly the same outfit he was wearing at her door during the night. 'Sorry about the noise,' she said. 'It shouldn't take much longer.'

He gave her and the tool a once over. 'Want a hand?'

Yes. No. 'I'm installing a security chain.' It wasn't an answer, it was making sure he knew.

He waited a beat. 'Not that I don't think you can do it.'

She smiled a little. He'd probably heard her swearing and thumping, too. She wanted the job finished, she just wasn't sure she wanted him in her apartment. She opened the door a bit wider. 'Did you know Talia?'

'The woman who used to live here?'

Carly nodded.

'Met her a few times. Wasn't around much when she was here.'

'Did she give you a key to the apartment? You know, in case she got locked out?'

'No point. If she locked herself out, I wasn't going to be much help from an oil rig.'

'True.'

'Is this about the cops last night?'

She wasn't ready to explain. 'I hope they didn't wake you.'

'I was already up.'

Dressed and tussling with an officer in her hallway. 'I saw you at the door.'

He slid his hands into his pockets.

'I was on the balcony,' she said.

'Right.'

'And you were arguing with the officer.'

'Yeah. That.'

Caution tightened Carly's shoulders.

Nate glanced along the corridor before explaining. 'I wanted to check you were okay.'

Carly remembered how that had turned out. 'What was the problem with the cop?'

He glanced the other way along the corridor. 'We've crossed paths before. It wasn't a happy occasion.'

'You were arrested?'

'Threatened with it.'

'What for?'

Eyes flicking away again, something shamefaced in it. 'It wasn't about me. It was my sister. A problem with her ex. I made some noise about it.'

Carly watched him a moment, thinking about the stocky build, the solid shoulders, the tense gruffness she'd seen in him on other days, and guessed he hadn't raised his voice to say *please*. Maybe it had stretched to swearing, some pushing and shoving like there'd been in her hallway. Forget what he was doing up at 4 am – did she want that kind of neighbour helping her? Asking questions, turning up in the night, hassling the police? She took a step back, wanting an excuse to shut the door. 'What was the problem?' she asked.

'I didn't think they were doing enough.'

'Is your sister okay?'

'She is now.'

Had he sorted out the cops or the ex? Maybe it didn't matter. He'd done something to help, it was more than Carly could claim to have done for the people she loved. 'So . . .' She tapped a finger out of sight, deciding. 'The door.' She opened it all the way, pointed at the jamb. 'I don't know if it's me or the drill but I've made a lot of noise without much result.'

His eyes stayed on her for another second before shifting to the timber. 'How's the bit?'

'No idea. How should it be?'

A tweak of an eyebrow. 'You want to give me a look at the drill?'

She passed it over.

'You won't get through anything with that. It's blunt.'

'Nice to know it wasn't my technique.'

'Can't comment on that. Haven't seen your technique.' Amusement flickered fleetingly through his gaze.

Ooh, a joke.

'Have you got a spare?' he asked.

'Just what's in there.' She pointed at the drill case.

He checked the contents. 'Wait here.' He handed the tool back and left, returning a minute later. 'This'll do it.' He held the power cord of another drill out to her. Had the holes done, screws in and the security chain installed in a quarter of an hour. 'Give it a try.'

Carly slipped the chain into its slot and pulled on the door. A loud thunk as the links straightened and caught. 'Perfect. Thanks.'

'These for the balcony?' He picked up the slide-bolt locks she'd bought.

'Yes.'

He didn't ask, just unplugged the tool, took the necessary pieces through the apartment and started on the other door.

He wouldn't do that if he was breaking in at night, right? 'Can I get you a coffee?' she asked.

'No thanks.'

'Glass of water? Juice?'

'No, I'm good.'

She hovered, trying to pre-empt his needs, passing parts and screws, matching his concise instructions with concise replies: *That one. This one?* Finally done, door tested and winding the electrical cord, he said, 'So what happened last night?'

Had he been burning to ask or leaving it to last? 'There was someone in my apartment,' Carly told him.

His hands stopped, his eyes lifted. 'Again.'

'Yes.'

Winding again, gaze dropping. 'How did they get in?'

'I don't know. Hence the extra security.'

'I take it you didn't leave the door open this time.'

'I'm wondering if that's really what happened last time.'

'What are the cops doing about it?'

'I spoke to some detectives this morning and they're sending someone from fingerprinting around again.'

He nodded, busied himself with packing up. He was at the front door when he stopped and looked back at her. 'I'm right next door, Carly. You could've called out.'

'I didn't know who it was.'

He hesitated, eyes not quite connecting with hers. 'You thought it could've been me?'

'I was scared. I didn't know who it was.'

'Hence the questions about the key?'

'Yes.' An apologetic smile.

She thought he might storm off or throw words back at her. He didn't, he just nodded, something sharp and raw in his eyes now. She wasn't sure what it was – but it made her feel bad for putting it there.

'Let me know if I can help,' he said.

'You've already helped a lot.'

'I'm right next door, Carly.'

11

———————

Carly woke with keys in her hand - on the sofa, the light outside was grey. She remembered the two-hour wait for the forensics officer and then sitting down to pull on shoes for the dash to her last class. Looking down she saw the laces hanging from the one shoe that had made it onto a foot. 'Shit.'

It was cold now and she flipped on the heating, checked the balcony door and stood to watch the encroaching darkness. Wind blew in blustering bursts against the glass. The ache at the base of her skull was gone and her mind was still, and for the first time since she'd woken with a man on her bed, she thought about it without the agitation.

Dean and Jacinda considered someone climbing up from the street. Or from another apartment. But why hers? She was two floors down from the roof, three balconies in from the corner. Not the easiest to get to.

And why now? She'd only been here two weeks, the apartment had been empty for months. Unless . . . her eyebrows rose. Unless it wasn't his first visit. Had he been here when the apartment was empty? Used a key or climbed over the balcony, making use of the place because no one was here? She glanced at her reflection. That only explained the first visit, an *Oops, someone moved in*. Not the second one, not after the squad of police that had been here both times.

Her gaze roamed around the suburb below. The streetlights were on, their glow pale in the early evening. The cluster of vacant warehouses loomed silent and watchful. Beyond them, bright squares of light marked bungalows and cottages. Occasional shadows passed behind drawn blinds like ghosts, the few uncovered windows like movie screens: a woman awash in steam as she cooked dinner, a teenager studying at a bedroom desk, a man drinking beer while he watched the news.

Carly turned her head, looking at her own home, lights on in the living room and over the kitchen counter. She imagined the east wall of the warehouse at night, its five floors of windows. How many of her neighbours had blinds or curtains? How much of her apartment could be seen from outside?

Was someone playing *Rear Window*? Watching through binoculars and amusing himself with the lives of strangers?

Feeling suddenly exposed, she took a couple of steps back, glancing up and around at the huge checkerboard windows. If there were curtains somewhere big enough to cover them, she couldn't afford them.

She switched a few bulbs off, skipped her nightly perusal of the view from the balcony doors and kept to one side of the expanse of glass, looking for faces at windows. When she went to bed, she left the ensuite light on and the door ajar – if he came back, she wanted to see him. It was meant to help her relax but the harsh white stripe around the door made her ankles and lower back ache, visceral reminders of the six weeks she'd spent in hospital after the fall – in pain and distraught, drugged and watched – and other brief, anguished stays in hospital, the last just five months ago.

Around two, she couldn't stand it any longer; she turned the bathroom light out and left the one at the bottom of the stairs on – not as bright but maybe she'd sleep. When she did, it wasn't hospital she dreamed of.

The moon is full and bright. Clouds like drifts of muslin float through its glow. The ledge is deep and level, wide enough for four. Wide enough to light a fire and stay warm all night. Only Carly is so cold her tears feel like hot water.

Debs? She was behind Carly, out of sight. The sharp stuttering of her breath had stopped. *Debs!*

Carly turned her face, found again the dark halo that had spread around Jenna's head. Adam's hand in Carly's was loose now, the blood drying and tacky. His panic had filled the canyon with sound. *The bone, oh fuck, it's sticking out.* He'd dragged himself to her, howling with pain, an artery spilling his life across Carly in a warm, fast gush.

Alone now, the shattered bones in her ankles and lower spine pulsed with fire. Pale shadows shifted and slid across the rock shelf. Carly's voice was barely more than a whisper but it was the only one in the canyon. *Take me too.*

CARLY SHOUTED Dakota a cappuccino in a break between classes, an apology for not turning up yesterday when they'd planned to visit the cafe.

'Dodgy curry, huh?' Dakota said, dropping onto the bench seat beside her, something cheeky in her grin. 'Sure it's not a hangover?'

'Not unless you can get one from a glass of wine and a takeaway.'

'Pity. At least you have a little fun before a hangover.'

Not always, Carly thought. 'That's the only bonus.'

'Did you get the assignment that was handed out yesterday?'

'I picked one up just now. Haven't looked at it, though.'

'We have to work in pairs. I thought we could partner up.'

Carly smiled, surprised. 'Are you sure? I don't have a business idea to contribute. Apparently that's an issue.'

Dakota cast a look over her shoulder, leaned in closer. 'Yeah, but I like talking to you. What do you think?'

'Yes. Love to.'

·   ·   ·

I NEED *my garage pass and my mail. Call me!*

Carly sent the text standing outside Howard Helyer's apartment. She'd already knocked and got no answer, but she listened at his door for a ping from a phone, wondering if he was in there and avoiding her. She heard only the weird hush of the foyer and the creaking-whispering that always made her think people were tiptoeing about just out of sight.

It was late afternoon when she headed across the suspended walkway on the fourth floor, an overcast sky turning the light in the atrium to an eerie glow. Her living room was bathed in a washed-out grey as she pulled out books and sat at the wrought-iron table. A knock at the door an hour later made her jump with fright.

Peering through the gap allowed by the security chain, she saw a tall, blond, absurdly handsome man.

'Charlie,' he said.

'Sorry?'

'Are you Charlie?'

'I'm Carly.'

'Right, right, Carly. I'm Howard.'

She wanted to smile – of course the conversation made no sense, and you just didn't see that kind of handsome walking around. But she leaned against the wall, kept the chain on its hook. 'Howard. At last.'

'Yeah, sorry about the mix up. I've had the flu.' He ran a hand through thick wavy locks. 'Actually, I think the drugs were the problem.'

Carly raised her eyebrows. That explained a lot.

'Oh, ha-ha, not those kind of drugs,' he said. 'I took some cold tabs and had some weird reaction. Just sort of flaked out and lost a few days. You probably thought I was, I don't know . . .'

'Hung-over.'

'Yeah?'

'Yeah.'

He shrugged, held up a large envelope. 'Got your stuff.' He sounded like a dealer, looked like a light-haired Superman in civvies.

Chisel-jawed, broad-shouldered and athletic enough to leap tall buildings.

'Great.' Carly held fingers up to the gap in the door.

He made no move to hand the package over. 'Got a minute?'

'Okay.'

'Can I come in?'

She hesitated, debating man-shaped shadows and his job as supervisor. Finally unlatched the chain and pulled the door wide.

He followed her to the living room, glancing around as though he was the landlord. 'Not much different to the last time I saw the place.'

Carly stayed near the hallway, more comfortable with the open front door at her back. 'When Talia was here?' Maybe she hadn't had much furniture either.

'No, when it was empty. The family had a bit of work done and I dealt with the tradesmen.' He took something from the front pocket of his jeans. 'You should have this.'

It was a key. Carly's heart thumped. She wanted to snatch it from him, she wanted to get the hell away from him. Opposing urges that held her to the spot.

'The cops came to see me at uni today,' he said. 'They asked if I had a key to your apartment. I said no, then remembered this one and rambled on about why I had it.' He shrugged. 'I'd forgotten about it. Here.' He let it drop from his palm to hers.

It was warm from his body. Like the hand on her throat. 'Did Talia give it to you?'

'No. Her dad. He came over from Perth after the accident. They had to pack up her things and make arrangements for selling the apartment. There was a problem with a couple of the walls.' As he pointed at the plaster on the long wall Carly shared with Nate, she wondered what kind of accident. 'There was a hole there and another one in the loft.' He made a circle with two hands, thumbs and index fingers together. 'And small ones where Talia hung pictures. There was a heap of them along here.' He indicated the stretch from the French windows to the hallway. 'It must have been like an art gallery when she was here. Her dad decided to get them all patched and have the whole place painted before it went on the market. Asked me to hold onto the key in case he decided not to fly back. And, you know, to let tradesmen in.'

Carly stiffened. 'You gave the key to tradesmen?'

'No. I let them in and they'd lock up on their way out.'

'So you're the only one who used the key?'

He ducked his head. 'Not ex*act*ly. I gave it to the painters once. They wanted to start really early and I was going out or away or something the night before, I can't remember now, but I . . . well, they let themselves in. Just that one time.'

'You mean they had the key overnight.'

'Until they gave it back to me.'

Her shoulders stiffened. 'How long did they have it?'

'Couple of days. Tops.' He held up a palm as though taking an oath.

It didn't matter how many days. An hour was enough to have a copy made. 'Did you tell the police?'

'Didn't need to. They returned it.'

'No, I meant today,' she snapped. 'Did you tell them about the painters *today*?'

'Oh, right.' He rubbed a hand over his chiselled jaw. 'Yeah, see, that's what I was rambling on about. I couldn't remember why I wasn't going to be here and that woman detective looked at me like I was spinning some story to cover my arse. I kept thinking, TV cop show, guy talks too much, sweats all over the place, gotta be the perp.' He huffed a nervous laugh. 'That was me. Sweating and blabbing. I wanted to handcuff myself.'

Even tense and impatient with him, Carly could imagine the scene and wanted to smile: Superman and Anne Long's deadpan face. 'Did you give the detectives the name of the painters?'

'I couldn't remember that, either, of course. But I've got copies of the receipts. I said I'd dig them out and let her know.'

'Can you do that?'

'Yeah, yeah.'

She'd heard that from him before. 'Tonight?'

He faltered, seemed to think past his own embarrassed explanation for the first time. 'You think one of the painters was in your
apartment?'

'Well the guy wasn't carrying a brush but it's possible whoever
was here got in with a key.'

'Oh, right. Whoa.' He froze for a second, as though the news had
shocked him to the spot. Then he hooked a thumb at the door. 'I'll go
look now.' He headed down her hallway in long, loping strides: Clark
Kent looking for a phone booth. 'Sorry about the key,' he said on the
threshold.

'Right.'

'It wasn't me, by the way.' He declared it with sudden gravity, then
grinned.

Hilarious. 'Howard, don't make another announcement of it. Keep
it to yourself this time.'

'Sure, sure. Yeah, sorry about that. Didn't think it through. Oh hey,
it was you who wanted the lights replaced, wasn't it? I'm free
tomorrow if you need a hand with that.'

She held back on an eye-roll. 'It's done.'

When she'd locked and chained herself in, she started to wonder
about his I'm-an-idiot show. A person could hide a whole other face
behind a smile and a steady voice – she'd done it for years, guilt and
anxiety tucked behind her *How can I help you?* at the post office.
Howard had a PhD, he was studying engineering and biomedical
science, there was no way he was stupid – and he'd had access to her
apartment for months. She got Anne Long's voicemail when she rang
the detective's number.

'Anne, it's Carly Townsend. The building supervisor had a key to
my apartment, he just gave it to me. He said he'd loaned it to some
painters. He's going to call you with their name but I wanted to make
sure you knew, in case he doesn't. In case . . . I don't know. In case it's
them. Or him. I'm just . . . not sure what to think. Can you call me
back?'

12

‘There were two painters and they moved back to New Zealand three months ago,’ Anne said when she finally returned Carly’s call.

‘Oh.’ Carly was silent for a moment. It was Monday morning and Carly had spent the weekend checking for messages, anxious about a painter with a key, hoping it was one of them and that the police found evidence and made an arrest. Hoping he didn’t use it again before that happened. ‘What about the real estate agent?’

‘It’s a large agency. We’re still talking to people.’

Carly watched a car pull into a space opposite. Its driver was one of the tradies from her class. They were both three minutes late now – he got out and set off at a trot. Carly stayed where she was. ‘What about Howard Helyer? He’s had a key for months.’

‘You said he returned it.’

‘He might’ve made a copy.’

Anne paused a moment. ‘Did your shadow look like him?’

Carly heard the sceptical emphasis on *your shadow* and felt heat creep to her face. ‘I . . . don’t know.’ Howard was man-shaped and lean but she wasn’t going to say that out loud. ‘What about the fingerprinting? Are there any results?’

'We're still waiting on those.'

'Even the first ones?' It had been almost two weeks.

'I'm going to get back to you on those, Carly.' It wasn't *I'll find out for you.* It sounded like *I'm not willing to discuss it now.*

And Carly was sick of not having the details. If Anne Long thought it would stop her worrying, she was wrong. 'When?'

'When there's something to talk about.'

'I . . .'

'I'll be in touch, Carly.'

'But . . .' The connection ended. 'And fuck you too.'

Carly tossed the phone at the passenger seat. Not the painters but possibly her building supervisor, a neighbour or any number of people in a large real estate agency that the police were taking their time talking to. Shit. She wanted it over, she wanted to sleep at night. At the very least she wanted information that would unwind the anxiety, not give it a reason to twist itself into more knots.

It wasn't just that, though. She'd come here to start again, to be someone else. Not the reckless Carly who had killed her friends and not the guilt-burdened version who'd waited thirteen years for fate to exact its punishment. Someone better, stronger and less selfish; someone worthy – but she wouldn't find that person if she was screwed around by a scary guy sitting on her bed.

THE NEW PARKING pass was great – it didn't make the garage any less creepy, though. It was a cave of poured concrete, low ceilings, wide columns, dim lighting, and cold like the inside of a fridge day and night. And now the fluorescent tube behind her designated spot was out, she noticed as she got out. She glanced around the shadows, tempted to make a dash for the lift, but she had things to collect from the back seat. Loading up with a shoulder bag, coat and folder, she bumped the door closed with a hip and bent to pick up her shopping bags. As its echo faded, she heard a voice.

'Hi, Carly.'

Swinging around, she saw a man standing in the gloom at the rear of her car.

'Damien,' he said.

All she registered was that her arms were tangled in bags and bulk, and she was hemmed in by a column and another car.

'From the community gardens,' he said. 'We met at the markets. Can I give you a hand with those bags?'

She flicked her eyes around. Where had he come from? 'No, I'm fine.'

'I can get the lift for you then.' He started towards it.

Carly followed, happy to keep a few steps behind him. He'd seemed nice at the markets, still did, she supposed, but it was dark down here and a man had climbed on her bed and she had no idea how he got in.

Damien tapped the button, waited until she reached him. 'Talia, the girl who lived in your apartment, I used to help her sometimes with her cello.'

Carly smiled politely, thought *Maybe she'd given him a key.*

'She had a three-door hatch and that thing only just fit in the back with the seats down.'

'Did you know her well?'

'I asked her to play at the community gardens open day two years ago. I thought she'd do a few numbers over lunch but she played for hours. It was fantastic, classical music among the vegies as people wandered around. We had a record number sign up.' He chuckled as the doors started to slide apart. 'I think some people thought she'd be there every weekend.'

Inside the small cab, he hit the buttons for two and four, Carly pressed into the opposite corner, shopping bags a barrier on the floor between them.

'You having a quiet one tonight?' he asked.

It was the Dickens celebration at the book club, but he didn't need to know that. 'Yes, you?'

'Got a ton of work to catch up on. I'll probably be drinking coffee at midnight to get through it.'

He was wearing dress trousers and a white shirt, nothing like his community gardens/markets look. 'What do you do?'

'I'm in IT.' He glanced at the floor indicator as the elevator slowed, shuffled backwards as it bounced to a stop in the foyer. It opened on someone else she'd met at the markets: Stuart, the uni supervisor. He took a second to eye Damien, then Carly, his head pushed forward by the slight stoop, face moving side to side like a bird with a long neck.

'Hey, how you doing?' Damien asked.

'Yeah, good.' He stepped in, filled the small space between Carly and Damien, turned to face the closing doors.

His presence was a conversation stopper. Carly felt wedged into her corner now, trapped at the back, her only way out blocked by two man-shaped, thin-ish neighbours. Her pulse drummed in her throat, her palms were suddenly slippery. She smelled the wind still clinging to Stuart's scarf and musky office on Damien's shirt. She tried to hold her breath. She wanted to get out and take the stairs.

As the lift slowed for the second floor, Damien said quietly, 'This is me.'

Stuart hadn't pressed a button. Was she going to be stuck with him to the fourth? But he was moving before the doors parted, head forward, leading with his shoulder, exiting stage right as soon as the gap was wide enough. Damien paused on the tracks. 'Shout you a coffee if you drop by the markets on Saturday,' he smiled.

He seemed nice but she wasn't sure. 'Do you bribe all your customers?'

'Wherever possible.'

CARLY COULDN'T FIND the earrings she'd bought at the markets. She'd searched the small box where she kept her few bits of jewellery, the bathroom, the half bath, the coffee table and the kitchen counter. She'd spent twenty minutes at it and was annoyed she'd been careless, more agitated than she should have been about losing them – knowing it wasn't really what she was stressing about.

Leaving for the book club without them, she walked the zigzag stairs to Elizabeth's apartment with a bottle of wine and *Great Expectations*, anxiety jittering in her legs. Carly had once been outgoing and confident but Charlotte was inside her tonight. She was uncomfortable in social gatherings, always felt as though her mistakes were tattooed on her face and hands. Charlotte hadn't let anyone close since the reckless, arrogant version of herself had killed her friends. It was self-imposed isolation – not just punishment, but because she was frightened to trust herself.

Carly had accepted Elizabeth Jennings' invitation because it was time, she reminded herself. Still, knowing it didn't cure the anxiety – thirteen years of undeserving and on the sidelines was hard to unlearn.

'Carly.' Elizabeth said it like an announcement, standing in her doorway and looking her guest up and down. She waited until Carly was in the hallway before curling a bony hand around Carly's forearm. 'I hear you had a nasty incident. Are you all right?'

'I'm fine.' She smiled like it was already forgotten, not wanting her 'incident' to be the topic of discussion.

'Good girl. Then not another word.' A brusque pat and Elizabeth was hobbling ahead of her, clapping her hands when she reached the living room. 'People, people, our guest has arrived.'

Carly kept the smile stitched to her lips for the faces that turned her way. It looked like a throng but as Elizabeth handled the introductions, Carly realised it was only six people. Christina, holding a platter of cheese and crackers, called, 'Hello, hello.' Carly recognised the man with funky angular glasses from the second-hand bookstall at the markets. There was an older man with a thick white moustache and dark bushy eyebrows and three other women. The one leaning on crutches was Brooke, Carly assumed.

Handed a glass of wine, Carly was offered nibbles and absorbed into the chitchat. Relieved they were more interested in catching up with each other than interrogating the newcomer, Carly took in Elizabeth's lovely apartment. It resembled Carly's and yet was entirely different. Same high walls and French windows but a bigger, reconfigured layout, maybe with two or three bedrooms, and decorated with beautiful, exotic . . . things.

Shelves dominated one side of the room and were filled with books and shiny pieces of porcelain and little sculptures and objects Carly couldn't identify, that she wanted to go over and touch. There were worn leather sofas, a coffee table with intricately carved legs, a battered dining table, a dresser with rows of tiny drawers.

'Three minutes to kick-off.' It was Roland, the older man, who seemed to think it was his duty to keep the glasses filled.

'Elizabeth said "kick-off"?' the man from the markets asked, a smooth, lilting accent in his voice.

'I stand corrected,' Roland returned. 'She said "call to order". But I thought my sporting analogy was more appropriate for the usual scrum.'

Scrum? Smile, Carly, they're joking, surely.

'Don't listen to him,' Christina told Carly, still holding the cheese plate. 'It's all in good fun. Elizabeth likes to play head girl and we like to shout her down.' She snorted a laugh. 'That's how it works, isn't it, Dietrich?'

The man from the markets nodded slowly, giving it serious thought. 'Exactly. When she asks you to speak, just be honest.'

'When she asks me to speak?' *Was it too early to leave?*

'Oh, definitely,' Christina popped a cube of cheese into her mouth and talked around it. 'Just remember. It's a book club, she can't give you detention.'

What followed wasn't close to the courteous debate Carly had expected of Elizabeth's book club. It was considered and well read, rowdy and opinionated, and pretty damn funny from where Carly sat. Bold statements were countered with shout-downs, academic commentaries were met with TV and movie references. There were long-winded diversions, including one by Maxine, a woman who lived on Carly's floor, that involved airport bookshops, a recent trip to Croatia and Turkish delight.

Elizabeth kept things moving, adding opinions, calling for order and finally cornering Carly. From the midst of a discussion about

Great Expectations and *A Tale of Two Cities*, she said, 'Carly, we haven't heard from you yet.'

It wasn't quite true. She'd voted for Gwyneth Paltrow in the movie version of *Great Expectations* and made a couple of attempts to speak up, urging herself to join in, unsure of when it was her turn, then waiting too long and finding the topic had moved on. 'I've enjoyed listening,' she said.

'Listening is an important quality in a book club, a timely reminder to some of our members.' Elizabeth aimed stern looks at Roland and Maxine. 'But listening is not discussing, Carly.' She watched Carly over the top of her glasses as though she expected an answer. When she didn't get one, she lifted a stubborn chin. 'I noticed you brought one of the novels currently under discussion. I'd like to hear your thoughts.'

Carly's mouth went dry. The room waited for her response. She cleared her throat. 'Actually, I've only read one Dickens novel so I don't think I qualify for an opinion.'

'I see,' Elizabeth said. 'But you've read *Great Expectations*?'

'Yes. I finished it this morning.' Fictional anxiety let her forget her own for a while. 'Which probably makes me more likely to remember the details but less likely to have something relevant to say.'

Carly had hoped it might bring a little humour to the moment but Elizabeth responded with a firm voice. 'The only relevance is that you have read the book, Carly.' Then to the meeting: 'I propose we conclude our current discussion and move onto the work our guest is familiar with. Who would like to begin? Christina?'

Not wanting to be singled out again, Carly found the volume required to be heard and offered short, brief sentences she hoped would keep Elizabeth at bay.

The meeting was closed exactly two hours after it opened, Elizabeth announcing supper would follow. She caught Carly's eye across the coffee table and sent her a single, unsmiling nod. Approval or disapproval, Carly couldn't tell.

She avoided the older woman at the post-discussion gathering, drinking wine with Maxine and Dietrich, learning the former was a university lecturer and the latter was German and writing a crime novel in his spare time. Carly's presence eventually prompted the subject of her new apartment.

'Why did Talia leave?' Carly asked. 'Howard mentioned an accident.'

Maxine exchanged a glance with Dietrich, 'She was in a car accident. A bad one.'

'Spinal injury,' Dietrich added. 'C-eight.'

'Quadradplegic.' Maxine raised her eyebrows in silent commiseration. 'Anyway, you bought a great apartment.'

Using a dessert platter as an excuse to move on, Carly carried it around, making her way to Brooke on the other side of the room, hoping cakes would get her some more information about Talia.

'Christina told me you were a friend of Talia's,' Carly started.

Brooke's eyes stayed on the selection. 'Yes.'

'I bought Talia's apartment.'

Brooke took a brownie, looked past Carly as she answered. 'Yes.'

It wasn't the first time Carly had been ignored at polite gatherings of neighbours, and her face stilled over the instinctive flare of shame it triggered. 'They're delicious,' she said and moved on.

She hadn't spoken to Elizabeth since the meeting broke up and braced herself for another curt retort as she lined up to say goodnight.

'Ah, Carly.' Elizabeth was standing by the dining table, leaning on her stick as she received her departing guests. 'I watched you thinking for an hour and couldn't bear it any longer. Such a pleasure to see you finally speak your mind.'

That's what it was about? 'I was . . . a bit daunted by the company.'

'My dear, if you've read the book, you've got the right to an opinion. Don't let anyone make you think otherwise.'

A pat on the back. It made her smile. 'I'll remember that.'

'Our custom is to have a majority decision on new members so I'm unable to offer another invitation yet, although I will be advocating for you. You'll be notified in time.'

After the boisterous discussion, Carly was surprised at the

formality – and that she wanted to be voted in. 'Thank you for the support. This is a lovely room. The shelves are the perfect setting for a book club.'

'Thank you, I like it. It reminds me every day of my wonderful life. My husband and I lived and travelled around the world for many years.'

Carly eyed them again, wondering at her chances of being seventy- or eighty-something and well travelled. She'd already wasted half her time. 'So many beautiful things you've collected.'

'They all have their memories. You must come and have tea with me. I can tell you some stories and try not to bore you.'

Carly saw herself to the door and started down the corridor. The hollow centre of the warehouse was cold and black, the echo of her footsteps coming back to her like another set of shoes on the timber floors. She checked over her shoulder to make sure it was just her, saw no one but picked up her pace as she started up. By the time she reached the fourth floor, she was power-walking. Head down and breathing hard, nerves tingling on the back of her neck, she swung off the top step and slammed into someone on the landing.

13

————————

Carly's screech and the clatter of falling crutches resounded around the deserted corridor.

'Oh, god, sorry,' Carly gasped.

'No, my fault,' Brooke said, hopping to the railing.

Picking up the crutches and passing them back, Carly wondered what Brooke was doing there – she lived one level down. And who took the stairs with crutches? 'Are you okay?'

'No, I'm fine. I wasn't sure which way you'd come up. I'd thought I'd see you if I waited here.'

'You were waiting for me?' She'd ignored her half an hour ago.

'Yes,' she said, her eyes sliding away like they had over the dessert plate, and she shifted her weight on her crutches, something closer to uneasiness than discomfort.

It made Carly think about internet searches and old newspaper stories. 'Why?'

'I . . .' Brooke dragged teeth over her bottom lip. '. . . wanted to apologise.'

Carly's eyebrows rose. 'To me?'

'I was rude tonight and I didn't . . . it's not . . .' She huffed a weak laugh. 'I didn't want you to think I was a bitch for ignoring you.'

An apology was a first. 'I thought you might've been short-sighted,' Carly smiled.

Brooke gave her a brief one back. 'I wish I could blame it on that.' She cleared her throat, took a breath, as though whatever she had to say was going to be difficult. 'Talia and I were friends. She was in a car accident last year and had to go back to Perth to live with her parents.'

'I heard. I'm sorry.'

Brooke turned to the railing, kept her gaze on the dark, empty beyond. 'I still get upset. She was so talented, such a beautiful person, now she can't feed herself. And I miss her. It's why I was, I don't know, tongue-tied.' She shrugged. 'Rude, really. I heard you talking to Maxine about her. I wasn't expecting it and it just all came back again.'

'Sure. Of course.' Something Carly understood.

'Anyway, I wanted to say welcome to the building. I didn't think I could do it at Elizabeth's without getting teary and I didn't want anyone worrying that I was upset. So, welcome. Your flat is lovely, we had some good times there. I hope you enjoy it.'

Carly wanted to ask about Talia's friends and keys but Brooke looked like she'd said all she could. Carly walked with her to the bridge over the atrium, Brooke told her she'd be fine from there. Carly understood about needing to be alone with those kinds of memories and left her to swing on her crutches to the lift. Opening her apartment, she eyed the long hallway and the darkness beyond. She'd toasted Talia for leaving – and Brooke's friend had walked out one day and never made it back.

It didn't feel good. It felt like the air was weighted with something dark and ominous. Carly walked to the windows, threw the doors open and let the cold winter wind rush through. She didn't want whatever it was touching her.

HE IS on top of her. All of him on all of her. The weight is suffocating. It is crushing the air from her.

Her breath is short, sharp and panting.

His is warm and wafting over her face.

She doesn't move. She doesn't know if she can, she just doesn't. His bones are hard notches in her flesh. Knees, hips, ribs. Feet beside her ankles are anchoring her legs together.

He isn't raping her. Not yet.

She wants to see his face. Searches the blackness, catches only dark on dark. A shape, head and shoulders. *Where is his fucking face?*

Anger. It doesn't loosen whatever has paralysed her but it feels like fighting. On the inside. She fixes her eyes on his darkness, willing him to go away. To fuck off and leave her alone.

He doesn't. He clasps a hand to her throat.

Choking, gagging, thumping in her ears. Her anger is replaced by bone-chilling dread. She squeezes her eyes. Hears him. Not a word, not even a voice. Just a husky, unhurried huff of laughter. It puffs across her eyelids. Her scalp ripples with fear. Panic is a high-pitched note in her head.

She waits for the air to be choked from her, for death to come. But the hand lifts, the pressure is gone, the skin cold where his fingers have been.

Now? Will it happen now? Will he cut her throat? Break her bones? Force her legs apart?

Tears leak from under her eyelids but she won't open them, she doesn't want to see him now. She just wants it over.

14

———

Carly's eyes were fixed on the security chain. It was slung across the jamb and fitted into its slide. She couldn't remember doing it. She couldn't remember getting here, on her haunches at the end of the hall. Just the urgent, panicked call to the police as she huddled in the corner.

There were aching, tender patches on her shins, her forearms, a shoulder, the top of her head. The tips of her fingers felt grazed. She was out of breath, she must have been running. The stairs? Through the apartment?

Two cops arrived – Dean and his partner. She wiped at tears as she explained. They did a quick, cursory sweep, no other officers turned up this time. When they were finished, Dean cocked his head at the front door and waited while his colleague disappeared into the corridor.

'How are you doing, Carly?' His voice had a harder edge tonight.

She tucked shaking fists under her arms, her tongue so dry it felt like there was paper stuck to the roof. 'You found nothing, right?'

'That's right.'

'He was *on top* of me. He . . .' She pressed fingers to her lips.

'You want to tell me what's going on?'

'I . . . he . . . You tell me.' It was his job to figure it out.

'I can see you're upset. I don't think it's an act.'

Carly stopped, blinked. 'An *act*?'

'There's been no one here, has there, Carly?'

Her mouth opened. Nothing came out.

'I'm not sure what's going on but you need to know the police aren't on call for your own personal issues.'

'My *issues*?'

A pause, something reticent in it. 'I don't know what this is about but I have to warn you that if you continue to call the police, you'll be facing a charge of public mischief.'

'*I'll* be charged? What about the arsehole who keeps breaking in? He's the one who should be charged.'

'Is that what it's about, Carly? You want someone charged?'

She didn't speak, didn't know what to say.

'It's not the right way to go about it,' he went on. 'If there's someone bothering you, an ex, maybe, someone you came here to get away from,' he raised eyebrows in question, 'there are ways of dealing with it. But not like this.'

She came here to get away from herself. 'It's not . . .' How did she explain that?

'There are laws about harassing people,' he said. 'If you need help with that, you can talk to me. Okay?'

'I *don't know* who it is.'

He nodded. 'If it's something else, Carly, you need to figure it out another way.'

'Something else?' Blood thumped in her throat. 'Like *what*?'

His voice softened but his eyes were hard and direct. 'People call the police for all sorts of reasons. It's not always about a crime.'

It took a moment to understand. Incredulousness made her pitch slide up. 'You think I'm *enjoying* this?'

'I don't know, Carly. Some people do.'

She stepped away from him, heat flaring in her cheeks. He thought she was needy, messed up, nuts. She'd come here to get away from that, too. She lifted her chin. 'That's it then?'

He produced a business card again and set it on the counter. 'My number, if it's something you want to talk about.'

She ignored it. Tried to sound more composed than she felt. 'Thank you for checking the apartment. I'd like you to leave now.'

He followed her down the hall, paused in the doorway. 'Look after yourself, Carly.' It sounded like an instruction.

She watched him to the stairs, angry and frightened and not sure she wanted to go back inside. A movement caught her eye, something passing through a strip of light under Nate's door.

He was awake again? How much had he heard? Was he was waiting for the police to leave before he checked on her this time?

She didn't want to see him, didn't want to explain what had happened – the man in her loft or the police accusation. Carly shut the door hard, engaged the lock and slid the chain into its slot. Her pulse was racing, her body trembling. She couldn't stand still.

Turning, pacing, she cut a path back and forth around the living room. Dean and his partner had lit up the place for their search and she left it that way, hoping the arsehole who'd been in her loft was watching her now. That he got her message: she was awake and alert, don't bother coming back. Because the police weren't going to stop him.

An *act*? *She'd* be charged? What the fuck?

On a pass of the French windows she stopped, looked the doors up and down. Both were locked. They were locked when Dean checked them. She swung her head, stared across the room at the hallway, remembering the security chain at the other end. It had been hooked on when she was waiting for the police.

Had she done it? Had he got in and she'd locked up after him?

She frowned, remembered staggering on the stairs and huddling at the front door and . . . nothing in between. Walking the steps, she stared at the nightlight she'd plugged into the power point at the bottom. It had been under the vanity in the half bath when she moved in, she'd forgotten about it until leaving lights on at night had caused more nightmares than sleep. Now, under the downlights, its glow was a tiny, rosy dot. Was it on when she stumbled down? She closed her eyes, couldn't recall. Felt instead her harsh breath at the front door.

Fear, yes, but more than that. Her lungs had been dragging for air like she'd been for a hard, fast walk. What had she done? How long could it have been from gasping out of bed to reaching the door? Twenty seconds?

Five minutes? An hour?

Carly lifted a hand to her pyjama top, something cold winding its way up her spine. The fabric was still damp with sweat – she'd done more than just run down the hall. There were bruises and bumps coming up and her fingertips were tender. Had she searched the apartment? Swept around the locks and barricaded herself in before she called the police? If she'd done that, which door had been unlocked?

She glanced around, thinking it through. Had the man on her bed got through the security chain and she'd relatched it? Or had he used both the front door and the balcony, in one and out the other?

She rubbed at a tender spot on her hip and another on the tip of an ear. Maybe she'd done more than lock doors. Maybe she'd seen him and tried to hide. Or run away. Or fought him. Had he hit her and knocked her out?

Dean's business card was on the kitchen counter. She wanted to call him, shout *What about the bruises?* Tell him to come back and take a look at her shins and arms, explain how they fitted his theory. Except she couldn't explain them either.

15

———————

'Hey, there.' It was Reuben at her side, a hand by her elbow as though she might need help to reach a seat. 'You look . . . pale.'

She was here most mornings windblown and without makeup. She must look as bad as she felt today – headachy and lethargic and freaked out. 'Had a big night. Just need a coffee.'

'Like that, is it? You want a quiet table and a double shot?'

She gave a grateful smile. 'Just coffee. I need to walk it off.'

'Each to their own when it comes to a hangover, I say. Two minutes, special circumstances gets you to the head of the queue.'

Instead of hyping her up, the coffee calmed her, easing the anxiety, making her feel more coordinated. She'd been aiming for the breakwater but didn't make it, needing to stop a couple of times to catch her breath and stretch the tightness in her legs. She paused again on the kerb opposite the warehouse, ran her eyes over its railings and windows, imagining a man in black climbing quietly, slipping over the edge of her balcony, lying on her and laughing.

Nate's door opened as she unlocked her apartment. 'Carly,' he called softly, half in and half out of the corridor. 'You okay?'

'Sure,' she lied.

'I heard the police at your place again and you were gone early. I wondered . . .'

'I'm fine.' There was no way she was going to tell him. Not now.

'Was it another break-in?'

'Just a routine check. You know, after the last one.'

He stepped a little further into the corridor. 'At 3 am?'

She hadn't thought that through. 'They saw my lights on and rang ahead. Being diligent, I suppose.'

'You were awake?'

'Yes. Sorry if they disturbed you.'

'They didn't. I just . . .' he cocked his head, a little reluctance in it '. . . wanted to make sure you were okay.'

She watched him a moment, wondering about that – awake at night, listening at his door, asking when she didn't want to tell. Grim moods and short on conversation. 'I'm fine.'

'DON'T YOU LOOK NICE TODAY?' Dakota grinned as she slid into the seat next to Carly's. The teacher hadn't arrived and the classroom was noisy with early-morning greetings.

Carly had thought about skipping another day, curling up on the sofa and sleeping off the aches, but the apartment felt tainted and she needed to remind herself of what she was doing here. Now she raised a doubtful eyebrow at Dakota's compliment – she'd had four hours sleep and fatigue felt like soup in her veins.

'Ye-ah. You've got the make-up going and the hair piled up and you're rocking that scarf.'

Carly lifted her fingers to the soft green fabric at her throat. *Rocking it?* 'Thanks.'

'So who are you trying to impress?'

That made Carly smile a little. Another man to screw up her life was the last thing she wanted. 'No one.'

'Oh, sure.'

'No, really. I had a late night, the make-up is to cover the black rings.'

'Good job then.' Dakota dropped her bag on the floor, picked up one end of Carly's scarf. 'And this is really pretty. New?'

'Yes and no. Two bucks second-hand.' A cheap, celebratory gift to herself the day after she arrived.

'Bargain. I love vintage. We should have a scrounge together sometime.'

Carly checked Dakota's face to see if she was serious. 'Sure.'

'We could grab a coffee somewhere nice then do a few of the second-hand places. I know some good ones.'

Dakota's enthusiasm made Carly feel jaded today - and reminded her that she'd been like that once too. That version of her hadn't always been reckless. 'Sounds like fun.'

CARLY HELD herself together with coffee and paracetamol, dragging herself into the apartment in the mid-afternoon, not caring now that it felt infected by the night before, only wanting to sleep. On the sofa, nowhere near the loft. Not yet.

Sleep came in surges of black slumber and half-conscious hazes, oblivion and meandering thoughts. She jerked awake feeling like she was suffocating, her body remembering the weight of him, her limbs too heavy to push him off. Then she slipped back under to the beat of the blood pulsing in her ears.

The last time her eyes flew open, the ache in her body had gone and she lay there, the dream still filtering through her. Feeling its substance, feeling *him*. Arms and legs, sharp bones and the pressure on her chest from another ribcage. Lean and muscular. Wide across the shoulders, thick through the thighs, feet reaching beyond hers.

A sound made the memory snap off as though the power had been cut. She sat up, nerve endings prickling, eyes towards the front door. Another, a dull thud had her padding across the apartment, standing at the deadlock, adrenaline tingling in the roots of her hair.

She heard footsteps, the brief rumble of a male voice, the tone suggesting swearing. Not right outside but close. She pressed her ear to the jamb. A clatter of keys. To her door? She straightened, fingers tingling, rechecking the security chain.

A vibration through the plaster as a door opened. Nate's. It slammed, the echo in the atrium humming for long seconds. Carly watched the wall that separated their living spaces, wondering if he was drunk or just mightily ticked off. His balcony door rattled in its frame, a clatter as one side banged open, two solid thumps she couldn't identify. Whatever was going on for him, it wasn't getting better.

Join the club, she thought. Maybe she should invite him over. Knock on his door and say *Shitty day? Me too. Feel like a drink?*

To what end, Carly?

Because shitty could be lonely. Because she had experience in that. Because the apartment didn't feel inspirational now and being here on her own wasn't so great.

Or was it something else? she asked herself. Was it that thing she did when it got bad? Turning to someone, anyone, when the loneliness was unbearable. Making more poor choices and living with them to hurt herself.

Outside, the afternoon was fading fast. Inside, darkness was creeping at the edges of the room. Carly switched on a light and poured a glass of red wine, her hand trembling a little. Adrenaline rush, she told herself. She took a sip. Her psychologist would be impressed – she'd recognised her failing and made a decision to keep it in check.

She held the glass up. 'Cheers, Carly.'

Locked inside with her own company, in the dark, scared of her bedroom.

'Yeah, well done, Carly.'

She stood to one side of the French windows, watching the street out of sight. Someone knew how to get into her apartment without waking her. Someone was amused by her fear. Someone might be thinking it would be funnier to hurt her next time.

Was fate playing with her now? Did it want to take this away from her too? She'd lived in fear for thirteen years of the retribution that would come for her.

And she'd paid her price. Three lives given for the three she'd taken. That score had been levelled five months ago. She'd suffered enough, she told herself. She didn't have to accept this too.

'I'D LIKE to add to my previous description of the man breaking into my apartment,' Carly told Anne Long the next morning.

She'd called ahead to ask if they could meet before Carly's class. 'No problem,' Anne had told her, then kept her waiting in the foyer for half an hour. The detective had skipped 'Hello' and 'How are you', going straight to 'Carly, come through.' Carly took it as a good sign, getting straight down to business.

'Do you know about the last break-in?' Carly asked. 'The one two days ago?'

'I've read the report from the officers who attended the scene.'

Carly eyed the folder on the table in front of the detective. She didn't know how police reports worked – whether it was just the facts or if Dean Quentin had added his own opinion. 'I've had time to think a little more clearly about the intruder. The last time, he was on top of me. Lying on me. It was still dark, I couldn't see, but I remember some details now.'

More had come back as she'd thought it through again in the loft last night. She paused for the detective to find a pen or open the file in front of her. She didn't do either.

Carly licked her lips, uncertainty creeping into her resolve. 'He's a bit taller than me, I'd say between one-eighty-two and one-ninety-two. He's broader than me but not by much. Lean and strong but not super muscly. I felt his top or jacket on my face. It was some kind of smooth nylon, I think. Cool to the touch. Not like a baggy, sweatshirt kind of hoodie. I think his trousers were a tight fit and I could feel the shape of his legs.'

Anne gave a nod. Not approval, just acknowledgement that Carly had come to the end. 'This was the third break-in you've reported?'

'Yes. So it's got to help, right?'

'I spoke to Constable Quentin yesterday.' It was a statement, as though there was nothing more to add.

Dean Quentin had called Carly a liar. 'He thought I was . . . He thought I might've known who was breaking in but I don't.'

'Carly, we ran a check on you following that call-out,' Anne said. 'Police records show you were scheduled in a mental health facility after an attempted suicide five months ago.'

Something hot and hard lodged in Carly's throat. She dropped her eyes.

'Is that right, Carly?' The tone was softer but insistent. Some kind of *We get it now and you need to fess up.*

Carly gripped the edge of the table. 'Yes.'

'I understand you've only recently moved here. It can be difficult establishing new medical arrangements, but I think you need to make an effort to sort that out now.'

'I'm not sick and I'm not making it up!' She lifted her chin. 'A man is breaking into my apartment. He's done it three times.'

'Without damaging locks or leaving fingerprints.'

Carly paused, frowned. 'No fingerprints?'

Anne opened the folder, pulled out a page and laid it on top. 'That's right. No fingerprints were found on either occasion your apartment was dusted.'

'But you said . . .' Carly stopped.

'Said what?'

Their last conversation as she'd sat in the campus car park ran through her mind: *I'm going to get back to you on those, Carly. When there's something to talk about.* 'Why didn't you tell me last week you didn't find prints?'

'I'm wondering why you thought I would, Carly.'

'What do you mean why? There was someone in my apartment.' She pushed a hand into her hair, held it there as she tried to figure it out. 'He must've worn gloves.'

'No, Carly. Gloves leave distinctive marks. Forensics didn't find any of those either. The only prints were from the officers who answered your call.' She lifted her eyebrows. 'And you.'

The last two words, the pointed expression on the detective's face, made Carly's heart pound. Anne Long thought Carly had invented the whole thing. That she'd called triple-O in the middle of the night, made up a story for a bunch of cops in uniforms and followed it through for forensics officers and detectives. That she'd done it *three times*. Possibly she thought Carly needed medication or another trip to hospital, but right now Anne Long looked like she didn't care what it was about just so long as Carly understood she'd been caught out.

Carly pressed her lips together, wanting to defend herself, realising there was no good place to start.

'I believe Constable Quentin has explained to you that any more unnecessary calls to the police could result in charges.' Anne slipped the page back into her folder as though its presence had been enough to prove her point.

'I don't know how he's doing it,' Carly said.

Anne met her eyes, said nothing.

'Look, I was in a bad way five months ago. I had a miscarriage, I was recovering from surgery and my husband . . .' *Left me. Told me he didn't know how I could live with all the deaths I caused.* 'Yes, I took some pills. I was sad and exhausted and desperate. Not crazy. I don't *need* this. I need to be able to sleep at night without being scared. This,' she waved an arm around, indicating the detective and the police station, 'I need it to *stop*.'

Anne stood, picked up her file. 'My advice to you is to get some help, Carly.'

16

—————

Carly drove. Back and forth along the harbour, back and forth to the campus, not stopping, not able to release her hands from the steering wheel. Angry, anxious, sobbing.

She'd thought moving away was enough. She'd thought she could leave the pain and grief behind and start over, be someone better. And now it was here with her, making her Charlotte again. Making her remember the day fate finally evened the score.

She was at work at the post office when the pain and bleeding started. She'd reached twelve weeks this time, longer than the first two pregnancies. Only three months pregnant but Carly had already ached with love. She took herself to the hospital – the baby had died, the night that followed was numbed by loss and nightmares. After the D and C the next morning, Carly still groggy with anaesthetic, the doctor spoke with Carly and Adrian. *You can try again.* It had felt like hope. But instead of taking Carly home, Adrian drove to her mother's house, parked in the driveway and told Carly he was done. *I don't love you enough to try again. I don't love you enough to stay around for your grief.* He left her curled under the doona in her childhood bedroom, the place she'd waited for broken bones to heal, where she'd mourned her friends and burned with shame. This time, the air was infused with failure.

Her first marriage was a disaster. It was a year after the night in the canyon, Carly fell pregnant and he felt obliged. He'd hit her once – it had felt like something she deserved. He walked away two weeks after she miscarried.

Adrian had never been a good husband; loneliness had made Charlotte accepting. Their first baby was unplanned, the sorrow when she lost it overwhelming. It brought back buried memories – that last day, their laughter on the ridge, their whispered last words – as though she was being reminded why she'd been punished. Adrian didn't want to try again but a yearning, a need to love and laugh again, had taken hold in Carly. Only she'd forgotten she had no right to happiness, not when so many others had been hurt by her actions.

You need to accept it's not going to happen now were her mother's words of comfort when she arrived home and found Carly where Adrian had left her. That buck-up-and-get-on-with-it attitude was the reason Marilyn never understood why Carly couldn't sleep with the lights on, why she still woke screaming from nightmares. Her words the next morning had cut Carly like a knife. *You're thirty-three, you've had two husbands and three miscarriages. Happily ever after is never going to happen, darling.*

Carly stopped at traffic lights, squeezed her eyes shut, tried to block it out. But the movie had started and there were more scenes to be played.

Memories had pushed and shoved in her mind all that day. She was exhausted but couldn't sleep without seeing the blood – of her friends, from her babies. The blood of six souls on her hands.

A horn blared behind her. Carly swerved back into her lane, tears wet on her cheeks. If she'd got in a car that day, it might've ended differently. But she'd had nowhere to go, no one to turn to. *It won't help to lock yourself away, Carly. Selina's coming over with the kids. We thought they'd make you feel better.*

A dam had burst then. *Don't speak to me. Don't speak to me!* Carly had yelled. She heaved a chest of drawers across the bedroom door, sat in a corner and watched the images of her life flash across the walls. She heard voices: a baby crying, her mother and sister demanding Carly come out and talk. She'd laughed at them. What the fuck did they expect from her?

While they murmured in the kitchen, Carly held little pills in the palm of her hand. A lot of them. Thought about tipping her head back, letting them slide into her mouth. Sleeping, long and black and silent. She'd sat like that for a long time. Exhausted. Hurting. Passive. Like she'd been since she'd walked that ledge and called, *Come on, it's fine.*

It was a police officer who pulled her out of it. Tony Feathermill. She'd been at school with him, he lived down the street. Marilyn had rung him, told him she'd seen medication and scotch in Carly's bag.

Tony Feathermill kicked in the door like he was raiding a meth lab. Ambulance officers followed. Yes, she'd taken pills. Some, two, three, maybe more, she couldn't remember.

This time, hospital had been a relief. She had a room to herself, there were staff to care for her, people with gentle hands and voices who passed her tissues when she cried. They pumped her stomach, discovered there was no need. The scotch was her mother's invention and she'd only swallowed three pills, she could've slept them off. She couldn't remember whether she'd decided not to take more or fallen asleep thinking about it.

She asked to stay and was there for a week – resting, refusing visitors, except Liam, her psychologist. And as she talked, she realised what fate had done. Three souls for three souls. It had taken from her what she'd taken from others. She'd cut short promising lives and shattered families. Thirteen years later, the score was even. She had paid her price.

Liam had talked about finally forgiving herself, pleased with her progress. But it wasn't forgiveness, it was release from prison. The one she built for herself when the police had decided there were no charges to be laid for the deaths in the canyon. Once it was gone, there was no reason to stay in Burden. It took her five months to leave. She needed to regain her strength after the miscarriage and the emotional trauma, and she needed money to make a new life work. When the house sold, she did the most assertive thing she'd done since she'd set off for that canyon – she bought her apartment. And now she was here.

Actually, she was at the campus, driving into the car park on automatic. 'Attempted suicide' wasn't on her enrolment form. There was no exchange of information between educators and police, at least not of that kind. All anyone knew of her was that she'd moved from out west and hadn't settled on a business idea. She was Carly Townsend, not damaged, guilty, anxious Charlotte.

She turned off the engine. Two lessons had been and gone since she'd walked into the police station. It was ten minutes into the next one and arriving late wouldn't go unnoticed. She checked her face in the rear-view. Her eyes were red-rimmed and swollen – she looked like Charlotte on a bad day. The urge was there to embrace it, to go home, cry some more, lose herself in reproach, fall back on old habits, but the gaze in the mirror locked on her own. *Go to class. Be someone better. Don't fuck it up.*

The teacher turned from the whiteboard as Carly stepped into the classroom. 'Glad to see you've decided to join us, Carly.'

The smile was easier than she'd expected. 'No wonder I had to wait three hours for a plumber, half of them are here.'

17

___

Carly put her mobile on the kitchen counter, paced to the windows and back. Picked the phone up for the tenth time. *Do it, Carly.*

'Adrian Townsend.' It was his distracted work voice.

'It's Charlotte.'

There was a silence on the other end that stretched beyond surprise. 'Charlotte. How are you?'

'I'm fine.'

'Have you spoken to Marilyn? She keeps calling to see if I've heard from you.'

Their first conversation since the house had sold and his thoughts went to Carly's mother, or maybe he was just sick of fielding her calls. Carly couldn't tell, she just twisted the knife a little more. 'You still seeing Danielle?' Three weeks after he'd left her – after he'd lost a child – Adrian had been in another woman's bed.

'Yeah, about that.' A pause. 'I was going to call but I thought it was better to wait, in case it didn't . . . well, no point if . . . So you've heard anyway.'

She didn't know what he was talking about, wasn't sure she

wanted to but she'd opened this door. 'No, I haven't. Why don't you tell me.'

'Fuck.' He didn't say anything for a while, his breath heavy on the other the line. 'She's . . . we're pregnant.'

Carly's lungs froze. Bile rose in her throat.

'Twelve weeks. Past the danger period now. We had the scan yesterday and everything looks healthy.' He said it as though Carly might be worried about Danielle. When she didn't speak, he said, 'You there?'

'I thought you didn't want kids.'

'I never said that.'

'That's right. You didn't want them with *me*.' Tears burned her eyes.

'Can you try to be happy for me? At least one of us gets to be a parent.'

Carly wanted to scream, just open her mouth and howl at the flat emptiness of her belly. But she hadn't called him to hurt herself. With Anne Long's doubting voice in her head, knowing there was no one else trying to figure it out, Carly had kept going back to Dean Quentin's words: *If there's someone bothering you, an ex, maybe.* She wiped the wetness from her face. 'Have you been in Newcastle?'

'What? When?'

She held onto his tone a moment, not sure if it was surprise or hedging. 'You still do business down here, right?'

'Yes.'

'When were you last here?'

A pause. 'Why?'

Business, she'd suspected, had involved women at times. 'I don't care what you do anymore. I just want to know if you've been here recently.'

'And I don't need to explain myself to you.'

'You do if you come to my apartment.'

'You think I might visit?' There was a snarky amusement in his voice. 'What, drop in for a bourbon and a fuck with my ex while I'm in town?'

Carly clenched her teeth. 'I thought I saw you here.'

'At your apartment?'

'Yes. I thought . . .'

'What?'

'I thought you might've wanted to see where I was. There's secu-rity here, you might've tried to get in, told someone you were my husband.'

'You thought I got into your building?'

She pushed two fingers into her forehead. 'Were you here?'

'I was in Newcastle overnight two weeks ago.'

A man had sat on her bed two weeks ago. He'd done it more recently than that – and Adrian was loose with the truth. 'Did you come to my place?'

'I went to a meeting and dinner. I stayed with a . . . friend. I didn't need help with a drink and a fuck. If you saw me, it wasn't because I was looking for you.'

She squeezed her eyes shut, ticked off, disgusted, but satisfied. 'Okay, fine. Have a good life.'

She tossed the phone at the sofa, crossed her arms, clenched her teeth. It was almost dark outside and she made a slow circuit of the view beyond the balcony – warehouses, streets, homes. Was someone watching back tonight?

The trill of her mobile pulled her eyes from the glass. Her mother, interesting timing. Long enough for Adrian to have called. Carly thought about ignoring it, but figured she may as well see it through or the phone wouldn't stop.

'Mum.'

'Finally you answer your phone. Are you all right?'

'I'm fine.'

'I just talked to Adrian, he said you didn't sound fine.'

'Are you ringing to get my opinion or hear for yourself?'

'I'm ringing to see how you are. Why do you have to be so temperamental?'

Carly took up her position at the window again. 'I'm fine, Mum.

The apartment's fine. The course is fine. The weather is fine. It's all fine.'

'Adrian said you thought he'd broken into your apartment.'

'I said I thought I saw him.'

'He said you were upset about Danielle and the baby.'

'Did he write a report or just ring to tell on me?'

'Charlotte, please, I'm concerned about you. This imagining you're seeing Adrian and the agitation, it's very worrying. Have you talked to someone about it?'

She didn't mean a chat over coffee with a friend. 'I don't need to talk to someone.'

'I knew it was too soon for this move. All that walking you did, not wanting to see Selina's children, not talking to me. You should think about coming home before it gets too much for you.'

Carly pulled in a long, deep breath. 'Mum. Stop.'

'You had a *breakdown*, Charlotte.'

Something *had* broken that day. The thread that had tethered her to Burden. To memories of dead friends. She never attempted to explain it to her mother; they'd barely spoken after Carly's stay in hospital. There was no point, Marilyn never listened, just like she wasn't listening now.

'I *live* here,' Carly said.

'You can just tell people you changed your mind. There's no shame in that.'

Carly's voice was loud. 'I'm not going back. You need to accept that.'

'Charlotte . . .'

She hung up, satisfaction and relief in the sudden silence. She watched the street for a good long while after that, trying to keep her focus on other things. People arriving home, lights coming on, curtains being drawn. Evening traffic. She recognised a figure heading from the shops, plastic shopping bags in each hand. Nate – hunched shoulders, slight limp.

A few minutes later she heard a noise in the corridor and turned away from the window, crossed the apartment and stood by the front door. At the sound of soft footfalls, she unlatched the security chain and took half a step into the passageway.

Nate was fumbling with keys, a bag of groceries at his feet. Only his head moved as he turned to look at her.

'Hey,' Carly said, her voice flat, a little hard, like it had been on the phone.

Maybe he heard it and mistook it for a complaint. 'Do you hear me when I come in?'

'Sometimes. Good day?'

He straightened, seemed to consider what to tell her. 'Usual stuff. You?'

'Just like old times. Feel like a drink?'

His eyes stayed on her, maybe weighing up the voice and the invitation. Not even close to flirting. 'Sure.'

'You drink red?'

'When it's on offer.'

'I'll bring a bottle.'

18

———————

Carly was in the corridor with the shiraz before she let herself think about what she was doing. A familiar mood had descended. She needed company, interference, something to block the thoughts that were gathering. Anne Long and her advice, Adrian, her mother – reproach would follow and she didn't want it.

Nate had left his door open. She knocked and went in. High ceilings, French windows, exposed brickwork, stainless steel. All the same features were there but they were turned around and out of place: the loft stairs on the opposite side, there were extra doors and a different-shaped kitchen.

'Wine glasses are underneath.' He pointed at the island bar. 'You pour while I put this stuff away.'

She liked his brevity even more tonight. Finding two large glasses, she poured a decent measure into each and set them on the counter. On the other side, Nate turned from the fridge and picked one up. 'Cheers.' He mimed a tap against her glass as though that was as close as he wanted to get. He took a single mouthful and went back to his unpacking.

Carly wound a path through his living room, eyes skimming matching leather seating, a low table, a large flat-screen TV. One wall was painted deep blue, a single black-and-white photo at its centre – a yacht under spinnaker. No cushions, no books, no knick-knacks, as though an effort had been made to select furniture and colours but the money or the interest had run out. Carly stood beside his windows and looked into the street. Same view, slightly different angle. If anyone was watching, they'd see her here – with her fit, muscular, male neighbour.

Shortening her gaze, she took in the reflection of the room. The groceries were gone and Nate was at the counter, fingers on the stem of his wine glass, watching her across the space. Probably wondering what the hell she was doing here. Don't be the weird neighbour, she told herself. The one who invites herself for a drink and then is tense and silent. She found a smile as she turned. 'Your apartment has a different layout to mine.'

'It's a two-bedder. One up, one down.' He pointed at the loft and a doorway she didn't have. 'Our ensuites are back-to-back. Nuts?'

'Sorry?'

'Nuts. Some people are allergic.'

'Oh. No, I'm not. Don't go to any trouble.'

'It's nuts and a bowl. Take a seat.'

She sat on one end of a sofa. Nate flicked lights on as he made his way over, slid the nuts onto the low table and took the chair beside her. 'You're my first guest. Lucky I picked up the dirty socks.'

'First ever?'

'Since I've been back.' He tipped his head from side to side. 'In a long time.'

Carly thought about the grimness she'd seen in him, wondered if he preferred to be alone or if no one wanted to visit. 'How's your knee?'

'No better, no worse.'

'Any news from the specialist?'

A hand moved to the kneecap, thumb kneading one side. 'I see him in a month.'

'Will he assess you for work?'

'For surgery. There's a chance it'll repair on its own. If it hasn't, I'll have to go under the knife.'

'What does that mean for your job?'

'Long recovery, depends how well it goes.' His shrug was tight-boned and brief.

She wasn't about to tell him to buck up, it'll be fine. 'Good luck.'

He nodded, glancing around as though looking for something else to talk about. 'I need to get some ice on it. Do you mind?'

'No. Please.' Carly munched on cashews as she watched his stiff-legged gait to and from the freezer, empathising with his pain and recovery, remembering what it was like to be fielding questions. As he positioned an icepack around the knee of his jeans, she said, 'What did you do before you worked on the oil rig?'

'Designed stuff. I'm an engineer.'

She raised her eyebrows. 'Is that what you do on the oil rig? Design it? Bits of it? Renovations and extensions.'

Amusement flickered on his lips. 'Bathrooms and sundecks?'

'I've no idea.'

'No. I'm a roughneck. I do grunt work, operate machinery, a bit of maintenance.'

Long hours, hard work and cramped quarters, he'd said another time. She'd come here for a better life, why did he leave for something worse? 'You didn't like being an engineer?'

'It's fine but I'll be heading back to the oil rig if my knee holds up.' He shrugged. 'The money's good. It paid off this place.'

She thought engineers were well paid. 'Is that what you wanted?'

'I wanted a lot of things. Mostly to leave.'

And now he was back here, poor bastard. 'I get that. Sometimes leaving is the only thing left to do.'

His eyes found hers. 'Yeah.'

'Will you stay if your knee . . . ?'

'Haven't thought that far. You?'

'I'm never going back.'

'An ex?'

'He's just part of it.' She hesitated, not sure she wanted the conversation to keep going in this direction. 'You?'

'She's just part of it.'

She took a sip of wine. He took a handful of nuts.

'Short conversation,' he said.

'And we were doing so well.' Except now he was tapping a finger on his glass, reminding her she'd invited herself. 'Maybe I should go.'

His gaze settled on her again. 'Or stay for a top-up.'

Did she want to? She glanced at the windows, the night beyond obscured by their reflections. More appealing than her apartment tonight. 'A top-up would be nice, thanks. Keep the ice on your knee, I'll get it.'

Refilling their glasses, she ran through a list of topics to keep the conversation on track. He hadn't asked her any questions yet but they were settling in, he would eventually, and she'd come here to stop thinking about the past. 'What did you design when you were in engineering?' she asked as she sat back down.

'Civil projects. Roads and bridges, mostly. A few storage facilities and warehouses.'

'Like this one?'

His eyes did a quick flick around. 'Nothing as interesting as this. Nothing I'd want to live in in eighty years' time.'

'The builders of this one probably thought the same thing.'

He nodded, the finger tapping the glass again. 'So, Carly, what's going on?' The tone was casual but his eyes were asking something else.

She shrugged. 'Drink with a neighbour.'

'I don't think you came here to talk about oil rigs and warehouses. They're not that interesting.'

'You'd be surprised.' She put her half-empty wine glass on the coffee table. Maybe now it was time to go.

'You were upset, I could see that. You want to tell me about it?'

Not at all. She wanted him to think she was his nice, smart, well-adjusted neighbour, to take her *I'm never going back* as a clean break.

But she'd plied him with questions tonight and kept him awake other nights. He probably deserved something.

'I had reason to phone my ex today. It wasn't fun. I needed to stop thinking about it.'

He nodded, slowly, like he was considering a response. Maybe deciding to tell her he was a good listener. She shuffled to the edge of the sofa, ready to leave.

'So . . . did you find the fish co-op?' he asked.

She smiled, grateful at the change of subject, impressed he'd remembered her earlier question. 'Yes, several times.'

'How about the Indian takeaway?'

'Had the butter chicken, avoided the vindaloo.'

He smiled. She smiled back. They chatted some more – about her course and the walk to the breakwater his knee wasn't up to, the cafe, the markets and the weather. Short, brisk summaries that kept her brain moving and seemed to warm up his conversational skills. He managed to speak in whole sentences, even laughed out loud once.

'Another?' Nate asked.

'No, I've had enough. I should go.' She was ready now. 'If I stay any longer, you'll never want another guest.' And she might end up in his bed.

He walked her to his door. 'Have a good night, Carly.'

'It'll be better now. Thanks.'

The memories had pressed hard today but she'd hadn't let them take over. And now she was going back to her own space, where she wanted to be.

Which would be perfect if only she wasn't scared of it.

SATURDAY STRETCHED AHEAD of Carly like a long road through a desert – just her and an assignment, alone in the apartment with its shadows and loft and agitation. Sitting at the small outdoor setting in the living room, she arranged pens and notebooks beside her laptop as though being organised would make a difference. She rubbed her neck, drummed a thumb on the keyboard and wrote . . . nothing. Got up and paced around. The space felt too small, too dim, too . . . oh, fuck it.

She was at the markets looking at handmade jewellery, blaming her tiredness on the lost earrings that she'd finally found in the fridge, when she heard her name being called.

'Over here!' Damien was manning the community gardens stall, the office clothes gone and the hat back on. 'Wish we had the egg-and-bacon-roll queue,' he called.

She worked her way to his table, more comfortable about chatting with him in a crowd with his plants.

'Have you signed the petition against the multi-storey car park?' he asked.

'No.'

'It's doing the rounds. So's the renovation proposal for the warehouse on the corner. Looking pretty green.'

'Oh, right.' Environmentally, not colour, she assumed.

'Heard any more from the police about the guy that broke in?'

Carly thought about how to explain it. He was community minded, maybe a little left wing. A simple *They think I made it up* might get some kind of can't-trust-the-bastards response. It would feel good to hear someone say it – except he lived in the warehouse and Chinese whispers might turn it into *She made it all up*.

'They're still looking into it,' she told him.

He nodded distractedly, his attention on a new customer as she waved and left.

She avoided the apartment a while longer, walking all the way to the breakwater, pushing through the weariness of bad sleep and old nightmares, lingering over coffee, imitating relaxation. The assignment was due on Monday, she told herself over a second coffee. She could finish it in a few hours if she got stuck in.

She was on the way home when she saw Brooke on a bench seat up ahead, the fat boot stuck out in front of her, something despondent in the set of her shoulders. Carly slowed, remembering the conversation with her after the book club. Carly sympathised with her grief, how could she not? But today she didn't want to be reminded of friends and tragedies, wondered if she could slip past unnoticed – and then Brooke looked right at her.

Carly waved, didn't see the tears on Brooke's cheeks until she'd stopped beside the bench. Brooke's attempt at a smile looked like she wished Carly *had* kept going and, for half a second, Carly thought about it. But they were three steps from the edge of the harbour and a drop into deep water. Alone wasn't always best. 'How are you doing?' she asked.

Brooke turned her eyes to the water. 'Having a bad day, actually.'

There was ice in the wind and Carly's ankles were aching, but she knew about bad days. 'Feel like some company?'

It was a while before Brooke replied. 'I was thinking of when I'll be able to walk along here again.'

It was a good start. Carly sat down beside her. 'How much longer are you in the boot?'

'A couple of weeks.'

'It's a long walk from the warehouse on crutches.'

Brooke hooked a thumb over her shoulder at a parking bay. 'I drove. It's an automatic, I only need one foot. I'd ask you how your walk was but I don't want to be jealous.'

Carly chuckled softly. 'Are you off work?'

'I work from home. I've been doing everything over the phone for the last four weeks.'

'You were lucky there.'

'Except now I spend my days stuck in the apartment staring at a computer screen and going a little crazy.'

'Not so good, then.'

Brooke turned her face to the harbour. 'I've been struggling with depression for a while. Since Talia's accident.'

'Not being able to get out and go for a walk makes it worse, doesn't it?'

Brooke looked back at her.

Carly's turn to shrug. 'I've been there, too.'

'Depression?'

'Anxiety.' Carly almost left it at that – she'd wanted to keep it to herself here but Brooke seemed alone in her struggle. 'I worry that something awful will happen without warning, that I'll lose people I love. It happened once, it's hard to forget.'

Brooke watched Carly a moment more. 'Do you take medication?'

'At times.'

'So it came back?'

'Comes and goes.' Sometimes better, sometimes worse.

Brooke pulled in a long breath. 'Talia had depression. Good days and bad days. Days she could hardly move. She thought it was something creative people suffered.' Brooke's shoulders lifted and fell again. 'I'm a graphic designer, I suppose that puts me in the same category. It's just, I feel like she passed it on to me when she left.' She gave Carly a wounded smile. 'Ridiculous, really.'

Carly wondered about the car accident, whether a suicide attempt had been suspected, but she didn't want to upset Brooke any more by asking. 'How is she doing now?'

Her voice broke on the words. 'Not so great.'

Neither was Brooke. Maybe she just needed to talk about Talia with someone who didn't know her. 'How did you and Talia meet?'

'We're both from Perth. She was . . . I had . . .' She stopped.

'You came over together?' Carly prompted.

'No, I didn't know her in Perth. I moved over with my boyfriend. When we broke up I was trying to find a flatmate to share the rent and someone told me the new girl on the fourth floor was from the west. I knew she'd bought her place . . . your place . . . but I fronted up and introduced myself, thinking she might know others from Perth looking for somewhere to live. After a couple of glasses of wine we were friends. It was a kind of instant connection.'

Carly nodded, interested in more than just letting her talk now. 'Was she like that? One of those people who has heaps of friends?' *Who was casual about who she gave her key to?*

'God, no. She was quiet, not really shy, just happy most of the time to watch everyone else having a good time. We were an odd match, really. She'd moved in the day before, I was the first person she met so maybe that was the connection for us, I don't know. She had a few friends at the Conservatorium but mostly it was about the music, not her, you know?'

Carly nodded. 'No boyfriend?'

'No. Not in the time I knew her. I never saw anyone else in her apartment. It was her practice space and her cello was worth a fortune. She was always a bit anxious about it getting damaged so we usually met at my place.'

'Sounds like she was lucky to meet you.'

Brooke shrugged. 'We would never have crossed paths back home. Her family is rich, her idea of a big night out was tickets to the symphony. I went to the local public school and a music festival is as cultural as I get.' She pinned Carly with her eyes. 'I was the lucky one. Talia found the smaller apartment I eventually moved into, encouraged me to freelance and taught me about classical music. I had the best deal. She got depression and drove into a tree.'

Carly laid a hand on Brooke's arm, lowered her voice. 'On purpose?'

'No.' She said it quickly, then shook her head as though thinking about it some more. 'No, I don't think so. Her parents asked me that too. A blood test after the accident showed she'd taken sleeping pills. Not enough for an overdose but she shouldn't have been driving.' Brooke pulled in a sudden breath, hands to her face. 'I feel bad about that. I could have driven her that morning. I don't understand why she didn't ask. She was only going to the Conservatorium and she was always careful about the drugs. She hated being on antidepressants and the sleeping pills made her too groggy for her morning practice. She only took them when she had to. Even then it was, like, half a tablet, and she'd do this whole time calculation so she wouldn't oversleep.'

'Does Talia remember taking them?'

'She can't remember what happened. The day before or the accident. She only remembers waking up in agony in hospital and being told she'll never play again.' A tear worked its way down Brooke's cheek. 'I didn't see her the night before. I wish we'd had our usual drink and Indian takeaway and I knew what she was thinking. And I wish she'd knocked on my door and asked for a lift.'

Carly knew all about wishing she'd done things differently.

19

'Carly, lovely. Come in.' Elizabeth Jennings stood back to let Carly through the door. She'd left an invitation for afternoon tea in Carly's letterbox two days ago. The eggshell blue stationery and formal wording had made Carly smile, then spend an hour drafting a reply that didn't sound like an RSVP from a Jane Austen novel.

Carly followed Elizabeth into the apartment, awed again by the shelves and their contents. 'So many beautiful things.'

They faced the wall together as though they were admiring a mural. 'Entirely self-indulgent, of course,' Elizabeth said. 'But it's my home and while I still can, I want to remember everything.'

It wasn't a vanity wall, there were no awards or brag photos. But there were photographs – some of people, others of exotic settings. And books, carved pieces, a tiny painting, three rocks, a bronzed shoe. 'You must have done a lot.'

'It's been a full life.'

'May I?' Carly asked, not wanting to assume that because they were on display they were open for close inspection.

'Please do. Take your time while I get the tea started. Or would you prefer coffee?' Elizabeth was already moving towards the kitchen with her walking stick.

'Whatever is easiest.'

Elizabeth's voice was firm. 'No, no, there'll be none of that. I'm prepared for both and a woman should make her preferences clear.'

Okay, then. Told again by the feisty older woman. There were several tea canisters on the counter, pretty tins that looked like something from an English TV drama. 'I'll have tea, thank you.'

'And tell me, Carly, are you adventurous with your tea?'

Did the occasional bag of Earl Grey count? 'What are you suggesting?' A slug of whiskey?

'As you are interested in my collections, I thought it an excuse to use a Turkish tea set I bought in Istanbul about thirty years ago. If we choose that path, we should do as the Turks do and drink it black and strong.' She flicked on the kettle with a flourish.

'I'm game,' Carly said. 'Is there something I can do to help?'

'You may stand on the other side of the counter and tell me about yourself. I'm interested in your name. Is it Carly with a C or a K?'

If that was all she wanted to know, Carly was happy to oblige. 'C.'

'Many years ago, I taught a Carlene, who was called Carly by her friends.' Elizabeth selected tiny tulip-shaped glasses with matching saucers. 'And there's Carla, of course, with the obvious diminutive to Carly. Are you either of those variations or are you simply Carly?'

'I'm none of the above. My full name is Charlotte.'

Elizabeth lifted her face, eyebrows raised. 'French and German origins, I believe. Feminine of Charles, meaning strong woman, if my memory serves. Is that you?'

Maybe once, not for the last thirteen years. 'I'm not sure I'm the one to judge that. It seems like a good thing to wish for your child, though.'

Using the benchtop for support, Elizabeth took a few steps along the counter, reached for a cloth-covered plate. 'I understand Charlie is the more fashionable shortening of Charlotte these days. I'm intrigued at your reasons for choosing a different contraction.'

The conversation was starting to feel like a visit to the school principal. 'I didn't choose it, really, and it wasn't short for Charlotte in the beginning. It started as a joke. I had a friend who was into athletics and was mad on the American runner Carl Lewis. I don't know if you've heard of him.'

Elizabeth paused in her preparations to give Carly a stern glance over the top of her glasses. 'Four Olympic track gold medals. 1984, Los Angeles, if I remember rightly. I was a history teacher and housemistress at a boarding school in my younger days. I used to supervise the resident sports students. History and sport. Sometimes I combine the two. Back to your story . . . Carl Lewis, go on.'

Carly grinned to herself, no problem imagining Elizabeth rounding up young ladies in checked tunics. 'Well, Carl Lewis won medals in different events, and I was involved in a lot of different things, and one day my friend called me the Carl Lewis of Burden.' After Jenna gave her the name, she, Debs and Adam had only ever called her Carl. She'd turned it into Carly when she started uni.

'I assume the reference to the impressive Mr Lewis was because you were doing these things at an exceptional level,' Elizabeth said.

Carly tipped her head from side to side. 'I suppose.'

Elizabeth gave her another glare over her glasses.

'Okay, yes, I was doing them well.'

'And what were these activities?'

'Tennis, hockey, cricket,' she shrugged. 'My friends and I used to ride horses and dirt bikes, go waterskiing.' She paused. 'And canyoning. I wasn't an expert at anything but I picked things up quickly.'

Elizabeth uncovered a plate of bite-sized cakes. 'And school, did you do well there?'

'I was a good student.' A's and B's, no problem qualifying for uni.

'You capitalised on your talents, I hope.'

An unfinished degree, divorced twice, no job, plagued by anxiety. 'It hasn't really worked out that way.' She folded her arms, preferring to keep the history to her name. 'Anyway, Carl became Carly and it stuck.'

. . .

CARLY POURED a third round from the silver teapot. She was sitting on the sofa beside Elizabeth, the elegant, carved-legged coffee table in front of them littered now with items from the shelves. Elizabeth had pointed and Carly had fetched.

'Dreadfully hot but the ruins, the history, more than made up for it.' Elizabeth was back in Turkey after describing the ramshackle shop where she'd bought the tea set. 'Clifford loved all that as much as I did so we hunted down as many archaeological sites as we could find.'

Clifford was her husband, gone ten years but clearly still present in Elizabeth's thoughts. He'd been in the diplomatic service and, with Elizabeth, had spent years at a time living in different countries. She spoke French, passable Spanish and a smattering of Japanese. Carly felt like a pumpkin in comparison.

'I'd love to travel,' Carly told her eventually. 'Actually, I'd be happy to leave the country and come back just to say I'd done it.'

Elizabeth made a tut-tutting sound. 'You need to dream bigger than that if you're going to get there.'

'I think it's likely I won't.'

'And why not?'

Carly shrugged. 'It's taken me years to get here.'

'And tell me, Carly,' Elizabeth placed her tea cup on the table and eyed her critically, 'are you planning to die before you're forty?'

There was reprimand in her voice, the tone of an older, wiser woman instructing the younger generation. It made heat creep to Carly's cheeks – she'd wanted to die more than once, she almost didn't make thirty-three.

Elizabeth patted Carly's leg. 'I do hope you're not one of these young people who thinks they have to achieve their life's dreams before middle age.'

'I've left my run too late for that.' Carly huffed.

'I see so many young people in such a hurry to get everything done, but life is a long time, Carly.' Elizabeth clasped her hands on her lap, her story-time pose. 'I had a disastrous love affair when I was at university. Shocking to others and almost ruinous to me. I spent twenty years as a history teacher at a private girls' school in the country, relegated, I assumed – and I expect to the assumption of most others who knew me – to spinsterhood. I met Clifford when I was forty-two. I skied on snow for the first time at forty-five, went whitewater rafting in Africa at fifty. I celebrated my sixtieth birthday on the Camino de Santiago in Spain and I was still at archaeological digs in my early seventies.' She reached out, gave Carly's leg a firm rap this time. 'It doesn't matter how slowly you start, Carly. Life is a long time. Remember that.'

Elizabeth's pale, watery irises hung on Carly's face for a moment, as though making sure her message had been received. Carly nodded, something warm seeping into her chest and threatening to fill her eyes.

'And now,' Elizabeth said, clapping her hands together, subject finished, 'perhaps you can carry the tray to the kitchen for me.'

Carly did more than that, stacking the dishwasher, wrapping the four little cakes they hadn't eaten, returning bits and pieces to shelves. Carly expected Elizabeth to complain about the assistance, but instead she leaned on her walking stick and gave instructions, her back still straight but her limp more pronounced. She pushed the leftovers into Carly's hand as she was leaving.

'I have to watch my weight with this hip,' Elizabeth told her.

'Are you in much pain?'

She made a scoffing sound. 'The doctor has increased my medication but I'm refusing to take it until I need to.'

Opening the door, Carly turned back. 'Let me know if there's anything I can do.' The refusal on Elizabeth's face made her add, 'You know, a bit of shopping, if something crops up. I'm in and out every day.'

Her face softened. 'That's very kind of you.'

'Thank you for afternoon tea. I really enjoyed it.'

'And I.'

'Take care, Elizabeth,' Carly said, torn between giving her a hug and scampering off before she got detention.

'You also, my dear.' She reached for Carly's hand and gave it a resolute squeeze before she went back in.

Carly stood for a moment outside Elizabeth's apartment, her throat growing thick. Along the corridor and up the stairs, the smell of Elizabeth's powdery perfume seemed to come with her, the sensation of the older woman's bony hand on hers lingering as though she hadn't quite let go.

Letting herself in, checking the lock and chain, Carly thought about lessons-in-life conversations she'd had with her mother and the edge of impatience in Marilyn's words: *Why can't you be grateful you didn't die too? It's time you thought about something else. You might never have children, you need to come to terms with that.*

Carly set the little package of cakes on the kitchen counter and burst into tears. It surprised her. The whole afternoon-tea episode had surprised her. Possibly Elizabeth was like that with everyone, telling any newcomer she could hold in her apartment about her shocking love affair and whitewater rafting and life being a long time. Maybe the other members of the book club had heard it a hundred times and were quietly chuckling among themselves that it was Carly's turn. But it didn't feel like that. It felt like Elizabeth Jennings had looked at her and understood. She hadn't asked why Carly didn't capitalise on her talents, hadn't told her what she should be doing with her life. She'd just gripped her hand, closing the distance of years and experiences, and passed a message of hope.

Carly went to the loft, pulled a cardboard box from the wardrobe, shuffled through its contents until she found the photo she'd kept safe but out of sight for years. She took it downstairs, glanced around for somewhere to prop it, eventually sticking it to the fridge with a magnet and standing back to look at it.

Four smiling faces, young and eager, dishevelled, with a touch of sunburn. It was before mobile phones and selfies, someone from the Rural Fire Service snapping it after a training session.

The sight of it made Carly's heart thump and her eyes burn. That day had been the best. Fun and funny, hot and sweaty and dirty. Damn hard work that'd filled Carly with satisfaction and achievement, made her feel part of a community, let her think she had something to offer in return. She'd been frightened to remember the four of them like that because of how it made her feel. Because of how she felt now, grief and shame welling hot in her limbs. But there was something else there, too. Happiness. The memory of it. Feeling the essence of that moment without being dragged down by everything that followed. Without her heart reminding her that six months later, Debs, Jenna and Adam were dead and Carly had become Charlotte: alone, anxious, lost.

20

Carly's arms and legs are spread wide. She is the Vitruvian Man and he is her mirror image, pressing her into the mattress.

His breath is on her cheeks, her lips. Deep and rough, as though it's being forced from his throat, as though he is trying to suck the air from her lungs and take it into his own.

There is a voice coming from inside her. *His face is close.* But she doesn't want to see. The darkness behind her lids is a comfort, a shield, a space he can't invade.

He moves. Something touches her cheek. It's warm, soft, gentle. The voice inside her shrieks.

His whisper is hot and moist against the shell of her ear. Slow and amused. 'Do you like it when I visit?'

Carly's mouth was wide open with the effort to fill her chest with air. Legs kicking at the covers, running before her feet touched the ground.

Her phone was by her bed but it didn't matter. She wasn't calling the police. They wouldn't believe her. They'd come and charge her.

Maybe they wouldn't come at all. She didn't know which would be worse.

Breath heaving, heart pounding, she found the safety chain in the darkness, the brass links a slack curve from the jamb to the door. She stared at it. She couldn't take her eyes from it. Could only feel the burn on her ear from the touch of his lips, the warmth of his breath on her face, the pressure of his hand at her throat.

'Carly?'

Soft male voice, little more than a rumble. On the other side of the door.

She scurried backwards a few steps along the hall. Out of reach, nowhere to run.

A knock. 'Carly? It's Nate. Are you all right?'

Her silence was filled with the hiss of blood in her ears.

'I heard noises from your apartment.' A pause. 'You okay?' Two more seconds. 'Carly? Is that you behind the door?' His voice this time was firm, demanding, slightly muffled as though he was talking into the hinges.

She thought of the mouth on her ear, the breath on her face. Didn't answer.

'Carly, if it's you, you need to say something or I'm breaking in the door.'

She swallowed at the sticky dryness coating her mouth, wiped the tears from her face, her voice high and tight. 'I'm okay.'

There was a shushing along the timber grain. Nate's voice when he spoke again came from lower down. 'Carly, what happened?'

She imagined him on his haunches, maybe his forehead resting on the door. She clenched her eyes shut. What the fuck could she tell him? *A crazy guy is getting through my locked doors.*

'Are you alone?'

She glanced at the darkness behind her, not sure. Not really. 'Yes.'

'Are you hurt?'

Bruises were throbbing. There was a tender bump on the top of her head. 'No.'

'Did someone get in?'

Her sob was a long, shuddering gasp.

'If you're scared, I can help.'

She *was* scared. Terrified. Of the man who'd been here. Of the locked door and what it meant. 'You should go.'

Nate was silent for so long she wondered if he'd left. Then, 'I could sleep on your sofa. Or you could sleep on mine.'

Nate would inspect her locks and ask her what happened and she *didn't know*. She shuffled a little further down the hallway as another thought flickered. He *might* know, it might be him. 'No. Please, you should go.'

'Carly . . .'

'Nate, just *go*.' It came out harsher than she'd planned but it was still the message she'd intended.

It had the right effect. There was another shushing on the other side of the timber, a footstep in the corridor. His voice again. 'I'm going to write my number down and slide it under your door. I'm ten steps away if you need anything. Just call me.'

Carly listened to his footsteps fade, wondered if his feet were bare. Hers were and they were freezing. Her whole body was frozen. It felt like the marrow in her bones had turned to ice. Maybe she'd shatter if she moved. Maybe something inside her already had. She had to get up, though. She had to check.

Hobbling through the apartment, bruises burning, she stopped in front of the French windows. There was enough glow from the night-light on the other side of the room to show her they were locked. Top and bottom, both doors, the way she'd left them when she went to bed. She tested them, sliding each bolt out of its casing and back. She pulled on the handle, yanked and rattled it, tried and failed to loosen the hold of the bolts.

Then she jumped away from them, as though the doorway was a ledge that had started to crumble. Stood and stared. Understanding at last. She hadn't re-locked the balcony doors in her panic. They were never opened.

'Fuck.' She pushed hands into her hair, agitation beating in her blood.

Okay. All right. So he didn't come in through the balcony doors. She hustled back through the living room, picking up her keys from the counter on her way to the front door, flicking on the hall light, squinting in the glare, a moment of alarm when she saw the slip of paper on the floor. Nate's phone number. She left it where it was, more interested in what the door would tell her, eyes shifting from the chain to its hasp, the deadlock to the jamb. The chain held when she tugged it. The knob didn't move when she tried it. Inserting the key, she opened the door as far as it would go, pulled against the chain. Did it again, harder, and then with a solid yank. She thought of Nate and his warning about breaking in the door. How hard would that be?

Did it matter? The man in her room hadn't got in that way.

Had he unlatched the chain? Was that possible?

She opened the door again, slipped fingers into the gap. There was enough room to get a hand through, but . . .

Fingers shaking, she typed in a Google search, found YouTube demonstrations on how to unlatch a security chain with a piece of string. Was that it? Simple and quiet. Followed by a stealthy path up to the loft, amusement at Carly's expense, then . . . no, no, the deadlock had been set and the chain engaged. How could he manage that?

She closed her eyes, felt the heat of his breath, the brush of lips. It had happened. It *had*.

Hadn't it?

She lifted a hand to her throat, under the hinge of her jaw where his fingers had been. Eyed the wall at her back, the one that ran from the front door to the French windows. Got up and gave it a shove. Pushed some more, all the way along the hallway and back up the other side into the living room. Then the other walls around the lower level of the apartment, knocking and flattening her hands on the paint. High, low. Then in the half bath, and standing on the toilet seat, reaching higher, then heaving at the ceiling and . . .

She caught sight of herself in the mirror. Hair a mess, face tear-stained. Dark ringed, pale, wild-eyed. And she spun away, the image burned onto her retinas.

Distraught, panicked, confused. She looked like Charlotte. No, worse than that.

She looked crazy.

'It's CHARLOTTE TOWNSEND. I need to speak to Dr Randolf.'

She'd paced and cleaned for three hours, not letting herself think about it. Not yet. Now the tremble in her hand made the mobile feel like it was vibrating.

'How are you, Charlotte?' Liam's voice was friendly, casual, as though she'd rung for a chat. 'I've been wondering how you were getting on.'

'Hey. Hi. Good and . . .' She sat on the sofa, elbows on her knees to hold them still. 'Not so good.' She rolled her lips together, fighting the rush of words, wanting to take it slowly. For his assessment of her. 'The apartment is great. Close to everything I need, including kilometres of walkway around the harbour.'

'Are you using it?'

'Every morning. Once a day at a moderate pace.'

'Nice to hear. And the not so good?'

'You said we could still talk. Professionally.'

'Yes.'

'It's not anything we've discussed before.'

'That's okay.'

'It's not the anxiety. It's there but it's not that.'

'Okay.'

She was stalling. They both knew it. He was giving his short answers, designed to make her fill the silence. Well, she'd phoned him.

'It's something . . . weird. I'm not sure what it is. Whether it's even . . . I just . . .' She pushed two fingers into the crease between her brows.

'Why don't you try to explain it to me.'

Pulling her knees to her chest, she found a place to start. 'A couple of days after I moved in, I woke up and saw a man standing over my bed.' She told him about the police, the forensics, the detectives; the replay a week and a half later when the man touched her face. Then the third time and not remembering how she got to the front door, Dean Quentin's *You'll be facing a charge*. The detective finding her mental health record, telling her there were no fingerprints. And last night – the man on top of her, the locks engaged. And the anxiety and memories that were making it worse.

As always, Liam was silent until she was done.

'So here's the thing,' she said, finally getting to the point. 'If there's no sign anyone has been here, if there's no way in or out, is it possible that everything that's happened, everything I've carried around with me, has broken something? That there's something screwed up and . . .' She pulled in a shaky breath. 'Am I losing my mind now?'

'Do *you* think you're losing you mind?' Liam asked.

'I guess if you're asking it's a good thing. If you thought I was crazy, you wouldn't, right?'

'Maybe.'

Oh. Great. She rubbed at the pain starting in the base of her skull. 'I don't know what to think.'

'Can you tell me more about what happens when you see the man?'

'I wake up and he's there. I'm terrified, so scared I don't move. Or can't. I'm not sure but I don't. I can't see him properly in the dark but I can feel him. On the bed, around me, touching me. On top of me. I just grit my teeth and close my eyes and wait for him to do whatever the hell he's going to do.'

'So you feel awake but you're not fully functioning?'

'No, look.' She dropped her feet to the floor. 'I know my dreams are intense, if that's where you're going. This is different. I'm *aware* of him, I know there's someone in the room and he's on top of me. My dreams, when I wake up, I remember them, everything about them. I might try to squeeze Adam's hand or check to see if I'm bleeding when I first open my eyes, but once I'm awake, I don't actually think I'm on a cliff or I've lost another baby. I don't ring for an ambulance.'

It took a second for him to respond, his calm voice a contrast to the alarm in Carly's. 'It's natural to be frightened and worried by something like that, but what you're describing sounds like an experi-ence called sleep paralysis. And, Charlotte, it's on the spectrum of completely normal.'

'Normal for crazy people?'

He laughed a little. 'Normal for normal people. It can be a symptom of narcolepsy, but we know you don't have that. I've read a bit about it, actually. One of the fascinating sidelines in researching your sleep and dream patterns. People who experience it tend to have an active dream life, like yours. They report not being able to move, someone sitting on their chest, feeling a presence in the room. All the things you've described.'

Heat flushed through her limbs. 'So you think it's a *dream*?'

'No, not a dream. It's considered a transitional state between sleep and wakefulness.'

'Uh-huh. Which is what?'

'Okay, let's see if I can explain it.' There was a rattle as though he was moving about, getting comfortable. 'When we're in REM or dreaming sleep, we're in a paralysed state, probably to stop us from acting out our dreams. You know, running in front of a car or choking the person beside us. Sleep paralysis is thought to happen when there's an overlap of REM and waking. The imagery from a dream makes it into your waking mind before your body has regained movement.'

Carly thought about the paralysed sensation that kept her still, the frustration that she didn't fight back, the certainty that someone was in the room. 'Okay. And?'

'And that's why it feels real. You are awake and you are paralysed, but the images are from your subconscious.'

Carly got up, stood at the windows and stared into the street below. She had a history of bad dreams and interrupted sleep. His theory matched what she'd seen and felt. She was relieved – and mortified. She'd called the police over a *dream*. 'Why now, though? I finally left Burden and I'm here, starting over.'

'Stress and fatigue are thought to be factors, and we already know they are the triggers for your nightmares. Irregular sleep patterns too.

But major life changes, situations that might make you feel unsettled or out of control, can contribute. And you're certainly in the middle of that.'

Carly rested her forehead on the glass, remembering their conversations before she left for Newcastle. 'You didn't think I was ready to move.' It happened faster than she'd expected: the house sold in two weeks, she found the apartment on her first visit, the course was starting and she wanted to be gone. And now . . . had she done this to herself?

'The question of whether you were ready doesn't exist anymore, Charlotte, because you left. It's now a question of how you go forward. How do you feel now you're there?'

'Worried, obviously, and not sleeping, but only because of the scary bastard I keep seeing in my bedroom. It's good here, though. The course, the apartment, the city. And there are some nice people. I think I'm making friends.'

'That's a big step for you, Charlotte. Perhaps you could try to think of these incidences like you do your nightmares, as a reminder from your subconscious that you're stressed or anxious and that you need to take care of yourself. Look up sleep paralysis online and do some reading. Knowing more about what you're experiencing usually helps to settle some of your anxiety. Try to go to bed at the same time every night.' He paused. She heard tapping on a keyboard. 'Just a thought,' he said. 'Does it happen around the same time?'

She hadn't checked last night but the police had asked on the other occasions. 'Between three and four.'

'I've pulled your notes up and I notice when you've had sleep issues before, you reported waking around the same hour, three-ish sometimes, around four or five other times, and the memories and circular thoughts would start.'

When it was bad, she'd paced the house and garden, sometimes wrapped in a blanket, sometimes she'd pull on clothes and walk the streets of Burden. She'd think about what she'd done, what she hadn't done, what she'd never do. 'Does that mean something?'

'It's interesting that the events you're experiencing now have occurred around the same time. It suggests you might've slipped back into a disturbed sleep pattern.'

'I'm not waking at that time on other nights, though.'

'Are you sleeping through?'

The first two nights in the apartment had been bliss. After she'd seen someone in the loft, she'd spent a lot of restless, anxious hours in bed. Lately, she'd spent more of the night awake than asleep. 'Not really.'

'You might be slipping in and out of deep sleep without becoming entirely conscious. That might explain the root problem. I have in my notes that your GP wrote you a prescription for sleeping pills a couple of months ago. Have you tried . . .'

'I didn't get it filled.'

Liam waited a beat. 'I've noted that when you took sleeping pills at other times, you felt it helped break the waking cycle.' It wasn't a question but he stopped as though he'd asked one. When she didn't answer, he prompted. 'Charlotte?'

'There were sleeping pills in my hand when the ambulance came to the house.'

'You didn't take them.'

'I took more than I should have.'

'We've talked about your account of that day.'

'Yes.'

'Do you want to talk about it now?' This time when she didn't respond, he went on. 'You said you remembered thinking about taking the first two but couldn't remember if you had.'

'Yes.'

'You said you took the third one because you were desperate for rest. You wanted to lie down but your body wouldn't stay still.'

She closed her eyes, the shouting and commotion of those fraught hours pressing at the edges of her mind. 'I know. It's what happened. It's just . . . I don't want to be there again.'

'Where?'

'Devastated and with an option.'

'You had more than one option. You chose another one.'

She had wanted to die on that cliff, had only lived because she couldn't get to the ledge and roll herself into the canyon. That day in her old bedroom, the door was busted in while she was weighing up the cost of the losses she was still enduring. 'I'm not sure I chose anything.'

'How do you feel about it now?'

'I don't want to kill myself, if that's what you're asking.'

'What are you worried will happen?'

She heaved out a breath. 'The usual. I'm worried I'll make the wrong decisions. That I'll be reckless and selfish. That I'll ruin everything.' Maybe she already had. Sleep paralysis, shit.

'All the more reason to make sure you get enough rest and look after yourself. You're strong, Charlotte. I believe in you. Think about getting the sleeping pills.'

21

Carly stood at the window, wanting Liam to be right. She didn't want a man breaking into her apartment and she didn't want to be crazy. But a dream?

Okay, not a dream, a nightmare finding its way into her consciousness. It explained the locks, the security chain, the lack of fingerprints, the lost time. It made more sense than anything else.

She glanced around the view outside, then turned and eyed the room. There was no one watching and there was nothing sinister in the apartment. She wasn't crazy and she wasn't about to be murdered in her bed. It was better than she'd hoped – and still scary. If it was in her head, she could be waking up with that shadow on her bed forever.

She wandered through the living room, thinking about the other dreams that plagued her that had a connection with real life. Memories from the canyon and losing her babies. Liam had helped her understand why her brain held onto those images and why it threw them back at her when she was frightened or anxious or stressed.

There were other themes that were replayed in her mind – running, laughing, screaming. And complex plots threaded with foreboding that left her agitated and fretful, the anxiety sometimes spiralling into panic attacks. Liam had encouraged her to examine them, to look for connections to her state of mind, use them as an indicator for her own mental health rather than worrying about what might happen to someone else.

The sleep paralysis visions could have been worse, she thought, climbing the stairs. She could have dreamed about spiders crawling all over her or Hannibal Lecter chewing off her face. There'd be logic in that – she hated spiders and *The Silence of the Lambs* scared the hell out of her. And she wouldn't have called the police. She would've opened her eyes and known it wasn't real.

Standing by the bed, she studied the space that at night was filled with shadows, wondering about the psychological connection between her and the man in her dream. He was in her bedroom but it wasn't about sex and he wasn't trying to rape her. Was she frightened of being alone? Worried about safety? Scared of the dark? Yes to all of that, but only since she'd seen him.

She hauled the sheets from the mattress, tossed them over the railing, stood in the ensuite and studied her image in the mirror. Not wild-eyed now, only weary. Whatever the hell her subconscious was up to, it wasn't what she came here for.

She met her own gaze in the mirror and made a decision: she couldn't stop her psyche from trying to screw things up, but she wouldn't let her conscious self do it.

THE LETHARGY HAD ARRIVED by the time Carly got to class, hanging around her neck like a weight on a chain. Sitting in the sun outside the campus cafe at the morning break she struggled to keep her eyes open.

'Any ideas yet?' Dakota asked, pushing a cappuccino across the table to Carly.

'For what?'

'A business?'

'Nothing yet.'

'I think we should work on it.'

Carly squinted at her.

'This assignment has been really useful,' Dakota said. 'I think we should be applying it to a concept for you as well.'

'Applying it to a concept?'

'Impressed?'

'It's a long way from *Dad's making me do the course*.'

'Ha-ha. I'm serious, though. We should both be getting something out of it. So, like . . . what are you interested in?'

Carly took a breath, blew it out, tried to work through the fuzz in her brain. 'A business that will support me.'

'No, I mean is there something you do, you know, a hobby, that you could turn into a business?'

'I walk. I read. Don't think there's anything in that.'

'Okay, then what are you good at?'

Screwing up. 'Nothing fabulous.'

'Come on, you must have skills. What have you been doing with yourself until now?'

Nothing she wanted to tell Dakota about. But her insistence was nice and Carly rubbed hands over her face, sat up a little straighter. 'I worked in a post office for years. Stationery supplies and mail delivery in a world that now does everything via the internet.'

'Right, I see the problem. Oh, wait, retail. You could open a shop.'

'Already crossed that idea off the list. I've had enough of standing behind a counter.'

'Fair enough. What's the time?'

Carly tugged at the sleeve of her jumper, saw her bare wrist and remembered. 'Don't know. I couldn't find my watch this morning.' She was sick of losing things – the earrings, a lipstick, her favourite bedsocks.

Dakota pulled her phone from her back pocket, checked the screen. 'Time to get back. Don't think you're off the hook though. We'll be continuing this conversation later, Ms Townsend.'

Collecting their cups, not wanting to discourage her, Carly said, 'I haven't really been thinking about it. Still settling in, I guess. I'll try to put some brain power to it.'

'Me too. It'll be fun.'

As they walked back to class, Carly glanced at Dakota's glossy blue-and-black hair, the piercings and funky boots, the bounce in her step. Carly had been a country girl, she'd never looked like that, but the grin, the lightness – Carly remembered having that. In another time, another life.

DETERMINATION AND RESOLUTION had got Carly to class but the effort to think and smile and make ordinary conversation had burned it up, and now, in the shadows of the warehouse garage, her nerves began winding up again. Stuart got in the lift at the foyer, nodding vaguely like he always did, head pushed forward on his long bird neck as he watched the numbers above the doors. She thought about saying hi, remembered their exchanges on other days – *Yes, we've crossed paths a few times* – decided she didn't have the energy. What kind of shit did he carry around in his head that he didn't notice other people?

He got out on the second floor. Carly hesitated a second or two then stepped out after him, walked to the atrium and peered through the evening gloom. The dim lights along the corridors made it feel like she was looking into a spaceship. Her apartment was up there, it was cosy and classy and tonight she dreaded going back to it. She headed for the stairs, delaying the moment a while longer.

Nearing the third floor, she heard footfalls above. At the turn, Nate swung down. They both stopped, eyeing each other from opposite sides of the landing.

'Hey,' she said, embarrassed about the last time they'd spoken – through her door in the middle of the night.

He took a moment to speak. 'Eaten yet?'

Not the response she'd expected. 'No.'

'I'm heading out to pick up Indian. Feel like sharing butter chicken and a couple of naan?'

She was starving and hot, spicy food sounded great but she watched him a moment, not sure if he'd decided to forget what had happened or if he was looking for a chance to talk. 'Thanks but I've got . . .' Vegemite and toast. 'Something waiting.'

He nodded, silent and watchful. Her face heated as she waited for him to broach the subject of last night. 'Sure,' he said. 'Need anything in Baxter Street?'

'No. Thanks, though.'

Another nod, another moment of silence. 'Okay.' He stepped past her and continued down. Carly watched until she couldn't see him, surprised and relieved it had ended there, wondering if he felt the same way.

Letting herself in, she turned the light on, hooked the chain, checked the locks, eyed the darkness at the other end of the hallway and felt her pulse pick up. Scared of the dark. Of going to sleep and waking up. Of herself. Fuck.

She should google sleep paralysis, she told herself. Calm her nerves, give herself something to focus on. She dumped her bag, tossed her coat and stood at the window. No fingerprints, she told herself. Locked doors, no one watching. It was just her. Alone for hours.

Her prescription for sleep medication was still in a drawer. As she thought about it again her hand curled into a fist, the memory of small, hard ovals in her palm. No, she didn't want the pills, she didn't want to feel like Charlotte. She didn't want the memories, either. Not tonight. Not if she wanted to sleep.

She went to the fridge, pulled a slip of paper from under a magnet. Nate's number, the one he'd pushed under her door last night.

'Nathan Griffin,' he answered.

So that was his name. 'It's Carly. Can I change my mind?'

A pause. 'Sure.'

'Papadums too?'

Muffled voices on his end. 'Done.'

.   .   .

'I BOUGHT a bottle of red while I was waiting.' Nate had hung his leather jacket over one of Carly's garden chairs and was unpacking takeaway containers on the table.

She collected plates and cutlery, taking in the muscled shoulders and biceps under his long-sleeved T-shirt, appreciating more than just his company. She needed conversation, not someone to sleep with, she warned herself. 'Great. I need a drink.'

Across the room, he lifted his head, a question in his raised eyebrows.

'Long day,' she said. And a few drinks might help her sleep.

They ate butter chicken and something deliciously spicy with vegetables, dipping and scooping with the naan and spreading pappadum crumbs over the table. She set the pace with the alcohol, finishing her first glass while his was barely touched, the food and alcohol helping to flatten out her anxiety. He kept the conversation moving: weather and the harbour, her car and the one he'd sold a few months ago, her study and his work.

'You're working?' she asked.

'Couldn't stand doing nothing.'

'Back to engineering?'

He shook his head. 'At the marina. Stripping back the timber on an old boat.' He leaned back in his chair. 'You always have this many lights on?' he said as though he'd just noticed.

The only light that wasn't burning in the apartment was the one above the stove. Now she looked, it seemed like overkill or reckless use of electricity. Carly gave a small grimace. 'Forgot about them.' She flipped a few switches, crossed the room and flipped some more. Sat back down and took another sip of wine. The loft and stairs were in darkness now, shadows pooled in corners, the hallway was murky and silent. She got up again, turned a couple back on, saw Nate watching her with a crease between his brows.

Be the calm, normal neighbour, Carly. It would look better if he was going to ask about the sobbing and thumping in the night. 'That should do it.'

'Sure.'

She picked up the wine bottle. 'Another?'

It took him a moment to answer, his dark blue eyes on her, a hint of *Maybe you've had enough* creeping across his face. Then he shrugged. 'No one's driving tonight.'

Crockery and cutlery clattered into the sink when Carly cleared the plates, a little woozy and unsteady. Nate opened the fridge to stack in leftovers. Maybe he'd leave now the meal was over. Probably better if he did, she told herself. She'd been awake since three – only she wasn't ready to close her eyes.

As he straightened, she held his wineglass out to him, took her own and wandered to her usual position at the edge of the windows, watching his reflection: one hand in the pocket of his jeans as he stood by the fridge, the soft fabric of his sleeves pushed up to his elbows. His face was turned towards her, the image not clear enough to read his expression.

'The windows make me feel a little exposed at night,' she said.

'I like being able to see out.' He crossed the room to them, stood dead centre.

Carly imagined what he looked like from the outside: solid, strong, undaunted. She did her circuit of the view - black bulk of the warehouses, soft lighting of quiet homes, the street below. 'I worry about who can see in.' Even now, bad dreams or not.

'Carly.' There was something decided in his tone.

She turned, resigned to his questions now.

'Whatever it's about,' he said, 'if you need help, you can ask me.' He took his hand from his pocket, patted the air. A dual message: *I'm not asking* and *It's okay*. 'I don't care about the cops,' he said. 'If they're part of it, it makes no difference to me.'

She took a breath, said nothing, no idea what conclusion he'd come to on his own.

'If it's something you've done, if you're in trouble, I don't care when or what. I want you to know that.'

Something she'd done? Did he think the police had come uninvited? That *she* was the problem?

'I just want you to know I'm here, next door. No questions, if that's the way you want it.' He raised his eyebrows, asking her to believe him.

'Nate, I . . .' It was so far from the conversation she'd expected that she didn't know what to say.

'I don't want you to think you're on your own, Carly.' He cocked a thumb at the wall between their apartments. 'And I don't want to sit in there doing nothing if there's something I can do to help. To stop it, if that's possible.'

He thought she was in danger, and the biggest danger was from herself. He finished his wine with a toss of his head and turned away as though she'd asked him to leave.

'Nate.'

'It's okay,' he said. 'You don't need to say anything. Now or any other time. Just don't forget I'm here.'

'Nate,' she called again as he started for the hall. She didn't want him to leave and not just because she was scared to be alone. She wanted to tell him it was simpler than he thought, that she hadn't done anything, that she was grateful for his words. She spoke quickly as she hurried across the room. 'It's not . . . I'm not . . .' She took hold of his sleeve, wanting him to know, at least some of it. But his eyes made her hesitate, wondering if he'd feel the same way if he knew it was all in her imagination.

So she told him something else. 'Don't go. Not yet.'

22

———

There was relief in Nate's eyes as Carly drew him back into the room. 'Thank you,' she said, wondering why it was important to him. 'For staying. For what you said.'

He nodded. Brevity. There was a lot to like about him. Her eyes lingered on him as she took a sip of wine, reminded herself sex hadn't been part of the equation when she'd asked him to stay. It didn't stop the concept slipping through her mind.

'What do you look at when you stand at your windows?' she asked.

'The harbour.'

Carly angled her eyes towards the wedge of sparkling lights. 'It's pretty.'

'What about you?'

'Down there,' she said. 'The warehouses, the neighbours, the street. I wonder if someone watches back.'

'Do you think anyone is?'

'I think I worry too much.' She turned her face to him. 'What do you see in the harbour?'

He stared straight ahead for a long time, lost in whatever was out there. His answer when it came was soft, low. 'The marina.'

'Can I see it from here?'

He came to her side, leaned close as he pointed. 'You can make out the straight line of lights along the jetty.'

Carly smelled curry and soap on him. And something unmistakably, appealingly masculine. A pulse of awareness joined the buzz of anxiety and alcohol. 'On the right?' she asked.

He nodded. 'In daylight, you can see masts and rigs, sometimes a mainsail as someone heads out.'

Boating terminology. 'You're a sailor?'

'Not anymore.'

She remembered the picture in his apartment, the big black-and-white of a yacht under spinnaker. 'The photo on your wall. Are you on that boat?'

'Yeah.' No hint of pride or pleasure in his tone. Maybe he regretted giving it away.

'No time anymore?'

He folded his arms across his chest, a muscle tightening at the hinge of his jaw. 'I was involved in an incident at sea. Someone died. I never went back to it.'

Without thinking, she reached for him, her fingers curling around his bare forearm. 'I'm sorry.'

He gave a single sideways dip of his head. Regret and sorrow and realism rolled into one small gesture. As if it was that simple. She knew it wasn't, she knew the shrug. It was shorthand for pain.

Turning to the lights, she imagined the kind of dark memories he might carry, of a drowning or a rescue gone bad or being adrift on wild seas. Visceral, terrifying memories like her own. She thought it explained his grim tenseness, that he gave up sailing, that he preferred a cramped oil rig to a nice apartment. But he worked in the middle of the ocean and on another man's boat – Carly had never ridden or skied or climbed again, and it had nothing to do with the injuries she'd suffered.

'I had friends,' she said, not sure why. 'Three friends. Best friends.' Maybe she just wanted to tell him something. 'I watched them die on a ledge in a canyon.' She closed her eyes. The warmth of his hand as it covered hers made her open them again. His thumb moved across her skin as though she'd said all that needed to be said. A still, silent moment that was breathtakingly intimate.

She wanted to feel what he knew, lifted her eyes to him. He raised his to the window, the muscle at the side of his jaw flexing. It made her hesitate, but her hand turned of its own accord, fingers slipping between his.

He didn't move. It wasn't rejection. It wasn't acceptance, either. Just a tight set to his mouth and the soft tangle of his fingers with hers. Carly closed the space between them, moved into the line of his gaze, seeing things in his face that she understood, that she felt herself – longing and lust, hesitance and restraint. And something harder and sharper in his eyes – resentment, anger, reproach.

As though he'd sensed what she saw, he straightened his fingers and pulled them from hers. Held up both hands and took a pace back. She didn't know if it meant *Get away from me* or *I'm trying to resist.*

'Carly, you've had a bit to drink.'

'You're being a gentleman?' she scoffed. 'You think I'm so drunk I can't make a responsible decision for myself?'

'No, look, it's not what I meant when I said I could help. I'm sorry if that's what you wanted.'

There'd been want in his eyes twenty seconds ago. 'You think I asked you to stay for a calm-down sex?' She'd asked it of other men.

'Christ.' He spun away, shoulders taut as he stalked from her. Halfway across the room he turned back around. 'This isn't what you need.'

'You think you know what I need?'

'Carly, listen.'

'No.' Her voice was loud, her legs stiff as she paced to him, incensed and disappointed now. 'You should leave.'

She marched past him to the hallway, paused to make sure he got the message.

Neither of them spoke until he got to the threshold. 'I can help with whatever is going on with you,' he said. 'But you don't want me like that.'

ANGER AND ANXIETY AND ALCOHOL. It was a shitty mix. Carly paced and berated herself. What had she been thinking?

She hadn't thought. She'd been alone and afraid and exhausted so she'd opted for sex with the first man to offer her sympathy. It was Charlotte's failing, her Achilles heel. But she wasn't Charlotte here.

And she should be grateful Nate had walked away. They lived either side of the same wall, they passed in the corridor – being rejected was embarrassing enough, it would be worse if she'd slept with him and wished she hadn't.

Except now she was alone in her apartment, left with her subconscious and the prospect of sleep. She opened her computer, tried to google sleep paralysis, but couldn't see for the alcohol or sit for the agitation. And all the time, Nate's last words kept replaying through her mind – *You don't want me like that.*

He wasn't being a self-righteous arsehole when he left. It was about him. A warning or an admission or . . . she had no idea.

'I'VE MADE A LIST.' Dakota unfolded a page as they walked to class the next morning. 'I've called it "Carly's big long list of things she could do".' She held the single sheet up.

Carly squinted from behind sunglasses, the glare off the white page reawakening her hangover. 'What is it?'

'I thought we could brainstorm business ideas for you.'

Carly caught a corner of the paper, glanced at the column of words. 'You think I should be a walking companion?'

'Well, no, not really. It was just, you know, off the top of my head. But that's what you're meant to do with brainstorming. Just chuck in ideas and see where they go.' She glanced at Carly, a little uncertainty creeping into her kohl-lined eyes. 'I was reading about the whole brainstorming thing last night and got thinking about you and, well, thought I'd give it a go. It was kind of fun, actually.'

'You were thinking up business opportunities for me last night?' When Carly was making a fool of herself.

'This morning actually. Over breakfast.'

When Carly was swallowing painkillers. 'Oh.'

Dakota grimaced. 'I hope you don't mind. You can, like, toss it if you want.' She took the page back, folded it over.

'No. It's a good idea. Come on, let me see.' There were a dozen or so items on the list. 'Walking companion. How would that work?'

'I don't know, it's just you said you walk a lot and . . . you could have clients who'd pay you to walk with them. Keep them company, make sure they go, that kind of thing.' She grinned. 'Include a coffee and cake break and make them pay.'

Carly nudged her with a shoulder. 'That's so sweet you were thinking of me.' It didn't make up for last night but made her feel a few steps further away from Charlotte this morning.

Okay, so sleep paralysis wasn't a term that people with stressed-out, over-analysed, first-world lives had come up with to explain weird dreams. Which was a relief.

Lunch with Dakota and a few more laughs on the way back to the car park had left Carly ready to face whatever Google could tell her about Liam's diagnosis. Legs crossed under the coffee table, the laptop open on top and an hour into her research, she was feeling an uncomfortable connection to other abnormal sleepers.

Sleep paralysis was a phenomenon that had been experienced frequently enough over hundreds of years for cultures around the world to develop mythologies to explain it. Mostly the folklore involved supernatural visits: demons, ghosts and devils who sat or lay on a sleeping person, pressing down on them, preventing movement and making it hard to breathe. It was called *Riding the Hag* and *Shadow People* and the *Incubus Effect*. The names gave Carly the chills.

She was grateful Liam hadn't insisted she was possessed by the spirit of someone in the building, which, according to Scandinavian folktales, was what had sat on her chest. Northern Spaniards would tell her it was a large dog. Fijians believed they were being eaten by the spirit of a dead relative. Japanese culture called the paralysis *kanashibari*, while the Mongolian term for it translated to 'pressed by the black'.

Carly checked off the similarities between the demon stories and her own. The weight on her body, the hand at her throat, the gasping, the paralysis and not being able to fight back. There was no mention of faces being touched, feeling the demon's breath or hearing it talk and laugh, but they were ancient stories, not a list of symptoms.

Modern science had, of course, debunked the mythology. Research showed sleep paralysis sufferers were often predisposed to panic attacks, like Carly. There were suggestions it explained alien abduction stories. At least she hadn't gone to the police with that one.

Studies had narrowed down three types of 'intruders': a man in a hat, an old hag, or someone with a hood. Dreamers couldn't see the faces and felt a deep sense of terror – all of which Carly had experienced and seemed to confirm Liam's diagnosis.

The good news was that it wouldn't kill her, the bad news that she might be one of the few that suffered repeated, regular incidences, and that it could happen several times in one night. Something to make her want to stay awake.

Except staying awake would make it worse – and not just the sleep paralysis. She'd been there before, strung out with insomnia and memories, walking herself into exhaustion in an effort to keep them at bay, jittery and fearful when she was still. The online advice matched Liam's: avoid stress and establish regular sleep habits. Sleeping pills might do that but having the prescription filled felt like a backward step – it was written for Charlotte, the version of herself she'd wanted to leave behind. And if . . .

She got up, stood at the edge of the window, telling herself the evidence for sleep paralysis outweighed anything else, but her eyes roamed the view anyway. No fingerprints, locks undisturbed . . . she wanted to believe it but her skin kept remembering. She touched her throat, her ear. She didn't want to be drugged and sluggish the next time it happened. Because next time the demon on her chest might do more than clasp his hand around her throat.

23

———

Elizabeth was sitting on her bench in the atrium when Carly returned from a walk the next day. Something about her stillness made Carly walk a little faster through the foyer.

'Elizabeth?'

The older woman's eyes were closed, her walking stick lying on the floor.

Carly dropped to her haunches, kept her voice low, worried about startling her. Worried she wouldn't respond at all. 'Elizabeth?' One gnarled fist clenched and unclenched. Carly touched the sleeve of the older woman's red jacket. 'Elizabeth?'

She raised her head, her gaze unfocused.

'It's me. Carly.'

'I know who you are,' she retorted.

Stroppy. Carly thought it was a good sign. 'Are you feeling okay?'

'Of course I am.' There was a moment of rearranging: shoulders, arms, legs. 'I was just enjoying the sunshine. You know I insisted they put this bench here for that very reason.'

Except there was more grey than sun today. 'Yes, it's a lovely spot.' Carly sat beside her, looking her over. Was there a problem or had she dozed off? 'Have you been out?'

'I have several items I must pick up in Baxter Street,' she said, fumbling suddenly around the seat.

Carly noticed an empty shopping bag, retrieved it and the walking stick. 'Are these what you're looking for?'

'Yes, dear. Thank you.' Elizabeth propped the rubber end of the stick on the floor, ready to hoist herself up – and just sat.

Carly took a guess. 'How's your hip feeling in this bad weather?'

'It's a damn nuisance.'

'I can go to the shops for you.'

'I'm perfectly capable of looking after myself.'

Obviously the wrong way to tackle it. 'It's just that I need to go myself and it looks like the rain might start any minute. I can take my car and pick up what you need while I'm there. Save us both getting cold and wet.'

'I wouldn't want to put you out.'

'A wise person told me recently that a woman should make her preferences clear.'

Elizabeth lifted her chin. 'Thank you, Carly. I would be grateful if you could make a few purchases for me when you are making your own.'

'It would be a pleasure. I need to grab my purse from upstairs,' she lied, trying to be discreet about helping Elizabeth to the lift. 'With weather like this it might be a good time to start that new medication for your hip, Elizabeth.'

'I've considered that myself. Perhaps I will.'

'I could pick it up for you now, if you like.'

CARLY WALKED to the shops in a light drizzle, happy for an excuse to avoid going back to the apartment for a while longer. She hadn't been into the pharmacy in Baxter Street before and took a moment to find *Prescriptions In* at the rear of the store. A man had his back to the counter, head down, reading. She cleared her throat, and was surprised when he turned.

'Oh, hi. I didn't know you worked here.'

Stuart, his neck looking even more birdlike in a conservative white shirt and blue tie, smiled uncertainly.

Oh for god's sake. 'Carly. From the warehouse. We've passed in the lift.' About twenty times.

He made a show of remembering. 'Right, yes. Only when they need me.'

'Sorry?'

'I only work here when they need me. Usually a couple of days a week. They'd like me to do more but, you know, the research.'

She nodded, undecided about him. Either he was brilliant or he wanted people to think he was. Maybe his memory was a clue to his brain capacity. 'At least it's handy to home,' she said.

'True. Actually, I've been working on a new project. I might have to cut back my time even more. Very interesting, this one.'

It seemed to be her cue to ask for details but she was damp and cold and she really didn't care. 'Well, that's nice. Can I give you my prescription?'

There was a second of hesitation before he took it, another as he looked it over. 'This script is for someone else. Did you have one for yourself?'

'No, that's it.'

'You're having this made up for Mrs Jennings?'

That's what it said. 'I'm helping her out with some shopping.'

'Mrs Jennings is on our computer, let me check her records.' He said it as though it was all a bit unlikely. He stooped to tap on a keyboard – maybe too much of that was the problem with his posture. 'I thought so.' Poking a finger at the screen, he looked up at Carly. 'This is a higher dose than her usual medication.' He held the script out to her like he'd trumped her.

'She's aware of that.'

'I remember she had some problems with this dosage. I notice it's dated several months ago. Perhaps I should call and discuss it with her.'

Carly was tempted to tell him Elizabeth's pain was worse, that she hadn't been able to walk to the shops, that she was intelligent enough to decide for herself. But Elizabeth was a proud woman and it wasn't up to Carly to discuss her symptoms, even with the local pharmacist . . . especially not with this one.

'You know what?' She took the prescription back. 'I'll sort this out with her. Thanks for your help.'

'I'll be here all day if you need any further advice.'

'THAT TOOK MUCH LONGER than I expected,' Elizabeth said as she opened her door, a little fresher than when Carly had left. 'I hope there were no problems.'

Carly hoisted two bags onto Elizabeth's counter. 'Not at all.' She'd ended up driving to a shopping mall to have Elizabeth's prescription made up, found a bigger supermarket and shopped for herself as well while she picked up her neighbour's few items.

'You left your flowers with my shopping,' Elizabeth said.

'They're for you.' Carly freed a bunch of pale pink lilies. 'They reminded me of your beautiful silver vase and the visits to the flower markets in Paris you told me about. I thought they might give you sunny memories in this overcast weather.'

For a moment, she thought Elizabeth was going to refuse them. The older woman simply looked at them without any attempt to take them from Carly's outstretched hand. Maybe she was annoyed at how her grocery pennies had been spent.

'My treat,' Carly added. 'I hope you don't mind.'

'Oh, Carly.' Instead of taking the flowers, Elizabeth reached for Carly's hand. 'How lovely you remembered my tales of Paris. You are a dear, dear girl.'

Carly waved a hand. 'They're probably nothing like the glorious blooms you can buy in Paris but . . .'

'They are perfect. Thank you. Come on, we must share. It's a big bunch, plenty for two vases. Your kind thought can brighten up two apartments.' She had the bundle of stalks on the counter, already opening the cellophane wrapping.

'I don't have anything big enough to hold them.'

'Carly, dear, I have enough vases to furnish every apartment on the first floor.' She pointed a bony finger at the shelves. 'Fetch me the silver one, will you? And the tall one in that cabinet.'

Five minutes later, Carly had filled them with water and Elizabeth had fussed over the arrangements until she was satisfied.

'There,' Elizabeth said, stepping back for a last appraisal. 'This one is for you.' She cupped her hands around the aged silver of the vase she'd found in a Parisian basement.

'I can't take that one.'

'Of course you can. My treat, as you say.' Elizabeth slid it across the counter towards Carly. 'May the flowers give you sunny thoughts also, and the vase the courage to imagine yourself in Paris. To follow your dreams.'

Why did this woman make her teary? Back in her own apartment Carly set the flowers in the centre of her little table, stepped back and looked them over as Elizabeth had done. She thought about the dream she'd once had for an adventurous life, which had died with her friends. What she wanted now was a life worthy of the ones lost on her account. She could find it here – if her subconscious didn't screw it up, if she did more than lie still when a man climbed on top of her.

'How did you break your ankle?' Carly asked Brooke. They'd met in the lift during the week – Brooke suggested a coffee on Saturday, Carly picked the cafe on the walkway. This morning it was warm enough to sit outside under a heater.

'I fell down the loft stairs,' Brooke said.

'Ow.'

'Yep.'

Carly thought of the nights she'd stumbled from the loft and the bruises she couldn't remember getting. Maybe she'd been lucky. 'Were you on your own?'

'It was the middle of the night and the phone was by the bed. I had to drag myself across the living room floor and bash on the wall to wake my neighbour. I was just glad I had decent pyjamas on,' she grinned. She looked like a different person to the one Carly had talked to at the harbour last weekend.

'Why were you up?'

She shrugged. 'I can't remember now. I figure I must have been thinking about work and went to check on something. I've woken up a couple of times standing at my computer with no idea what I'm doing there. One of the drawbacks of working from home. But here's a piece of advice – turn on a light before you go downstairs in the middle of the night.' Brooke's eyes flicked past Carly. 'There's a guy over there who keeps looking at you.'

Wariness tingled across Carly's shoulders. 'Someone from the warehouse?'

'I don't think so. Why?'

Because if she wasn't dreaming, someone knew how to get into her apartment. 'I . . .'

'He's quite nice-looking and . . . yes, he's coming over.'

Carly wanted to escape the cluster of tables and heaters but as she turned in her chair, a body filled the space beside her.

'Carly?' Dark hair and eyes.

She knew him, she'd seen him. Somewhere. Was it *him*?

'Dean,' he said. 'Constable Dean Quentin. I came to your apartment a couple of times.'

Shit. Fuck. 'Sure, yeah. Sorry, I didn't recognise you.'

'No problem. Most people only notice the uniform. I saw you over here and thought I'd drop by on my way out.'

Carly shot Brooke a quick glance. 'Right.' She got to her feet, hoping to keep the conversation private.

'How are you now? You're looking better.'

Every time he'd met her she'd been in pyjamas and hysterical. And he'd carried handcuffs and a gun and threatened to arrest her. 'I'm fine, thanks.'

He gave Brooke a nod, looked back at Carly and lowered his voice. 'I've been on day shift for a couple of weeks but I've been checking the log. There were no more call-outs to your apartment.'

'No.'

'I'm glad to hear it.'

Carly didn't comment, not sure if he was repeating his earlier warning or giving her a pat on the back for being well behaved.

'The situation you had, is it sorted now?'

He'd accused her of making up an intruder for entertainment – he might not have been far from the truth. 'It's . . . I'm . . .'

'I meant what I said, Carly. If you need to talk to someone about it, if you're scared, you can talk to me.'

And tell him what? She was scared to go to sleep and she wasn't sure why?

24

'E-Greeting cards,' Dakota said, looking up from her list.

Carly shook her head.

'Something in e-publishing.'

'Such as?'

'I don't know, but you read and you're good on the computer, you could put them together.'

'That's specific.'

'It's brainstorming, not a recipe.'

Carly grinned. 'We should get back to class.'

Dakota tucked the page into her pocket. 'So you found your watch?'

'In the cutlery drawer.' Carly rolled her eyes as she dropped their coffee cups in a bin.

'I've started on Round Two, by the way,' Dakota said.

'Round Two?'

'The "Anything Carly Showed Interest in List". We can start culling that when I cut your hair.'

Carly ran a hand over her ponytail. 'Won't you need to concentrate?'

'Nah, if I make a mistake, I'll just cut more off. You'll look good with short spikes. Just kidding.'

CARLY TURNED to see what the commotion was about at the other checkout. The owner of the little supermarket in Baxter Street was towering over a woman who was bustling and huffing to get around him.

Oh dear. It was Christina.

Carly watched for a moment, catching a few words: 'I did not,' from Christina, '. . . haven't paid,' from the owner. Christina was shoplifting? Then the scuffle was over, and as Carly paid she saw Christina leaving, weaving a little, bumping into the automatic door as she passed through. Christina was drunk and shoplifting?

Outside, the afternoon air was cold enough to steam Carly's breath. Christina was leaning against a parked car, a hand to her forehead, getting wet in the rain. Maybe she was sick.

'Christina?'

The woman looked up and flushed. 'Oh god, oh damn. I'm so embarrassed.'

'Are you okay?'

'I'm mortified. That man thought I was stealing rolled oats. Who steals rolled oats?'

'You're in the rain, Christina. Come and sit down.' Carly took her elbow and steered her to a seat outside the pharmacy. She didn't smell of alcohol but she was unsteady and loose. 'Do you feel all right? You seem . . . not quite yourself.'

'Bernard's away. That's what's wrong.'

She needed a carer? 'Does Bernard usually do your shopping?'

Catching her breath, pulling herself together, Christina laughed a little. 'No, he's a milk and bread man only. It's just, well, I get muddleheaded when he's not around. Never tried to steal anything. He won't be happy if he finds out.'

'He'll be mad at you for that?'

'Not cross. He worries about me. Ever since that business with the farm. He knows I don't sleep well when he's gone. That's what this silly thing with the oats is about. It makes me dreadfully off the air.' She shook her head like she was shaking out the cobwebs.

So Bernard was her husband and maybe she took sleeping pills when he was away – maybe one too many this trip. 'You want to share my umbrella on the way back?'

Christina patted at her shopping bags. 'I had one. Somewhere. If you don't mind.'

She bumped and bounced off Carly as they crossed the road, Carly eventually linking an arm through Christina's and holding her close.

'Is it nightmares?' Carly asked, thinking about the violent robbery at Christina's farm.

'Yes and no. All part of that nasty post-traumatic thing they said I had. Just a lot of trouble sleeping when I'm alone, really.'

It didn't sound like sleep paralysis but it felt like company. 'Do you worry about security in the building?'

'No, no. The security is excellent. Oh, except for that recent incident, you poor thing.'

'The police said there'd been other break-ins. A year or so ago.'

'Oh, yes, and that. I'd forgotten about that.'

Possibly Christina didn't need to be reminded if Bernard was still away, but the police had told Carly next to nothing, and if the hand on her throat was . . . 'Do you know what happened?'

'There were two or three, from memory,' Christina started as they made their way arm-in-arm towards the warehouse. 'In about just about the same number of weeks. Phillipa Bakewell was the first, I think, and Tobias on the second floor. Yes, and Lola Matthews, which was a little awkward, as it turned out, because her husband had left her for another woman and she'd been keeping it a secret. Hoping he'd come back, I heard, which didn't eventuate. Their apartment went on the market quick smart after that.'

'They were robbed?'

'Oh yes, I think so.'

'At night?'

'That's right, now I remember. Tobias saw someone in his apartment, and after it happened again to poor Lola the security doors were adjusted so they'd close without having to be pushed.' Christina stopped at the entrance to the warehouse, at the bottom of the stairs opposite said security doors. 'I could do with a push myself today,' she puffed. 'You go on ahead, if you like. I'll be out of the rain from here.'

'No, I'll wait. Make sure you get up the stairs,' Carly smiled like she was joking.

Christina took a couple of deep breaths and hauled herself up and through the doors. 'Now that I'm thinking about it,' she said as they crossed the foyer. 'There was that other woman a few years ago who made a big fuss about security. What was her name?'

'What was the fuss?'

'Something about an ex-husband. Oh yes, Maggie something, east wall, I think. She said her ex had got into her apartment one night and, well, I don't know. He scared her, that's for sure. Probably why she left him. She didn't stay long after that. Lost a fair bit of money on the rent she'd paid in advance, I heard.'

Carly hit level five in the lift.

'You don't need to come up with me, Carly. I'll be fine from here.'

'Are you sure? I don't mind.'

'The cold and the rain and a nice chat and I'm feeling a bit less muddle-headed.' Christina pulled a face. 'Still mortified, of course.'

'No need.' Carly stepped out on her floor. 'Let me know if you need a hand with shopping while Bernard's away.'

'Thank you, Carly. I'm sure I'll be fine.'

Personal shopper, Carly thought as the cab closed. There were enough residents in the warehouse to keep her in work.

She locked her door, hooked up the chain and walked through the apartment, thinking about the other break-ins. Christina's version wasn't the eight or nine over six years that Anne Long had mentioned. Maybe Anne was being casual with the numbers, maybe there were others that Christina didn't know about.

Maybe they had no relevance to Carly's 'intruder'.

The only relevance was that Christina had reminded Carly what could happen if she didn't get some decent sleep. She made a cup of the camomile tea she'd been drinking. Had another after dinner, then got on the floor for some stretching and deep breathing before bed. She kept the lights low as she undressed and cleaned her teeth, slipped under the doona and told her subconscious to relax.

CARLY LURCHED FORWARD, down. The stairs shuddered. She slammed into the wall, hit the handrail, missed a tread. Grappling as she fell, slowing herself, she slipped and tumbled until the floor hit her in the back like a thwack from a cricket bat.

She lay for a moment, one foot in the air, the ankle wedged between two steps. *Brooke*, she thought, taking half a second to assess for pain before yanking her leg out and scuttling away on hands and knees. She was around the corner into the mouth of the hallway before she remembered.

Sleep paralysis, Carly.

Knees to her chest, sweat hot in her hair, she touched her cheek, her ear, her throat. *Was it?*

She reached for the switches above her head, squinting as the hallway and living room filled with light, flicking her gaze around the walls, the stairs, the loft. She was alone. Like every other time. Terrified and sobbing and doing it to herself. What more evidence did she need?

Pushing to her feet, she pitched left and right down the hall as she stumbled towards the front door, sinking to the floor again. The same place she'd ended up every other time, comfort in the tight, familiar corner.

Sounds in the corridor froze her breath. Footsteps. Approaching, retreating, coming back. Then a tap on the door.

'Carly? It's Nate.' His voice was little more than a murmur. 'I heard noises from your apartment.'

She wiped her face with the heel of her hand, didn't answer.

'I know you're on the other side of the door, Carly.'

She didn't want to talk to him. Didn't want comfort. She wanted the night to end and the day to start, to be outside and walking and past it all.

'Let me help, Carly.'

She remembered his words the night he bought the Indian take-away, before she tried to kiss him. *I don't want to sit in there doing nothing if there's something I can do to help.* There was nothing he could do to help. It was all in her head. She didn't want him to know what was wrong with her.

'I'm okay.' The tremor in her words made it a lie.

The next time he spoke, he sounded as though the door was all that separated their faces. 'I thought you fell. More than once. Are you hurt?'

Injured, no. Aching, everywhere. She spread her hands, saw half-moons carved into her palms from her nails. 'No.'

'Are you alone?'

Was he thinking intruder or a one night stand that got out of hand? 'Yes.'

'I'm right here, Carly.'

She could almost feel him. And she wished he'd go away so she could wait out the night in her hallway corner. Alone, the way she'd done it for years. 'You don't need to be. It's the middle of the night. Go home, Nate.'

'No questions. Like I said.'

He'd told her it didn't matter what she'd done. But it mattered to her – that he wanted to help someone in need and she was only scared of the dark. That he was brave and she was broken. 'Go home, Nate. Please.'

'I don't want to sit in there with you here like this.'

His frustration lit a spark. She fired words back, glad to feel something other than misery. 'It's none of your damn business.'

'Carly . . .'

'Go away and leave me the hell alone!'

25

Stuart was behind the dispensary counter in the pharmacy. It made Carly falter. She was buying sleeping pills; she didn't want a discussion about the medication and the dates and the doctor who'd written the script. But she had to get to class and she couldn't do the terrified stumble down the hall again. She needed to sleep tonight.

He stood at the counter for a minute, stooped over a keyboard, before he pulled his eyes from the screen. 'Can I help you?'

She waited a beat. 'Carly. From the warehouse.'

A small shake of his head. 'Of course.'

He took a moment to read her script, looked up at her as though he was making his own assessment. She found a brochure on the counter to study.

'Carly is short for Charlotte,' he said.

'Yes.'

'You're not from around here.'

'No.'

He squinted at the script. 'Burden.'

'Yes.'

'North-west, isn't it? Past Tamworth.'

Okay, he got a point for that. 'Most people have never heard of it.'

'I guess I'm not most people.'

That's for sure. 'I'm a little short on time. How long will it take?'

He nodded as though she'd asked for advice. 'Have you had this medication before?'

'Yes.'

'I notice the script was written several months ago. Have you started any other medication in that time?'

'No.'

'You should check the contraindications if you do. Even if it's a herbal supplement.'

'Okay.' She checked her watch, hoped it would prompt him.

'Do you have any other questions before you start on it again?'

She hadn't asked any to start with. 'No.'

'You can come back and ask anytime.'

For god's sake. 'Thanks.'

He straightened and smiled as though his job was done. 'It'll be about ten minutes. I noticed you looking at the vitamins. Do you need some advice while you wait?'

She held up a hand. 'No, really. I'll just have a wander.'

'THE COURTYARD?' Carly tipped her head towards the area beyond the campus cafe.

Dakota pulled a face. 'It's friggin' freezing outside.'

'It's not that bad, and I've got gloves if your delicate constitution can't handle it.' Carly picked up their coffees and started walking.

'My delicate constitution could do with a blanket and a gas heater.'

Carly needed the cold to fight the post-sleep paralysis aches and tiredness. Dakota zipped her jacket to the throat and wound her scarf around her throat until she looked like she was wearing a neck brace.

'Hand over the gloves.'

It was Newcastle, never as cold as Burden, but Carly found the gloves in her bag, feeling a little guilty she was subjecting Dakota to it.

'Did you mention why we're out here?' Dakota cupped the gloves around her cappuccino.

'I needed something to wake me up. I couldn't keep my eyes open in that last class.'

'You should've said. I could've slapped you. It would've been warmer.'

Carly grinned. 'I'll remember that next time.'

'You look a bit shit today, if you don't mind me saying.'

'I do mind. I'll have my gloves back now.'

'Is it the sleep thing again?'

Carly hesitated. 'Sleep thing?'

'A while ago, you weren't sleeping. I wondered if it was that again.'

A shrug. 'It comes and goes.'

Dakota scooped foam from the top of her cup. 'How does it work? You don't sleep at all? You wake up and stare at the ceiling for hours? Walk the floor? Read until your eyes hang out?'

Carly didn't want to think about it. 'A bit of all of that.'

'Not much fun.' It sounded like a throwaway line but Dakota reached out and laid her hand on Carly's arm.

It surprised her, made her think about telling Dakota about the sleep paralysis. She just wasn't sure her easygoing twenty-year-old attitude would make her feel any better. 'I have . . . nightmares. I don't sleep afterwards.'

'Not fun at all.' Dakota gave Carly's wrist a comforting squeeze, must have felt her watch underneath. 'How's our time?'

It would be nice to dismiss the subject so easily, Carly thought as she hitched her sleeve. 'Another five before we need to start walking.' The chill air felt good on her hot skin so she pushed up the other sleeve, hoping a few goosebumps might help her energy levels.

'Hey.' Dakota pulled the arm to the table.

There were four dark ovals on the pale flesh above her wrist. Companions for the ones on her knees and shins and the green one brewing on her hip that she could feel through her jeans. 'Bruises.'

'Well, yeah. What did you do?'

Bounced off the steps and the floor. She looked at her other arm, at the long, thin bruise that seemed to grow from her watch – that one had got stuck in the rails. 'I slipped on my stairs.'

'Ow.' Dakota ran fingertips across the four ovals. 'Did someone grab you?'

'What do you mean?'

Dakota spread her hand on Carly's forearm, the pads of her fingers finding the four marks as though they were a guide. 'My brother used to give me bruises like that with a Chinese burn.'

Something slithered along Carly's spine. *A dream, not real . . . A dream, not real . . .* But the warmth of Dakota's palm reminded her of another hand, gripping hard, holding her down. She snatched her arm back, rubbing the sensation away.

'What?' Dakota asked.

'Nothing. I . . .' Carly pushed at her sleeves, covering the marks like they were shameful. 'I . . .' She'd fallen down stairs, crawled around like a baby. Any number of things could've put those smudges there. 'We should go now. Keep the gloves, you can give them to me later. Tomorrow, whenever.'

Dakota hooked her bag over a shoulder. 'You okay?'

'Yeah, sure. Let's go.'

CARLY STOOD at the bottom of the stairs eyeing the railing that ran to the loft. Stainless steel, the top bar a circular tube, vertical bars underneath like the rungs of a ladder. They were wide enough for a fist to pass through, close enough to stop a kid getting its head stuck. Last night, they'd stopped her from falling into the kitchen below.

She looked again at the dark ovals on the inside of her arm, held her forearm to the railing, comparing the struts and bruises. She sat on the steps and moved her arm about, trying to find an angle that would explain them. She walked to the top and looked down. It must have happened on the stairs, she'd bounced like a pinball.

Maybe the four bruises were from more than one bump. She

mimed slipping and twisting and thwacking the handrail so that her forearm hit several times but it didn't feel like it had last night.

Studying the marks again, she glanced around for something else with knobs or protrusions – but it was a staircase, just steps and railing.

She'd tumbled and lurched about, there was no accounting for bruises sometimes, she told herself. She gave her arm a brisk scrub like the lesson was done and she could rub it out now. Sleep paralysis, she recited. Classic indicators: sense of menace, weight on the chest, choking sensation. She lifted her forearm, touched her fingers to the ovals, aligning the tips to the marks.

'Fuck.' Fuck, *fuck*.

Then she was on her feet again, checking the deadlock, the chain, and across the room to the French windows. The doors were locked. They were locked this morning. They'd been locked every damn time. *Sleep paralysis, Carly*. Awake and asleep at the same time. Scaring the shit out of herself. She must have done it to herself, then. Right? Frightened, panicking, standing at the windows and holding herself so tightly she bruised her own arm. It had to be that.

But what she remembered was the weight of a man on her body, his breath on her face, his hands pinning her down.

AN EDGY UNCERTAINTY hummed inside as Carly stood to one side of the French windows once again. Not thinking about the bruises now, exhausted by the round and round of theories and possibilities. By sleeplessness and dragging fatigue.

She watched lights come on in the neighbourhood, traffic and pedestrians until they thinned to a trickle. The woman stirred at the stove, the man drank beer in front of the TV, the teenager had her feet on the desk and a keyboard in her lap. Carly thought about the sleeping pills on her counter, undecided – about holding them in her hand, about bruises she couldn't explain, about whether sleeping through the night was safer than waking.

A figure in the street made her lift her chin for a better look.

Shoulders hunched in a jacket, slight hitch to his gait. Nate. A twinge of guilt as she remembered his voice on the other side of the door – and her own, *Leave me the hell alone.*

He was moving awkwardly, and not just from his bad knee. The pub he hadn't recommended was around that corner, perhaps he'd had a few. He held a palm to his forehead for a moment, staggering a little. Maybe he'd been drinking for a while. Then he turned to cross the road and she saw blood on his face.

Swinging the balcony door open, she watched from the railing as he stumbled down the kerb, a hand grazing the tarmac as he struggled to stay on his feet. She was four floors up, a shout wouldn't help, so she waited to see where he went. When he'd disappeared into the warehouse entrance, she grabbed a towel and headed for the door.

She'd never seen him in the lift but she stood at the doors, figuring he wouldn't take the stairs if he couldn't cross the road without falling. Except there were no sounds from the cogs. Leaning out into the atrium, she searched the foyer below. If he was there, he wasn't making any noise.

She made plenty hammering down the stairs, hurling herself around the turns, then pulling up suddenly at the bottom, a prickle of nerves across her shoulders as she remembered the bruises on her arm.

The forest of columns was eerie in the gloom, and deserted. 'Nate?' Her voice bounced softly around the hollow centre of the building. There was only silence in its wake. Moving quickly, quietly, she headed for the security doors, saw him under the light in the entry bay – on the ground, slumped against the wall.

26

———

He smelled of alcohol and cigarettes and blood. One leg was out straight, as though it had slid from under him. The other was bent, supporting the arm that was holding one side of his face.

'Nate?' Carly squatted beside him.

He looked up. There was blood between his fingers.

'I saw you from my balcony.' She wadded the towel and held it out to him. As he pressed it to his face, she saw a dark, congealing blob forming on his eyebrow. 'Are you hurt anywhere else?'

He shook his head.

'What happened?' She was thinking hit-and-run, a fall.

'Someone's fist.'

'Oh my god. You were assaulted?' Carly glanced warily into the street. 'Are they still out there? We should call the police.'

'No.' It seemed to cover all her questions. He shifted, tried to get up, stopped with a hand to the wall, pulling in deep breaths.

She grabbed an elbow, hoped he wasn't about to throw up. 'Do you need an ambulance?'

'No.'

'You might need stitches. You could be concussed, you're slurring a little.'

'It happened at the pub. I'm pissed.'

Oh, right . . .

'Someone hit me. I hit something.' He got both legs under him, waited a second before pushing upright. 'A table, I think. Possibly a chair. And the deck. I definitely hit the deck.' A couple of unsteady steps.

Carly grabbed hold of him again, pushed the security door before remembering she'd only planned to wait for him in the corridor. 'My keys. I left them inside.' Goes to bleeding man's aid, gets locked outside. Good job. 'Have you got yours?'

He patted his jacket, almost pushed himself over. Leaned against the wall and tried again. She wasn't sure if it was alcohol or concussion, only knew he was never going to find them slapping like that.

'Here, let me.' She pressed palms to his pocket flaps, felt cold leather and solid chest. Felt her way down, searching for compartments in the lining and the pouches he stuffed his hands into.

'Jeans?' She glanced up, found his eyes on her.

Without shifting his gaze, he opened one side of his jacket, the warm, musky scent of his skin filling the space between them. She hesitated and then briskly, like his body under her hands wasn't making her mouth dry, she felt the front of his thigh, reached around to a back pocket, fingers skimming thick denim and the curve of firm buttock. She tried the other side, up to her shoulder inside his coat, cheek resting on the soft fabric of his shirt. 'No keys.'

He watched her for a long, silent moment.

'Okay, well . . . I'll buzz.' Carly pressed Christina's number. 'Hi, it's Carly. I've locked myself out.'

'I was only thinking of you tonight.'

'Great. Can you . . .'

'I've pulled out some books I thought you might like.'

'I'm locked . . .'

'Novels, mostly. Come and get them anytime. We could have a coffee.'

'That'd be great. Christina?'

'Yes, hon.'

'Can you buzz me in?'

'Oh for god's sake, what am I doing blathering on like that? It must be freezing out there. Here you go.'

Carly turned to Nate as the door clicked. 'Christina from the fifth floor. Apparently she's got a library up there.'

'Why are you here, Carly?' It didn't sound like *here on the doorstep* – it was more like *here at the warehouse* or *in Newcastle*. Maybe even *here in his life*.

'To get you inside,' she said.

Nate staggered along beside her, veered away before they reached the lift.

'It's this way.' She grabbed his arm.

'I'm taking the stairs.'

'You're bleeding.'

'I always take the stairs.'

'Give yourself a night off.'

'I don't *deserve* a night off,' he growled.

It made her wonder about the raw look she'd seen in his eyes at other times. She softened her voice. 'Everyone deserves a night off when they're bleeding.' She gave his arm a tug. 'You can go back to beating yourself up tomorrow.'

There was something defiant in his eyes as he resisted.

'Besides,' she added, 'there's no way I can get you up those stairs. There's fucking hundreds of them, in case you haven't counted.' She hustled him around, grateful for his unsteadiness as she steered him across the foyer.

'It's not meant to be like this,' he said when she'd pushed him into the lift.

'No. You're not meant to come home like this. Drunk is okay. Everyone needs to do that sometimes. But not concussed and bleeding and peeled off the front step. That's not good.'

On the fourth floor she got him out and stared across the atrium at her door. It was wide open. She'd left it that way, she remembered, only planning to go as far as the lift. But there were bruises on her arm and it was night and quiet and an open door was as good as an invitation. She glanced around the dim corridors as they crossed the walkway. How long had she been gone? Ten minutes?

Nate stopped outside his place.

'You'll have to come to mine,' she said.

'I'm okay.'

'You're bleeding and wobbly and you have no keys.' *And anyone could have walked into mine.* Even drunk and concussed, she'd feel better if he was there.

'This isn't right. It's all fucking wrong.'

'It's fine. I can clean up your eye and you can sleep on the sofa.' He slowed as they got closer. What was the problem? 'Nate, it's okay.'

'It's not. I fucked up. You shouldn't have to do this.' He propped on the threshold, a hand on the jamb.

'I'm already doing it.' She cast her eyes down the hallway, wished he'd keep walking.

'No, Carly. I should be helping *you*.'

Something tight and shameful caught in her chest then. She'd told him to leave her the hell alone this morning. 'You *have* helped. This . . .' She touched fingers to his bloodied temple. 'Dragging you up here – awful for you but it's a circuit breaker for me.'

It consoled him enough for Carly to get him to the living room and into a chair. 'Wait here a minute.' Flicking lights, she ran up the stairs, checked the loft and the ensuite. No one there. Scaring herself again.

Nate sat on the toilet lid in the half bath while she washed his wound. Breathing through her mouth so she didn't catch the copper smell of his blood, telling herself she hadn't done it to him. He kept still as she worked, only pulling in a sharp breath when she sluiced it with antiseptic.

'I think you might need a stitch,' she said, her torso pressed to his shoulder in the tight space.

'Tape it.'

'It'll leave a scar.'

'It won't be the first. Tape it.'

She didn't argue, glad to have it covered. 'Have you eaten dinner?'

'Don't go to any trouble.'

'I'll take that as a no. Omelette okay?'

Ten minutes later, he was out of the shower and back in the same clothes as she handed over a plate of eggs and toast. He'd opted for bourbon instead of painkillers and she topped up his glass, poured one for herself and sat on the coffee table while he ate on the sofa. He still smelled of second-hand cigarette smoke and blood but it was faint under the clean soapiness. There was a rip in the knee of his jeans, a piece of skin missing from a knuckle and a knot of swelling on his cheek. But it was the deep purple bruising starting around the eye that spoke of the violence behind it all. It made the small, brown smudges on her arm seem inconsequential. Seemed to confirm she had done them to herself. She waited until he'd put down his fork before asking, 'So what happened?'

'I got hit.'

'No kidding. Did the other guy?'

'No.'

'You didn't swing or you missed?'

He ran a finger around the edges of the bandage on his head. 'He wanted to take a shot at a kid so I got in his way.'

Carly frowned. 'A kid? A little kid was at the pub?'

'Some skinny young bloke with brand new ID and no brains.'

Not a bar brawl then. 'You stood up for a teenager?'

'Don't make it something it's not. I didn't get anything I don't deserve.'

He thought he deserved a punch in the face? Carly had thought she'd earned the slap from her first husband but she hadn't stepped in front of his hand. What had Nate done? 'Just wondering. Does it make it go away or bring it all back?'

He hesitated. 'What?'

'Whatever makes you step into a punch aimed at someone else. Does the pain block it out or make you remember?'

'You studying psychology now?' A small, chiding smile. 'Are you trying to forget or remember when you're crying at your front door?'

She felt the stab of pain he'd intended to inflict, thought, *fair enough*. If he deserved anything, it was an explanation. 'Coming here has put distance between me and what happened. The other night . . . nights, it's something else. I'm sorry I told you to go to hell.'

He nodded.

'I'm sorry you think you deserve to have your head caved in,' she said. 'My experience runs to that, too, and I can tell you that physical pain doesn't take it away. It's just another load you have to carry around.'

He took a mouthful of bourbon, nursed the glass in his hands. 'Your friends, the ones who died?'

Carly wasn't sure she wanted to talk about them. 'Yes.'

'Did you kill them?'

She took a sharp breath, snapped her face away, guilt and shame pounding in her chest like it always did.

But Nate must have taken it as a 'no'. 'Then your experience can't tell me anything.'

It made her look back at him. He'd killed someone? Reckless and unthinking or . . . she dropped her eyes to his calloused hands. Had they pulled a trigger? Thrown a lethal punch? Held someone's throat and squeezed? She lifted fingers to her own, saw him watching her, waiting.

And she got it – he wanted her to recoil in disgust, even fear. It was another way to hurt himself, she knew all about that. So she kept her face still as she sipped her drink.

'The boating accident you mentioned?'

He glanced away, like she had. 'I never said it was an accident.'

He wasn't planning to talk about it either, that much was obvious. Which was fine because she hadn't wanted to push fingers into his wounds, just let him know he wasn't the only person on earth dealing with a burden of shit. 'Is that why you're up at three o'clock in the morning when I'm at my front door?'

His eyes found her face again. 'Yeah.'

'The dark hours suck, huh?'

A softening of his lips. 'Yeah.'

'How's your head?'

He poked roughly around the bandage. 'Sore.'

'It will be if you do that to it.' She took his wrist, pulled his hand away. 'How about trying to sleep now?'

He left his wrist in her grasp, gave an upward nod.

'If you wake up before dawn,' she added, 'turn on the lights and I'll come down and we won't talk about it.'

'You don't need to do that.'

'I might be grateful for the opportunity. Let's see what the night brings.'

He caught her fingers as they slipped through his. 'Thanks.'

Carly held her breath, aware of the heat in his touch, the roughness of his skin, of something intimate in the connection. Then he released her, an apology in his eyes, as though her silence had been a reprimand.

She wanted to tell him it was all right, that it didn't have to stop there. 'I'll find you a blanket.'

Carly moved quietly around the loft, cleaning her teeth, changing into pyjamas, aware of Nate one floor below, only a staircase separating them. Was he thinking of her as she peeled off her clothes? She was thinking of him and his hands – that for a brief, cold moment she was naked and he was warm.

His words replayed in her mind as she lay in bed: *I never said it was an accident.*

There were awful ways to die at sea. Awful ways to survive, too. Lots of ways to feel responsible. That would haunt your memories and make you stay awake at night. And screw with your mind.

27

———

Nate was still asleep when she came down in the morning. She scrawled a note: *Gone to class. Help yourself to breakfast.* Set it on the coffee table and took a moment to observe the sleeping body on her sofa. The etched lines of his face were softer in rest, the tight grimness smoothed out, something gentle and less hurt in its place. She could smell the warm sleepiness of him. It made her think of waking beside a man, still hungry for him. *You don't want me like that*, he'd said. Except she did.

CARLY WAVED AT MAXINE, who was waiting by the lift on the fourth floor, and the nice woman who wore the bright headscarves as she made a turn on the zigzag stairs. Stepping into the corridor on the first level, she spotted little Alice and her dad in the foyer below, heading out to work and daycare. The girl's singsong 'Hi' as they passed Stuart echoed upwards like the tinkle of a bell. Carly grinned at Stuart's response, glancing around like an egret as though the greeting might have come from voices in his head.

She knocked a cheery rat-a-tat on Elizabeth's door. Since finding her asleep on the bench, Carly had dropped by every couple of days, asking if there was anything Elizabeth needed while Carly was at the shops – the older woman probably wondered why Carly was always running out of stuff. She waited thirty seconds and knocked a little louder. When there were no shuffles from the other side, she pressed her ear to the timber, hearing voices, a radio or television.

Crossing the corridor, Carly looked over the railing. The bench seat was empty. Carly checked her watch, decided to give Elizabeth a minute or so – she was slow and it was cold and damp this morning. Maybe she was in the shower or ignored callers this early. Or out already. Before eight, with the radio going?

Checking her watch again, thinking about parking prospects at campus, Carly gave it one more try and left.

At lunchtime, Dakota pulled out the Big Long List. 'Tutor.'

'Of what?'

'No idea. Student counsellor.' Fast, terse, hungover.

'I don't have any advice to offer,' Carly said.

'You could have told me not to drink so much last night.'

'I might've if you'd rung.'

'I was going to. I pulled out my phone to tell you to get your arse down to the pub and meet some of my friends. Then someone handed me a drink and the next time I looked at my phone it was almost midnight. Fortunately for you, I was sober enough to remember your sleep thing and decided I wouldn't be a very good friend if I woke you up.'

Carly grinned, happy to be thought of in so many ways. 'Fortunately for me.'

'So this cheerfulness – you had a good night then?' Dakota asked.

'I had an . . . interesting night.'

'Weird dreams?'

'No. The guy next door got beaten up. I rescued him from the street entrance, he bled in my bathroom and slept on my sofa.'

'So how old is this neighbour?'

She shrugged. 'Mid-thirties.'

Dakota raised an eyebrow. 'Nice-looking?'

'Not this morning.'

RAIN PATTERED, the windscreen wipers beat a steady rhythm. More jazz than Hollywood horror flick, Carly decided. It was late afternoon, the little supermarket in Baxter Street would be open for another hour. She could drop by Elizabeth's on the way up, make a quick trip on foot if Elizabeth needed anything. Nate might be home by then. If he dropped by, she'd see how it went, she told herself again. Don't drive it. She was Carly now, not Charlotte.

Reading a text from Dakota in the lift up from the garage - *Vintage specialist??* - she was grinning as the doors slid open on a crowd in the foyer. More people than Carly had ever seen in one place at the warehouse. Little groups of them, quiet and still in the grey light of the atrium.

Christina appeared, hair damp, tiny raindrops sparkling like glitter on her green cardigan. 'Oh, Carly.' She came all the way into the lift, took Carly's elbow and steered her forward.

'Is there a meeting?' Carly asked as Christina led her past small groups, wariness making her glance around. Howard Helyer was talking to a man in a suit. The guy with the bike was at the bottom of the stairs, toes turned up in his cycling shoes. Ahead of them, Dietrich acknowledged Carly with a nod. Brooke was there and she was crying. Carly's feet slowed.

'George Pankowitz rang me,' Christina said. 'He thought I might've had a key. We had to chase down Howard. It took a while but, well . . .' She paused, her voice thick and trembling as she finished. 'It was too late anyway.'

Carly's mind caught on *key* and Howard and thought *Nate*. Oh god. Had someone come after him? Got through the security door and beat him up? She swung her head, searching for him among the crowd. Maxine, Roland, Stuart, Alice's mother. No Nate. Movement above caught her eyes. Figures were at the railings overhead: two there, another four higher up. Had someone thrown him over? He'd told her he deserved to get hurt. Had he jumped?

Carly dug her feet into the floor, turning Christina to face her. 'What? Tell me.'

Taking her hands, Christina said, 'It's Elizabeth. Carly, honey, she's gone.'

'What?'

'She passed away. The ambulance has just left.'

The air evaporated from Carly's lungs.

'She knew everyone in the building. All these people are here to see her off.' Christina dabbed at the droplets of moisture in her hair. 'Some of us went out to the street to watch her go.'

Carly looked closer at the faces now, saw what she hadn't before. Shock and sadness. 'There was an ambulance?'

'It was George Pankowitz. Her neighbour.'

'Someone *killed* her?'

'He heard her radio going when he came back from golf,' Christina went on with barely a pause. 'He thought it was strange she was playing it so loud. He knocked a few times and thought she must've forgotten to turn it off as she went out. But when it was still going hours later, he got worried. That's when he called me. Did I tell you that already?'

Carly took a breath, wishing Christina could be concise for once, understanding she probably needed to talk this time. 'And what happened?'

'Oh, I can't stop seeing it.'

'Where was she? In her chair?' A peaceful passing with her memories?

'I thought she might've slipped in the shower and she wouldn't want George to see her like that. I thought I could put a towel over her first or . . .' A sob as Christina pushed a tissue under her glasses. 'She was on the floor beside the bed. She'd pulled the bedside table over. There was blood all over . . . Everywhere. On her face, her nightie.'

Carly shut her eyes on the image, on other images of bloodied bodies. She wound an arm around Christina's shoulders. 'I'm so sorry you had to see that.' More pictures to join the ones that were already keeping her awake at night.

'She must have fallen first and was trying to get up,' Christina said. 'Her clock radio was on her chest, she was holding it there, as though . . . as though it was all she could do to call for help. It was so loud I could hear it from the front door.'

Carly had heard it too, and the memory of it now slid through her bones like a chill.

'Maybe she wasn't feeling well,' Christina was saying. 'Maybe it was a heart attack. The ambulance people can't say . . .'

Carly pushed her voice through the choking sensation in her throat. 'I knocked on her door this morning. I could hear the radio then. I thought . . . oh god.' She'd thought about getting a car park at the campus. Reckless, selfish.

'What time was that?' It was Dietrich. He was beside Carly now. Brooke, too, her eyes bloodshot and glassy.

Carly looked from one to the other and felt as if she'd failed them. Failed everyone here. 'I'm so sorry.'

Brooke took Carly's hand. 'She was such a lovely person. So lovely and bossy and . . .'

'What time did you see her?' Dietrich asked.

'I didn't.' *Oh god, I just left.* 'It was just after eight. I could hear the radio from out in the corridor and I . . . she didn't answer so I . . . *left.*' Carly covered her face with her hands, a familiar shameful heat filling her chest. 'She might've been alive then. She might be now if I'd . . .'

'You mustn't blame yourself,' Dietrich said.

'Oh, Carly.' Brooke squeezed Carly's hand some more.

Christina fussed, passing Carly a tissue, patting at her hand. 'Oh, no. No, no, no. You mustn't think like that. It was lovely that you went to see her, she would've liked that and of course you didn't think anything about the radio going like that. Who would?'

George, obviously, and anyone else who'd been involved in the search for a spare key. Carly had thought of herself.

'Well,' Christina said on a huge sigh, 'I don't know about anyone else but I could do with a drink right now. Would you like to join me?' The sweep of her glance included Brooke, Dietrich and Carly.

Brooke nodded. 'Yes, a cup of tea.'

'I think this calls for something a bit stiffer,' Christina said.

'I can't . . .' Carly started. 'You go up. I need to . . .' She stepped back. 'Walk a bit.'

Carly strode to the stairs, her vision blurring as she took the first flight two at a time. She didn't look back, didn't want them to see the tide that was threatening to burst. Hurrying quietly past Nate's apartment, she opened her door, pressed her back into the corner and let self-reproach pour from her in an agonised groan. She held her stomach, doubling over as though she was injured, the bag falling from her shoulder, its contents scattering across the floor.

She stayed there, dragging in breath, tightening fists in her hair until it hurt. Sounds from the corridor made her straighten. Just someone passing but it dragged her from her pocket of pain to feel the agitated, faltering breathlessness that was starting inside her. *Christ, not now.*

She scattered the detritus from her bag as she stalked up the hallway, trying to ward off the panic attack. Arms folded, hands clenched, she continued around the living room, pacing it out as though she was walking to the breakwater – until she saw it. The vase. The flowers gone now, just the empty etched silver that Carly hadn't returned.

Fuck. *Fuck.* What had she done?

If she'd checked properly, Elizabeth might be alive and Christina wouldn't have seen her friend's bloodied body. But she hadn't, and Carly had spread grief and shock like it was a disease she'd carried from Burden.

She sucked at the air, keeping her eyes wide, her focus on the apartment instead of on other places she'd been. The unopened packet of sleeping pills was still on the counter. It was early evening, the light was fading inside and out – and yeah, she wanted to sleep tonight. Not just because of the man that trampled through her subconscious. She wanted to close her eyes and see nothing until morning.

Snatching up the packet, she drew out a foil sheet of pills, punched two onto the palm of her hand. Two small discs. She could barely feel them in her palm, no weight at all, and yet her breath was shallow, her heart thudding. Fear, memory, shame, yearning.

She held them for a long time. The hum of the lift was a distant vibration. Quiet knocks and taps and muffled voices drifted to her. A louder, closer *clack* made her head snap up.

It was followed by soft, urgent footfalls . . . in her hallway.

28

———

'Carly?' It was a forced whisper.

She closed her hand around the pills, fingers forming a fist as she backed up along the counter. Movement in the hallway. Then the voice again. 'Carly?'

It was Nate. He was at the edge of the living room, a strip of white plaster above one eye. 'You okay?'

'What the fuck?' she snapped. 'How did you get in?'

'Your door came open when I knocked. I saw your bag and keys on the floor and thought something might've . . .' He paused. 'Thought you might need help.'

She hadn't closed the door properly? Tiny hairs rose on her neck. 'I'm fine.'

Nate came further into the room, slowly, as though he wasn't sure he should. 'I came to see if you'd heard about Elizabeth.'

She scrubbed a hand across her damp cheek. 'Just taking a moment to fall apart.'

He waited a beat. 'Shall I go?'

'No.' *God, no.* Half an hour ago, the thought of team-grieving had made her pound up the stairs in need of solitude. Now her own company scared her. 'I'm done now. Stay.' She borrowed Christina's words, a flat, hard-edged pitch to it. 'Don't know about you but I need to follow that news with a drink. Something large and alcoholic.'

He hooked a thumb towards the hallway. 'I'll close the door. You want to get your stuff from the hallway?'

She had pills in her hand, trembling in her knees. She didn't want him to see either. 'It's not going anywhere.' Turning, walking around the counter, clinging to bravado like it was a life vest keeping her head above water, she called after him. 'I've got bourbon and bourbon.'

'I'll have bourbon then,' he called back.

She opened her hand, tossed the pills into the sink, ran the tap and washed them down the drain.

'Dry, if you've got any,' Nate said, in the living room again.

'Nope, only ice.' She dropped cubes into tumblers, remembered as she unscrewed the bottle that she'd been avoiding the whiskey in case it made the dreams worse. Right now, she didn't care what happened in four or five hours when she tried to sleep. Hopefully she'd be too numb to think. Covering the ice with golden brown liquid, she carried both glasses to the windows, making Nate join her, not wanting empty space around her.

'Did you know Elizabeth?' she asked as he took his drink. Was he sad or a bystander?

'Only to say hello. She'd bail me up in the foyer sometimes, ask about the job, my knee. We exchanged a few gripes about limping.' He paused, something gentler in his voice when he spoke again. 'I used to wonder if she made notes. She remembered everything.'

'I was in her book club. She told me her memories.' *She helped me remember my friends.* Carly lifted her eyes to his reflection. 'I knocked on her door this morning and didn't wait to see if she was okay.'

'You want to talk about it?'

'No.'

'You want to go somewhere and not talk?'

'No. I want . . .' She let the sentence trail away.

'What do you want?'

Carly shifted her gaze from the window to the man beside her. 'I want to turn it off.'

'Turn off what?'

'Everything. All of it.' Every bloodied, bleeding moment that filled her head.

He didn't speak for a long moment, his eyes steady on Carly. She'd said more than she wanted, didn't want to explain it, was tempted to back away and change the subject. But she saw there was no judgement in it, no *She should feel accountable* or *She needs to get past it*. There was nothing in it but recognition.

'It's part of you,' he finally said.

Her skin felt hot, sharp. Her breath was ragged. In front of her, close enough to touch, Nate was motionless. In her space.

'I don't want it anymore,' she said.

'No.'

'It hurts.'

'Yeah.'

It wasn't his fault but he was telling her to wear it. 'I'm fucking tired of it hurting.'

He held her eyes and said nothing more.

Her heart thumped, blood crashed in her veins. Without thinking, without choosing to, she reached for his hand, interlaced her fingers with his and closed the distance between them.

He didn't move, didn't speak. It wasn't uncertainty, he was waiting to see what happened next or for her to make the next move, or maybe he thought she was deciding. She didn't know, didn't care as she pressed her mouth to his.

Sensation fired through her like an electric charge. His lips were soft and firm under hers. Hot and salty. And still he didn't move, as though she might change her mind if he did, his answer coming only from the tilt of his head and his tongue when she parted her lips.

She leaned into him then, felt the solid muscle of his chest press at her breasts, his belt buckle at her waist, his thighs against hers. Unwinding their fingers, she slid her hand around his back, pulled him closer, kissed deeper. And finally he moved, wrapping his arms around her, enclosing her within his bulk. It felt safe, warm, anchored. The things she'd needed for thirteen years. It felt like her bones were alive, her flesh was on fire, her mind pinned to this moment.

The glass in her hand fell to the floor. If it broke, she didn't hear it, her senses consumed with the skin under her fingers as she slid her hand beneath his jumper. He groaned quietly against her mouth. She tugged at the hem of his top. He pulled away, only enough to form words.

'The windows.'

She turned her eyes, saw the darkness outside and the reflection of their bodies on the glass, imagined the view from the street and what they were about to do. Holding onto him, not wanting to let go, she pulled him with her, away from the balcony, dragging the jumper over his head as they reached the sofa.

He released her to throw it off, cocked his chin at the loft. For half a second, she thought about it: climbing the stairs single-file, enough time for her to think about what she was doing.

'Here,' she said. 'With the lights off.' She lifted a hand to his chest, ran the palm across wisps of hair pooled in the centre. 'Maybe not all the lights.'

From the glow of a single, soft bulb, Carly watched as he peeled away her layers of clothing, pushed at what remained of his. She drew him down to her, the sofa at her back, his weight on her breasts, his legs between her thighs. He lingered there, drawing out the moment, holding her gaze in the gloom as he slid slowly inside her.

She closed her eyes, felt only Nate now. Hard inside her. The touch of his tongue as it traced a line from her shoulder to her ear. His palm as it left her breast. Fingers stroking her throat. The gentle pressure below her jaw . . . and her mind leapt to another dark place.

Gasping, twisting her face away, she snatched at his fingers. '*No.*'

Nate lifted his face. He was still inside her, held by her legs around his hips, confusion and concern in his eyes. She wanted to push him away and haul him closer, her body hungry even as her mind tossed back images of another man who'd hovered above her.

'Carly?'

He lifted his torso from her, the cold of the room suddenly between them. Her gaze flicked to the dark windows, his glass on the coffee table, the bourbon gone. She didn't want alcohol to numb her or herbal tea to make her sleep. She wanted Nate – around her, inside her, so there was no room for grief or fear.

'Not like that,' she whispered.

'Tell me what you want.'

She pulled him upright, kneeled over him. He understood that, kept her close as she rocked. Held her as her breathing grew short and sharp, as he buried his lips in her neck and groaned.

THEY ATE at the table as though it was a date. Placemats, cutlery and tinned soup. They talked about nothing that counted, the sticking plaster above his eye peeling at the corners. Nate stacked the dishwasher while Carly sat on the kitchen counter in his shirt. He stood in front of her when he was done and ran his hands along her thighs.

'What are the bruises about?' he asked.

She slid his hands higher, away from the mass of dark splotches around her knees. 'Just bruises.'

'Are you sick?'

'What? No. I fell down the stairs.'

'How many times?' He wasn't making a joke, it was disbelief.

What could she say? That it was from crawling on hands and knees, terrified of the ugly, scary things in her mind? She wanted him to stay, not find an excuse to leave. 'It's a long way down from the loft.'

'My sister said the same thing. Tried to tell me she'd walked into a door once. Turned out it was a door with a fist.'

His sister. The one Nate had gone to the police about and ended up being threatened with arrest. Carly could see his concern, but she didn't want to explain it. Not tonight, anyway. 'It's not what you're thinking. No one comes here and pushes me down the stairs.'

'Who put their hand around your throat?'

A man without a face. 'It's not . . .'

'You were scared.'

'Not of you.'

Nate took her wrist, held the forearm under the light, the four ovals dark under the brightness. 'My sister had these, too. They're grab marks.'

She wanted to snatch her hand away, but her eyes clung to the bruises, something fearful winding its way into her brain. 'I have bad dreams,' she told him. Told herself. 'I stumble around sometimes. I fell down the stairs. It's what you hear in the middle of the night.'

'Sleepwalking?' The question was doubtful.

'Something like that.' That was as close as she wanted to get to it before she tried to sleep. 'Can we not talk about it?'

He ran his fingertips across the marks on her arm, either weighing up her explanation or wondering how far he should push.

Carly didn't let him decide. She pulled him between her legs, slid her hands around him. 'Exhaust me so I sleep tonight.'

She took him by the hand, led him up the stairs but paused at the top. A glow from the living room cast soft shadows at the edge of the loft but the gloom beyond it made her uneasy. She wanted to see Nate here, not the man who scared her. She flipped on the lights, making sure it was only Nate who was with her when she pressed her skin to his.

Afterwards, his arm around her waist as he curled at her back, the climax still humming in her muscles, Nate murmured into her neck, 'Is it turned off now?'

Carly thought of the kind of answers that other men had wanted to hear: *You're a good lover, the sex was great, it was exactly what she needed.* But she remembered Nate's face when she'd told him what she wanted, the sense that he'd understood. 'Yes.'

'For how long?'

It was a question only someone with experience would ask. 'I don't know.'

'Will you sleep tonight?'

Whether she did or didn't, this was better than herbal tea and soft music. 'I want to.'

'Doesn't always work that way.'

'No.'

His hand slid from her waist, explored the curve of her hip, her thigh. 'Is it better if I stay or go?'

She didn't know and she wasn't sure what she wanted but she was intrigued about him. 'What do you want to do?'

'I want to make something better, not worse.'

'Something?'

'Anything would be a start.'

She turned to face him, wondering what he meant. Saw only that his eyes didn't meet hers. That was fine, she understood about needing to do something right, only . . . 'Sleeping here might not be a comfortable experience. I wake a lot. Confused sometimes. Sometimes scared.' She smiled a little, tried to make light of it. 'You know, of the dark. Like a kid.'

'And tumble down the stairs?'

'Yes. Once.'

'It's okay, Carly. I won't let you fall.'

Fall. A split second of sensation, of dropping into space, battered by rock, by fear and shame – and then it was over, as though he'd caught her. She reached out, touched a finger to his lips. Who was this guy?

29

———

Nate was awake when Carly got up to shower and ready to leave when she went downstairs. The tape was gone from his eye, the swelling below it barely there now, a thick scab and a purple slash around his eye the only evidence of his beating.

'I've got an early appointment,' he told her.

She wondered if it was an excuse to leave. What was the protocol when you'd slept with a neighbour who had a shower and change of clothes five metres away? 'You want coffee first?'

'I should get going.'

'Sure.' She walked him to the door, shared an awkward smile, not sure how to finish it. A kiss? A friendly embrace?

'I'll be around later,' he said and left it at that, open-ended.

The apartment felt large and quiet with him gone. She ate cereal standing at the windows, watching drizzle fall in a fine mist. The street below was dark with rain, the sky heavy with fat clouds. The kind of weather that would have made Elizabeth ache. Carly shook her head. It was fine for Nate to tell her he wouldn't let her fall – but he wasn't here now and she had two hours to fill before class.

She took her laptop to the sofa, planning to go over some study notes, then found her fingers poised above the keyboard and Nate's name in her head.

She typed *nathan griffin yacht*, pressed Enter and got plenty of hits. Newspaper articles, TV reports, inquest findings and a Wikipedia entry. She glanced over her shoulder at the wall they shared, then clicked on the first item.

It was a story from the online version of a Sydney paper, a detailed piece written three years ago at the end of an inquest into the death of Vivien Clements - it was a woman who drowned in Nate's boating incident. She was twenty-eight when she died, the same age Carly would have been at the time. According to the article, Vivien Clements' body was never found after the yacht *Flamingo* capsized forty nautical miles off the New South Wales coast. Carly skimmed a few paragraphs in search of Nate's name . . . *and Nathan Griffin, of Newcastle, 31 at the time of the incident, was skipper and survived six hours in the water before being rescued.*

Carly sat back from the screen. Not just an 'incident', not just memories of open water and waiting for rescue. Nate had been in charge and a woman had died. Guilt, blame, reliving, second-guessing. Things Carly knew about. She remembered his comment last night: Make something better, not worse. On other nights – *I never said it was an accident. I don't deserve a night off.* She got up, paced a bit before reading more.

Flamingo was a fifteen-metre racing yacht, fresh from the builders' dock, custom-built for sixty-eight-year-old Gerald Fitzgibbon. He'd commissioned Nate to skipper for him when it was sailed from the Sunshine Coast in Queensland to Lake Macquarie, north of Sydney. Fitzgibbon had organised five crewmembers, one had dropped out at the last minute. Nate asked Vivien Clements, *an experienced sailor and Griffin's girlfriend . . .*

Carly pulled in a sharp breath. Vivien Clements had been Nate's girlfriend. And she'd died crewing on a boat that Nate was in charge of. Something burned in Carly's chest – for Nate, for his words last night, for the pain in his eyes.

Scrolling quickly through the article, she found a photo of Vivien

Clements. A black-and-white shot on a windy dock, her hair blown to one side of her face like a dark flag. Not glamorous in any way, a hint of toughness in the life jacket slung casually over her shoulder, a smile that seemed on the verge of laughter, something easygoing and fun in it. Carly's gaze flicked across the room to the photo she'd put on the fridge: four fun-loving faces that no longer existed.

The report talked about weather conditions that were 'challenging, not extreme', said there was inexperience in the crew and severe seasickness. The new radio failed late in the afternoon and weather warnings of a deepening low were missed. Around 9 pm, the boat was being hammered with five-metre waves. Fitzgibbon, attached to the boat by a harness, was washed overboard. Vivien went to his aid but she needed Nate and another crew member, fifty-two-year-old Lucy Sabouni, to drag him back on board. Suffering broken ribs, Fitzgibbon was helped below in considerable pain. Lucy dislocated a finger during the rescue. With two other men badly affected by seasickness at that stage, Nate, Vivien and the injured Lucy were the only crew on deck.

A single, massive wave flipped the yacht. The sick and injured crew were trapped in an air pocket inside the cabin. Gerald Fitzgibbon was helped to the surface by the other two. On deck, Nate, Vivien and Lucy, attached to *Flamingo* by harnesses, had been thrown into the sea.

A hand to her mouth, Carly read the story Nate had told the court of the minutes that followed.

Underwater and following years of boating procedure, Nate unclipped his harness, used a knife from his belt to cut himself free of ropes, followed the upside-down deck to the rail and worked his way to the surface. Coming up on the windward side, he was battered against the hull by waves, gagging on seawater as he shouted for his crew, his voice drowned out by the wind. He fought his way around the stern to the lee side and began shouting again, a single word, 'One'. Lucy responded quickly with 'Two'. Fitzgibbon and his friends called Three, Four and Five. Vivien Clements never answered.

Tears burning her eyes, Carly left the laptop and stood at the windows. Restless clouds jostled and shoved, an umbrella sheltering a pedestrian made a red hole in the grey street. The inquest had determined the faulty radio prevented Nate from making an informed decision about the worsening weather. It recommended no charges be laid. It didn't matter what the official decision was, she thought. Nate had floated on a black ocean, responsible for terrified members of his crew, shouting for his girlfriend and hearing only the howling rush of wind and waves.

Did you kill them? he'd asked Carly about her friends. There'd been no inquest into the deaths on the cliff ledge, the coroner had decided the fall was an accident. It hadn't mattered. She knew what happened, that she'd goaded them into going, that they'd drunk too much the night before, that their laughter had rung around the canyon only hours before their screams. She heard again the voices that haunted her dreams. Carly's own: *Come on, it's fine.* Debs' last words, like an accusation: *I'm cold.* Adam's as his hand grew weaker: *I wanted to be a dad.*

What did Nate think about when he stood at his windows and remembered? There were no last words from his girlfriend, just an endless silence in the dark. Something else Carly knew about. How did he look at the water and bear it? How did it not screw with his head?

30

———

Sunlight sparked red and gold fireworks behind Carly's eyelids. The hush of the foyer, the expanse of the atrium above her head, the sense of space around her made sitting on Elizabeth's bench feel like meditation. Maybe that was why Elizabeth had done it every day. Carly rested her head on the wall at her back, grateful the week had finally ground to its end.

If lack of sleep and stress were an invitation for the man in black to scare the hell out of her, then he'd missed a prime opportunity: anxiety, guilt, a sadness that had seeped through the warehouse like a gas leak, then yesterday the funeral and wake. Nate had come and gone from her apartment, had spoken no words of endearment, never kissed her goodbye, just knocked on her door at all the right moments.

Today, the sun was shining, the sky was gloriously blue, and in a couple of hours Dakota was cutting her hair. She'd have a laugh with her friend, apply some brainpower to her Big Long List, have a few drinks. Be normal and maybe sleep like a normal person tonight.

'Good afternoon, Carly.'

She opened her eyes. 'Roland.' He was returning from the markets too, carrying a shopping bag, wearing a tie and sports coat –

a man from a different generation, who'd struggled with his emotions yesterday. 'How are you today?'

'I'm well, thank you,' he said formally, like he always did.

'I'm tired,' Carly told him. 'It was a long, sad day.'

'Indeed, it was.'

'But the wake under the atrium was lovely. As were the words you spoke about Elizabeth.'

He sat beside her, said nothing, lips pressed together under his moustache.

Carly patted his hand. 'I love your suggestion of a plaque for the bench. I think Elizabeth would be chuffed.'

He nodded, small movements, more to himself than Carly. 'Thank you for that.' He cleared his throat, stood again. 'Well, I'll leave you to it.'

Carly probably should have caught the lift too, put the cheese she'd bought in the fridge, but it was nice here. The vastness, the gentle silence somehow letting her anxiety take a break.

While she sat, people stopped or just waved as they passed. The personal trainer in a dress instead of leggings. The guy with the scary tatts on his neck, the woman with the angular haircut. Christina, out of breath and still talking as she hurried past. Dietrich. Stuart. Brooke, who propped her crutches against the wall and joined Carly on the bench. Then Dakota.

Surprise drew Carly to her feet. 'You're early.'

'Nope,' Dakota called, turning a circle as she made her way across the foyer. 'This place is awesome.' She set down a shopping bag that clinked as it touched the floor.

'I sat down for a minute and people just . . .' Carly shrugged and made the introductions. 'Dakota's about to hack into my hair,' she explained to Brooke.

'And pour her too many drinks.' Dakota gave her bag a jiggle. 'I've got Coke and dry for the bourbon and chocolate for later. Or before. Or now, if anyone's up for it. So . . . are we making it a party?'

Brooke glanced at Carly. 'Oh no, it's all right. You two have plans.'

Right now, Carly didn't care if the haircut was awful, Dakota was good to be around – maybe for Brooke too. 'We need someone to help us eat the chocolate,' she told Brooke. 'And you can be my moral support when Dakota starts with the scissors.'

DAKOTA HAD QUIZZED Brooke about her crutches and her job and her alcohol preferences by the time they reached the suspended walkway on the fourth floor. 'Shit, that's a long way down,' Dakota said, leaning out.

'Everything's a long way down in this place,' Brooke said as she clomped past.

'Would you die if you fell over there?'

'According to the work safety brochure I just designed, there's a ninety per cent fatality rate for falls from twenty-five metres. And according to my calculations for the photos of the atrium I put up on my website, it's close to sixty metres from the foyer to the glass in the ceiling.' She stepped into Carly's hallway. 'I am fond of useless information.'

Dakota closed the door, pointed a finger at each wall. 'Which side is your bleeding neighbour?'

Carly cocked her head at Nate's.

'The scary guy?' Brooke said.

'He's scary?' Dakota asked.

'He's not scary,' Carly said. 'He cut his eyebrow and I cleaned it up.'

'He got punched in the head,' Dakota corrected, following Carly and talking to Brooke.

'Talia and I used to call him the Scary Guy because he always looked like he might yell at you if you talked to him.'

'Maybe someone else thought he was scary the other night,' Dakota suggested.

'Maybe he yelled at someone,' Brooke said.

Dakota and Brooke were laughing like they'd already had a drink when they spilled into the living room.

'He's *not* scary.' Carly's voice was a little snappy. Dakota and Brooke pulled up short.

'Right, right,' Dakota said. 'He's nice.' She turned to Brooke. 'Carly thinks he's nice.'

Carly blushed, feeling suddenly awkward, aware that it had been a long time since she'd had friends to entertain.

'Wow. You live here?' Dakota made a show of looking around. 'A view, a shiny kitchen and cool stairs to a *loft bedroom*. I want to live here.'

Brooke had walked to the centre of the room, her back to them as she stood. She'd been here before, Carly remembered. With Talia. 'Brooke?'

Her voice was quieter. 'I wasn't sure how I'd feel coming here again.'

'Are you okay?' Carly asked.

She turned. 'Yeah, I am. It looks different to the last time I was here.'

Did she want to remember or forget? 'It's had a coat of paint since then.' Open-ended, so Brooke could decide.

'Same colour, I think. It seems bigger, though. Talia's cello took up a lot of space.'

'Who's Talia?' Dakota asked.

Carly explained the history for Dakota, who decided the information should be followed by bourbon and chocolate. While she searched kitchen cupboards for glasses, Carly joined Brooke at the window, looking back into the room.

'She used to play here,' Brooke said. 'Where the light was best.'

'Did she play for you?'

'Sometimes. She was shy but she didn't mind an audience.'

Carly remembered Howard's comment about the holes in the plasterwork. 'The walls must look bare now. I haven't got any pictures to hang.'

'Talia didn't have many. Some framed concert posters that meant nothing to me and . . .' Her eyes wandered around the room, a smile starting as a finger came up to point. 'There was a huge canvas of a treble clef over there. And one of my photos that she'd framed and hung over there.'

Carly frowned. 'What were all the holes for then?'

'I don't know. Where were they?'

She pointed at the long wall. 'Howard said they had to be patched up before the place was painted. He thought it must have looked like an art gallery in here, there were so many.'

'Not a gallery, but . . .' She hobbled forward a few steps on her crutches, faced Nate's apartment. 'She used to Blu-Tack sheet music to the wall. Usually just a few pages here, where she practised, so she could read it without having to turn pages, I suppose. Then,' Brooke lifted a crutch, pointed along the plaster, another smile starting. 'That's right, the last few times I was here, the pages stretched all the way to the hallway. I think there were even a couple down by the front door.'

'Pages of music?' Dakota said, offering chocolate around.

'Yeah.' Brooke took a chocolate. 'She said she was learning a complicated piece and it helped to have the music there in front of her all the time.'

'Weird. Carly?' Dakota held the bowl out to her.

She took one, the chocolate softening on her tongue as she imagined Talia putting up her pages: balling up the gum, pressing her hands to the walls. Pushing at the plasterwork . . . like Carly had, shoving and knocking, searching for a way in. 'Howard said there were some other holes, bigger ones.' She joined the tips of her thumbs and index fingers together, like Howard had to demonstrate how big.

'Oh, yeah. Here.' A jab at the air with the rubber end of Brooke's crutch, as though that might have caused it. 'Talia was trying to find the stud for a hook. It was low down, though, and we joked that she'd done it practising kickboxing. It was a running gag for a while. She covered it up with a page of sheet music as a laugh, you know, because she'd have to get on her knees to read it.'

'There was another big hole in the loft,' Carly said.

'Was there?' Brooke laughed. 'Talia's hands were meant for strings and a bow, not a hammer and nails.' As soon as the words were out, her smile fell. 'And now she can't use them at all.'

Carly wanted to ask more, like when had Talia had gouged the hole? Did she explain why she'd been looking for a stud so low on the wall? Had she been worried about security? But Brooke's lips had thinned to a tight line and she was turning away, asking Dakota if she'd poured the drinks. And what right did Carly have to ask Brooke to dig around in her sad thoughts.

'I'm not sure about bourbon and scissors,' Carly said.

Dakota lifted a wedge of hair and snipped. 'No laws against drinking and cutting.' She'd produced the Big Long List and invited Brooke to join the cull. Ten more jobs were crossed off, a few drinks had stretched to all evening.

Brooke and Dakota exchanged phone numbers before Brooke left a little wobbly on her crutches. 'Text me when you get home,' Carly called from the front door. 'So we know you haven't fallen down any more stairs.'

It was after eleven when Carly found a pillow and blanket for Dakota and left her bedding down on the sofa. In the ensuite, she dropped a sleeping pill onto her palm, thinking about it, like she'd done every night since she'd bought them. She went through the for-and-against for tonight: she wanted to sleep while Dakota was here versus bourbon and sedatives weren't a good mix. Then the usual arguments: she wasn't sure knocking herself out would prevent it, that she wouldn't kill herself falling down the stairs if she was doped up, that she might be safer if she could wake up. And she tossed the tablet into the sink.

Carly's eyes snapped opened on black, alarm firing in her chest. She turned her head, searched the darkness. A muted thunk and her feet were on the floor and she was moving with stealth across the room.

The timber cold on her soles, the glow of the nightlight trailing up the stairs.

At the railing, peering into the drop on the other side, the space seemed to rush at her with scary images: a figure looming over her, blood pooling around a head, holes in a wall.

A sound like a sigh.

'Dakota?' she called quietly.

The answer came as a quick, quiet thud. It made Carly's scalp tingle, her mind skitter across scenarios: someone getting in, getting out, finding Dakota, hurting her.

'Dakota?' Firm, clear this time.

'Shit.'

A breath. 'You okay?'

'Getting a glass of water.' Another bump.

'Turn a light on.'

'Didn't want to wake you.'

'Too late.'

Stainless steel flared under the bulbs, Dakota's face appeared below scrunched against the brightness. 'Is it morning?'

'It's the creepy dark hours.'

'Oh. Go back to bed.'

'Going.'

From under the doona, heart beating hard, Carly listened to Dakota moving about, watched the wash of light from below, then the gloom that followed. Thinking about other nights and the black-on-black shadows that had paralysed her. She wanted to be this Carly, the one who moved without hesitation. For the first time in years, she wanted to be the Carly she used to be.

31

Carly was buried in an assignment when a knock at the door made her lift her head for the first time in an hour. She kept the security chain hooked up as she opened the door.

'Got a second?' Nate asked.

'We might need more than that,' she said as she unlatched the locks. Then she saw the bag at his feet.

'I'll be gone overnight,' he said.

'Okay.'

'I'm staying with my sister.'

'Right.'

'In Maitland.'

She leaned on the jamb, wondered what this piecemeal conversation was about. There'd been no discussion of relationship status, no suggestion from either of them that empathy and sex had made them a couple. It had been both reassuring and disconcerting. Carly had a track record of wanting too much, too early. Part of her wanted to push this time too, flapping wings in her chest urging her to hold onto him, to make it something she could hide in like she had at other times. Another part of her was intrigued by their suspended state, the sense that whatever was going on between them hadn't happened yet. Now he was telling her his plans and making it her business.

'Okay,' she said slowly.

'Just letting you know,' he said. 'In case.'

In case she woke up screaming during the night. Not the same as *In case you wondered where I was.* 'Thanks.'

He smiled.

'You should do that more often,' she said.

'Stay with my sister?'

'Smile like that.'

'I can't do everything.'

'Can you kiss me before you go?'

He glanced along the corridor first. It made her expect something brief and obligatory but it was long and slow, his mouth covering hers as though he'd been waiting for an invitation.

'Call me if you need to.'

'I'll be fine. I'm a big girl.'

She went back to the assignment but couldn't concentrate, his parting words stuck in her mind. No relationship status didn't mean things were different. Did Nate think she couldn't cope on her own now? Or was he hoping she'd let him in the next time she woke sobbing and crawling through the apartment at three in the morning?

It hadn't happened in almost two weeks. It hadn't happened since she'd been sleeping with Nate. Hilarious if sex was enough to make her subconscious behave. She hadn't told him what it was about, she figured there was no need when he wasn't asking. Perhaps no need at all if his body had sorted the problem out.

She hitched up the hem of her trackpants and ran fingers along her shins – the bruises were almost gone. She pushed back her sleeve: no trace of the four ovals on her forearm. She placed her fingers there again. Yes, they were grab marks and she'd put them there herself. Freaked out to the point where everything else was a blur. Sleep paralysis and anxiety.

Hours later, she stood in the ensuite in her pyjamas, the foil sheet of sleeping pills in her hand, and suspended the nightly debate. The buzz of the weekend with Dakota and Brooke had lasted right through Monday, the talking and laughing like a new form of energy. Tonight, she'd finished her assignment, eaten a healthy meal, drunk herbal tea and taken deep meditative breaths. Not as enjoyable as Nate in her bed, but slumber was creeping at the edges of her awareness and she felt . . . good. A whole lot better than she might have expected three days after Elizabeth's funeral.

She was a big girl, she told herself. Her subconscious had just needed to remember how to do it. She tossed the blister pack back on the sink.

He is weight and heat and bone-sharp pressure. Straddled on top of her.

Inside, she recoils. Outside, her body is pinned in place. Fear beats through her like a vibration.

Voices are clamouring in her head. Words and warnings and cries of alarm but she shushes them. She must concentrate. She must see. She must . . .

His breath on her face is unhurried, faintly sweet. Hers is bucking in her chest. Does he feel it? Perhaps he likes it. Perhaps it's why he's here. To feel her bucking beneath him.

He lowers himself to her. Hips to hips, ribs on ribs. Her breasts feel naked, exposed, tender.

His voice comes on a flutter of air across her cheeks. 'You're good tonight, Carly.'

It is praise. He is pleased with her. She wants to scratch his eyes, ball her fists and slam them in his fucking mouth.

'You don't let me down. You're my best, Carly.'

Vomit burns her throat.

The light, gentle touch to her face jolts through her like an electric shock. She snaps her face away. A sharp, instinctive thrust. It hurts her neck, makes her gasp in pain and surprise. It breaks the long, stretched-out moment under his spell.

She thrust her head the other way. The hand on her cheek finds her throat, pushes hard under her jaw. Not choking her, holding her down. Noise comes from her mouth, a gagging, retching that doesn't sound like her. Doesn't sound anything like the screaming, cussing, seething inside her. She is thrashing under his hand, shoulders jerking like she's fitting. The fingers at her throat dig under her jaw. Is he feeling for a pulse? Maybe she is fitting. Maybe this is what it feels like: great shudders of angry, explosive energy.

A guttural grunt. It comes from him. He's pushing her into the mattress. A fist on her chest, shoving at her sternum. Something hard in her gut makes the air huff from her lungs. A knee, his knee.

Her hands flap at her sides. Useless, strange things, as though she has borrowed someone else's and can't control them. They make contact, nails dragging across cloth. Then it's gone, her wrist restrained. He is strong, she is limp. It's restraint, not a fight. But she can't stop struggling. Not now that she finally can.

It's too weak to hurt him. It's pathetic. He holds both her wrists in one hand. Pins them to her chest. His other fingers are wound into her hair, twisting, wrenching until she thinks her scalp will lift off.

'Be still.' It's a harsh whisper.

She has no choice. In her silence, she can hear him panting from exertion.

'Breathe, Carly.'

She grits her teeth, closes her eyes, inhales.

32

———

Carly kept a shoulder to the wall as she turned into the hallway, scurrying to the front door, following the instinct that had taken her there every time before – escape, neighbours, Nate's voice. Pressing her back to the tight corner, her eyes found the security chain in the darkness, its telling curve from jamb to door. *It was a dream*, she told herself again. *A fucking dream, Carly.*

Still, she stayed where she was, listening to the silence of the apartment. She should've taken the sleeping pill. She should take one every night. She couldn't trust herself, with or without them.

There would be no voice on the other side of the door tonight. No cops, no Nate. Just Carly and the scary images in her mind.

She stayed there for a long time, the agitation contained in the taut parcel of her body, fear hissing in her limbs. But the chill of the apartment eventually found her, seeping through the sweat on her pyjamas, settling into the soles of her feet.

A little unsteady, she made her way down the hallway, rubbing absently at her forearms as she glanced around the light and shadow of the living room. Nothing moving, nothing out of place, the view beyond the windows dark and sparkling.

The French windows were locked like she knew they would be.

The glass reflected her new haircut flattened by sleep, dark rings under her eyes, fist rubbing at her sternum as though she had indigestion. She lifted her hand away and it fell to her sleeve, scratching on reflex as if she'd been bitten by mosquitos and couldn't resist. Except it wasn't itchy. It stung.

She pulled up a handful of sleeve. The light from the street was dim but Carly's skin was pale, the perfect backdrop for the two red streaks on her forearm. She didn't move, didn't breath, just stared at them. One was long and crooked, from the inside of her wrist almost to her elbow. The other was short and straight, dissecting the first.

With trembling fingers, she felt the raised, hot, broken skin. 'Fuck.' She tugged at the other sleeve, a cold rush down her spine. Three angry welts, side by side. 'Oh fuck.'

She wanted to rub them off, scratch them out, cover them up. Remembered the tingling on her chest under her pyjama top and pressed a hand to it. *'Fuck.'*

The light in the half bath was brilliant. It washed the colour from her skin, made the weal on her chest look crimson. A curve, like a large apostrophe above the flesh of her left breast. Memory shuddered at the back of her mind. Thrashing, grappling, hands that flapped.

It was a dream, it was a dream, it was a dream.

Leaning closer to the mirror, she saw a spot of blood at the top of the apostrophe. Under the light, there were more dots of blood on her arms, one mark like a perforated line on a tear-off brochure.

And suddenly her whole body itched and stung. She lifted her top, inspected her stomach, checked her back in the mirror. Dropped her trousers, ran her eyes over her legs, her buttocks, closed her eyes briefly before examining between her thighs. Not there, thank god. Only her arms and chest.

Six scratches.

She checked under her nails for skin, saw in the mirror the fear that bloomed in her eyes in the second before she ran. To the doors, checking the locks. Flicking on lights, running her hands across the plaster, pushing, knocking, wanting to see inside it. Remembering a hole in the wall. Talia had made it and she'd covered it with sheet music. She'd had pages and pages of music stuck to her walls and lots of holes that had to be repaired. Has she done this too? Had she found the way in? There'd been another hole in the loft.

Carly took the stairs two at a time, stopped breathless at the top, alarm sparking like fireworks in her blood. She eyed the rumple of bedclothes, the pillow on the floor, lifted her arm and peered again at the damage. And something forceful charged at the corners of her mind.

Thrashing, jerking, flailing. Hand shoving at her chest, wrenching her hair.

Like a wave that started in her feet, a tingling, sweating numbness rushed upwards. She gasped for breath, grappled for the railing, holding it with both hands as the stairs swam and pitched in her vision. Panic. A flood of it, filling her with molten fear. She couldn't stay in the loft, didn't want to fall to her death so she gritted her teeth and forced herself to move. Knees juddering, palms slippery, planting her feet carefully, cautiously, all the way to the bottom. Her vision blurred, her breath came in gulping, hitching breaths. She lurched as far as the kitchen before she hit the floor.

CARLY WAS CURLED on her side when her breath finally slowed to something close to normal. Sweat was cold on her skin, tears dry on her cheeks. There was a crumb near her face and the starburst shape of a water droplet. She heaved herself upright, shaky and weak. The fear that had fizzed and shouted was quieter now, subdued as though it had been slapped.

You're good tonight, Carly.

She fingered her cheek where the warmth of the words had fluttered.

You're the best, Carly.

She wanted to be a better person, a worthy person. Was it a nasty mind game she was playing with herself? Or . . .

She dropped her hand to her chest, felt the tenderness of the graze.

Had someone done it to her?

DEAN QUENTIN WAS WAITING for her at the enquiries counter in the police station, just off night shift and changed out of his uniform. He hadn't asked why she wanted to see him, his smile as he shook her hand was a mix of professional gravity and pleased-you-called. He directed her to a couple of chairs in a corner.

'How can I help?'

Now she'd left the apartment, the agitated pacing had reached its limit and the heavy-boned fatigue was settling in. It made the station feel overheated and sweat prickle in her hair. 'It's about the break-ins.'

He watched her, waiting for more.

She'd thought about Nate and Liam before Dean Quentin, decided she didn't need sex or reassurance, she needed someone who could do something. 'It's still happening.' She unwound her scarf, fingers trembling. 'Actually, it hasn't stopped, I just haven't called the police. Last night, it was . . .' She dropped the coat from her shoulders, searched the ceiling for an all-encompassing description. 'It really scared me.'

He nodded.

'You said I could talk to you. And, I guess . . .' She spread her hands, palms up.

'You're ready to do something about it?'

'I want it to stop.'

'That's a good start.'

Relief made her relax enough to smile.

'Can you explain it to me?' he asked.

'That's the thing. I'm not sure I can. It's why I'm here. To get another opinion.'

'Is it someone you know?'

'I've no idea. It could be. It's dark, I can't see properly, I'm not really . . .' Awake. Asleep. '. . . sure. And then it might be . . .' No one. An invention.

'But you think someone is there?'

'Yes.' In her heart, even though it didn't make sense – *yes*. Yes, she did.

'Where do you see them?'

'In the loft.'

'Is that the only place?'

'What do you mean?'

'This person, they're not at your apartment, are they?'

She frowned.

'What's really going on, Carly?'

She stalled for time, pulling her arms from the coat, draping it across her lap, trying to understand his question before she answered. Did he think she was exaggerating the story so he'd listen? 'I don't know what's going on. That's why I'm here.'

He shifted his shoulders as though adjusting his approach. 'Tell me what you know then.'

'I wake up and someone is in my bedroom. It's dark, I can't see properly. He lies on top of me then he's gone.'

He ran his tongue over his bottom lip, doubtful.

'I know,' she jumped in before he said anything. 'My doors are locked, there were no fingerprints. I've also called my psychologist and I'm not crazy.' She forced a laugh. Dean's expression didn't alter. 'Look, I haven't called triple-O since you warned me. I don't want to be arrested for being scared. But I *am* scared and you said I could talk to you.'

He folded his arms. 'Okay, Carly. We're talking.' It wasn't *This better be good*, not entirely.

She took a breath and another, urging herself to be calm, to at least sound calm. 'I'm asleep, I wake up in the early hours and I see a man. It's not every night, once a week usually. Two weeks this last time. I can't see him but I can feel him on top of me. He touches . . .'

'Carly, I've heard this.'

'I know, I *know*. You need to understand all of that before . . .' Her bag slipped to the floor, spewed keys and a lipstick at Dean's feet. She wiped sweat from above her lip. '*Shit.*'

'It's okay. Leave it for the moment.'

She righted her bag, rubbed at her sleeve, her bones aching.

'You okay?' he asked.

No. 'Yep. Sure.'

'You need to tell me something new, Carly.'

Frustrated and angry now, she yanked at her sleeves, her volume climbing as she shoved her forearms at him. '*This* is new.'

His eyes dropped to the marks on her skin.

'And this.' She pulled the neckline of her jumper down to reveal the red curve on her chest.

'They're scratches,' he said.

'Yes.'

'How did you get them?'

'I don't know. I found them this morning. I think he did it.'

'What do you mean you found them?'

'It's what I'm trying to tell you. I woke up in the loft with a man on top of me. I struggled this time, he left and I found these. It must have happened when he was trying to hold me down.'

She wanted him to stand and shout for detectives but he'd been to her apartment three times – locked doors and no fingerprints. She figured the best she could expect was an offer to take another look. It was what she'd come for.

He didn't do anything more than look at her for a long moment. She took it as a good sign, that maybe he was thinking about it. Finally, he took hold her wrists. 'Did you do this to yourself?'

'What?'

'Did you hurt yourself, Carly?'

She tried to pull her arms back but he held on, turning the scratches to the light from the fluorescent above. 'No,' she ground out.

His voice was gentle. 'Maybe you thought you needed these to make the police take notice.'

Carly snatched her hands away. 'What the fuck?'

'It's okay, Carly.'

'No. It's not. You think I gouged myself for attention.'

'I've seen it before. Scratches, cuts, broken bones.'

'That's not what happened. I didn't do this.'

'You think it was the man in your apartment?'

'Yes.'

'You *think*.'

Her jaw tightened. 'I don't know. That's why I'm here. He was trying to hold me down and I was struggling. Then I was running to the front door. I felt stinging on my arms and I found these.' She lifted her forearms again, kept them out of his reach.

He didn't speak.

'It's sounds ridiculous, I know, but . . .' She swung her face away, unable to talk to his doubt any longer. 'I just want to know what's going on. You said I could talk to you, I thought you might help.'

It took him a long moment to decide. 'You said you had a psychologist.'

She faced him with a glare.

'If you give me a name, I can make a call for you.'

'I don't want a psychologist. I want someone to look at my apartment.'

'If your doctor isn't here, I . . .'

'I meant *you*,' she cried. 'Will *you* check my apartment? Please.'

He glanced at his watch. 'I've got some time now. I can take you to see someone. If you don't . . .'

'No.' Carly stood, tore her coat from the chair. 'I don't need to see anyone.' This was a mistake. A big fucking mistake. She snatched up her bag.

'I know some people at the hospital. I'll go with you.'

'The *hospital*?'

A step towards her. 'There's a psychiatric unit there, Carly. You need to get some help.'

She backed away. 'Don't touch me.'

He raised his hands, something cautious and soothing in his tone. 'I won't. It's okay, Carly.'

Christ, he thought she was losing it. She was holding her handbag to her chest like a shield – she looked like she was losing it. 'This is not what you think. I haven't slept. I'm tired, not crazy.'

'Carly.'

As he moved towards her, she stumbled away, almost falling as she bolted for the door.

33

———

It was late afternoon when Carly woke groggy and cold, the lethargy only a ghost in her bones now. She'd come back to the apartment, taken her first sleeping pill in six months and slept like the dead on the sofa. She now stared blearily at her few pieces of furniture, the French windows, the view. She hated it all. Hated the loft and the long hallway and the exposed bricks and the stainless steel kitchen. Hated how it felt now. Hated that this was fucked up too.

There were sounds from Nate's apartment. Carly looked at her arms again, wondered what he would say. He knew things that others didn't understand, about pain and grief and reproach. About wanting to feel and not feel. About being crazy and still sane.

Outside, afternoon was becoming evening, the approaching darkness making her skin prickle with apprehension. She couldn't stay here again, not with scratches on her arms and no idea how they got there. Maybe she needed protection. Maybe she did need to go to a hospital. Maybe she *needed* to know what Nate would say.

Carly took a packet of crackers. Nate opened his door, eyeing them with amusement.

'Are you looking for cheese to go with that?' he asked.

'I thought we could pool resources.'

He pulled his door wide. She smelled soap and deodorant on him as she passed, rubbed at her arms as she stood at his kitchen counter. He pulled out wine glasses. She said, 'Can we talk first?'

They sat by the windows. Carly rested her elbows on her knees, the ends of her sleeves tucked into the palms of her hands. She told herself to do a better job this time.

'I have nightmares. Bloody, awful dreams. I've had them for years, since my friends died. When I came here, I started dreaming about a man in my apartment, in the loft. It's why the police came, I thought it was real. It's what you hear on the other side of the wall – I wake terrified, running for the door, thinking someone is there. Last night, he was on top of me, whispering to me. I tried to fight him off. When I woke up, after I'd freaked out and calmed down, I found these.' She pulled up her sleeves, showed him her arms.

He looked at them, something suppressed about his expression, as though he wasn't sure what he was meant to say.

She opened the top of her shirt, revealing the gouge on her chest. 'They're scratches,' she said. 'I don't know how they got there. Every time I have the dream, my doors are locked and nothing is disturbed. It's just me, scared and half asleep and convinced someone is in my apartment, on my bed.' She ran a palm over the scratches on her forearm. 'I don't remember doing this and there was no skin under my nails.' She raised her eyes to him. 'I don't think I did it to myself. I'm scared of what it says about me if I did. But if it wasn't me it was the man from my dream, and that makes no sense.'

Nate pulled in a breath, the sound of it uncertain, doubtful.

'Don't say anything yet,' she told him. 'Right now, I need you to listen.'

He sat back in his chair like he was settling in for a long story. 'Okay.'

Wishing she had a drink now, she said, 'Six months ago, I took a bunch of sleeping pills.' She worked her way back, keeping it simple. It took a while, it was a long, painful tale.

When she was done, she walked to the windows. It was night now, the neighbourhood below in the glow of a quiet evening, lights from the harbour twinkling in the distance like sparks of hope. Nate hadn't interrupted her flow and didn't interrupt her now.

'People judge what they see,' Carly said, turning around. 'I've hurt people and hurt myself. I have anxiety, I wake screaming, I fall apart sometimes. I came here to start again, where nobody knew any of that, so I could find out for myself who I am.' She pulled at her sleeve again, held out her arm. 'I look at these and have no idea. I showed them to a cop today and he offered to take me to a psychiatric ward.' She felt it again – the humiliation, the doubt. But it was time to get to the point. She sat on the coffee table, knee to knee with Nate. 'If I'm hurting myself, I don't know I'm doing it. If someone else is hurting me, I don't know how. Either option is pretty fucking scary.'

Nate took a long time to speak. Maybe waiting to see if she was finished. Maybe deciding how he was going to handle it. Whatever it was, it made her nervous. He leaned forward, took both her hands. 'You're not crazy,' he said.

'You haven't seen me when I wake up from those dreams. When I'm frightened, I *feel* crazy.'

'Frightened can look crazy. I know.'

His voice was firm but it was his eyes that loosened the rigid ball of trepidation inside her. She thought of him in the ocean at night, calling for a woman he loved and trying to keep his crew alive. 'I'm scared, Nate.'

He shifted to the edge of his chair, knees either side of hers. 'I don't know what's going on, Carly, but you're not sleeping in your apartment tonight.'

She didn't know if he thought she was a danger to herself or she was in danger. It didn't matter. He'd heard her story and hadn't jumped to conclusions.

'You should change your locks tomorrow,' he said. 'I can do it, if you want.'

'You think someone is getting in?'

'I think you should eliminate possibilities.'

'Should I tie my hands together, too?'

He watched her like she might have the answer written on her face. 'You didn't do it accidentally, there are too many scratches for that. It's possible you did it in your sleep, but it's both arms and your chest – that's some deep sleeping. It's possible the dream you remember was some kind of hallucination. I don't know anything about that stuff but you remember a struggle, so, theoretically, you could have imagined that and fought yourself.'

'"Stuff" meaning mental illness?'

'No idea. Let's find out what's happening before you worry about that.'

She nodded, wanted to kiss him for that.

He reached for her hand, held it between both of his. 'I was in a yacht that capsized at sea because a wire in a radio was faulty. We had years of experience, we took every safety precaution and my girlfriend drowned.'

'I'm sorry.' For his loss, for already knowing.

'Things happen that you can't predict,' he said. 'That don't make sense until you get all the facts. Even then . . .' He tipped his head, didn't finish the sentence. 'We could set up a camera in the loft.'

'THIS ONE SOUNDS GOOD,' Carly called down her hallway. She was googling motion-sensor apps for mobile phone cameras while Nate replaced the deadlock on her front door. 'Fifteen shots per second instead of video. Uses less memory, saves straight to cloud storage and it won't send me broke.'

'Download it and we'll give it a trial run. I'm almost done. How's the coffee coming?'

'Brewing.'

On the balcony with mugs, they agreed on a contingency plan: if she thought there was someone in the apartment, if she could lock herself into the ensuite or wardrobe, she would phone Nate and he would let himself in with a spare key. If it happened another way, if he heard sounds of a struggle or thought she was hurting herself, he would use said key to get to her.

'I've been thinking,' Nate said as he wound the new key onto a ring with his others, 'about the wiring and plumbing.'

'You think now is a good time to call in a plumber?'

A small smile. 'We should check your manhole.'

'Have I got a manhole?'

'Somewhere. Mine's in the ensuite ceiling.'

She looked up, wariness tightening her shoulders. 'You can get into the ceiling?'

'There's only crawl space between the floors,' Nate said. 'But if we're eliminating alternatives, it's worth a look. You should have a key for it.'

It was on the ring Howard had given her; she'd thought it was for a garbage chute. The manhole was in her ensuite, too, disguised as a ceiling panel above the vanity. She'd noticed the small brass disc that covered the keyhole when she moved in, had figured it was heating or electrical-related and forgotten about it.

'I had some rewiring done last year,' Nate told her when he'd fetched a ladder from the storeroom and propped it in front of the basin. 'Had a bit of a crawl around up there.'

The cover dropped down on a hinge, dust falling like ash, leaving a black hole in her ceiling. Nate took the torch from Carly, his head and shoulders disappearing into the dark space.

'What's there?' she called.

'Wiring and plumbing.' His voice was muffled. His feet shuffled about as he shone the torch beam around. 'More wiring and plumbing.'

'That's it?' she asked as he started down.

'There's nothing but pipes and conduit.' He stopped halfway, held a corner of the manhole cover. 'Look at this.'

There was something written in the layer of dust. She squinted, tipped her head, felt a jolt when she finally worked it out: *Talia 14/11/18.*

'Talia was up there. Last summer.' Carly tried to work out the timeframe. 'A month or so before her accident.'

'She wrote on the manhole cover. It doesn't mean she got into the ceiling.'

'I suppose, but why open the latch in the first place?'

'She might've figured out what the key was for, like you just did.'

'She might've been looking for the same reason we are.'

'Can't rule that out. Doesn't look like anyone else has used it, though. The only other marks in the dust are mine. And it's a one-way lock. You can only open it from the bathroom side.'

Carly stared up into the void, arms folded, wanting more.

'Take a look for yourself,' Nate said.

The air as she reached the opening was warmer, dry, musty. She'd imagined blackness stretching in all directions, huge and endless like the warehouse. What she saw was a low tunnel that ran in a straight line across the top of the apartments along the east wall, enough room, maybe, to crawl on all fours. The walls on either side were formed by single lengths of timber, the light from her bathroom creating a plume of illumination through the manhole. No discarded balaclavas or glinting rats' eyes. No footprints or scrape marks in the thick layer of sticky dust that coated everything.

'Filthy and creepy up there,' she said as she climbed down.

'Impressive, though. The warehouse was built before concrete or steel was used in this kind of construction.' Nate pushed the manhole cover back into place. 'Those huge timbers up there are the original beams, they hold up the fifth storey. The ceiling in there is the strip flooring of the apartment above. It's the same on every level. This ceiling,' he touched the one above his head, 'was added in the renovation. Before the warehouse was renovated, the timbers were exposed and you would've been able to count the rows of parallel beams from here to the atrium.'

'How far did you get when you were up there before?'

'Just a couple of apartments over. You can't put any weight on the ceiling and I figured my neighbours wouldn't appreciate me dropping in.' He folded the ladder. 'Satisfied?'

'That no one came in through the ceiling, yes.' She stepped back into the bedroom. 'And that the doors were locked.' She eyed the bed and tugged her sleeves over the scratches.

'Wait and see, Carly. Get your mobile.'

They rigged a makeshift stand for it on her chest of drawers opposite the bed.

'Let's do a test run.' Nate tapped the screen, activating the motion-sensor app.

As Carly walked into the frame, there was a quiet, continuous ch-ch-ch of the camera taking its fifteen shots per second. It stopped and started when Carly sat on the bed, and again as she lay down.

'Hold it there a second,' Nate said.

While he fiddled with the phone, memories began filtering back: grappling and gasping, the pain in her neck as her head snapped away.

'Try a small movement,' Nate said.

She slid a leg out of the ball she'd curled into, the ch-ch-ch of the shutter reaching her like a whisper. *You're good tonight, Carly.* 'Are we nearly done?'

Nate was tapping on his own phone now. 'In a minute.'

'What are you doing?'

'I've connected to the cloud file. Just checking it's uploading. Close your eyes, have a rest, all that posing must be exhausting.'

Relax. She focused on the seam of her jeans, the weave on her mattress, Nate's boots . . . and Nate as he watched her, unaware she was watching him back. His phone in his palm, his head lowered as though reading it, his eyes on her. It made her pulse pick up. Not a beat of desire but a tap of uneasiness. Something about his presence, his silence . . .

And then she was standing, moving out of the shot. 'That's enough.'

'The pictures are uploaded. You want to look?'

She was already on the stairs. 'Not now. Not up there.'

.   .   .

'You don't have to do it tonight,' Nate said as he shoved his dish-washer closed.

Carly's squeezed her interlocked fingers, anxiety like a small animal scurrying around her ribcage. 'I need to know.'

'When you're ready.'

She'd spent two nights in Nate's bed. 'It probably won't happen tonight.'

'No.'

She rubbed a hand across the back of her neck.

'We could test the motion sensor over a whole night,' he said, giving her another option. 'Make sure it works when you're ready to stay there on your own.'

She had to sleep in the loft again sometime. 'Okay. Let's do it.'

As she set the phone up on top of the chest of drawers, Nate said, 'Don't switch it on yet.

'Why not?'

'I want to take your clothes off without having you distracted by a camera.'

'In that case.'

He peeled away her pyjamas, walked her naked to the bed like he was leading her onto a dance floor, the sex slow and sensuous and unreserved on her covers. It felt like a statement, like he was reclaiming the loft for her.

Afterwards, as Nate set up the camera, Carly pulled her pyjamas back on before sliding between the sheets. If it happened tonight, she didn't want to see pictures of herself terrified and naked.

34

'Still snapping?' Carly sat up as Nate collected her mobile from the chest of drawers.

'Two-hundred odd photos and still downloading.' He held it out to her. The screen was black. 'How can you tell?'

'I checked on my phone.'

It had seemed logical for Nate to have access to the cloud file, but now, after being photographed in her sleep, Carly wished he'd waited for her before looking. She switched on her phone. 'Anything interesting?'

'Just you.'

Tapping the screen. 'What do you mean?'

'You move a lot. Toss and turn. You rose onto an elbow once.'

'Onto an elbow?' *On a good night?*

'It doesn't mean anything. Not yet. Take a look on the laptop, the images are hard to make out on the phone.'

Downstairs, she flicked through grainy thumbnail pictures, a time stamp indicating the hours that had slipped by. Around 3 am, her scattered movements turned to restlessness. As Nate lay curled beside her, she tossed and jerked about for half an hour. At 3.37, her head rose from the pillow, the elbow pushed into the mattress, her face aimed at the camera. For five minutes. Did she do that on other nights?

Did she do more than that – and scare the hell out of herself?

The last shots were of Nate waking and walking naked towards the camera, turning before he reached it, his back to the lens as he faced the bed for fifteen frames before he turned it off.

'FROM THE SOMEONE YOU MET?' Carly asked, watching the smile on Dakota's face as she read a text message.

'Yep.' She pushed the phone into her pocket, looking uncharacteristically coy.

Carly unwound her scarf, the warmth in the courtyard outside the campus cafe finally making it through her winter layers. 'Made any decisions about him yet?'

'Still a maybe but edging towards approval.'

'Ticking the right boxes?'

'So far.'

'Has he got a name?'

Dakota made a face. 'Bruno. Don't laugh.'

'Wouldn't think of it.'

'How's your scary neighbour's eye?'

'Not black anymore. A little pink scar right here.' Carly touched her eyebrow.

'Bet you had to get close to see that.'

Carly hesitated . . . and reminded herself friends shared. 'Yeah, I looked pretty close.'

'I knew it.' She tapped her coffee cup to Carly's. 'Good for you. Hope he ticked all the right boxes for you.'

'Hope you're not about to ask which ones.'

'Ee-uw, no. Must be easy being next door, though. No biggie getting home at 4 am. No early-morning oh-no-I-need-new-clothes.'

'That's true.' That part had been easy. 'Possibly too easy.'

'Oh, so he didn't tick *all* the boxes?' Her tone was still flippant.

Carly couldn't match it. 'It's not that.' She thought about the photos on her laptop, not the images of her raised on an elbow, but others before and after that. Of two bodies nestled together, Nate cuddling into her back, Carly with an arm or a leg draped across him. Not like new lovers but already settled into cosy, familiar sleeping positions. Like a couple. Like she'd done in another life with men who'd started out wanting to save her. 'I have a tendency to jump too fast.'

'I guess it depends where you jump to,' Dakota said.

Carly wondered if a twenty-year-old was the right person to explain it to. 'I've been married twice. I'm bad at relationships. I screw them up.'

'Maybe you don't screw them up. Maybe you just choose the wrong guy.'

'Same result either way.'

Dakota stirred her coffee for a moment. 'You don't have to jump, you know. You could just, you know, shuffle forward on your butt and lower down slowly.'

Carly smiled. It sounded sensible, but could she? She never had. And now? When she didn't know what was happening, when she was scared, when Nate was the only thing that made her feel safe, could she shuffle – when it was possible the man in black might never return if Nate stayed with her?

NATE HAD a bakery box in one hand, a bag of groceries in the other. 'Steak and apple pie.'

Carly stood at her door and thought about shuffling, telling him she had study to do, that she was ready to stay on her own. But it was a good-looking man with food.

Over dessert, Nate said, 'I'm going to my sister's again tomorrow.'

'Nice.'

'I won't be back until late. Not much before midnight, probably.'

'Right.'

'Will you be all right on your own?'

The question made her pause. She'd been worried about slipping into togetherness because she was scared to be alone, that her neediness would screw things up. But his question flipped it around. She wasn't a child, she could be on her own. It was part of the reason she was here, to prove it. 'I'll be fine,' she said, not sure if it was the truth.

'Call if you change your mind.' Nate said at her front door the next morning. 'Or text.' He kissed her. 'Anytime.'

'I've got the message.'

She could still feel him on her skin as she watched him to the stairs. He'd murmured to her as they made love on the sofa last night: 'You don't have to be afraid.' And again in the loft as he'd stroked the soft flesh at her throat, following the curves of her face with his lips. Shadowy memories had played at the back of her mind as her body had ached and arched beneath his. Fear and pleasure, shuddering and breathlessness.

His presence stayed with her all day, his smell in her hair, his voice in her ear and the raw, sensual tenderness inside her. Underneath it all, like a thread stitching it together, was apprehension – for what might come in her apartment tonight and what it would tell her.

SHE CAN HEAR his steady breath. Her dread is harsh and hot. Something she doesn't understand is deep and pulsing within her.

The bed shifts. He is above her now. She can't see him but she knows. She wants to open her eyes but they won't move, so she waits. It won't be long. She knows that too.

Warm, sweet breath on her neck, her hair, her face. A sharp gasp in her chest as the hand finds her. Firm and possessive, on her throat. Her breath quickens. Fear and . . . desire. He chuckles quietly. Amused, pleased. Shame washes over her.

He lowers himself, his weight presses the swell of her pubis, the mound of her breasts. Behind her lids she sees light and colour, a man above her. Muscular, freckled shoulders, thatch of hair on his chest, nipples puckered and dark. Rocking slowly, rhythmically. Watching her.

He has a face. It is Nate's face.

The whisper is warm across her lips. 'Don't be afraid.'

Her breath catches. Fear and desire.

Wetness snakes a trail, cheek to temple. Her eyes open on darkness. Searching, straining for clarity.

'I can taste you.' His tongue is in her ear, sliding, probing, worming its way into her head. Through her brain, reaching a memory. She is astride him, setting the rhythm, the blue of his irises is dark and sated and on her. Nate's eyes. Nate's hands on her. Desire driving the thrust of her body.

She stiffens at the sound of his guttural chuckle. The memory dies and she is beneath him, prostrate, pinned like an insect. She can't see his face now but she knows. It is Nate and she has done this. She brought him here, she wanted him.

Her stomach pitches with disgust. A sound comes from her throat. Not a word, just the force of effort as she twists her face away. As her arms bend at the elbows and her fingernails scratch across smooth, thick fabric.

'*Fuck.*'

There is surprise and alarm in his exclamation. His body jerks, rears away. Something falls hard across her throat, crushing her neck into the pillow, her jaw jammed shut, teeth locked together. She can't breathe, beats her hands against the covers.

'Fuck. *Fuck.*' Panic in his voice. The pressure at her throat driving down, crushing her windpipe.

She stills. Scared to move, needing to breathe. Blood pounding in her face, her ears. A buzzing, speckling fog creeping at the edges of her awareness. Muscles slackening as though the air she needs is to keep them inflated.

Then the choking eases, just enough for her to gulp at the air, chest and shoulders heaving.

Her eyes are open on blackness, his shadow. He is sitting on her, straddled across her pelvis. There is a bar across her throat. Her arms will move if she asks them, she feels that, only she doesn't. She listens to the agitated, unnerved stuttering of his lungs.

There is something less than black in her eyes now. She blinks at the suggestion of light, wanting it to show itself. Senses indecision in him – kill her or rape her or not? Enjoy it rough or kiss her and tell her not to be afraid?

Anger itches in her veins, the cry that slips from her mouth is pitiful.

The bar lifts from her throat. 'Carly?' It is a whisper.

She's not sure she can speak but she won't answer. Fuck him.

Fingers probe the hollows under her jaw. A shout in her head: *He's checking my pulse!* She turns her face away. A sharp snap, a thrust of her shoulders. Then her hands are grappling, scrabbling, hitting. It is not in her mind, she can feel the bursts of contact under her fingers.

He is grabbing for her arms, her elbows, her wrists. Trying to hold her, pin her. Grunting, swearing. A palm covers her face, shoves it sideways, pushing it into the pillow. She is flinging her arms, pitching herself, wrestling him without skill or aim or strength.

Fighting for breath, for life.

35

She found the top step when she tipped over the edge, clutched at the bars as she tumbled downwards. On her feet again at the bottom then tripping, scuttling to the wall, cringing there.

Not a fucking dream. Someone had jammed fingers against her pulse. Acid leapt to the back of her mouth. She retched, forced it down, searched – kitchen, windows, stairs, the dark space above the edge of the loft.

Was he still there?

Legs clumsy, something wrong with a foot, she stumbled to the kitchen, fumbled along cold stainless steel, found what she wanted: the handle of a long, sharp knife jutting from the block on the counter. It felt too light and too heavy. The wooden handle was slippery in her palm. She needed two hands to stop it shaking.

What now? What the fuck now?

The answer came from the hallway. Noise at the front door, the flat of a hand slapping the timber. The voice from the other side froze her blood.

'Let me in. Carly, let me in!'

Nate. Oh *fuck*, it was Nate.

Carly pressed her back to the wall at the end of the hallway, its length between her and the front door.

The door rattled. She watched it and waited. Whatever Nate had done, however he had done it, she'd taken him to her bed, given him her body – and a key.

The clunk of the pins inside the lock reached her through the silence. A metallic thump as the chain caught, his voice louder through the gap.

'Carly, it's Nate. I'm coming in.'

She heard the bump and scrape of metal on timber. Boltcutters. Then the door flew open and the shadow of him stepped inside.

She watched it pause on the threshold and knew something else. Something important. She wasn't crazy. It was real, it was cruel. And she had a knife in her hand.

'Carly?'

'Stay back.' Her mouth was dry, her tongue slow.

He found her in the dimness, came closer. 'Are you hurt?'

'I've got a knife.'

He stopped. 'Is there someone here?'

'You, Nate. You're here. You let yourself in with a fucking *key*.' She lifted the blade – a threat.

Edging past her, walking backwards towards the lighter gloom of the living room, he held up a palm. 'Carly, it's okay.'

'No, it's not.' She moved with him, staying close, not wanting to lose him in the shadows.

'I won't hurt you.'

'No, you won't.'

'You can put the knife down.'

'*No.*'

He stopped in the open space at the bottom of the stairs, reached for the wall. A light came on, blazingly bright. 'Your hands are bleeding.'

Was blood making the knife slippery? She wanted to shift her eyes to it, didn't move her gaze from him.

'Did you cut yourself, Carly?' He didn't mean by accident.

'It's not *me*. I didn't do this.' Victory in her tone. Something edgy and uncontrolled in her muscles. Making her move, pace and retreat, feet shuffling like they were on a dance floor, something wrong with one of them. 'It's you. I know it's *you*.'

'No, Carly.' He glanced over his shoulder, stayed where he was.

'Don't pretend. Just *don't*.'

'Tell me what happened.'

'You *know*.' Swaying, stepping, breathing hard.

He moved in as she danced away. The knife flared under the lights as she slashed at the air.

He showed his hands. 'It's okay, it's okay.'

'You tried to *choke* me.' She swung again.

He caught her wrist and pulled her close. Strong, fast, the fat blade in the space between their chests, its sharp, lethal tip aimed at the ceiling.

'Not me, Carly.' His voice was low and calm. 'I wasn't here. I don't know what happened but it wasn't me.'

She breathed hard, eyes on the fingers tight around her wrist. 'Liar.'

'You want to hurt me?'

Her breasts touched his forearm with her inward breaths. Her pulse bucked and surged in her veins. 'Yes.'

'Then do it. Cut me. I don't care.' He changed the pressure of his hold, angled the point of the blade at himself, pushed at her hand until the tip of the knife touched the hollow under his jaw. 'If that's what you need, if that will fix it, do it.'

The knife slipped from her hands, clattered to the floor, skittered away. She'd killed once before, she couldn't do it again.

Stepping back, out of his grip, she saw the blood, bright red under the light, smeared across her hands, drops of it on the pale blue of her pyjama pants. The shaking started then. Great rolling tremors that quaked through her spine, spiralled out to her arms, her legs. She swayed and stumbled.

Nate caught her by the elbow. 'Let me help you.'

She wanted to keep her distance, but any strength for resistance was gone and she let him guide her to the half bath, lurching as pain drilled through her foot. Nate sat her on the toilet lid, ran water over her hands, inspected the right one where blood oozed across the palm and dripped into the sink.

'Tit for tat,' she said.

He glanced up.

'First you, now me.' Her voice sounded strange. A knee jiggled. She pointed at his eyebrow. 'Taking turns to bleed.'

His eyes flicked over her face as though he was trying to read what was written there.

'I didn't do it,' she said. 'I mean I did, I must have, but not to myself. Not on purpose.'

'You had a knife.'

Her voice was loud. It echoed in her skull. 'I didn't cut myself.'

He lifted her sore foot to his lap, pressed gently around the ankle. 'I think you sprained it.'

'I broke it once. I broke both of them. I fell down and broke myself.'

Nate said nothing to that, just tugged at her sleeves, ran fingers across her forearms, lifted her hair and touched her throat. Then, finally, said, 'What happened, Carly?'

'I saw you,' she whispered.

'Tell me everything. Tell me like I don't know.'

'How you pinned me down? How I fought you?'

He pushed at her sleeve again. 'Is that how you got this?' A pink welt stood out on the inside of her upper arm.

She snatched it back. 'Maybe it was when you shoved your arm against my throat until I couldn't breathe.' She squeezed her eyes on the memory.

'Carly, can you wait here? Just stay here? Okay?' Then he was gone.

She heard him on the stairs, on the floor above. She didn't wait, she stood, clutching the sink as her head spun, lifting her eyes to the mirror. There was a raw scratch on her cheek and red welts on her throat. She reeled away from her reflection, spilling into the living room, stumbling into the TV, bumping the kitchen counter.

Then Nate was sitting on the coffee table in front of her. He was holding her undamaged hand and she was shaking her head.

'What did you take?' His voice was firmer, insistent. 'What are these?' He shook the foil blister pack.

'Sleeping pills.'

'Did you take them all?'

'I didn't take any.'

'There are only two left.'

'I washed them down the sink.'

'All of them?'

'No, one of them. One every night. I push one out then toss it down the drain.'

'You took something, though.' When she shook her head, he held her chin, searched her eyes. 'Okay.' Something grave in his voice. Her mobile in his hand. 'Okay.'

'No.' She grabbed the phone. 'You don't get to look first.'

'You do it then. On the laptop.'

Her hands were shaking. She couldn't remember the password, he had to sign her in to the cloud file. The first pictures were taken just after 1 am when she'd activated the app. There were small groups of shots as she'd settled into a restless sleep. At 3.17, a longer batch. Images of Carly as she rolled towards the camera, lifted a hand to her ear, head raised off the pillow. Then nothing. No more photos.

'Where are the rest?' she asked.

'That's all there is.'

She straightened, leaned away from him, anger and fear tightening her chest. 'You *deleted* them.'

'No, Carly, listen. I found your phone on the floor in the loft just now. I came straight back down. It takes a couple of minutes to get into the file with the mobile. This is the first time I've seen the pictures.'

'My phone was on the floor?'

'Yes. With everything else that was on top of your dresser. I think you cut your hand on the glass from a mirror.'

A memory: sharp corners, toppling, tumbling. 'I knocked the phone down?'

'It stopped shooting before that. It stopped shooting here.' He pointed at the last photo, her head slightly raised from the pillow.

Carly's pulse tapped. 'I saw you.'

'Something woke you.'

'My eyes were closed.'

'And then the motion sensor stopped.'

36

Nate stayed with her through the early hours of the morning doing little more than watch her as she paced the floor, hobbling and agitated and frightened. She didn't care, it didn't matter – because she *knew*.

Someone had been there. Someone had almost choked her. Someone had slammed her into the chest of drawers. And the knowledge was like free fall – exhilarating and terrifying. It wasn't her, she didn't need a psychiatric ward, she wasn't fucked up, someone else was. A man who knew her name, who'd had his hands on her, who was amused by her fear. Who could get into her apartment.

Was it Nate? She didn't think so. Not now. The image of him had been in her mind. And yet, when he tried to put his arms around her, she shoved him away and scuttled out of reach. She didn't know why, didn't try to understand it, just kept up the pacing, giving the anxious, edgy energy an outlet so it didn't spiral out of control.

When the early morning sun stretched deep into the living room, Nate joined her at the windows. 'You look a bit better.'

'My throat hurts and I'm bruised all over.'

'You seem more rational.'

'Sorry about the knife. I was scared.'

'It seemed more than that. It seemed . . .'

'Crazy?'

His eyes held hers for a moment. 'What did you have for dinner last night?'

'What?'

'Dinner. Amuse me.'

'Stir-fry and a glass of red.'

'Here?'

'Yes. Why?'

'You were hyper. Totally wired. Ever since I came in. Pacing the floor and talking at the speed of light.'

She turned her face away. Anxiety could look like that.

'Sleeping pills wouldn't do that,' he said.

'I told you, I didn't take any.'

'I'm wondering if you took something else.'

'Got stoned and forgot to mention it?'

'No. You said it's happened before so maybe it's something in your kitchen, or an allergic reaction or . . .'

'Shock.'

He turned his face to the view, eyes aimed at the marina. 'You're right. It was probably shock. You scared the hell out of me with that knife. What's the name of your friend with the books?'

Carly frowned. 'Christina?'

'I want to call her, see if you can stay with her today.'

'I've got classes.'

Nate watched her a second, touching her for the first time since she'd pushed away from him, running a finger gently across the scratch on her cheek. 'I don't think you should be driving today.'

Something cold slid along Carly's spine. Talia had put holes in the walls, she'd written her name in the dust on the manhole cover. She'd gone out one morning and driven her car into a tree.

'The apartments on the top floor are all three- and four-bedders. They have bedrooms with ensuites on the lower levels,' Nate said.

Carly's gaze wandered around her own lower level. 'And?'

'You could sleep in one of them instead of a loft.'

. . .

'I TOOK A SLEEPING PILL,' Carly told Christina over lunch. 'Woke up disoriented and stumbled into a chest of drawers. Knocked over a mirror and fell on it,' she shrugged. 'Not so clever. Then I tripped on the stairs when I went looking for a bandage.' She'd then slept in Christina's downstairs bedroom for three solid hours.

Christina pushed another sandwich towards her. 'What happened to your face?'

'I must have scratched myself in the bumbling around.'

Carly stayed for the day, working on an assignment at Christina's dining table while Christina sat opposite writing reviews. It was easier than Carly expected, not chatty and annoying but productive and cooperative.

Nate called during lunch and again in the early afternoon, asking how she was, what she was doing, who was with her. It made her think of his questions about the sleeping pills, made her feel monitored. She'd been there before, didn't want to be there with him. He sent a text a little before four. *Don't go home yet.*

Not planning to.

Forty minutes later, he sent another. *Don't leave till I get there.*

Christina looked up from her keyboard. 'What's the frown for?'

'Nate checking in. Again.'

'I think his interest might be a little more than neighbourly.'

If only she knew. An old aggravation made Carly want to tap out *Don't tell me what to do.* But she sent nothing: passive aggressive non-commitment.

Five minutes later. *Carly?*

Still at Christina's.

Wait there for me. I need to show you something before you go back.

She hesitated before replying. Was it something pertinent to going home or an invention to make her stay? She wanted to ask, see what he came up with but, well, there was no reason to make a point of it now. *Christina invited me for dinner.*

She met Bernard, Christina's husband, when he got home from

work. He poured wine as Christina retold the sleeping-pill/hand-cutting/stair-falling story, not a hint of eye-rolling at Christina's hand-to-chest retelling. Carly liked him for that.

'Why sleep on your sofa tonight when you can stay in a comfy bed here?' Christina said. 'You can prop up that foot properly and not worry about breaking your neck just getting to the kitchen.'

Carly wanted to be independent, stoic, the things she'd come here to be, but the thought of another night in her apartment – with a twisted ankle and no quick escape – made her accept the invitation. It was almost ten when she pre-empted Nate with a text: *I'm staying the night at Christina's.*

She figured he'd reply or call, a *How are you doing?* or *No need for me to rush back then*, but nothing came and at ten thirty, in bed, needing sleep and sick of waiting to hear from him, she dialled his mobile. Left a message: 'Sleep well, see you tomorrow.' Told herself she'd wanted him to back off, she couldn't have it both ways.

She still hadn't heard from him when she left Christina's the next morning but as she stepped from the lift, hobbling on her sprained ankle, she saw his apartment was wide open. Carly knocked on the door jamb, heard a muffled bump, saw a shadow move through the light at the end of the hallway and felt suddenly, acutely aware that she couldn't run and hide.

A woman appeared. 'You after Nate?'

Thirty-ish, jeans and knee-length boots, short blonde hair, something sharp in her tone. Carly felt questions and doubt start to gather. 'Yes.'

'He's not here.' The woman talked as she walked towards Carly. 'He won't be back for a few days. Possibly more.' Her voice was curt, the volume as loud at the door as it had been at the other end of the hallway. It sounded like anger or umbrage. 'Are you Carly?'

Maybe it was an accusation. 'Yes.'

'Nate mentioned you. I'm his sister, Bec. Look, I'm really sorry. He's in hospital. Someone beat the shit out of him.'

Carly's heart banged into her ribs. 'Who . . . wh- . . . how is he?'

'Yeah, sorry, I should've told you that first.' Bec took a breath and heaved it out, something Nate-like about the way she reined herself in. 'He's got concussion and a broken jaw, a couple of fractured ribs and his knee . . .' The sigh was fury. 'The bad knee is totally screwed. It's when, not if for the surgery now.' She turned abruptly, started back down the hallway.

Carly hobbled behind, trying to keep up – with the pace and the information.

'He's sedated for the moment,' Bec picked up a mug from the kitchen counter. 'Because of the head injury. They did a CT scan and there was no brain damage but he was agitated and in a lot of pain and apparently that's what they do. I thought I'd pick up some stuff for him. Have a coffee while I'm here. I've been at the hospital most of the night.' She paused, looked Carly over. 'Are you okay? Do you need a chair?'

'No, I'm fine.'

'Can I make you tea? Coffee?'

'No, thanks. What happened?'

Nate's sister shrugged. 'Some kids found him and called an ambulance. Near the marina.'

Eyes slipping to the street beyond the glass, Carly remembered watching him cross the road on another night with blood on his face. 'Had he been to the pub?'

Another shrug. 'He was found at seven. I don't know where he was before that.'

Carly had been sipping wine, ticked off because he'd checked up on her, because he hadn't called when she'd wanted him to – and his bones were being broken. 'What are the police saying?'

'They think someone took to him with a metal bar.'

Carly's hand flew to her mouth.

'They think it might've happened in a laneway and he managed to crawl to the waterfront before he passed out.'

She blinked hard, tried to think of something useful. 'A couple of weeks ago, he stepped into a fight at the pub around the corner. Someone split his eyebrow open. Maybe they had another go at him.'

'Do the police know about this?'

'He didn't go to the police.'

'Were you there? Do you know who it was?'

'No. I found him afterwards.'

'You should tell the cops.'

Carly hesitated. If they checked her name, they wouldn't believe her. 'I don't know anything.'

Maybe the pause sounded more defensive than truthful, because Bec took a moment to look Carly over again: scratch on her cheek, bandage on her hand, only a sock on her sore foot. 'How did you get hurt?' It wasn't concern, she wanted to know if it might've involved Nate.

Taking a breath, ready to repeat the easy answer, Carly hesitated again. Nate said he wanted to help work it out. Maybe he had. Maybe . . . what? Someone in her loft, three thirty in the morning, scaring a woman while she slept – and Nate beaten with a metal bar on the street in the early evening. Within walking distance of a rough pub and drug users in derelict warehouses. 'I fell down my stairs.'

His sister watched Carly a moment longer, heaved another breath before she saying, 'You want to help me look for some clothes for Nate?' She rinsed the mug. 'PJs, if he's got any,' she said as she climbed the stairs. 'Some clean clothes, T-shirt, trackpants. With any luck, he'll be awake to put them on today.'

Carly held onto the handrail as she trailed behind, head down as she negotiated the stairs with her limp, only looking up as she reached the top.

'Socks and jocks, too,' Bec said from the wardrobe. 'Any ideas where to look?'

She didn't answer. Her eyes were fixed on the ceiling. On a square hole that opened into the black void above.

'Yeah, I don't know what he was doing,' Bec said from the other side of the room. 'The cover is on the bed.'

Bec didn't mean the bed cover. She meant the dirty white square that had sunk into the thick padding of the doona. A vent cover. Carly lifted her gaze from it to the black hole in Nate's ceiling, her pulse picking up as she peered at the darkness beyond.

37

Carly saw the whole tableau now – the stepladder positioned under the vent hole, the toolbox on the floor, its lid folded open, a screwdriver across its top shelf. Nate had taken the vent cover off.

Nate had access to the ceiling.

'Can you look for a razor?' Bec said. 'And toothbrush and toothpaste.'

'Sure,' Carly said, staring at the scene a moment more. The ladder had five steps, high enough for someone to peer into the ceiling, but the square wasn't much bigger than her laptop. A squeeze to climb through.

'You okay?' Bec asked.

'Yeah. Razor. I'll check the ensuite.' Carly frowned in the doorway, remembering, rethinking. It was her bathroom but in reverse. Their lofts were back-to-back, mirror image. She lifted her face to the hole again. It was in the space between the bed and the side wall, opposite the ensuite and built-in wardrobe. Carly didn't have a vent there. There were no vents in her ceiling.

Had Nate put this one in? When? She'd slept four nights here, couldn't remember seeing it. Had she even looked?

She heard Nate in her head: *Mine's in the ensuite ceiling.* He'd meant the manhole. She peered up at it, the brass key plate in the same place as hers above the vanity. She looked back out to the bedroom. The vent was off to the left, far enough left that she had to stand in the doorway before she could see it. Too far left to open into the tunnel Carly had seen through the manhole.

'Found it yet?' Bec called.

'Still looking.' What had Nate said about the tunnel? *Those huge timbers up there are the original beams, they hold up the fifth storey.* There would be more beams up there, parallel rows of tunnels in the ceiling.

Carly stared at herself in the mirrored cabinet. Nate had a hole in his ceiling that opened into a long, dark tunnel that ran above her apartment.

'How are you doing?' Bec was at the door.

Carly pulled open the cabinet, no idea what she was looking for as her gaze ran across packets of soap, shaving equipment and bottles of . . . pills. A bunch of them, Nate's name on the label. *What did you take?* He'd said. *I'm wondering if you took something else.*

'Drop them in here.' Bec held up a small overnight bag.

Carly grabbed a razor, and toothbrush and toothpaste off the vanity, flipped them into the bag. 'I'll just be a second.' She pointed at the hole above the bed. 'I want to see what's up there.'

'Now?'

'Maybe the cover should go back on while Nate's in the hospital.'

Bec made a face. 'Rats?'

Carly hadn't thought of that. She made a face back. 'Could be.'

Bec looked at the opening for a moment as though deciding how much time she had or whether Carly should be left alone in her brother's bedroom, or imagining a stream of rodents spilling out of the ceiling. 'Yeah, okay. I'll hold the stepladder so you don't twist your other ankle.'

At the top, standing on tiptoes, only the crown of Carly's head made it into the hole. If her shoulders had reached, she'd have to turn on the diagonal to get through, corner to corner. If Nate had used this ladder to get into the ceiling, it would've been a tight squeeze. She craned her neck to peer into the space. No tube or chute for air conditioning, no rats either. Just the sensation of dry air and space.

'Careful of traps,' Bec called. 'He might've been setting baits.'

Yes, maybe that was all he was doing. She felt cautiously around, felt only the stiff padding of insulation. No wires or pipes – at least not within reach.

'Anything?' Bec asked as Carly climbed down.

'No.' Nothing that told her why Nate had taken the cover off.

'No droppings?' Bec asked.

'Not that I could feel, thank god.'

'Should we screw the cover back on?'

'I don't think my arms are long enough. We'd have to get a ladder from the storeroom in the foyer.'

Bec checked her watch. 'Next time, maybe. I want to get to the hospital. Are you coming over?'

She was Nate's neighbour, Bec suspected they were more. Twenty minutes ago when Bec told her Nate was in hospital, Carly had wanted to go straight there. Now she'd seen a hole in Nate's ceiling.

She checked her own watch, as though deciding how much time she had. 'I need to be somewhere soon. I'll go over later.'

Maybe not even then.

THERE WERE DRIED drops of blood on the floor where Carly had waited for Nate in the dark with a knife. There were more at the bottom of the stairs, smeared where she'd fallen. A rust-stained tea towel in the kitchen sink.

She needed a change of clothes and a shower but the loft seemed dark and ominous at the top of the stairs. The last time she'd been there, she'd been attacked and terrified.

She closed her eyes, remembering Nate in the moments after he arrived – inviting her to drive the knife into his throat. Voice calm, pain in his eyes.

He had a fucking hole in his ceiling.

Anger heated her fear but she cautioned herself. She was frightened and confused, burned by men who'd hurt her – and it might be just rats. Dread was always her first instinct, that hot, oily ooze of fear through her veins before the anxiety started. But what if he'd pulled the cover off to try to figure it out – how someone could get into one of the apartments, how they could do it silently and without being seen. Carly wanted it to be that, but . . .

She eyed the wall that separated their apartments, lifted her gaze to the loft above, thinking about their back- to-back ensuites. If he was getting into the ceiling through his vent hole, how was he getting into her apartment?

She crossed the room, stood under the loft and looked up. Their bedrooms were mirror image. Her ensuite was on the right, Nate's was on the left. His vent was on the right side of the room, she didn't have one. Unless . . . the vents weren't mirror image. Unless the vents had been put on the same side of every loft, regardless of layout. She turned around, kept her eyes focused up, picturing what was there. Nate's vent was on the right. On the right of her loft, there was an ensuite and . . . the built-in wardrobe.

She hop-skipped the stairs, loped across the room, slid the wardrobe open and looked in. The storage was deep enough to take a step inside, the top shelf low enough to reach with an arm extended over her head. Like the rest of the loft, it had no natural light, but it was dark like a dungeon in there. Carly flicked a switch and the rack of bulbs above the doors came to life.

Stepping in, peering past the shelving, Carly eyed the dark empty space that went all the way to the five-metre ceiling, black beyond the reach of the bulbs. All she could make out was the straight line where wall met ceiling.

After a detour downstairs for a torch and painkillers, she shone a beam around the upper reaches of the wardrobe, the circle of light bouncing and jerking before hitting its target, shining straight and still like an accusation.

It wasn't a vent, at least not the same as Nate's. It was a rectangle about twice as wide covered with a grate of tiny squares.

Carly stared at it for a long time. She moved the light around, too, checking the walls, the shelves, the floor. But kept going back to the trapdoor – yes, it was a trapdoor with two little knobs on one side.

In line with the vent in Nate's apartment.

Fuck. Oh, fuck.

She looked back into the loft, positioned herself where Nate must have stood at night, saw the chest of drawers where the mobile had sat, aimed at the bed. The sheets had been straightened since then, the doona pulled up. He'd done that while she paced the floor downstairs with her cut hand and twisted ankle. Clearing up the mess left after she'd fought back. She remembered the surprise in his panicked exclamation. And his arm against her throat.

A hand flew to her mouth as she lurched across the room, her throat filling with bile.

NATE'S GIRLFRIEND had drowned off a boat he skippered. He'd called her name in the darkness and she never answered. His new neighbour, Carly, was the same age as the woman he'd loved. He'd called Carly through the door and she'd told him to go away.

Carly stood at the French windows, her gaze on blue sky while her mind reeled with dark thoughts.

Cut me. I don't care, Nate had told her. Had he broken in and scared her so she'd need him? Had he wanted to redeem himself and save the girl this time? Sleep with her so it was closer to the original version of his tragic story?

She didn't pace up and down, she didn't need an outlet for the anxious energy – she needed to remember what had happened this time, to figure it out.

Nate had been outside her door every time she'd stumbled terrified through the apartment. He'd told her he was known to the police for an argument over his sister's ex – and Carly had taken his word for it. Nate had attached her security chain and changed her locks. The visitor in black never came when Nate was in her bed. The motion sensor app had worked all night when he was there and it had stopped when he wasn't, moments before she was attacked.

Before *Nate* attacked her.

'Fuck. Oh, fuck.'

Not fate coming for her. Carly had done this herself. She'd reached out when she was lonely and scared, repeated things that had hurt her before. She'd behaved as though she'd learned nothing.

She tightened the arms that were folded across her chest, held on like it was a restraint. Her skin felt dirty, the view too bright, the apartment dull and ugly. The police hadn't believed her. Neither had Liam. Nate, though, had been clever. He'd listened, he'd empathised, he'd let her think he was trying to solve the puzzle while he kept himself out of it. Then he'd left the warehouse with his vent open and didn't get back to close it.

Anger threaded its way into her thoughts. And something else, something she recognised, that she'd tried to cull from her personality. The drive that had put her friends on a ledge that collapsed beneath them. The part of her that had pushed, cajoled and manipulated to make things happen. All through school, she'd wangled permission to parties and camping trips, she'd got them into the Rural Fire Service when it wasn't taking recruits. She'd got herself into a uni in Sydney. And she'd talked Debs, Jenna and Adam into going to the canyon when none of them had wanted to be there.

Nate hovering in her thoughts, Carly saw again the moment before she'd sealed their fate: Debs, Jenna and Adam turning as one to her. *Do we stay or do we push on?* For thirteen years, Carly had been haunted by her reckless, arrogant confidence. Only that wasn't what she felt as their eyes looked at her again. They weren't relinquishing the decision to someone else, they weren't waiting to be told what to do. Not all of them, not Debs. They'd looked at Carly because she got things done, she found a way. She talked parents around, she hustled transport to get them where they wanted to go, she found the best climbing gear at discount prices. They never trekked until she'd analysed routes, assessed the risks, mapped the path. They'd looked to her because if anyone was going to get them down, it was Carly.

It wasn't shame or guilt winding its way through her now. It was the same emotion she'd felt standing on that cliff face in the darkness. Resolve and purpose.

It wasn't over. Nate was in hospital and he was coming back. There was no fixing it but she could change it. Now, while he was in a bed, before he tried to stop her.

You should tell the cops, Bec had said. She'd meant the fight Nate was in two weeks ago. But Carly could tell them other things, show them her bruises and what she'd found in her wardrobe. The police had been to her apartment, there were official records of the break-ins ... yeah, and they could look up her file, escort her to another wing of the hospital. Have her sedated, too.

No, she needed more. She needed to get in the ceiling and see how he'd done it. Take photos and find evidence that proved Nate was crazy, not her.

38

———————

It was miraculous Howard was home. He headed across the foyer to the storage room like Superman without a cape: long, emphatic strides, jaw squared, happy, he said, to take a break from his studies. Carly limped along behind, making sure he didn't get distracted while he collected a ladder.

'Where are you painting?' he asked as she unlocked her door.

'Up in the loft. Sorry, there's another set of stairs.'

'No problem. I'm going to miss these call-outs.'

'Are you going somewhere?'

'The UK.'

'Oh, when?'

'Next semester. I'm taking up a position in the physics faculty at Bath University.'

'Nice.' Not the physics but the Roman ruins and the new start.

'So you'll have a different me next year. The body corporate is advertising this month.'

Carly hoped they found someone who would actually supervise. 'Okay, well, thanks for the news and the ladder.'

When he was gone, she stood at the bottom of the stairs and eyed the gloom above. Her ankle ached, the cuts on her hand stung. She drank a glass of water, ate a biscuit, not sure if she was hungry or nervous. Vents and rats and solid black ceiling space. What the fuck was she doing?

She should be calling a real estate agent and getting the hell out, not climbing a ladder. She should follow in Howard's footsteps and escape to Bath University. Any university. Finish the social science degree she'd begun, forget sustainable work and live the student life on government allowances and loans, degree after degree, uni after uni, so she never had to stay, so she could leave when she made a mess of it.

She glanced at the view, at the cold, crisp day outside, the wedge of harbour in the distance. The French windows, the rustic brick, the sheen of stainless steel. Her apartment. It was hers. Brooke and Dakota had laughed here. Christina dropped by. Elizabeth's silver vase was gleaming on the kitchen counter. She'd given it to Carly for courage to follow her dreams.

This place was her dream.

It took some manoeuvring to wedge the A-frame ladder through the sliding door and into the wardrobe. Carly was sweating before she'd started up. Grimacing, she pushed her sore foot into a walking shoe and laced it loosely, then tied her hair back, pushed her mobile phone into the back pocket of her jeans, picked up the torch and climbed.

It was like rising into a fog – visibility dropping, the atmosphere close, the sounds of her hands and rubber soles on the metal treads bouncing off the walls of the wardrobe. She stopped three rungs from the top, the trapdoor an arm's length away and looked down. Her feet were just about level with the top shelf – if she was more agile, uninjured and less frightened, she could possibly climb the shelving, stand on top and reach the trapdoor. Was that how Nate did it?

Wanting both hands free in case she overbalanced – something that felt like more than a possibility as she tried to keep the weight off her sprained ankle – she slid the torch strap over her wrist, the light swinging and bouncing around the wardrobe as she reached for the grid of tiny squares. A slight resistance when she tugged, a snick as a magnetic catch released. Slowly, cautiously in case it fell, in case something fell out, Carly eased it down. It was hinged on one side; she smelled dust as the trapdoor passed her face. Remembering Talia's name on the manhole cover, she lifted the torch and took a closer look at it.

The frame was white, a fine wire mesh covered the grid of squares. There were no names, only fingerprints, but not in the dust – there wasn't any dust. The cover was clean, really clean, as though it had been wiped recently. The prints were dark smudges from dirty fingers. Someone had been there.

Carly's torch went up first, then her hands, holding on as she climbed to the top of the ladder. Head and shoulders in the ceiling, she shone the light around. It didn't tell her much, its weak beam casting only a small, pale circle on flat surfaces. What she saw, though, was another tunnel: sides formed by massive beams, ceiling formed by the flooring above, the base a giant checkerboard of timber framework inset with pads of insulation. Beyond the short, filmy play of her torchlight was a wall of blackness.

Uneasiness prickled across her shoulder blades. Nate was in hospital and sedated, she reminded herself. The worst that could happen was falling through a ceiling. Breaking a leg. Or her neck. Or rats. Shit.

'Don't think about it.' She said it out loud, talking to the anxiety that was fidgeting in her muscles. 'Do it now.'

She hauled herself up and sat on the timber frame that surrounded the vent, the ceiling so low her scalp was pressed to the floor above. A bubble of pale light glowed around her, the dust made her nose itch. It wasn't entirely black beyond the torch beam. There was a patch of weak greyness in the direction of Nate's loft. The dim glow from the open vent in his loft leaking into the pitch blackness, she guessed. Her destination.

She tested the plasterboard between the checkerboard framework, feeling a slight give. She'd have to stick to the cross-timbers – only she needed a few seconds to think about how. They were too narrow to crawl along one without toppling, too wide apart to spread her knees across two, and the next cross-timber was more than an arm stretch away. She pushed the torch onto the padding ahead of her, squatted at a T- intersection and lurched forward with her undamaged hand . . . banging her spine on the ceiling before thumping onto the next timber. Then hung there as though she was playing Twister and deciding how to get her feet to the yellow dots. She thrust sideways and sat in one motion, butt on a cross-timber, beam at her back.

'Like that,' she said quietly.

Favouring her injured hand and ankle, she repeated the lurch and thrust five times before she was looking into Nate's apartment, lit only by the daylight from the living room below. Carly pulled the phone from her pocket and took photos: of the tunnel, the hole with its missing vent cover, the view into Nate's apartment.

The flash barked at the darkness, filling the space with bursts of white, giving her a glimpse of what lay ahead. More tunnel, more timber grid and insulation. A lot of it, probably all the way to the corner of the warehouse. It made her feel trapped and exposed, too big and too small. Made her wonder what Nate felt when he was up here. He'd been a sailor, he'd travelled the ocean at night – vast, open spaces with stars in the sky, wind in his face and water rolling beneath him. Why had he come here in the first place? He said he'd had rewiring done last year. Had he found it then? Had he got into her apartment when it was vacant, saw Carly when she moved in and decided to get to know her better?

'What the fuck, Nate?' He couldn't answer, maybe he never would, but the sound of her voice in the blackness was reassuring.

The plume of light from her wardrobe hovered like a ghost in the distance. A little creepy but quite bright now that her eyes were accustomed to the dark. She rubbed her knees and started back. Overbalancing twice, a knee and then a hand dropping onto the plasterboard, snatching it up again and holding on tight so she didn't topple the other way.

Finally back above her own wardrobe, she sat, breathing hard, sweat and dust on her face and hands, and a buzzing in her muscles. Not anxiety. It was exertion, exhilaration. More than that. She felt strong, energised, bold, able. Words she hadn't applied to herself for a long time. She flexed her throbbing ankle and her sore hand, looked back to where she'd come from and forward to where the tunnel headed. Nate was in hospital, he couldn't reach her here, not today. And she wanted to see what was down there, how far she could get. She flicked on the torch and kept going.

CARLY LURCHED and thrust until she found another vent set into the insulation. It was the same as Nate's: square, louvered slats instead of wire mesh and caked with grey-brown dust. Had he replaced the one above her wardrobe and kept it clean so he could slide in and out easily, noiselessly? Wondering if this one was inside a wardrobe or above a bed, Carly dropped her cheek to it, tried to peer through. Saw nothing.

Glancing back only briefly, she continued on, lunging into the shadows to the last apartment, two doors down from Carly's. She knew she'd reached it when she saw the vent set into the insulation - a rectangular hole with a wire-mesh cover, the same as hers except for the solid coating of dust. She shone the beam down, caught the shapes of shelving and stacked boxes, the outline of closed doors. Alternating vent covers? Maybe Nate *hadn't* replaced hers, but he'd kept it clean.

She was out of apartments to crawl over now but kept going. Three more lurches and she saw a brick wall up ahead in the gloom: the corner of the warehouse. It was what she'd come this far for, to touch it and say *Been there, done that.* She tossed the torch one more time, its beam shrinking to a coin of light on the insulation, and hefted both hands to the last cross-timber. As her weight transferred over them, she stopped, not sure why, her body responding to an instinctive brake. Then she felt it – a whisper of cool breath on her face. She smelled a trace of something earthy in the air, a strand of hair tickling her temple. Reaching for the padding beneath her, she found the torch, aimed it – and her stomach pitched.

It was the end of the tunnel, and the space where the insulation pillow should have been was a drop into nothingness. A black hole, literally.

'Don't do anything stupid, Carly,' she breathed.

Slowly, awkwardly, she lowered herself to the insulation, spreading her weight across the plasterboard, her face at the edge of the abyss. Played the light around the hole. No roof, no floor, at least not that she could see with a torch.

The two massive beams that formed the sides of the tunnel continued all the way to a brick face opposite. On her left, above and below the beam, was a stud wall, its pale timbers stretching up and down into darkness like endless ladders. It was the outside of the last apartment on the next wall, Carly guessed. The black hole was the void between the two corner apartments.

She tilted the torch down, saw only darkness. It was possible the hole was only as deep as the loft below her, five metres. Except the slight upward breeze carried a hint of the outside world – the dankness of decaying earth, the tang of exhaust fumes. Possibly it dropped four storeys to the bottom of the warehouse. In which case, rats weren't the worst thing that could happen in the dark.

Wriggling backwards, the insulation scratching at her clothes, Carly climbed onto the cross-timber behind her, shimmied across it to the wall and sat. Mouth dry, adrenaline sparking in her veins. Jumping as her ringtone shattered the silence.

'Carly, it's Bec.'

Her voice in the darkness felt like company but Carly was wary – it was Nate's sister, she was at the hospital with him. 'Bec, hi.'

'Everything okay?'

She glanced left and right: eerie tunnel, black hole to oblivion, sitting on a two-by- four so she didn't fall through plasterboard and break her neck. 'Sure.'

'Right, good, well, I'm with Nate,' she said, something tight and forced in her tone.

It made Carly wonder what Bec knew. 'How is he?'

'He's awake. He can't talk but he wants you to know some things. He's written them down. He wants me to say them for him.'

An apology? An explanation? 'I'm listening.' It didn't mean she'd accept it.

There were muffled noises on the other end, a question or confirmation. 'He has the building plans,' Bec said.

Carly frowned. He was telling her how he got into her apartment? Did he feel bad about it now he'd spent a little time in hospital? Convenient for his sister to be doing the talking. 'Right.'

Enunciating as though she had a learn-to-read book, Bec said, 'He found it. He has marked them. I should get them. What?' A pause, muffled words.

Listening to the offstage conversation, heat started to smoulder inside Carly. Dread and fear, her usual fuel – and an anger that felt like oxygen.

'Nate, it's okay. Calm down,' Bec said. Then louder: 'Carly? He wrote, "You should get them". I thought he meant me but he means you. *You* should get them.'

'Get what?' She had no intention of getting anything for him.

'Uh-huh, that's right,' Bec said, then dropped her voice, spoke quickly. 'I don't know.' Another pause, brittle brightness in her tone. 'This one? You mean Carly. Okay. Carly, are you there?'

'Yes.' But not for long if the conversation kept going like this.

'Nate says you should look at the corners.'

Carly shifted the torch beam to where the stud wall met the brickwork. 'At the corners?'

'That's right.'

'What corners?'

'So you've got all that?'

'No. I . . .'

'Good,' Bec said. 'I've got to go now. His doctors are here.' A pause. 'Thanks. Bye.'

Carly stared at the screen. Heard a tinny voice and lifted it to her ear just as Bec spoke again – hurried, hushed words. 'I'll call you back.' Then the line went dead.

39

Bec's tight voice and the muffled asides with Nate seemed to hover in the darkness as Carly shuffled around, getting into position for the lunge-thrust back. *Get what?*

The mobile barked again.

'I'm so sorry about that.' Bec's voice was low this time, as though she was trying not to be heard.

'Where are you?' Carly asked.

'In the corridor outside Nate's room. Where are you?'

'In a library.' This place was quiet like one.

'Right.' Bec hauled in a shuddering breath. 'Sorry. I'm upset. It's Nate, he's . . .' Another shaky intake. 'He's been awake for a couple of hours and really confused and agitated. There's a specialist with him now.'

Carly squatted on a junction of cross-timbers, the ceiling pressed to the back of her head. 'What sort of specialist?'

'A brain woman. For the concussion. Because of the confusion and agitation. Look, I wanted to apologise about that phone call. He was insisting I ring. I promised I'd call you but he was getting worked up about it. I thought it might help if he heard me actually say it to you. Sorry it didn't make any sense.'

Some of it did: he had building plans, he'd found the tunnel – and now Carly had, too. The rest, she figured, was some kind of confused admission. 'Did it calm him?' Was that why he'd insisted, so he could get it off his chest?

'More or less,' Bec said. 'He's better than when he came to. He thought you were in hospital. Or dead. He was going nuts. I had to call for help. A couple of nurses had to hold him down until I convinced him I'd seen you this morning. It was awful.'

Dead? 'What did he think had happened?'

'I'm not sure, exactly. His jaw is bandaged up, he can only make sounds through his teeth and he was upset and getting the shits with writing everything down.'

Hard to explain what he'd done with a notepad and pen. 'Maybe he was thinking about my sprained ankle and cut hand.' Maybe concussion had made him think it was worse.

'No, it wasn't that. He remembered you'd fallen down stairs. It was something else. I think he thought you were with him when he was beaten up. Seriously, Carly, he thought you might've been dead.'

Carly shifted on the timber, thinking of his texts yesterday afternoon. *Don't go home till I can get there.*

'The doctor says there could be memory loss,' Bec said. 'She said he could be associating his injury with the last thing he can remember.'

He'd left his apartment with a hole in the ceiling. 'What does he remember?'

'You, obviously, but . . . he's not making a lot of sense. He's agitated and angry. Mostly because we can't understand. Before the doctors came, he kept writing, "Tell her. Tell Carly". Underlining it and tearing the page out of the notebook and putting it in my hand.'

Tell me everything. Tell me like I don't know. It's what Nate said to Carly when he was cleaning her wounds, checking her for bruises, asking how many sleeping pills she'd taken. He'd refused to leave her, he'd wanted Carly to stay with Christina because she had a bedroom without a loft. 'Does he remember what he did yesterday?'

'He remembers being with you and he remembers getting beaten up.'

Would he tell Bec if he remembered taking the cover off the vent to crawl around in the ceiling?

'My brother is a fallen hero, Carly,' Bec said, regret in her tone now. 'He was everyone's good guy until that boat went down. Skipper for this boat, navigator for that boat, the man with all the answers when his mates had a problem. Just about everyone he knew slept a night on his couch sometime or another. Then it all went to shit. His girlfriend's family blamed him for putting her on that yacht. The cops blamed him for being negligent. He was looking at manslaughter charges until the inquest. No one wanted him on their boat and he didn't trust himself to go anywhere near one. I know him, Carly, I've seen what he's been through and if you were with him when he was attacked, his first thought would be about you. Whether he'd gotten you hurt, whether he should've saved you too.'

Carly ran her teeth over her bottom lip, realising she knew the man Bec was talking about. The man who carried his pain across his shoulders like he was wearing it, who watched the marina so he would remember. She turned her head, looked towards her apartment, the ghostly plume of light barely visible. Nate had been beaten up and was worried about Carly. He'd told her not to go home until he was there. He said he had building plans, had found *it*. She'd thought he meant the tunnel she was sitting in.

'Bec? Have you still got the message he wrote down?'

'I shoved it in my pocket.'

'Can you read it to me again?'

'Hold on.' There was a pause. 'Okay, here it is.' She went through it slowly, like a poem. 'I have the building plans. I have found it. I have marked them. You should get them. Look at the corners.'

Carly focused the circle of torch beam on the insulation at her feet. 'It is separate sentences or commas in between?'

'Sentences. Each one on a new line.'

'Like bullet points?'

'Yes, five bullet points.'

'Five separate ideas.'

'I guess so.'

Carly aimed the light at the end of the tunnel. Okay, she was look-ing. Two corners in the hole to oblivion, two beams meeting brick-work. Oh, and a third corner – the north-east corner of the warehouse.

'Carly, I've got to go,' Bec said. 'I want to talk to the specialist before she leaves. Will you make it in later?'

Five minutes ago the answer would have been no.

'Yes.' Maybe. She wasn't sure. She felt as confused as Nate's words. She pushed the phone into her pocket, rubbed at the dust that was gritty on her face. Was he confused? Guilty and confused? Or . . .

Carly got to her knees again, wanting to be back in her own apart-ment now. Nate, the fallen hero. He'd told her it didn't matter what she'd done, that he couldn't bear to be next door when he could help, that he'd make sure she didn't fall. She'd believed him. She'd believed him right up until she'd found the trapdoor in her wardrobe.

But the words Nate had written for Bec to read, his agitation that Carly was dead or injured – it didn't make sense if he'd been getting into Carly's loft through a tunnel and scaring her.

She shifted ideas around as she lunged and thrust. If Nate's message wasn't about guilt, maybe it wasn't all that confused.

If he wasn't confused, maybe it was Nate being brief – five concise ideas – and maybe he thought Carly knew what he was talking about.

If Nate wasn't the bad guy, maybe he thought she trusted him.

I have the building plans. I have found it. I have marked them. You should get them. Look at the corners.

She kept the words afloat in her head as she thrust on, heaving, bumping her spine, overbalancing.

Building plans – meaning renovation plans for the warehouse.

It – he'd found the way into her loft through the vent.

Marked them – maybe he'd circled her vent on the plans. Carly had seen building plans before, there were always pages of them. He could have marked more than one page.

Get them – the plans, from wherever he had put them. In his apartment?

The corners. Which corners? The corners of the pages he had marked?

She paused, looked up. There were corners everywhere – the tunnel, the vents, the grid of timbers, the void at the end. How many corners can you find in this picture? She peered into the darkness beyond the reach of her torch, imagined the crawl space all the way to the other end. *Look at the corners.* Did he mean the ones at either end of the east wall?

Was it a warning? Get the plans and be careful in the corners because there were deep, black holes. Would he expect her to come up here? She'd put her head inside the manhole in the ensuite and declared it creepy and dirty. He'd probably expect her to be scared. No, he wanted her to *look* at the corners, not beware of them.

She shook her head, started again, saying it out loud. 'I have the building plans. I have found it. I have marked them.'

Okay, he'd marked the access to her apartment on the renovation plans.

'No, wait.' There was only one vent in her loft, not a *them*.

If Nate wasn't the bad guy, if it wasn't Nate getting in, there had to be another access point – a way into the tunnel from somewhere else. She glanced over her shoulder. There were seven apartments along the east wall – seven vents.

You should get them. 'The plans.' Yes, she wished she had them now. *Look at the corners.*

She sat on her haunches, rubbed her ankle. She could use the vent to get into Nate's apartment and search for them. Except Nate had used a stepladder to look into the ceiling and Carly wasn't tall enough to get back up once she'd climbed in. She rubbed the bandage on her palm. Why draw her attention to the corners of the plans if he'd marked them? Wouldn't she see his notations?

She repositioned her feet, ready to push forward again. He said *corners*, not 'the corners of the tunnel' or 'the corners of the page'. Just corners. She closed her eyes, imagined plans, the bulk of the warehouse. It was a huge cube, lots of corners. But what if she stood in front of it, out on the street, and Nate said, 'Look at the corners'?

She raised the torch, shone it back towards the brickwork. She'd look there. Where the walls met.

What was in the corner?

Nothing. It was empty space, blackness up and down.

The hairs on her arms rose. The sensation she'd felt as she hung above the plasterboard. She'd felt a cool whisper on her face, smelt a hint of something in the air. From the void.

Nate told her to get the plans and look at the corners of the warehouse. He didn't expect her to come up here, he thought she'd see and understand.

She ran a hand over her hair, letting the ponytail slip through her fingers. The apartments were designed like Lego bricks. If there was a void where the east and north walls met, there were probably matching ones at the other three corners. No roof, no floor. An upward breeze, something earthy in it. A pulse picked up in Carly's throat.

Was Nate was telling her there was another way into the tunnel? Up or down the shaft at the corners of the building?

Had someone had used the void to get to her vent?

40

––––––––––

It wasn't Nate who'd used the void. Not when he could get into the tunnel through his own vent. Not if he'd made his sister ring Carly from his hospital bed to tell her there was access at the corners of the warehouse. If Carly had deciphered it right.

'Who, Nate? Who?'

If he knew that much, he would have given her a name instead of cryptic bullet points, right?

She was almost back to her apartment now, the plume of light from her wardrobe oozing into the darkness, but she shone the torch in the other direction. Where did the void go? How could someone climb it?

The renovation plans must show it. They had to be in Nate's apartment. Bec had a key but she was at the hospital. After he'd locked himself out, Nate had told her Howard held a key for him, too. Carly could probably convince him to let her into Nate's apartment, but she was covered in dust, she'd have to clean up, change clothes and it would take time – and she was here now.

'Photos. Police. Game over.' She turned around.

She wouldn't call the cops. She'd go down to the station and let pictures of the void be the proof. Done. She could sleep without fear, have her new life back.

Back at the void, on her stomach again, she thought about the couple who lived in the apartment below, two doors along from her. Late twenties, renters. Maybe one or both had found the tunnel and decided to have some fun. Why scare the judge next door when he could send you to prison? When a single woman was the next one along?

She shimmied forward until the timber edge was pressed to her ribs, her head and shoulders stretched into nothingness, a waft of air feathering the sweat and dust on her face. Then she pointed the dim light of the torch into the shaft. Straight down was dense, unyielding black.

Taking her time, working the torch beam around, she strained for details in the weak glow. Moved the light up and down the pale timbers of the stud wall until something caught her eye. A dark patch, a hole.

Had someone come out of there? How? It was in the middle of an abyss. She aimed the torch at the brickwork opposite her, looking for another one. Then at the brickwork on her right that was above and below the timber support beam. The light was almost back at the tunnel when she saw . . . she squinted. A strip of metal. And another. And . . . her breath caught.

It was a ladder. Metal rungs attached to the bricks. Evenly spaced, one after the other until they disappeared downwards into the darkness.

'Oh shit.'

She aimed the light up. There were more rungs on the other side of the beam. The tips of her fingers tingled. The glow juddered. The earthy smell on the faint movement of air made her stomach roil.

Had someone climbed four storeys in a dark shaft to get into her loft? To lie on top of her and whisper in her ear, lick her face and shove his arm across her throat?

She closed her eyes, tried not to see it in her head but her mind went there anyway – a black figure clinging to the rungs, rising slowly through the dark.

'Who the fuck did that?' Her whisper slipped into the darkness as she saw another version – the black figure, agile and fast, scuttling downwards like a spider. She shook her head, fumbled for her phone and took photos, snapping quickly, the flash bouncing around the walls, her nerves jangling.

Then she reversed fast, bumping knees and spine as she lunged away, the hint of earthy air still in her nostrils, on her face; the solid, dense black of the void like a presence at her back. Coming after her, filled with . . . *him*.

IT WAS mid-afternoon when Carly passed the sign to Nate's hospital ward, her skin still tingling from the heat and scouring in Christina's guest shower. She'd tossed her filthy clothes into the ensuite and told Christina she couldn't manage the stairs in her own apartment. She wasn't going to use her ensuite when there was an open doorway to her loft.

Checking beds as she wandered the corridor, Carly walked past a patient with a bandage that looked like a nun's coif, stopped and turned back, needing a couple of seconds more before she was sure the bruised face was Nate's.

The relief in his bloodshot eyes as she crossed the room confirmed what she kept telling herself – it wasn't him, he'd tried to figure it out. She wanted to feel good about that, but the sight of him made joy seem like the wrong emotion. He lifted a hand from the blanket as she reached the bed. She took it as she sat on the edge, noticed grazes on the knuckles as she interlaced her fingers with his.

'I'm sorry I couldn't get here earlier.' Sorrier she hadn't trusted him.

He gave a small nod. The swelling circling his left eye looked like a fat purple worm curled under the skin.

'You can't talk?' she asked.

A shake of his head. The left side of his face was misshapen, a dark, multi-coloured bruise creeping up from the bandage at the jawline.

'Is it bad?'

He lifted his other hand, tipped it side to side.

'Can I kiss you?'

He pointed at his forehead.

His skin was warm, he smelt of cotton bandage and antiseptic. He was wearing a white hospital gown, there was a cage on the bed under the covers protecting his knee. Tears burned her eyes.

'I didn't get the building plans,' she said. 'But I found the vent in the top of my wardrobe.'

A nod, relieved.

'And I looked at one of the corners.'

Quizzical frown.

'I got into the ceiling and saw it.'

The crease between his brows deepened and he reached for the table by the bed, stopped and grunted, holding his ribs.

'Hold on.' Carly wheeled it to him, waiting while he used a notepad and pen.

Don't go back there, he wrote.

She nodded. She didn't plan to. 'The corner, it's a huge void.'

He wrote again. *Ventilation shaft. Big fans. Top and bottom.*

The cool upward breath of air. 'Did you see it?'

On the plans.

'I thought you went up through your vent hole.'

Just shone a torch around.

She nodded again. 'There are rungs attached to one of the walls in the void.'

Maintenance.

It made sense if there were fans. 'It's a way in and out.'

His eyes stayed on hers: acknowledgement.

'Where is the entrance?'

Stay out of there.

'I intend to.'

A softening of his face, his shoulders. He looked weary, sore.

It made Carly hold back on her questions, take up his hand again. 'Thank you,' she said. 'For finding the plans. For sending me the message.'

He watched her a while, his eyes marbled with red veins, something more than tiredness in them. Then he wrote again. *They said they knew where you were.*

'Who?'

He pointed at his face, his knee.

'The person who beat you up?'

Two fingers held up.

'Two people attacked you?'

One watched.

Carly wanted to swear, but clenched her teeth as her fingers tightened on Nate's. 'Why were you in the lane?'

Someone left a message at the marina. He used the tip of the pen to point at an earlier sentence.

She read it again. *They said they knew where you were.* 'The message was that they knew where *I* was?'

He nodded.

'That's why you thought I was hurt?'

Another nod.

'They said my name?'

Said my girlfriend.

His girlfriend had drowned at sea. Carly raised her eyebrows. 'I'm your girlfriend?'

The one who watched used your name.

Something sweaty and cold crept along her spine. Was the assault about her? 'He said "Carly"?'

He nodded.

'Carly Townsend?'

A shake.

'What did he say about me?'

Don't go back to your place.

'He said I shouldn't go home?'

Another shake. He underlined the previous sentence.

'You think it's about the man in my loft?'

Don't think it's safe.

'But there were two of them in the lane. There's only one in my loft.'

No shake, no nod, just a hard glare.

Were there two men in her loft? One on top of her, one watching? 'Nate?'

Don't go home.

'What aren't you telling me?'

Nothing.

She glared back.

A feeling. DON'T GO HOME.

41

———————

Nate wouldn't expand on his 'feeling', wouldn't tell her what he thought or what the guy in the lane had said about her, finally writing: *Please Carly. Something else.* It didn't make her feel any better but he was bruised and bandaged, he had first rights on changing the subject.

So for half an hour more they played yes or no about his injuries: it was a hairline fracture of the jaw, didn't need to be wired shut, no solid food for a month. His knee was ruined, he'd have surgery before a steak. Two cracked ribs, a few stitches in his scalp under the bandage, a dislocated finger from landing a punch. Uniformed police had been around but there wasn't much to tell – he didn't see his attackers, didn't know who'd left the message, couldn't remember what was said. Detectives would be coming later. Then Carly talked while Nate listened and by the time she'd told him about her day with Christina and meeting Christina's husband, Nate's eyes were unfocused and the lids drooping.

When she kissed him goodbye, he caught her arm, gave her a pointed stare.

'I won't go back to the warehouse,' she told him. 'I'll call Dakota. See if I can stay at her place.'

She sent a wave from the door, stepped into the corridor and leaned against the wall, shaken by the sight of him, horrified it might be about her. He'd gone in search of answers, he'd got hold of building plans somewhere. Maybe the man in her loft had seen Nate asking for them or caught the flash of his torch in the ceiling or . . . she ran a hand across her mouth. The man in her loft had never come when Nate was with her. If he'd climbed a maintenance ladder to get to her, had he beaten Nate up to keep him out of Carly's bed?

Whatever it was, she felt responsible. He wasn't dead, she had that to comfort her – but his injuries were on her account.

She wiped her eyes, manoeuvred around an obstacle course of medical equipment in the corridor and a meal trolley parked near the nurses' station. Past it was a gathering of people with clipboards, and a tall, broad-shouldered woman standing to one side. Detective Anne Long.

Carly felt a flush of humiliation as she remembered the end to their last conversation. *Get some help.* She dropped her eyes as she got closer, hoping to pass without the cop recognising her, then a patient in a wheelchair rolled into the corridor, halting Carly beside the detective.

'Busy in here this afternoon,' the cop said.

'Mmm.' Carly feigned fascination in the ward bed that was now holding up the wheelchair.

'It's Carly, right?'

Great. 'Yes.'

'Thought so.' The detective sounded impressed with herself for remembering.

Carly pulled her mobile from her pocket, started tapping the screen, sending a message if the cop felt chatty. From the corner of her eye, she saw Anne Long swap a notebook from one hand to the other. Carly glanced at the photo she'd pulled up, one from the tunnel, and said, 'I'm visiting a neighbour. He was expecting a detective. Nate Griffin. Are you looking for him?'

'I'm seeing a Nathan Griffin, yes. Do you know what room he's in?'

Carly pointed down the corridor, thinking about evidence and building plans and injuries. Hers and Nate's. 'Fourteen B.' She looked back at the cop, not sure how to begin. 'He's got a broken jaw and can't talk but he's doing okay with pen and paper.'

Anne Long took a long look at her. 'Are you the girlfriend?'

The girlfriend mentioned in the message left at the marina or his actual girlfriend? Carly wasn't sure on either account. 'I guess.'

She waved a finger at Carly's face and the bandage on her hand. 'This happen last night too?'

Carly touched the scratch on her cheek. 'No. I fell down the stairs in my apartment a couple of days ago.'

Beside them, the wheelchair patient gave a hacking cough that made the orderly behind him check the progress of the bed still blocking the corridor.

'So how are you, Carly?'

Anne Long's tone suggested her question was more than time-filler now, and Carly wondered if Dean Quentin had filed a report about her visit to the police station with the scratches on her arms. 'I'm fine. About Nate's . . .'

'The last time we spoke, you were going to sort out some new medical arrangements,' the detective said. 'How did you go with that?'

Carly glanced at the patient and orderly beside them, at a nurse also waiting. No one looked at her but heat touched her cheeks like two warmed stones. She wanted to tell the cop she never did have a damn problem, but a sharp, defensive retort wouldn't help the proof she had in her hand. 'Fine, thanks.'

'Good result then.'

It was smug. A reminder of who was right and who was damaged. It made any boldness Carly still felt from lunging around a ceiling shrink away. She glanced at the picture of the tunnel on her screen, saw it from the cop's perspective. It could have been taken anywhere – inside, outside, on a screen stage, in the back blocks of Istanbul. And as the ward bed started to move, Carly changed her mind about showing the collection to Anne Long. It wasn't enough proof to make a cop believe Carly was well and sane and someone else was crazy.

.   .   .

THE LAST RAYS of sunlight blazed through the windscreen as Carly drove to Dakota's house, squinting in the glare and batting at the tears threatening to spill.

Nate was in hospital, the police thought Carly needed psychiatric help and she couldn't go back to her apartment because a man could get in and hurt her. Lick her face and laugh at her. Choke her, rape her, kill her.

Stopping at traffic lights, her hands curled around the steering wheel and throttled it. Squeezed and thumped it, her heart pounding, dread building, agitation itching and biting under her skin. She wanted to get out and walk it off, block it out, but she needed to think about the problem that was causing it. Figure it out, find a way to convince the police it was happening.

It was someone who knew about the ventilation shafts. And who knew Carly. Who'd seen her or met her or crossed paths with her.

How did he do it without waking her? Did he time it so he got in and out while she was in her deepest sleep? Or did he stay up there, above her wardrobe, listening and watching and . . . ? Oh shit. How many times had she stood in front of her shelves in her underwear? She'd had sex with Nate in the loft. Uninhibited, energetic sex. Had the shadowy presence listened to them? Laughed or jerked off at the sounds from her bed?

Nausea swam in her gut. She wanted to be sick but that involved pulling over and getting out and she was scared – of being followed, of being alone and exposed in the darkening evening. It was trembling, anxious Charlotte all over again.

She shifted into gear, took a left turn. Made herself focus. The visits to her loft had started three days after she moved in. Maybe it wasn't about her. Maybe it was the apartment. Or the creepy space above the lofts. Had he discovered the tunnel, found 419 empty and spent six months perfecting his silent entry and exit? Then Carly had arrived and he discovered another opportunity?

If he'd spent hours up there, he might have left something behind. Food wrappers, empty water bottles, something to pee in. A fucking bar fridge. She hadn't seen anything like that in the tunnel but it might be up there, somewhere. Evidence of him. In that dark, scary place.

She took a right into Dakota's street. You could leave, she told herself. Put the apartment on the market, get a student loan and go to university. Somewhere else, somewhere new, somewhere she could start over. Again. With rules so fate wouldn't be tempted to find her: don't buy, don't live anywhere great, don't make friends, don't like it too much.

There, number fifteen, Dakota's place. Carly pulled to the kerb, wiped her face and sat. Scared and angry and immobilised by it all.

A knock on the window made her head snap around. There was a face at the glass, a man staring in.

'You Carly?'

Her eyes flicked to the door, making sure it was locked.

'I'm Peter. Dakota's father.'

Thinning blond hair, ruddy face, nothing like Dakota.

'You're staying over?' he asked.

Would the man from her loft know that? She talked to Dakota only twenty minutes ago. Carly nodded.

He watched her as she stepped from the car, keeping her distance as she reached back in for her handbag. 'Everything okay?' he asked.

'Just needed a minute. Been a long day.' She followed him down the drive, ducking under the branches of a tree, spooked by its shadows. They walked through a garage into a cluttered kitchen that smelled delicious. She should eat, Carly told herself. She hadn't eaten since breakfast.

'Dakota!' Peter yelled.

Carly jumped.

Dakota appeared grinning in the doorway, then frowning as she came closer. 'What happened to your face?'

'The fall down the stairs.' It was the excuse Carly had given when she called to beg a bed for the night.

'And this?' Dakota lifted Carly's bandaged hand.

'Yep.'

'You did a good job.' Her voice was matter of fact but she ran gentle fingers over the bandage. It made Carly want to cry again. Then Dakota had moved on. 'Hope you like soup.' She lifted the lid off a pot on the stove. 'It's lamb and beans.'

The three of them ate at the kitchen bench, Carly feeling like a teenager staying over with a friend and getting checked out by the parent. When Peter left to watch TV, Carly told Dakota that Nate was in hospital, kept the details to the assault and his injuries. Dakota got up and fetched a jar from a cupboard. 'Eat chocolate. It'll make you feel better.' She slid it across the counter. 'Eat Nate's share, too. No solid food for a month. Shit.'

'Yeah, shit.'

'Bet you didn't move here for this, huh?'

To be scared to go home? Responsible for someone else's pain? Not trusted? It was what she'd left.

'Carly, what's wrong?'

'It's just been a shitty day.'

'Okay, I'm listening.'

The shitty day line was meant to steer Dakota away from the subject, but Dakota didn't hedge. And Carly wanted to talk now. She was tired of herself, of the police, of her fear. Maybe just tired. She took a breath and a chocolate, just held onto the ends of its wrapper as she spoke. 'I came here to find a better me.'

'Well, that's cool.'

'Only I don't like who I found.'

'Oh.' Disappointment. 'How did you want to be?'

'Brave. Assertive. Happy.' She untwisted the chocolate wrapper. 'The bits of me that I used to like.' Before she'd become brash and reckless, then damaged and anxious.

'Personally, I think you're great. But, okay, why can't you be that other you?'

Because Carly couldn't change what was on her police profile, because Nate was hurt, because a man could get into her apartment. 'I think it's too late.'

Dakota tipped her head in doubt. 'You've only been here a few months.'

And she'd been Charlotte a long time. 'I don't know how to do it now.'

'But you remember how you used to be, right? The brave, assertive, happy bits.'

'Yes.'

'So be like that.'

'I don't think it works that way.'

'Sure it does. I mean, if you know what bits of the old you that you want to be, then when you do something, think about that and just, you know, be that.'

If it had been anyone else Carly might have rolled her eyes, but it was Dakota and Carly chuckled. 'Just like that?'

'Yeah. Why not?' She picked up a chocolate, plopped it in her mouth and talked around it. 'You said it's been a shitty day and now you feel shitty too, and maybe you think the old you might have gotten through a day like that without letting it make her feel shitty. Because she was happy and assertive, right? So if you want to be like her, you could think about a better version of everything that's just happened. Your neighbour was found by those kids – yay. He has a broken jaw and not brain damage – yay. You have an excuse to keep dropping around to his place with pots of soup he doesn't have to chew – nice. He needed knee surgery anyway. And you have a very clever friend with chocolate and a spare bed and a list of career options to keep your mind off your shitty day.' She picked up her mug and tapped it against Carly's. That simple.

CARLY'S EYES SNAPPED OPEN, momentarily confused by purple walls and black curtains. Then she saw the bottles of hairdressing supplies and a foam head, remembered she'd stayed at Dakota's and fell back to the thought that had woken her.

Carly would climb the ladder.

Twenty-year-old Carly would get on that ladder in the void. Without a doubt. Probably without hesitation. Possibly with a shout of *Hell, yeah!* Energetic, agile, persistent Carly. Who'd ridden trail bikes, joined the Rural Fire Service and went rock climbing. Who wasn't afraid or anxious or ashamed. Who didn't spend her life on the verge of tears.

Be that.

Thirty-three-year-old Carly sat up and swung her feet to the floor. She'd laughed at Dakota's simplistic advice. But maybe it was that simple. *If you know what bits of her you want . . . be that.*

Climbing the ladder might give Carly everything she needed. Evidence of someone getting in, an access point that suggested who, fingerprints, signed documents, backpack, bar fridge. Proof she could take to the police, a way to make it stop and claim her life back.

And if it did none of those things, if she had to leave the apartment, start over again, climbing the ladder would still give her something she needed.

It would give her a chance to be the person she wanted to be.

42

Younger, eager Carly got instructions from her cautious older self and stopped at a hiking store on the way back to the warehouse. Not thinking about the cost or the risks, she bought a brighter torch with a head strap and a smaller one with a belt clip, eighty metres of rope, a harness, carabiners and a belay device that would stop her descent if she fell. It felt like a hundred years since she'd even thought about climbing anything, and this was a ladder, not a sheer cliff face, but it was a long way down and the fall would hurt the same.

'Have an awesome climb,' the guy in the store said as he handed her the receipt.

'WHAT THE FUCK ARE YOU DOING?' Carly paused on the bottom rung of the A-frame in her wardrobe, shoe laced a little tighter around her sprained ankle, a fresh bandage on her cut hand as she tipped her face to the gloom above the shelves – and climbed.

Snick as the trapdoor came down. She hitched her butt over the edge of the vent frame and pressed a button at her forehead. A brighter, wider beam filled the width of the tunnel and lit the way like a headlight.

As she pulled her feet into the ceiling, apprehension began to gather. It was nine-thirty in the morning, she told herself. He came at night. He'd only ever come at night.

That she knew of.

On her haunches, anxiety sparking, she listened to the silence. *You need to do this, Carly.* Or go back to Burden.

It only took a few minutes to reach the void, the lunging familiar, her ankle loosening up as her body warmed with the exertion. On her stomach again, pushing her head out over the drop, she tipped her forehead down to shed light on the drop beneath her.

Under the brighter beam she could see a yawning, rectangular space. Red brick, pale stud walls, the hint of something less black in the bottom, too far away for the torch beam to define.

She uncoiled the rope and reached into the void, both hands suspended in the updraught, her hips anchored behind the last cross-timber, instinct insisting she was about to fall. Whoosh of air, black space filled with screaming. She shook her head, shook it off, slung the rope around the closest rung of the ladder and fastened a knot, fed the other end through the carabiner and the belay device. Spent some time checking and rechecking her gear, fingers trembling, mouth dry. Sipping water, glancing into the abyss, telling herself to be brave, assertive, happy, goddamn it. Then slowly, cautiously, keeping her butt anchored to the lip of the tunnel, she found rungs with her hands, then feet and, before she thought about it, before she her memory threw back the last time she was on a rope, she thrust her torso into the void.

Adrenaline swept through her veins like splinters of glass. She gulped at the air. Hung for long, paralysed moments. Skin tingling, scalp damp, fear wedged in her throat like a hunk of unchewed bread – and something steely and euphoric pulsing inside her.

Hell, yeah.

Her goal was the bottom of the ventilation shaft. Carly felt the way with her feet, one rung at a time, dropping her head every few steps to aim the torch into the space below. The brickwork in front of her face was cold and held the tangy smell of masonry. The stud wall on her right – the outside of apartment two doors down from hers – was close enough to touch with her elbow. It was about five metres to the next tunnel below it, but it felt like half a day before it appeared as a wide, black mouth below her.

The ladder ran out where it reached the beam above the third floor and started again underneath it. On the way back up, it would be safest to climb into the tunnel to reach the upper set of rails. The way down, though, was a short abseil – easy in theory, but as Carly prepared herself, soles of her shoes flat to the wall and her hands clasping the last rung, she heard Debs' voice and froze. Not words, but laughter. Loud and raucous, like it had been from the top of the canyon that last day.

The water in Carly's stomach tried to come back up. A hiss droned in her ears. In Carly's mind, Debs chucked her gear to the ground. 'You should come home more often, Carl. I'm a lazy-arse when you're not here to kick my butt.'

'Well, you're here now.' Carly whispered the words she'd crowed back then.

'And thank god for that,' Debs replied. 'I forgot how fucking brilliant this place is. So stop pissing around with your gear, get yourself on that rope and let's do what we came for.'

Carly fingered the harness at her waist, remembering how it had started. Remembering *that* Debs, not the one she saw in her dreams. Wondering what she'd say to her now.

'Well, you're here now.' Carly said it again. Then held the rope, released the rung and leaned out. Walked down the wall and pressed her body to the next section of ladder. Like she used to do it. 'Like I came to do.'

THE BOTTOM of the void looked flat and grey in the torch beam now. She sensed more than she saw as she descended – a change in the sounds that bounced back at her, cooler, fresher air moving across her face and, eventually, a soft, rhythmic whir, as though the shaft was a giant mechanical lung.

Finally, she hung above a concrete floor in an empty room, elated to have made it, disappointed that was all there was. The fan, she now saw, was on the outside of the wall, in a unit fitted into what must have been a doorway in the original warehouse. A thick layer of dust clung to every surface, as if the space was the filter for every piece of fluff, lint and microfibre that was sucked from the apartments above.

On the wall behind her was a door.

She descended the last rungs, disconnected from the rope and took photos – of the ladder going up and the door leading out – then she stood at the door and listened. The only sound was the hum of the fan.

The door pushed into another dim space. She tipped her head around, let the torch on her forehead light the narrow, windowless room beyond. There was a group of machines huddled in the middle. One looked like a ride-on floor waxer, another some kind of hoist on wheels. She couldn't identify the others. Maybe they were Trans-formers waiting for a signal to reassemble into weapons.

There was a second door on an adjacent wall. Carly opened it and recognised the light and shadows on the other side. The foyer. Its centre was ablaze with sunshine, the columns closest to her casting long, dark shadows that seemed to point right at her. A man with a large box on a trolley was waiting for the elevator. Up above, someone was on the stairs.

Surprised, relieved, already thinking about catching the lift back up, Carly had taken a step out before remembering the harness around her waist, the powdery dust covering her clothes, and the fact she didn't have a key to her apartment.

At the bottom of the ladder again, head down as she reconnected the rope, Carly saw footsteps in the dust. Hers. Which meant the man in her loft hadn't walked through here. She grimaced at the darkness overhead – no evidence and a hard climb up.

She had to pause twice before she reached the first tunnel, her thighs burning with each upward step. Sitting on the edge of the first-floor tunnel, flicking her gaze around the void as she gathered herself for the next set of rungs, she saw a hole at the opposite corner. Just like the one she'd seen yesterday from the fourth floor tunnel. In the stronger beam of light, she saw two rows of rungs around the brick walls, foot- and handholds that led to the opening. What was there? she wondered. It was short-lived, though, replaced with *I'm not climbing over there to find out.*

She stopped three times on the next section, breathing hard and blowing on the blisters in her palms. On the ladder to the third floor her thighs and arms burned, her neck ached from looking up and her sprained ankle pulsed inside her shoe. At the crawl space she rolled over the lip and sunk on her back into the insulation. It was scratchy and stunk of dust and she wanted to keep going but her body refused.

Somewhere further along the padding, Brooke's ceiling opened into this passage. The giant beams on either side held up the apartments on Carly's floor. She aimed the torch at the timber above her. Strip flooring for the living room above. Her own living room was three apartments from the void. Had he come through her floorboards?

She sat, shone the light down the tunnel. There was no hatch in her floor, nothing to suggest he'd got in from underneath, but she was here and her body ached from climbing upwards and she didn't want to go home empty-handed.

It was the same as the tunnel above: beam walls, insulation and cross-timbers, square vents like the one in Nate's bedroom and rectangular ones like the trapdoor in her wardrobe. The third one along made Carly sit back on her haunches.

Its white frame was clean except for a couple of smudges on one side. Just like Carly's.

Blood beat in her ears. Was this *his* apartment?

She glanced up. The apartment overhead was hers. Did he live beneath her?

Leaning over the vent, shining the head torch through the grid, the shelving appeared in the glow below. She pulled the small torch from her harness and angled the beam around. There were rows of neatly stacked boxes on the top shelf, clothes hanging below. Long items. Dresses. And one very high-heeled boot by the door, on its side. Carly frowned, ran her beam across the top shelf again. They were shoe boxes, lots of them.

Okay, a man could collect shoes, but the one boot could see was a stiletto. And there were dresses. Maybe the man in Carly's loft was the shoe-collector's partner. Or a cross-dresser. Or . . . Splaying fingers across the vent, she gave it a push. *Snick.* It dropped away on a hinge, opening into the apartment below – and she heard his breathy voice again. *You're my best, Carly.*

'Does he visit you, too?' she said aloud.

She glanced back at where she'd come from, skin prickling. This vent and Carly's were the third ones in from the void. Maybe he lived in an apartment between here and the void, with easy access to both of them. Or nearby or . . . She turned, lighting the way ahead of her, towards the other corner of the warehouse.

'Maybe it's not just us.'

43

———————

It took twenty minutes to reach the opposite corner of the warehouse. There was a void in the corner, she counted nine vents along the tunnel, five of them rectangular grids, all of which opened with a snick. Three had been cleaned recently. Carly took photos of them all.

On the way back, she sat above a rectangular vent trying to remember if Brooke's door was the third or fourth from the corner. She shone the torch around the wardrobe, looking for a piece of clothing that was familiar, wanting to call down *Get out of there.*

She didn't though. The idea that it wasn't just Carly, that a man in black had crawled through here too, and dropped silently into other apartments, had filled the darkness with something new and poisonous. There was urgency to her lunging as she headed back to the void, her gasping and thrusting reminding her of the scrambling escapes from her bedroom. She'd sprained her ankle and Brooke had broken her leg. Carly had pushed at the walls of her apartment and Talia had left holes in the plaster. Talia had opened the manhole and written her name in the dust. She'd driven into a tree with sleeping medication in her system and Nate had asked Carly what she'd taken and told her not to drive.

Was she seeing connections that meant nothing? Brooke had no memory of how she'd fallen down her stairs. She wasn't scared in her apartment and she hadn't had nightmares.

Maybe Carly had it wrong. Maybe she didn't want to be the only one. Maybe the vents had been cleaned for . . . what? Maintenance? Who would know?

'Nate. Maybe.'

THERE WAS something new inside Carly as she followed the corridors to Nate's hospital room. Calmer, bolder. Not the same as brave and assertive but it felt good.

'Have you seen yourself today?' she asked him.

Nate shook his head.

'Probably best if you don't.' The swelling was a little better but the mass of bruising had spread. Deep purples and bright greens ran a mottled track from his eye socket to his chin. The bandage around his head looked like it was holding his face together.

He watched as Carly sat in a chair then made a throaty sound, pointing at her, waving his finger up and down.

She'd tried to hide the soreness in her muscles, it obviously hadn't worked. 'I'm a bit stiff. The spare bed at Dakota's.' She shrugged. 'How are you?'

He pulled his hospital table closer, wrote on the notepad. *Glad to see you.*

'Sorry I didn't get here sooner.'

You went back to the apartment.

It wasn't a question. Had he seen the change in her too? 'Yes.'

Another noise from his throat as he tried to talk.

She took his hand, wanting to reassure him, but he turned hers over and found the blisters. He touched them gently, grunted. *What?*

'You're not going to like it.'

He made a face that said *What the fuck* and *Don't do it again* and *I care about you.*

'I know, I know. But I'm okay and it's an intriguing story, if you can ignore the danger.'

Deep frown, louder grunt.

'Yes, it was dangerous but I need you to not freak out so you can help me understand what I found.'

Eyes wide, pointed look.

'I won't tell you if you do that.'

He glanced away, took a few sharp breaths, looked back and nodded.

There were plenty of times he wanted to interrupt. Carly could see it in the stiffening of his spine and the twitching of his lips. He picked up the pen a couple of times and Carly pushed his hand back, wanting to tell it all before the details got lost in other explanations.

'In the end, I needed to rest in the tunnel above the third floor and I found something I didn't expect.'

She told him about the three clean vents, showed him the photos she'd taken. Nate shook his head: no reason for the vent covers to be cleaned for maintenance. More head-shaking when she asked him about building inspections or electrical work, heating or air flow or the big fans in the ventilation shaft. No obvious reasons for the vents to have been wiped down.

'What are the holes on the other wall?' On her way up the ladder, she'd seen them on every level.

Pre-fab chutes.

She frowned. Waited while he wrote an explanation.

The beams run parallel to the east and west walls of the building, forming the tunnels you've been crawling through. The vents draw air from the apartments, which is pulled towards the ventilation shaft by the fans at the top and bottom of the void.

When she'd finished reading, he raised his eyebrows at her. She nodded that she understood. He wrote again.

Along the north and south walls, where the ends of the beams butt up against the brickwork, there's no way for the air to escape. A metal chute was attached underneath the rows of timber to collect air from the apart-

*ments. The holes you saw from the ladder are the ends of the chute where
the air empties into the void.*

Carly took a couple of seconds to think about airflow and access.
'So there would be vents opening from the apartments into the pre-
fab chutes?'

A nod.

'Big? Small?'

Same as all the other vents probably.

Carly tucked a strand of hair behind her ear, a bigger, uglier
picture forming in her mind. 'If someone has worked out how to get
into the ceiling tunnels, they've got access to apartments on the east
and west walls. If they've crawled around more than one tunnel,
they've been in the void. Which means they've seen those holes.' She
paused, thinking about the hand- and footholds that led to the pre-
fabricated chutes. 'I'm wondering how many other apartments they
can get to.'

That's a lot of crawling around.

'Yes. It would be a bizarre way to spend your time. So is climbing
into a woman's loft while she sleeps.'

Understanding and apprehension were in Nate's eyes as they met
hers. The arrival of the dinner tray interrupted their silent exchange.

'I thought about telling Howard,' Carly said. 'But it might be him.
It might be anyone. It might be more than one person. There might
be a team crawling around up there.'

Nate lifted the lid on his dinner tray, made a face at the soup and
reached for his notepad.

Tell the police.

'They think I'm nuts.'

Show them the photos.

'That will convince them I'm nuts. It's just pictures of ladders and
vents and creepy tunnels. The climbing gear is mine so, if anything,
it'll look like I'm peering into people's apartments and trying to
blame someone else. They'll probably charge me with trespass or
stalking as they drive me to the psychiatric unit.'

Nate tipped his head, reluctant agreement. *Don't go home.*

'Believe me, I don't want to, but I can't couch-surf forever. And,' she held her hands out, palms up, 'I need to know what's going on up there.'

Stay out of the ceiling.

She didn't say anything. Yes, it was dangerous up there but it wasn't just her now – and it wasn't his decision.

I'll be out in a day or two.

She frowned. He could barely sit up without help. Did he think he could do more than Carly in that condition? 'You can't walk. You're having surgery soon. You're not going to be able to do anything.'

It was the wrong thing to say to the man who'd tried to protect her, and the sharp, pained look on his face made her want to take it back. She ran a hand over her hair, wanting to give him something. 'Can I sleep in your apartment?' It wasn't a solution, just somewhere she could think about her options.

Too close to your apartment. Dakota? Christina? Brooke?

'I've run out of stories to explain what's going on.' And she didn't want to try out the real story until it made some sense.

Bec?

She lived an hour out of town, and what story would cover her need to stay at Nate's sister's house? 'If I screw the vent cover back on, he won't be able to get into your apartment. He won't know I'm there. If he crawls by, he'll only know I'm not in my own loft.'

He watched her a moment. Indecision, frustration, concern.

Carly lifted the lid on his soup again. 'You need to eat something. Come on, I'll help you.' She picked up his spoon.

You are not feeding me!

'I'll swap you then – your key for the spoon.'

BROOKE PHONED as Carly was walking to the hospital car park. 'I've spoken to Dakota and Christina and heard all about your fall and Nate. I've cooked a beef casserole and it's ready whenever you can get here.' Her voice was firm, determined to help.

It made Carly feel like a link in a chain. It felt nice, and she wasn't ready to be on her own in Nate's apartment yet. 'You're brilliant. I'm on my way.'

Brooke showed Carly in, handed her a glass of wine and ordered her to sit. 'The rice is almost done, have something to eat while we wait.' She pushed crackers and a bowl of dip across the kitchen counter. 'Do you want to talk or are you sick of explaining it?'

'Maybe we could talk about something else.' Carly glanced around, saw two oversized computer screens on a messy desk, mismatched furniture and a large print of the warehouse atrium. Despite them, it felt like déjà vu. 'I didn't realise your apartment was the same layout as mine.' She lifted her eyes to the loft. Where was her ceiling vent?

'Talia and I used to laugh about that. Same apartments, different style. She was organised, I'm clutter-city. Oh, here,' Brooke stepped away to the fridge, pulled a photo from under a magnet. 'This is Talia.'

It was a snapshot of a woman holding a cello. Late twenties, mass of tight, dark curls that fell past her shoulders, pale skin and plump cheeks that were dented with dimples from a smile. Her feet below the instrument were bare, legs either side of it in faded jeans with frayed hems. Possibly she looked sophisticated and gifted when she was performing but here she looked casual and a little cheeky. It made Carly wish she'd had a chance to meet her.

'It was taken in your living room,' Brooke said.

Carly picked up the snap, saw the shadow of the French windows on the four sheets of music stuck to the wall behind Talia. It must have been before she lined the plasterboard with her pages. 'I found her name written in dust under the manhole cover in the ensuite,' Carly said.

'Oh yeah?'

'Her name and a date. It felt like a message, only I didn't know what it meant.'

'What was the date?'

'Fourteenth of November. Last summer.'

Brooke's eyes slid up and away. 'Oh. Only a month before the accident.'

'Any idea why she was up there?'

She shook her head. 'Why were you?'

'Just taking a look.'

'Maybe that's what Talia was doing. Did you write your name too?'

'No.' But maybe she should have. Maybe it meant something that Talia had. A record that she'd been there? 'Would you mind if I used your bathroom?'

'No, go ahead.'

'Actually, two birds, one stone: would you mind if I used your ensuite? I'm having problems with my shower screen, maybe you've got the same one.'

'Go for your life. Want to check the manhole while you're there?'

Carly laughed as she climbed the stairs, no intention of using the ensuite, thinking about what Talia had left in the apartment – holes in the wall, her name on the manhole cover and . . . the nightlight. Carly had found it in the half bath, she'd assumed whoever had packed up Talia's apartment had decided she didn't need it. But why did she have it in the first place? For the same reason Carly was using it?

Carly pulled the torch from her pocket as she headed for the wardrobe, took a step inside and aimed the beam up. The vent was there, shrouded in darkness. Moving the glow around Brooke's shelves, she saw short and long hanging space, shoes and boots. Nothing Carly remembered seeing from above, but it looked different from this angle.

Over beef casserole, Carly considered telling Brooke about what she'd found, what she suspected, but she didn't know anything for sure – and why freak her out with stories of intruders in her ceiling and questions about Talia if Carly was wrong?

As Carly walked back to her apartment, a full, white moon hung above the atrium, flooding the huge, hollow centre of the warehouse in a ghostly glow. She stopped at the turn in the zigzag stairs and ran her gaze around the layers of apartments and corridors.

Who knew about the hidden spaces in between? About the vents that looked into people's lives?

The third floor was a little below her, Brooke's door closed now. Carly counted eight others in the row – she'd crawled across all of them today, peered into five, opening the hatches and inspecting their belongings. Over on the left lived the woman with the shoe collection. What size was she? Maybe Carly could borrow a pair. A smile flickered on her lips, then she remembered the man in her loft and her face dropped.

How did he do it without waking people?

Carly had woken. She'd called the police. Anne Long had told her that other residents had reported intruders, sometimes more than once. Had he stopped visiting them or got better at not waking them? He'd called Carly his best. Maybe he didn't get so close to the others. Or maybe she was a light sleeper. Or . . .

None of it made sense. Her theories screamed of psychosis and invented worlds with bad men in secret tunnels. There were special wards for people with those kinds of fantasies. And yet . . . she angled her eyes to where she'd emerged from the equipment room. The tunnels existed and bad things had happened. To her. Maybe to Brooke and Talia. How many others?

Two weeks ago, she'd stood in the foyer with her neighbours on a bad day. Elizabeth had died getting out of her bed. The official version was that she'd tripped and hit her head, perhaps a little unsteady from new painkillers. Elizabeth had a loft but she'd slept in a bedroom off the living space. Did it matter? If you could get into a loft, you had access to a whole apartment. Maybe Elizabeth *was* groggy – and maybe she was scared. Scared and groggy. Scrambling out of bed, terrified of what was in the room with her.

Carly ran her eyes around the corridors until she found Elizabeth's door on the first floor. She'd lived in the centre of the north wall. There was a pre-fab ventilation chute that ran along that wall. With vents that opened into the apartments.

And now Carly needed to see it for herself.

44

———

It was almost 10 pm but it didn't matter – it was always night in the ceiling. The only thing that mattered was that it wasn't close to three thirty. That was when he came. And Carly didn't want to be in the tunnels if he was roaming around tonight.

She ran the rope through the carabiner and belay device, dropped her legs into the void and found the ladder with her feet. It had been cold outside when she returned from the hospital and the wind had picked up since then, but the ventilation shaft felt the same as before: mild temperature, the updraught a whisper across her face. The difference was that a hot, pressing need to know was overriding her fear as she made the long climb down to the pre-fab chute above the first floor.

Getting to it from the ladder was the first problem. The chute was on the wall opposite and there were hand- and footholds for maintenance workers to make their way around, but it involved a big sideways step over a long drop. It reminded her that the place was designed for people using regulation safety gear who worked with a buddy in case of accidents.

Don't think too hard about it, she told herself.

Her arm was at full stretch before she felt the cool metal of the handhold in her palm. She stuck out a shoe, found the step, hung for a second, spread across the corner like an insect. *Don't think about it.* She pushed off her back foot too hard and slammed the bricks, hitting a knee, roughing up her cheek, the smell of dust and cement filling her nose.

'Okay, breathe. You made it.'

The next two along the straight wall were easy. At the mouth of the hole she ducked her head to shine the light into the chute. It was an endless, square metal tube. Like something from a movie, space stations or spies, *Aliens* versus *Mission Impossible*. The kind of thing you watched with a hand over your face thinking, *No way would I get in that.*

Well, she was here now.

Climbing in was easier than it looked and sitting at the lip, the back of her head pressed to the roof, she unhooked the rope, tied it to the rung outside, turned onto her hands and knees and crawled.

The apartments along here were two- and three-bedrooms, and Carly had no idea how they were configured or how many vents to count before she got to Elizabeth's wardrobe. It was a minute of slow progress before she reached the first one.

Nate was wrong, the vent wasn't the same as the others and it didn't look into the apartment below. It was in the top of the pre-fab chute, opening into the ceiling cavity above – and it was just a large, rectangular hole covered in a grating of a wide-weave wire. Sticky with grime, the cover was riveted to the metal chute and didn't budge when Carly pushed.

'Maybe I'm the only idiot to do this.'

She crawled past three more vents, inspecting each, telling herself to keep going, less and less convinced she should. The next one changed her mind. When she slipped her fingers through the grating, the cover lifted straight up, separating from the chute.

Carly sat up, her head and shoulders rising through the hole into the space above. Shining the torch around, she saw another tunnel with beam walls and insulation padding. There was brickwork, too, where the big beams butted the north wall. Ahead of her, she could see a hole in the insulation where it had been cut around a vent.

Climbing carefully from the chute, Carly lunged her way over. It was rectangular-grid variety and dropped down with a *snick*. The doors of the wardrobe below were closed, the shelves were empty. Elizabeth had had neighbours on both sides, a couple of nieces had packed up her clothes and personal belongings last week. Which meant she was looking into Elizabeth's apartment. And Elizabeth had died stumbling from her bed.

He'd been here too.

Realisation made Carly reel back from the vent with such force she toppled onto the insulation pad, catching her thigh on a cross-timber, ripping a hole in her leggings.

'You fucking arsehole.'

Anger made her voice loud, possibly loud enough to carry into the apartments below. She didn't care. She wanted to storm about, stamp her feet, throw something. She had to settle for kicking the timber wall.

She should go, she told herself. Take photos, get back to Nate's, write it all down, make a record of where she'd been and what she'd found. Lock herself in before it got too late, in case the bastard from her loft decided to climb into the ceiling tonight.

But she just sat on the timber beside the vent above Elizabeth's wardrobe. The apartment was empty, Elizabeth's memories were gone, the woman Carly had known for only a few weeks was ash in a jar somewhere – it didn't make sense for Carly to feel close to her here but she did. And she dropped her head in her hands and let the tears roll through the dust on her cheeks. For the friend she'd lost, for the thought of what might have happened the night she died. For the weight of what Carly knew now and the absence of anyone to tell.

Life is a long time, Elizabeth had told Carly.

Long enough to move on again? Because Carly couldn't stay in the warehouse. Not now. Not when the police thought she was making it up. She could board up her vent, warn Brooke and Christina, maybe knock on doors and try to explain about the man in the ceiling to the other residents she thought were vulnerable. But she couldn't stay.

You need to dream bigger if you're going to get there. Elizabeth had meant Paris, but Carly's dream had been here. In this warehouse, with these people, friends it had taken her a long time to find.

'And now this is screwed up too.'

It wasn't Carly's fault this time but that was no consolation. Carly knew what was going on, that made it her responsibility.

She tipped her head against the timber at her back, rubbed her leg where the leggings had ripped. Go home, she told herself. Work it out there. Maybe he'd turn up and she could restrain him, knock him out, call the police and prove he existed.

'They'd probably arrest me for assault.'

As she pushed to a crouch on the cross-timber, her heel slipped from the edge, something sharp scraping a heel.

'Ow.'

Reaching down to the flap of skin that had torn, she noticed blood was already between her fingers. She angled the torch on her forehead, saw more blood on her palm, checked the hole in her leggings and uncovered a scratch on her thigh that was oozing crimson. Great, one nail sticking out and she'd found it twice. Thinking about rust and tetanus shots, she slid her hand between the insulation and the cross-timber and found something that was definitely not a nail.

She couldn't angle her head torch to see what it was in the shadows, so she switched on the small torch and blinked at the glint of metal, understanding what she was looking at but not why it was there.

It was a latch. The kind you might see on the front of a toolbox. She must have caught her tights and heel on the clip. But . . . it was a *latch* in a ceiling.

She flipped it up and a tiny crack showed in the timber. She pushed a fingernail into it, but something further along was holding it down. Dragging the insulation away, she found a matching latch. Flicked it up and pulled.

Carly's jaw dropped. The entire top of the cross-timber lifted like a long, thin lid, tipping up and back on tiny hinges.

It was a box. Handcrafted and divided into sections. She stared at it for long seconds, trying to make sense of it. Lots of sections and the sections held . . . packs of cards? She picked one at random.

Not playing cards. They were square and white. She turned the pile over and a hot surge of adrenaline made her head spin and her vision darken. She squeezed her eyes, pulled in a breath, hoping her brain had misread what she'd seen.

It was a photo. Glossy, overexposed, weird angle. The kind of shot that was produced on the spot by a Polaroid camera. Of a bed, a person asleep under sheets, which were pulled and bunched under the chin. Carly knew the white hair and lined face. She was sitting above her apartment.

There were countless cards in the box and as Carly held the stack in her hand, something tight and agitated picked up inside her. In the first picture, Elizabeth's eyes were closed, her cheeks slack, her lips slightly parted. The next, Elizabeth on her back, the sheet gone, her nightgown pulled straight, hands arranged on her chest like she'd been laid out at a funeral home.

'You *bastard.*'

She pressed the wad of photos to her chest, not wanting to see, not wanting to make it real. But it was too late for that. Teeth tight, she worked her way through the pile, skimming the images, some sense that they needed to be seen, for someone to comprehend what had gone on.

Different nightgowns, different poses. Sheets, blankets, a doona at times. Taken over time, through changing seasons. Sometimes underwear and skin. Some poses almost respectful, others hideous and humiliating.

When she'd finished, she straightened the cards, wedged the pack into its place in the box, curled her fingers into fists and squeezed. Until her hands shook and her knuckles ached and her lungs burned from lack of oxygen. Elizabeth was eighty-three. She had a bad hip and couldn't see without glasses. Why her? What was the point?

'What is your *fucking* point?'

The crack of her anger bounced off the walls, trailing into the tunnel. It's echo reminded her that she was in a cavernous and secret place and that someone else, someone cruel, knew how to get there. She glanced around, alarm sparking as the shock of what she'd found filtered into reality. This was evidence, tangible proof that someone had been here. It was also a warning. This was not a lark, a bit of crawling around ceilings and screwing with the residents' heads. The man in Carly's loft had targeted specific apartments, taken photos over a long time, built storage, carried it in here and concealed it. Carly didn't know the first thing about criminal profiles but his seemed pretty goddamn obvious: well-planned, meticulous, patient, agile and bizarrely, exceedingly twisted.

And she did not want to meet him in a ceiling.

She started to lower the lid and changed her mind – those photos did not belong here. She pulled stacks of them and pushed them into the pockets of her jacket. She couldn't take them all, there were too many, but she zipped in as many as she could. Relatched the lid and headed for the ventilation chute. Moving fast this time, ignoring the bruises on her knees and the burn in the backs of her legs, not thinking about Elizabeth, staying focused on the job of getting back.

It wasn't until she hauled herself into the tunnel above her own floor that she started to think about other vents. She stopped at the first one, felt around the timber. Then the next one. Then, crouched above her own, she noticed what was different. Around the first two vents there was a single piece of timber along each edge of the vent cover, forming a frame. Here, the border was doubled, two pieces of timber all the way around.

And there were latches tucked down the side of the thick padding of insulation.

Electricity buzzed in her veins. She took a breath and blew it out. Flipped open the box.

'You fucking bastard.'

About two-thirds of the tray held white cards: section after section, starting at the left. A filing system.

'You twisted, screwed up, tiny, worthless nothing of a man.'

She didn't want to look at herself. She wasn't leaving them here, though. Unzipping her jacket, she laid it on the insulation and stacked the bundles of photos face-down in its centre without looking at what was on them. Then she rolled it up, tied the sleeves together, *snicked* open the vent and dropped it into her wardrobe.

45

———

Carly took a large mouthful of red wine and stared at the balled up jacket on Nate's coffee table. She could smell him – on the soap from his shower and the long-sleeved T- shirt she'd found in his drawer. She wished he was here, wished someone would tell her what to do. Another swallow of wine and she pulled the jacket towards her.

She hadn't planned to look at the photos. As she'd stowed away the climbing gear, she'd thought about burning them in the sink. About packing a bag and leaving. Getting in her car and driving, finding an on-site caravan up the coast or a cheap hotel in Sydney, somewhere she could get distance to think. She'd thought about the police, too, but not for long. It was a long tale about dark spaces and a twisted man with treasure boxes hidden in ceilings – and it was past midnight. It wouldn't matter how calm and logical she was, a call like that would be another big, black strike against her. Calm and logical might even make it worse.

Now, as she unwrapped the stash, she could see the original stacks holding loosely together. She took another gulp of wine and began setting them out on the coffee table. Face down. She wanted to be organised before she fell apart.

Fourteen little piles lined up like a card game. She could tell not all of them were photos: some cards were slightly bigger and matt cardboard. When she was done, she drained her glass, refilled it and set it on the floor.

'Okay, time to do this.'

SHE STARTED ON THE LEFT. A pile of five photos. Carly steeled herself and turned it over. Frowned. The top one was a close-up and it wasn't demeaning or horrifying. It was a picture of a watch. Her watch. On someone else's arm.

She slipped it to the back, eyed the next one. An earring, sitting on the palm of a hand: the one from the markets that she'd lost and found. Then a mug with lipstick on the rim. Her green scarf neatly folded. And a single black sock on the pink of an insulation pad.

Carly glanced along the row of stacks. He'd scared her in bed and stolen stuff from her life to photograph? Was that it?

She picked up the next pile and got her answer. The first picture was a circular glow surrounded by darkness, Carly's bed at its centre. The covers were removed and her body was spread-eagled on the sheet. She was wearing pyjamas, thank god. She'd never woken naked, but it didn't mean . . . She flipped to the next photo. Face down and spread-eagled. Different pyjamas. Then a nightie hitched to her waist, dark thatch of pubic hair. Then a pyjama top unbuttoned, her breasts bared. Eight pictures, same angle, different nightwear, her body exposed in some, arms and legs straight and wide in each. The way she'd been when he was on top of her.

She stood up in a rush, paced away. Paced some more, hand over her mouth. She saw a tube of rolled paper on Nate's dining table – the building plans. She saw the wine on the floor, wanted to gulp it down, wasn't sure it would stay there.

'Oh, fuck.' She ran for the half bath and vomited in the toilet.

She boiled the kettle, searched Nate's kitchen, discovered a bottle of Scotch and added a slug to her tea. Thinking as she moved stiffly about. The circle of light was a flash from a camera. He'd taken her bed covers off, arranged her body, stood over her and snapped photos. It would have taken time, the flash would have been bright. Why hadn't she woken up?

The third stack was more photos. She skipped it and picked up the fourth, turning over cardboard squares.

Plain white except for the small, neat handwriting in impossibly straight rows. Carly squinted at the lettering. She couldn't read it all, a lot of the words seemed to be abbreviations. She understood what it was, though: dates, times, durations, activities, observations. The bastard had documented her like a goddamn science experiment.

Three weeks ago, he'd written:

02.50: 3 min intvl, vis. response nil, mus slack, 60–109, bpm & resp incr on full contact. Impr result.

Carly had brought her laptop with her and opened it now, googling the abbreviations. It didn't give her all the answers but she took guesses at what it meant – at 2.50 am, there was a three-minute interval (no mention of what for), her vision or visual response was nil, her muscles were slack, her pulse ranged between 60 and 109 beats per minute, and it and her respiration increased on full contact. According to the arsehole in her ceiling, it was an improved result.

She wondered if the three-minute 'interval' meant he'd arrived and waited three minutes to see if she'd wake up. The vision or visual reference was unclear. Possibly he checked her eyes, possibly he made a visual check of other responses. The rest, though, was appallingly obvious.

He could rearrange her body and clothes because she was slack and unresponsive. Her pulse and breathing had shot up when he was on top of her. And the result was better than earlier ones.

Carly rubbed at the hollow under her jaw again, remembering the thump of her pulse and the loud hiss of her breath. Maybe it was better she'd slept through the unbuttoning of her pyjamas, of her nightie being lifted and his hands on her.

Maybe if she'd woken, she could've kicked him in the face. Why the hell *hadn't* she?

She flipped through the rest of the stack – there were eight sets of records. One for every visit to her loft, she wondered?

She went back to the photos, found shots taken around her apartment. Close-ups of the inside of the pantry and fridge, her DVD collection, the contents of her bathroom cabinet, boxes of tampons under the basin, the tangle of knickers and bras in her drawers. Had he taken them as she lay drugged in bed? Or had he come back at other times? There was probably a name for it, voyeurism or something like it. Whatever it was, it made Carly glance warily at the windows and the neighbourhood beyond.

A gulp of Scotch-laced tea. Another stack of pictures. This lot made her burn. She supposed it was the comedy reel, the gotcha shots, the kind you take when you are fourteen at a slumber party and someone drops off to sleep. Not shaving cream hair and drawn-on moustaches but close. Carly, asleep with her finger up her nose, others with a hand on her crotch, scratching her arse, middle finger salute. Three photos in a row – see no evil, hear no evil, speak no evil.

'For fuck's sake. How old are you?' That thought made her pause.

The body on top of her had been strong and lean. He'd have to be agile to get in and out of the vents and through the pre-fab chute. A slim, fit older man could do it, but would he take arse-scratching photos? Would a 40- or 50-year-old who was organised and calculating enough to keep vent covers clean, plant hidden storage and detail pulse and respiration be juvenile enough to push her finger up her nose for a laugh? Because that's what it was. The arsehole was laughing at her. Collecting data, keeping files and having his own private joke.

Was that what he did to everyone he visited? How many other double rows of timber were up in the ceiling? How many ugly collections of photos were up there?

Another stack of cards got her more neat, straight writing, but this time there was a different collection of data. Dates, measurements of some kind, acronyms and abbreviations scattered across the card: mcg, FEN, PPF, MDL, INO, Sal d., Aya, THC.

Googling 'acronyms', she found a site that searched by category:

medical, military, science and technological. Carly doubted she'd need military terms but any of the others might help.

FEN stood for Family Education Network, fentanyl and Far East Network. She searched the medical term fentanyl and found: 'a potent, synthetic opioid analgesic with a rapid onset and short duration of action'. The simple description said 'A fast-acting anaesthetic.'

Carly pressed her hands to her chest as though the drug was surging through her now. Only she wasn't getting drowsy – her skin was itching and her heart was pounding, her tear ducts welled and her legs wanted to move. To escape. But it was too late for that.

'He *drugged* me? I was *drugged*?'

Carly searched the other acronyms. There were no answers for some, but what she found told her plenty. Sedatives, hypnotics, hallucinogens and psychoactive drugs. Various combinations with measurements in micrograms.

Head spinning, face burning, she stood, paced, tried to get it under control. She straightened chairs, wiped Nate's counters, checked the front door was locked. Remembered other mornings she'd stalked her apartment, unable to keep still.

She'd thought it was her anxiety, her baggage. You *seem more rational*, Nate had said hours after she'd threatened him with a knife. She told him she was scared, he said it seemed more than that. *You were hyper, Carly. Totally wired.* He'd asked what she'd eaten, had wondered aloud about an allergic reaction.

'I thought it was *me*,' she snapped at the empty room. She'd felt it all before. 'I thought it was my brand of craziness.'

At the laptop again, she searched the drugs, found a grab bag of side effects – confusion, anxiety, memory loss, erratic heart rate, weakness, muscle stiffness, dry mouth. It explained a lot: the pacing, the lethargy, her thirst, why she couldn't tell the police exactly what had happened. It made her think again about the three-minute interval and the visual/vision response. Had he waited three minutes after the drugs were given then checked her eyes? Had she been temporarily blinded? Was that why she couldn't see him or the nightlight? Or was it memory loss – maybe she had seen the flash and didn't remember. Maybe she was so out of it, the light didn't register. Maybe she'd been aware of it all and the images had been washed away on her bloodstream.

Not all of it, though. She remembered him on top of her, breathing on her face, whispering in her ear. She'd thought that was the beginning and the end, a man in her loft who fled when she woke. Now she wondered about the order of events and when the drugs had kicked in. Did he pose her body on the bed and take photos first or did he do that after he'd spread himself over her? She never saw him leave, the room was always empty when she stumbled for the stairs.

She rubbed her arm, thinking about injections – she'd never felt that kind of soreness. Wait, one of the acronyms, INO had stood for inhalation. Was she breathing the stuff in?

She thought about asthma inhalers and plastic tubes under her nose. And gas tanks and scuba divers and oxygen tents and . . .

'Fuck.' She got up, walked away from it. 'Enough. You've seen enough.'

She showered again, scrubbing at her skin, wondering about seeing a doctor for blood tests and the long-term effects of drug concoctions and the acronyms she hadn't been able to decipher. She thought, too, about the treasure box above Elizabeth's apartment.

Did he visit Elizabeth the night she died? If he'd given her sedatives and opiates, it wasn't just scaring an old woman. It was murder.

46

Carly didn't think she'd sleep and wasn't sure she wanted to, but sometime after three, cocooned in Nate's doona on the sofa, her eyelids wouldn't stay open.

It wasn't really slumber, though, more of a deep, physical silence as her brain continued to tick. It mulled over the time and labour involved in crafting a box that passed as a piece of timber. With compartments for storing information that would leave no electronic footprint. Repeating the process over and over. Climbing in and out of the walls of the warehouse, indulging a hobby for a long time.

Then, slipping back and forth between thoughts and dreams, Carly saw torchlight bouncing off walls and pictures of Elizabeth, and of herself, naked, smiling as a camera flashed.

She rehearsed conversations with police in which she handed over bundles of cards, explaining how she'd found them in her ceiling. In some versions, Dean Quentin or Anne Long would flick through the pictures of Carly spread out on the bed; others, they'd tell her she'd disturbed evidence and destroyed fingerprints. Every time, she wanted to snatch it all back, humiliated, shamed, doubted.

Brooke kept sliding into Carly's thoughts, standing at the top of her stairs, but it was Carly who fell.

Christina was there, too, trying to leave the supermarket with her packet of rolled oats, talking about nightmares and being muddle-headed.

And Talia, with her tight, dark curls and frayed jeans, stowing her cello in her three-door hatch and driving into a tree.

By 7 AM Carly had reached the harbour, her energy sparked by an angry, purposeful agitation. Her sprained ankle hurt but she didn't care. She was in bright sunlight, filling her lungs with fresh air, stretching the aches and pains in her muscles and joints from crawling through that dark, shadowy place.

She wasn't going to the police with the evidence she'd found. She would not sit with Dean Quentin or Anne Long or any other goddamn cop and watch them flick through those humiliating photos or explain how she'd found them. She didn't know what she was going to do yet, but that was not going to happen. It felt like the first decision made. It felt strong and determined. Perhaps it was the only thing to feel good about today.

Waves were pounding on the breakwater but she didn't have the patience to watch it. There was something at work inside her – a solution, maybe, or just a violent, throat-tearing scream. Whatever it was, it needed space and energy and she pushed on, retracing her steps.

She wanted to talk to a doctor. She wanted to know what her apartment would sell for. She wasn't going back into the ceiling. More decisions. Steps towards a conclusion.

'Not using our furniture today?' Reuben asked as he delivered her breakfast.

Carly was standing under a heater, her gazed fixed on a container ship being tugged towards open water. She'd ordered eggs and toast and strong coffee – something to sustain her for however the day turned out. 'I can't afford to get too settled,' she told him.

'Got a lot on?'

'A lot on my mind.'

'Good to get that sorted then.'

'Yes. It needs to be done today.'

Because it would end today. She had not come here to see friends hurt and killed, to be questioned and doubted, to wait for the next awful event. She would not live like that again. The only decision now was how to end it.

In the warehouse, Carly stepped off the lift on the third floor and knocked on Brooke's door.

'I wanted to say thanks for last night,' Carly told her.

'My pleasure. How did you sleep?'

'All night. How about you? How did you sleep?'

'Me? Fine.'

'Okay. Good.' Carly fiddled with the cuffs of her sweatshirt, wanting to warn her.

'You want to come in?' Brooke asked.

It wasn't only about Brooke, though. It was Elizabeth, maybe Talia, too. 'No.' Carly should be sure before she opened that wound. 'No, I've got to go.'

'Okay.' Brooke nodded, frowning a little. 'What's happening?'

'Nothing. A class.'

'Oh. You seem . . .' Brooke tipped her head side to side.

'What?'

'Like you're on a mission. I thought you might've had a presentation or a job interview or . . .' She shrugged. 'I was going to wish you luck.'

'We should wish each other luck. For the hell of it. We deserve it, right?'

'Yeah, why not. Good luck to us.'

Carly pulled her into a hug, felt Brooke's surprise at the tightness of the grip, saw the question in her eyes as Carly waved and walked away.

Heading down the corridor, she picked out the third door from the corner. The woman with the shoe collection. Carly had sat above her wardrobe and looked into her life. A man in black might have done more than that. She could knock, explain there was someone getting into her loft, drugging her and taking pictures. But she should know more before she passed on that shocking news.

Carly counted four doors on Christina's row before she knocked.

'I was wondering how you were getting on.' Christina was in slippers, a mug of tea in her hand when she opened her door.

'I thought I'd come up and show you.' Carly did a little jig, proving her ankle was recovered, waving her arms like it was a magic trick.

'Would you like to dance in here for a coffee?'

She'd like to board up all Christina's vents. 'I'd love to but I've got a class. It's just, I'm missing a book. I think I left it in your library the other day. Would you mind if I take a look?'

'Of course not. Come in.' Christina walked ahead down the hallway. 'I'm just spooning muffin mixture into a pan. Do you mind if I keep at it?'

It saved Carly from explaining what she wanted to do. 'Only if you promise to keep one for me.'

She didn't know if access to the ventilation shaft had been set into every loft room or just spaced evenly through the ceilings, but it didn't really matter. She skipped the library and found Christina's bedroom, felt a twinge of guilt about letting herself in. Reminded herself as she opened the wardrobe that she wasn't climbing through a vent. She shone the light up and found the rectangular hole in the ceiling. Bastard.

'Not there. I must've left it somewhere else,' Carly said as Christina was sliding the muffins into the oven. 'What flavour am I getting?'

'Lemon and coconut.'

'Yum. And I've been thinking,' Carly said as Christina walked her to the door. 'We should do something together the next time Bernard is away. See a movie, maybe.'

'That's very kind but you don't have to do that. You've got your own young friends to go out with.'

'No age limit on friends, Christina. We could have a bite to eat afterwards and discuss it. Brooke might like to join us. It could be our own movie club.'

'Well,' her face broke into a girly grin, 'yes, that might be nice. I do get a little out of sorts when Bernard is away.'

It wasn't her fault. 'Great, good. When is he away next?'

'Wednesday week.'

'I won't forget.' Carly was already over the threshold but she stepped back and wrapped Christina into a hug too. 'Thanks for the muffin. And for the bed the other night. And the books. Take care.'

She turned and left before Christina could ask what it was about, not sure herself. Not sure if she was saying sorry or goodbye. Maybe both.

Back at Nate's, she showered, changed and left again. There was a class at nine thirty – she'd missed two days but that wasn't why she was going. She needed to put some distance between her and what she knew, think about something else for a while, give her brain a chance to work its way to wherever it was going, without the warehouse and the ceiling and the evidence everywhere she looked.

And she needed to remind herself of what she had here – what she'd achieved and where it could go.

'THANK GOD YOU'RE BACK,' Dakota said as Carly slid into the chair beside her. 'That essay is due at the end of the week and I think I've written a thousand words of utter bullshit. I figured you'd tell me if it was.'

'Because I'm rude and patronising?'

'Because I'll buy you lunch if you read it and tell me what you think.'

Not today, she couldn't do it today. She didn't know if she'd be able to after today, either. 'Sure.'

Carly listened without taking anything in, drawing rectangles on her page, covering them with grids of tiny squares. She sat on a bench in the sun at the break with her eyes closed, face tipped to the light, soaking it in like she'd been starved of vitamin D.

'You got happy thoughts in there?' Dakota asked, arriving with cappuccinos.

'Not sure happy thoughts are what I need.'

'What do you need?'

A solution, she thought but said, 'Not sure. I took your advice, though.'

'Should I apologise?' Dakota pulled a face.

It made Carly smile. 'After I left your place yesterday, I decided to do something the old me would have done. Like you said,' she made quote marks in the air, '"Be that".'

'What did you do?'

Abseiled down a ventilation shaft. 'Something completely outrageous. And it felt good. Liberating. Exhilarating. Thanks for that.'

'Any time.'

'It's just . . .'

'Uh-oh.'

'It opened a door I didn't expect to find and now I don't know what to do.'

Dakota chewed her lip, maybe wanting the outrageous details but hearing Carly's evasion. 'What do you *want* to do?'

It was an easier question. Still, Carly lowered her eyes. 'I want to forget it. I'm good at that, I did it for years. But the old me is talking now. Just throwing her opinion into the mix and complicating things.'

'What is the old you saying?'

'That I opened the door so it's my job to close it.'

'What do you think?'

'That it's harder than I thought to *be that*.' Brave, assertive, happy.

'Well, I guess if it was easy, you would've *been that* before now.'

Carly lifted her gaze, settled it on Dakota's face. She was young and honest and frank. She reminded Carly of herself, before the night on the cliff. Maybe it was why Carly kept asking a twenty-year-old with a stud in her eyebrow and blue hair for advice. Carly had been brave, assertive and happy at her age, and she'd tried to erase that person. She'd thought it was what had sent her friends to their deaths, but now, looking at Dakota, she saw Debs' face again, the one

Carly had remembered yesterday as she hung from a rope. Brave, assertive, happy. The four of them had *been that*. It wasn't what had killed them, it's what had made them friends. And Carly had been too scared or too ashamed to *be that* without them.

'Thanks,' she said. 'And I'm pretty sure you don't need me to read your assignment. If it's bullshit, I'd be very surprised.'

Carly drew more rectangles and grids through the next class, listening to the activity in her head instead of the teacher. Whoever was getting into the ceiling had to be stopped. The police could do it but they didn't believe her. Turning up at the station with what she'd found last night won't change that. Photos of her spread-eagled on a bed wouldn't make the story any more believable, not after her last conversation with Dean Quentin, and she didn't want them added to her police file. So . . . she needed evidence. Better, more convincing evidence.

She needed to get back in the ceiling.

47

It's Nate. Where are you?

Carly checked the shadows in the garage before typing a quick reply. *Home.* That's all she wanted to explain – he wouldn't be happy about what she was planning and there was an urgency to it now. She wanted it done and over. She almost sent the text then changed her mind, figured something to soften it might make him worry less. *How's your face? Knee?*

His answer came as she waited for the lift. *I'm at home. You're not here. Where are you?*

Too late to stop him worrying. If he was in his apartment, he'd seen the contents of the treasure box lined up on his coffee table.

Be there in 5.

He was in his doorway on crutches, his face grim as Carly crossed the suspended walkway. The bandage around his head was gone but his face was still blotched with bruising and swelling. She was glad to see him out of bed but wished he'd stayed in hospital – she didn't want to discuss it, the photos or her next step. He said nothing until she was standing in front of him, then pulled her hard against him. 'Christ, Carly.'

The words were pushed out through clenched teeth. Carly

couldn't tell if it was anger or the broken jaw but the intensity of his embrace felt good. After long, scary hours alone with the evidence from the ceiling, it felt like a rescue, and she held fast for a moment – because it wasn't going to last for long.

'You look terrible,' she said when he'd let her go. 'I can't believe they discharged you.'

'They didn't. Where have you been?' He asked for the third time, anger in his voice muffled behind his closed jaw.

'To class. Why are you here?'

He shut the door and started down the hallway on his crutches.

Ignoring her? 'Nate.'

He stopped in the living room, spoke without looking at her. 'I was worried about you. I thought you might try to get back in the ceiling.' He turned hard eyes on her, pointed across the room. 'What the fuck is that?'

The files from the treasure box were still lined up like solitaire. 'How much have you seen?'

'Enough to know it's fucked up.' The unbruised parts of his face had paled, sweat shone on his forehead.

He should have stayed in hospital. She didn't have time to play nurse. 'Nate . . .' She reached for him.

He pulled his arm away, swaying a little. 'Where did it come from, Carly?' There was a guttural edge to his voice now. He was in pain, she could see that. Not just from his injuries. There was frustration and fear in it, too, and something that made his eyes shine with wetness.

She made an effort to soften her voice. 'You need to sit down.' He didn't move.

'The ceiling,' she said. 'I found it in ceiling. If you sit down, I'll tell you.'

She found his painkillers and got water, telling herself to explain it calmly – an argument would take longer. She made him swallow the drugs before she started, then told him about climbing into the metal chute.

He shook his head, an *Are you fucking kidding?*

'If you start with that, you'll exhaust yourself,' she snapped. 'Just listen.'

He sat back in his chair, hands gripping the armrest. When she got to the part about the wire cover that lifted off, a line appeared between his brows and deepened as she talked him through Elizabeth's vent and finding the latches and the treasure box.

'There were photos. I didn't look at them all, I couldn't. I just crammed what I could into my pockets.' Carly pointed at the jacket on the floor. 'They're still there. I still haven't looked. I found those instead.' She aimed her finger at the stacks on the coffee table.

'Where did you get them?'

'In another timber box, the same as the other one. Above *my* loft.'

His gaze ran across the line of cards. They were photos, she told herself. Nate had seen her naked, he'd touched her body, what did it matter if he saw them? Her vision shimmered anyway. She'd been drugged, manhandled, exploited, demoralised. She didn't want him seeing that.

'Carly . . .'

She should tell him about the drugs, but stood and stepped away from him to the windows.

'Carly?'

'It's has to be someone who lives here.'

Nate took a second to respond, maybe wanting to know more, finally following her train of thought. 'Because of access?'

She waved a hand at the coffee table. 'A lot of work has gone into this. In the ceiling and wherever the boxes were made. I called the police the first time only three days after I moved in. I've only been here two months and there is a handcrafted box with ordered files above my apartment. This system was already in place. It was refined and well rehearsed before I got here.'

She sat down again, using her hands to explain the rest. 'I counted five drop-down vents in the tunnel below mine. If we take that as an average for each floor, multiplied by the number of storeys in the warehouse, that's twenty-five wardrobes he has access to on the east wall alone. If we assume he's doing it on the west wall too, where the beams also run along the top of the lofts, that's fifty apartments. I don't know how many are occupied by women who live alone but if it we take a guess and say a quarter, that's twelve or thirteen women keeping him entertained.'

Carly pointed at her jacket, the photos still zipped inside. 'He visited Elizabeth, too. She lived on the north wall. You can only get there through a long, metal chute.' She paused, the words hanging in the air between them. The reasoning, now that she'd said it aloud, had firmed the anger and resolution inside her. 'He's been right through the building, Nate. He can do it without stepping out of the walls. He's taken a lot of photos. He's been doing this a long time.'

Nate's eyes stayed on Carly, a focal point while he thought. Then they dropped to the coffee table, then to Carly's jacket on the floor.

'A long-term resident,' he said. 'Probably someone who's been here from the start.'

'Which is why it's not a team. A team couldn't keep it hidden for that long. But one man . . .' She shrugged. 'It's someone agile, lean and fit. He molests his neighbours and walks in and out of the building, which means he's ordinary enough not to get noticed as the freak around the warehouse. He knows things about people and doesn't let on, so maybe he's the guy who avoids everyone. Or maybe he gets in our faces and enjoys the joke. Have you seen the notes?'

'What notes?'

Carly pulled a card from a stack. 'He writes up his visits like a science experiment. So he's intelligent, probably well educated. And this.' She picked up another and handed it to him. 'There are drugs listed, so maybe he has a medical or science background. Maybe access to drugs, but,' she shrugged. 'You can get anything over the internet. If he's been at it for years, he's probably got an account with a regular supplier.'

Nate said looked back and forth at the two cards, a frown deepening.

She sensed the questions building in him – the shorthand, the abbreviations, the things she'd had to google – and bypassed them. 'My bets are on Howard.'

The frown didn't move as Nate lifted his face and stared at her.

'There are others on my list,' she said. 'But Howard ticks all the boxes. He's been here since the beginning. He's the supervisor, he can go where he likes, he's never around when you want him, and he's good at playing dumb. Plus, he's got degrees in engineering and science, the right body shape and he'd have no problem crawling around the ceiling.'

Nate pulled his teeth across his bottom lip. 'Who else?'

'The guy on two who locks his pushbike to the stairs and never talks to anyone.' She was uncomfortable about pointing the finger at people she'd gotten to know – and at the same time nauseated at the thought it might be someone she smiled and waved at. 'Damien from the community gardens, who works in IT and is unusually friendly. Stuart, who's a little odd and works at the pharmacy. Dietrich, the German guy, who's writing a crime novel and looks like he'd have no problem climbing around a ceiling. And then the guy might keep a low profile and I've never even seen him anywhere but in my loft.'

Nate eyed the cards she'd pulled, the others on the coffee table, her jacket on the floor.

Carly glanced at the ceiling, anxious and impatient. 'Why not Howard?' she asked.

'He's got keys to most of the apartments,' Nate said. 'Why would he use vents to get in?'

'A challenge? His own private science experiment? Maybe it doesn't have to make sense. Nothing else about it does.'

Nate placed the two cards on the table in front of him, laid an index finger on each. 'Do you know what all this writing means?'

She jerked to her feet, snatched up her jacket.

'Is this what he did to you?'

'Not now.'

'You said there were drugs. He gave you drugs?'

It was the difference between them. Nate wanted to remember, Carly wanted to hide from it. She wrenched the evidence from Elizabeth's apartment from her pockets, started stacking it on the floor.

'He can't hurt you here, Carly.' It was an attempt at reassurance, but as he grappled with his crutches, something else took over. 'He won't do this again.' He picked up a card and held it in a fist. 'This . . .' He stopped, breathed hard. 'Tell me, what did he do to you?'

She sat back on her haunches and watched Nate struggling to his feet. How the hell was he going to stop it? 'He checked my pulse and breathing. My vision, the slackness of my muscles. He arranged my body on the bed and took pictures.' She flung a stack of notecards at Nate. 'They're the details of what he gave me. Sedatives and anaesthetics and fucking hallucinogens. Concoctions of them. All written down, nice and readable, which is really useful for understanding why I just laid there while climbed on top of me.'

'Carly, it's okay.'

'*Don't tell me what it is.*' She shouted it, took an angry stride towards him, the toe of her shoe scattering the pictures she'd stacked. 'I thought it was me, I thought I was the screw-up. And it was *him*. He *drugged* me. So I'd lie still for him. So he could take photos and sit in the ceiling and get off on it. So I wouldn't remember what he whispered in my ear or that his hot, rank tongue was on my face.' She scoured a hand across her cheek as though it was still wet with his salvia. 'Except I did remember. For whatever reason, his concoction didn't work like he wanted it to. And I moved. I scared him that last time. And now I've found his stash in my ceiling.' A hand pressed to her chest. '*I* know.' The other hand stretched towards Nate. 'We know.'

'We give this to the police.'

'No.'

'This is . . .'

'I'm *not* giving those pictures of me to the police. I won't have that on my file too.'

He watched her in silence. She glared back at him. He must have understood the body language and decided not to push it. 'What about those?' A nod at the scattered pictures on the floor.

Elizabeth humiliated. Drugged and exposed. Thank god she never knew.

'It'll get their attention,' Nate said.

Carly squatted beside them. It was evidence. Close-ups and wide-angles, white thighs and breasts, mouth open, dentures missing. Elizabeth wouldn't know who saw her now. Carly walked fingers across the photos, seeing only Elizabeth's essence this time: glittery rings, a pale blue shawl, her glasses folded on her side table. Carly picked up a picture, a pair of red slippers in shot. Elizabeth had been wearing them on one of the days Carly dropped in, hobbling up the hallway with her stick, proud and determined. 'No.'

'She's dead, Carly.'

'That's right. She can't make that decision for herself.' Carly picked up her jacket and turned for the hallway.

'What are you doing?'

Nothing had changed. 'I'm going back up there.'

48

Nate blocked her path. 'No.'

Carly held up the photo of Elizabeth that was still in her hand. 'It's not enough.'

'It's plenty. The cops see these photos of Elizabeth, they'll have to look.'

'The last cop I talked to asked if I'd got psychiatric help, the one before that thought I'd scratched my arms for attention. They see these and they'll want to know how I got them, what I was doing in the ceiling, why I was peering into people's wardrobes. They'll want to know where I keep my straitjacket.'

'I'll go with you, we'll explain together.'

'The crazy girl and the angry man. Yeah, that'll work. They'll question us both. We're neighbours, they'll probably think we're in it together. Or that I've roped you into my plea for attention. Or it's what got you beaten up. I don't know. But they won't send patrol cars and set up floodlights.'

'One look up there and they'll know.'

'Yeah, maybe. And how long will it take to get them here? It won't be this afternoon. It won't be tomorrow, either. They'll talk among themselves, ask us more questions, think it over, solve other crimes.

And in the meantime, Howard or whoever the hell it is will be up there again. Drugging our neighbours and taking photos. It might be Brooke next. Or he might discover I've emptied the treasure box above my loft and do more than drug me.'

Nate scrubbed a hand across his head. Carly could see that he saw her point – and he didn't like it.

'I'll just go to the third floor,' she said. 'I'll look for boxes, take photos and come back. Then we can go to the police. With all of it. Enough to convince them.'

'You shouldn't be up there on your own.'

'Who's going to come with me? Not you. You can't walk.'

That didn't come close to convincing him. It only made anger burn in his eyes. 'You're not going up there, Carly.' It was loud, an order, like he had the right.

'I need to do this, Nate.'

IT WAS LESS than a day since Carly had been here and she knew more this time. It made the darkness and dust seem sinister, tainted. It made her angry and committed. She stepped off the ladder into the tunnel above the third floor and shone her torch down its length, wariness tickling at the hairs on her neck.

Unhooking the rope, she started the long lunge-thrust to the other end. Her sprained ankle was a little less painful but the rest of her body was sore: legs, back and shoulders tight, blisters on her hands, tender spots on her knees. Progress was slow. She saw a double row of timbers around the vent above the shoe collector's apartment and felt success and repulsion – it was evidence for the police and it meant the woman below had been molested.

The latches were slightly different, maybe an earlier model, but the system was the same: hinged lid, divided compartments, cards and photos. Carly withdrew a picture, not happy about being a witness to someone else's humiliation but wanting to confirm it was what she expected.

It was. Ignoring the tangle of sheets, she focused on the face, recognising the woman – blonde hair, freckles, large bust. The first compartment of notecards detailed drugs and dosages, the next physical observations. Carly took photos of the box, the filing system, pictures and notes. Close-ups and wide shots, just like *him*, the flash filling the tunnel with bolts of white light. She pocketed samples, too – one photo, one each of the notecards – put the rest back the way she'd found it. Glanced briefly over her shoulder at the ventilation shaft before continuing on.

Her muscles had warmed up by the time she reached the next clean vent and the treasure box beside it. She checked a sample photo, her eyebrows sliding up with surprise. It was a man: forty-ish, beard, no one she knew. She pulled more, wondering if a woman lived there too. But it was just him, spread-eagled, exposed. Women weren't the only targets.

Carly stayed only long enough to take pictures and kept going, hustling now, urgency in her movements, fear a cold hand on her back.

At the third clean vent, she snapped the latches, lifted a photo and dread sent its oily wave through her. Brooke, eyes closed, exposed. There was no cast on her leg but it was there in others. He'd continued his visits when she was injured? Remembering Brooke's 'bad day' by the harbour and how much better she'd looked in the weeks that followed, Carly flipped through note cards, looking for dates. There – almost a month ago. Last words: *Injury impeding results. Subject suspended.*

'Subject?' she whispered. 'Brooke is not your fucking *subject*.'

She collected samples, took pictures, started back. She had plenty of evidence now. Three different people drugged and photographed, three treasure boxes, three vents. Plus Elizabeth's stash. And if Carly added her own, it would be part of a crime, not a black mark against her name.

The way back seemed so much further. Her body was a mass of pressure points: toes, glutes, inner thighs, lower back. Her shoulders and neck felt like they'd been crushed in a vice, the blisters stung. She kept overbalancing, tearing more skin as her knees and her hands slipped off cross-timbers onto the insulation. She'd counted four vents, only two to go, twenty metres give or take. Another slip and she paused, rubbing grazed skin, looking ahead. In the torch beam, it looked like a kilometre of shifting shadows. Beyond it was the tortuous upward stretch on the ladder. She needed to stop for a breather or it would take a lot longer.

Cautiously spreading her weight, she straightened her muscles across the rough padding. Closed her eyes and thought about Nate. He had been angry and silent when she left. It was her turn to understand what was inside another person. He was frightened she wouldn't answer when he called her name in the dark; he wanted to save her from drowning but she'd drown in her own self-reproach if she didn't do this. She needed to figure this out, collect the proof, stop what was happening to her friends, to the community she cared about, to *be that*, better, worthy . . .

Her eyes snapped open.

She'd heard a shush and the whisper of its echo. It seemed to come from all around her. Quiet, distant maybe, but loud when the only other sound was the beating of her heart.

She rolled to a crouch on the nearest cross-timber, head swinging one way then the other, bracing for a figure in the darkness. All she could see was the glow of her torch bouncing across the walls.

'Time to go,' she whispered and froze as a bright, white beam lit the tunnel. Soundless, weightless. It came from the shaft she'd climbed down, threw the shadow of her body to the insulation in a crisp, elongated silhouette. Eyes tightening in the glare of a high-voltage globe, she felt like an actor on a stage, a thief in a floodlight. And she was blinded to anything beyond it.

But someone was there. Someone had flicked the switch and was holding the beam, still and silent. Getting a full, clear image of Carly.

Him. It couldn't be anyone else.

He didn't move, the beam steady, the brilliance relentless, the silence stretching. She wondered if she should start the conversation. *Hey Howard, is that you?* Or *It's okay, I won't tell anyone.* The voice, when it finally came, turned her veins to ice. So low it was almost a murmur.

'You're a disappointment, Carly.'

A man's voice. She couldn't tell if it was Howard. Didn't pause to ponder it as she turned, hands, knees, feet scrabbling to get away. Crawling, lunging, wide crabbing steps. The jerking of torch beam made the tunnel sway, made her feel as though she was tumbling – and, she realised, illuminated her progress for him. She flicked it off, the way ahead now lit by the beam at her back.

Was he looking for her or on a regular outing? It could be either or both. He might have discovered her rope at the entrance to the tunnel or her treasure box emptied of its booty. And now he'd found her.

His light turned her shadow to a hunched figure moving ahead of her, like something from the underworld leading her to oblivion. She listened for him beyond the thumps of her lunges and the jolting gasp of her lungs and heard nothing. She remembered Howard carrying the ladder up to her loft yesterday not even breathing hard. Had he wondered what she was up to? Worried that she'd fought back on his last visit?

What did it matter? He was behind her, he'd seen her, he had a lot to protect up here. And there were some ugly ways in this ceiling to stop a person from exposing his secrets.

A vent ahead in the shifting gloom – like the one above Nate's bed, Carly saw as she got closer. She slowed, thinking about pressing her lips to the slats and calling for help, and as she crouched above it and drew breath the shadows disappeared. In the blink of an eye, the space around her turned to dense, solid, suffocating blackness.

The sudden blindness made her rear back from the vent, tumbling into the timber wall of the tunnel at her back. Her ears took over and the sounds in her head became loud and alarming. Her heart crashing, blood thumping, air hissing in her lungs. And some-where underneath it all she heard noises from behind.

He was moving across the timbers, and not with her clunking, faltering progress. It sounded easy, practised. He'd been doing it a long time, maybe he didn't need to see. Maybe he thought unfathomable blackness would slow her. She'd started two apartments ahead of him. If it was Howard, he was tall and strong. He could reach her in a minute, pick her up and throw her headfirst down a vent.

Feeling her way, eyes wide in the darkness, hands scraping and scrabbling along timbers, she found the next vent. She could push this one open, drop down feet first. It was five metres to the floor, she might break an ankle, smash a knee, but she could drag herself. And if no one was home? If he came down after her? She'd be trapped and he could kill her and leave without a trace. Nate would know how he did it, but what good was that if Carly was dead?

Panic roaring in her ears, she clawed forward, missing and overstepping, groping in the insulation, wondering if falling through the plasterboard might be the best option. Crashing through someone's ceiling, breaking a hip or her neck, maybe just killing herself and saving him the trouble.

She couldn't tell where he was. She'd lost count of the vents, no idea how many ahead or how far to the next corner and the deep void that was there. Would she sense it before she lunged straight in? She wanted to flick on her light. She wanted to know where he was. But she fumbled on, body scraping and bruising and burning.

She could hear breathing now. It sounded close, it sounded like it was all around her. She couldn't tell if it was an echo or he was on her heels. Only that it was steady and regular. That he was fit and agile.

Something froze her. She couldn't say what it was. The same internal radar or change in atmosphere or the angel on her shoulder that had stopped her from lurching into it yesterday. Whatever it was, she didn't question it when it shouted a warning in her head. Stretching a hand past the next timber, she felt the black, cool nothingness of the void. Somewhere out there was the ladder.

As she arranged herself on the lip of the tunnel, she wondered if the darkness made it better or worse. She couldn't see the hole that could suck her down or the rungs that would hold her to the wall.

She couldn't see him, either. He was there, though, lunging, breathing, coming after her.

Impulse made her want to go down – shorten the fall, find the door out. *Up, Carly, go up.* Safety was there: her own apartment and Nate. You've done this before, she told herself. Reach out and up, find the second rung, haul yourself up like a kid on the monkey bars.

Crouched on the last cross-timber, hip pressed to the wall of the tunnel, fear and darkness held her in place. Ninety per cent fatality from here. If she overbalanced, if she missed the rung, if her fingers slipped, she was dead. On the floor in a room no one ever checked.

'Hey, Carly. Having fun?'

49

———————

His voice was a whispered growl. It carried in the darkness, wrapping around her like a chill wind. It was close and distant, behind and below. She couldn't wait any longer. Out and up. Her fingertips found cold metal, her palms locked around it. Then she was blinded by dazzling, eye-crunching light.

Shock jerked her left hand from its hold. It was only for a fraction of a second, but her body had been moving across the abyss and her mind leapt into the free fall. Panic exploded in her muscles. Her knuckles slammed brick, a thumb snapped back, skin tore from her elbow. Then her arm was around the rung, her body jammed against the wall, heart slamming her ribs.

She turned her face to the light. It wasn't where she expected it, not right there on the edge beside her, but it was close, three or four quick lunges away. All she could see of him was a crouched torso and limbs below the glare of the beam. Lean, lithe, silent, like a jaguar ready to pounce.

It scared Carly more than the lethal drop, and before she'd thought about how to climb she was doing it, hoisting her weight up, reaching up for the next rung. She flicked on her head torch. He knew where she was, she may as well see where she was going. She was juddering with fear and exertion but she moved as though the upward breeze was pushing her. The tunnel she was aiming for was a dark rectangle above when the abyss below was filled with light.

'Move,' she ordered through gritted teeth. 'Move. *Move.*'

His feet made ringing sounds on the metal, tapping a faster beat than hers. The span of his light inched further ahead of her, as though it was a net being thrown over her, waiting for the right moment to pull her back down.

'Are your legs burning, Carly? Can you feel the lactic acid building?'

His voice rebounded around the walls. It didn't tell her how close he was, only that he was barely out of breath. She was gasping, mouth wide open, chest too tight to fill. Slowing, feeling like she was pushing up through water.

'Nearly there now,' he said.

It wasn't Howard's voice. She didn't know whose it was.

Hands on the top rung, her head above the mouth of the tunnel, she glanced down. The light was blinding. She could see hands on rungs in its glow. A dozen steps down and moving. *Do it, Carly. Do it now.*

A thrust sideways, hips crashing on the cross-timber. She threw a leg, got the knee into the tunnel and shoved forward onto the insulation. As she pushed away from the ladder with her other foot, a hand closed around the ankle. Hard, tight. He was wearing a glove. His fingers reached all the way around. It was her good ankle, she kicked it. He held fast, a shackle pulling at her leg so she couldn't thrash.

'Good girl,' he said. There was a smile in the voice. Patronising, superior.

'Fuck you.'

The body behind the glare rose higher, the lower half of his torso coming into view, arms and legs gathering to climb into the tunnel. Clothed in black, something tight like a wet suit. The pull on her ankle shifted as he moved. She wanted to shake her leg free – except he was on the ledge, it might knock him off and take her with him.

He kept hold of her ankle as he climbed in, pushing her backwards to the wall, arranging himself opposite, casual, one knee up, like an impromptu meeting on the floor. He tipped his head back then and she saw the face underneath the light.

'It's *you*.'

'And here we are,' Stuart said.

Stuart, university researcher, part-time pharmacist, strange needy guy who tried to impress. He'd undone Carly's pyjamas, touched her body, drugged her, taken photos. She wanted to be sick, wanted to lash at him with her nails. Did neither as she breathed hard and watched him.

'So you discovered my research,' he said.

He was wearing an all-in-one suit, fitted to thin and surprisingly well muscled body, a long zipper down the front. There were matching booties on his feet, excess at his long, craned neck that looked like a hood folded down. The man in black she saw in her loft.

'It's a pity,' he said. 'You were excellent.'

She swallowed, breathed, worked at focusing on that.

'Consistently good responses,' he said. 'Especially with the plant derivatives. I had high hopes for you as a long-term participant. You disappointed me in our last few sessions, though. I blamed myself initially. I thought I must have overestimated the effect of the benzo, but you didn't take it, did you?'

Carly's forehead tightened with a frown.

'Benzodiazepine. Your sleeping pill.' He watched her, a smile spreading his lips. 'No, you didn't take it. I have to ask, though. Discounting that anomaly, how did you find it?'

She couldn't keep her silence. 'Find what?'

'The experience.'

'You drugged and molested me.'

'I'm interested in subject response when it's available,' he went on. 'I don't know about you but I find that particular dream experience fucking mind-blowing.' He raised his eyebrows, a question of their shared experience.

He still held her ankle. She wanted to break his nose with her foot but his amused, casual tone filled her with fear. 'You hurt people,' she said quietly.

A nod, acceptance. 'There have been some losses. It's the nature of an experiment of this kind.'

Experiment? Losses? Carly sensed the void at her side, his hand tight on her skin, and wondered if she was his next loss. Pushing down her terror, trying to dredge up something she hoped would pass for a genial expression, she said, 'I hope you don't consider me a loss, just because I found out. I was frightened before, that's why I was fighting you. But I understand now.'

Blinking, nodding, his lips widening. She thought it was a good sign, until she heard the flat, hard edge to his voice. 'Nice try, Carly.'

'No, listen. I could help. I could give you my responses.'

He huffed, scorn and contempt. 'I've heard your responses when you're fucking your arsehole neighbour. Like a rutting zoo animal. Except you like it on top, don't you, Carly? Buck-naked and riding hard.'

Her face snapped away.

'Yeah, I've watched. I thought about taking photos but I prefer to arrange those scenes myself. How's your neighbour enjoying the hospital?'

She frowned back at him.

'He was proving a persistent visitor in your bed so I thought a chat in a quiet laneway might give me some time to correct your dosage.'

'It was you?' Nate hurt on her account?

'And a friend. I can't take all the credit, my hands weren't made for that kind of work. A wasted effort, I see now.'

The wrench on her ankle came without warning. Stuart dragged her across the insulation, close enough to twist a fist into the front of her top and craned his long neck until his face was in hers. Smiling, amused. 'Looks like it'll have to be an overdose.'

She shoved at his hands, pushed at his chest, aware of the black drop beyond her elbow. She raised her voice, hoping the sound carried to the apartments. '*No!*'

He slapped her face, hard. It knocked her to the insulation. It felt like he'd torn her cheek open. There was no smile when he spoke. 'Don't fight it, Carly. It won't hurt.' He tightened his hold on her jacket, pulling her upright.

'No, *no*.' She tugged away from him, saw the void and found herself back in his grasp.

'No one will believe I've killed myself.' It was a lie but she said it anyway, hoped Stuart hadn't seen her hospital record.

'People believe what they're told. Drivers have accidents. Old ladies mix up their medications.'

His face was so close she could feel his breath on her skin. It wasn't the first time but there was a light between them now. She could see the pale streaks in his brown irises and she wasn't drugged. 'Drivers. You mean Talia.' Had she found him too and he tried to get rid of her?

He dipped his head. 'It was a new blend. It obviously didn't agree with her.'

The anger she'd felt on other nights, that had been trapped within her, was hot on her skin and tightening her jaw. 'And Elizabeth?'

'I told you she wouldn't like the stronger medication.' He dropped away from her as though the dispute was over now and she'd go with him willingly.

She swung an arm out wide and slammed the side of his head with bunched knuckles. 'You fuck!' It rocked him sideways. She went with him, shoving with both hands, hitting him again, catching his chin hard. 'You fuck. You *fuck*.' He held a hand over his head like a shield. Carly rose to her knees and pressed forward. She didn't know how to punch, that sport had never reached her. There was no skill in the blows she aimed but they pounded throat and sharp bones. He laughed, like he had in her loft. She found his teeth with her fist and drew blood.

Then the air was heaved from her lungs. The knee he thrust into her gut lifted her, drove her away. A hand out, Carly caught a cross-timber – and felt the nothingness beyond on her fingertips. She scuttled backwards, stopped by the beam wall at her back.

Stuart's fingers closed around at her ankle again. Blood coated his lips, his teeth were bared in a grimacing smile. He didn't take his eyes off her as he got to his haunches, moving towards her, head pressed to the timber above. The hand on her leg travelled with him, inching upwards, forcing her knee wide and into the void. Carly hunkered hard against the beam.

'Have it your way then, Carly. Forget the overdose.' He glanced over the edge. 'Not as easy to explain, if it comes to that, but my work is safe here.' He fisted a hand in the front of her jacket.

Beneath it, Carly's heart thumped against her ribs. The edge of an abyss. She'd been here before. With friends, laughing and terrified. *Come on, it's fine.* She'd killed them and she'd wanted to die. She'd craved it for a long time but she'd only been broken – bones, heart, mind. She'd been on another ledge in the bedroom at her mother's house, pills in her hand, broken then too, not strong enough to fall one way or the other.

Here again, she thought. Grief and shame, like before. Elizabeth was dead and this man had exposed Carly – her damage, her fears, her body. She'd come here to this ledge, she'd made that choice, but what had happened wasn't her fault. And that made other things burn bright inside her.

Rage, loathing, retribution. And as Stuart lifted her from the wall, gathering his strength to lever her over, she felt them sharp like knives. Sharp like the memory that opened behind her eyes. The photo on her fridge was old but Carly was in that moment now, sweaty and exhausted and exhilarated. The person she once was, who'd tried to save her friends, who'd survived a freezing night on a cliff. Three faces smiling with her: young, sunburned, full of daring. Full of life. They'd taken risks, all of them, and Carly had been left to live with the consequences. She'd spent thirteen years wishing she could make things right.

Maybe that had changed her. Maybe it was enough to change the ending. Maybe all that mattered was that she knew.

She let her hands drop, pushed them into the insulation as

though it was the last sensation she would ever feel. Drew up a knee and slammed the sole of her shoe into Stuart's chest.

It caught him on the right side of his ribcage. Not hard enough to knock him down, only to push him off balance. He struck out a hand to catch himself, but it was beyond the lip of the tunnel, suspended over the void, and as he leaned, as the weight of his shoulders tipped towards it, he realised his mistake.

Carly saw the flash of alarm in his eyes. He flung himself towards her, grappling at her jacket, her legs. His feet came out from under him, a hip thwacked the ledge as it dropped out and over. There was a grunting from his throat, rasping as his nails scratched at her, at the timber. Fingertips white on its edge.

In the fleeting seconds it took, Carly saw how it could end: her blistered hand extending, the painful grip, the heaving and pulling, a life saved . . . Then she saw it again: hand and grip, a twist in the other direction and Carly feeling the weightlessness of the fall.

She could save a life and she could lose her own.

She could follow old friends into death or help new ones.

She could take a risk and live or die with consequences.

Making a decision, shifting closer to the edge, she took a breath, gathered her strength and slammed with her foot. Reaching into the ventilation shaft, snapping Stuart's head back. And, like a ledge breaking away, he was launched into the void. Arms and legs flung wide for the briefest moment before his body crumpled into the brickwork. A guttural, involuntary sound pushed from him, the light on his head coming away and illuminating the way before it hit the bottom and went out.

Carly watched the rest in the beam of her paler light, his black shape rebounding downwards like a crumpled cut-out of a person. Leaning out, peering over, she waited – for a noise, a flicker of light. Her eyes eventually finding the contours of a shape on the flat concrete floor below.

Ninety per cent fatality rate. He was dead. She'd killed him. She'd kicked him in the face and shoved him into an abyss. Risk, consequences. Lives lost and saved, and as she watched, she wondered what poisonous concoction would rise up and engulf her this time.

The trembling started in her hands. She pushed away from the edge, her breath spasming in her chest.

'Fuck.' She'd killed him. 'Oh fuck.'

The back of her hand stung from his gouging. The nail of her middle finger was torn away. There was skin missing from knuckles, an elbow. Blisters and splinters. A hot welt on her face from his slap. She pressed a palm to it and felt something reach through her.

He was going to kill her. An overdose or thrown to her death.

Stuart. No last name.

He'd killed Elizabeth and destroyed Talia's life and felt nothing. He'd beaten up Nate. He'd made Brooke fall down her stairs. He'd drugged his neighbours and photographed them for his own fucked-up experiment. And he was dead.

Him instead of Carly. Him instead of her friends.

And now it was over.

She turned away from the void, got to her bruised knees and crawled. For a long time, everything hurting, no idea how many vents she passed. Thinking about conversations with police, explanations and evidence, discussions with residents, meetings and counselling and media. Consequences.

Then she was above Nate's loft. The cover was off, the light was on. Carly looked down as Nate hobbled into view, her face bruised and swollen by the man she'd just killed.

'Carly.' It was barely more than a whisper, as though he was afraid she wouldn't answer.

'I'm okay.'

He made sure she didn't fall, just like he said he would. Helped her through the narrow hole, onto the stepladder and to the bed, where he held her as adrenaline and shock rattled through her.

Stuart was dead, she was safe. She wanted to feel relief or guilt or horror at what she'd done. But she didn't. She only saw Stuart's handiwork: the treasure boxes concealed in the ceiling, the rows of cards filed inside, the photos she'd seen and the hundreds still up there.

She imagined Christina's face once she knew, Brooke's depression, the woman with the shoes. She remembered the wake under the atrium to celebrate Elizabeth's life and the way this would change things.

Carly had stopped Stuart. She'd protected people – she didn't want to hurt them now.

Finally lifting her head from Nate's shoulder, she said, 'Do you remember that first night we had takeaway?' she asked Nate. 'At my place.'

'Yes.'

'You wanted to know what was happening. You said it didn't matter what it was, it didn't matter what I'd done. Do you remember that?'

'Yes.'

'Do you still feel that way?'

He watched her for a long moment as if he was trying to predict what his response would mean. 'Yes.'

She didn't know if she had the right to ask or if it was a burden that would damage him more, but she thought he would understand. 'If anyone asks, tell them I was here with you all day.'

50

'This is the last box,' Carly told Bernard as she set it on top of the two others on the trolley. 'It's only the last bits and pieces from the kitchen now, Christina and I can carry them.'

'I'll get this lot into the lift then.' He wheeled the load around and pointed it towards the hallway. 'Are you going to lock up now?'

'The place is empty and clean, no point prolonging it.' Still, Carly stood a moment in the living room, watching him trundle the long hallway to the front door, turning and running her eyes over the soaring ceiling, the exposed brick, the stainless steel and, finally, the wedge of harbour beyond the balcony that was bathed in afternoon sunshine. She'd miss this place.

'There are two muffins left over,' Christina said from the kitchen. 'I've packed them in plastic for later.'

'Thanks. And thank you for your help today.' Christina had baked and brewed in her own kitchen then turned up late in the morning with lunch and rubber gloves to feed and help with the last wipe-over of the apartment. It was a lot different to the last time Carly had moved, when she'd packed in stony silence and left behind more than she took.

'Happy to be useful.' Christina ripped off her gloves. 'That's the kitchen finished then. The only thing left is a walk-through with the broom on our way out.'

Carly pushed it ahead of her down the hall, only pausing for a brief glance back along its length before pulling the door closed, giving it a tug and shove to make sure the lock had engaged.

Bernard had held the lift for them and they squeezed in with the trolley. 'We'll miss having you just downstairs,' Christina said.

'You can visit anytime. Ring ahead and I can have dinner waiting,' Carly joked.

The doors opened on to the foyer, Carly leading the way through the geometrical shadows to Howard's apartment. It was Carly's now, at half the market rent for as long as she filled the job of building supervisor – she'd admitted to being low on maintenance skills but on first-name basis with a classroom of tradies. It wasn't about the cost saving, though; she wanted to make sure her neighbours were safe, and do it better than Howard had. She would be there for three years at least, while she completed the social science degree she'd started a dozen years ago. Maybe longer if she was still keen on doing her Master's after she'd worn the cap and gown.

When Howard left for the UK two weeks ago, Carly cleaned and painted his two-bedroom apartment, discovering his record keeping was as hopeless as his supervising. She'd already started a new database for residents, adding the tenant who was moving into her place and updating old records.

The first she'd refiled was the information on Stuart Mayberry, owner, south wall, second floor, whose death just over a month ago had shocked the warehouse. A cleaner replacing supplies in the storage room had noticed a funky smell, investigated, and found Stuart's body at the bottom of the ventilation shaft in the south-west corner of the building.

Police believed his body had been there for around three days. They'd found a rope tied to a ladder in another shaft and concluded he'd been climbing and fell. For almost everyone at the warehouse it seemed a bizarre thing to be doing, but it matched information from

Stuart's university colleagues in the school of Biomedical Sciences and Pharmacy, who said he was an experienced member of their caving team.

'The table's arrived,' Bernard called.

Carly left Christina unpacking crockery, reaching the hallway as Dietrich walked backwards through the front door, heaving one end of the dining table Carly had found with Dakota in a second-hand store. Now it was here, it looked huge. 'Wait till you see it, Christina,' she said. 'It's got dents and gouges and paint slops. It's fabulous.'

'Where do you want it?' Nate asked, managing the other end easily, his limp improving every day.

'Right here.' Carly stood between the kitchen counter and the wall, where it would fill the space and seat a dozen people with a few extra chairs.

Christina looked it over with a frown. 'Needs a bit of work.'

'Just a good scrub,' Carly said. 'The scars are its history. It looks like it deserves a good home, don't you think?'

'Chairs! Coming through!' They appeared ahead of Brooke, two stacked together and towering above her head. She'd lost five kilos now she was walking again. She was off the antidepressants and looked happy. She'd wielded a paint brush with Carly a couple of times during the last week and had developed a sudden interest in cycling since she'd started chatting with the guy who chained his bike to the stairs. Brooke set her load down and looked around at the stacked boxes and jumble of furniture. 'You sure you want to do dinner here tonight?'

'So long as no one minds a hint of disaster with their lasagne,' Carly grinned. 'It's already made and taking up room in Christina's fridge.' And it felt like something she had to do to mark another end and another beginning.

There'd been no official signing-off on Stuart's activities in the ceilings and no funeral to mark his passing. A cousin in Adelaide had made arrangements for the body to be transported across the country for burial. Carly hadn't signed the card that went around: she'd written her name in neat, clear handwriting at the top left hand side, like the start of a list. Maybe thinking it was to fit all the names, or maybe because no one seemed to really know him, the other residents followed suit and when it was finished there were five rows of names. Carly knew by then which ones he'd visited at night, knew also that he'd betrayed them all.

On the pretext of needing to tie up business with the apartment, Carly had called the cousin. She'd only had to ask a few questions before Phil Mayberry got talking about the relative he hadn't spoken to for three years, as though he felt responsible for providing some sort of explanation for Stuart's unusual death.

'I keep thinking about him up there in your ceiling,' Phil had told her. 'He was always a strange guy.'

Stuart was five when his high-achieving parents divorced and began a long custody battle for their only child. He saw his cousins once a year – the quiet, scrawny, nerdy kid in a big, boisterous family gathering. 'He used to have this calm smile all the time. He got smacked in the head with a tennis racket once and smiled like he didn't know what else to do.'

According to Phil, when arguments started, Stuart would stand back and watch as though he was keeping out of the firing range. 'He started half of them. We all knew he did but it sounded like we were picking on the shy kid if we accused him. He'd steal toys and hide them, pinch the cricket ball so the game couldn't be finished, push the little kids over and walk away. My sister nearly drowned once, she said Stuart had pulled her into the pool but he denied it and no one saw him.'

The last time Phil spoke to his cousin was at Stuart's mother's funeral. Stuart had talked about some ground breaking research he was working on, something about human trials and on the verge of multi-million dollar grants and making a valuable contribution to science.

'I couldn't get a handle on what it was all about,' Phil said. 'Couldn't tell if he was really smart or I was really stupid. Turns out he was only a research student and his own father couldn't get home from Europe for his funeral.'

Carly knew nothing about psychology but after hearing Phil's stories, she'd found terms likes 'antisocial behaviour', 'narcissism' and 'self-serving cognitive distortions' on the internet and figured there was probably an explanation there somewhere.

She'd suggested to Phil that the ropes and harnesses found in Stuart's apartment be donated to his caving team – the Polaroid camera that had been stowed in a backpack she'd smashed and thrown away. After meeting two of his friends in the storage room one afternoon, watching as they picked over the equipment, Carly had understood a little more about Stuart.

'It's good gear,' one of them told her.

'So you guys worked with Stuart?' she'd asked.

They told her they'd been pharmacology research students with him. The conversation got complicated with medical references but Carly got the gist. There were a number of long-term projects being run at the uni and an opportunity for students to shift between them, depending on funding levels. Two got her attention. The first was to do with developing new delivery methods for inhaled medicines – according to Stuart's friends, there were several devices that were proving promising that they told her they'd tested on themselves. The other was a comparative study on psychoactive properties in naturally occurring drugs. Carly remembered Stuart's words in the tunnel, telling her she'd had *consistently good responses, especially with the plant derivatives*. Her assumption was that he'd made use of the plant-based and manufactured drugs being tested in the research and done his own comparisons on his human lab rats in the warehouse.

Both of Stuart's friends were students and cavers, and Carly wondered if they knew what he'd been doing, or even if they'd been up in the ceiling with him. Stuart had told Carly he'd found *that particular dream experience fucking mind-blowing* and she'd speculated whether the three of them had trialled the drugs together – and whether one of them had broken Nate's jaw. But both were a little like Stuart, not even close to brawny or thug-like, and Stuart had access to powerful drugs. She figured it was more likely he'd made other friends, the kind that had a market for his concoctions and who knew how to use a metal rod on a man's head.

By three o'clock, Carly had convinced everyone to go home. Except Nate, who was sitting on the new dining table swinging his legs when she returned. 'Clean the table or reassemble the bed?' he asked.

'Am I insane?' she replied. 'Hosting a dinner party for eight the day I move house?'

'Yes.' He caught her with his feet, pulled her between his thighs and kissed her.

The police had conducted a door-to-door canvass of residents after Stuart was found, asking what they'd seen or heard in the days before his fall. Nate was in Carly's apartment when Constable Dean Quentin came by.

'I was here for the interviews, thought I'd come by your apartment myself,' Dean told her, filling her threshold again.

Carly didn't know if the body in the ventilation shaft had made him wonder about her story, but she invited him in like an old acquaintance, introduced him to Nate, his face still bruised and swollen, his knee surgery scheduled for the next day. They'd sat around her low table with coffee and some of Christina's muffins.

That was five days after she'd climbed out of the ceiling filthy and shaking and shocked. True to his word, Nate hadn't asked what had happened up there. Carly had told him, though, the next morning, after she'd scrubbed her skin raw and slept all night – a deep, black, uninterrupted slumber. And after they'd made love in the loft, naked and brazen, because Carly – the Carly she'd found in the darkness – refused to be shamed by the man who'd watched them. With no attempt to rewrite it or defend it, she told him everything. Then she'd told him how she wanted it to end.

Perhaps she had no right to decide. Perhaps the other victims had a right to cry and rail, make statements to police and talk about it, have nightmares and appointments with psychologists, be the subject of media scrutiny and targets for internet trolls and never feel safe in their home. But Stuart was dead, he couldn't answer for his sins . . .

and Carly knew what it was like to survive, how it felt to have her pain part of a collective memory, and how a person could lose their life without dying. And she thought Stuart's victims deserved to keep what he tried to take for himself – their privacy.

Yes, it was for Carly, too. She didn't want this on her record – the climbing around in the ceiling, the photos and drugs, the kick that had launched Stuart into the ventilation shaft. Charges, a trial, possibly a prison term. Nate didn't give her an answer until Dean Quentin put questions to him.

'I don't remember much from around then. I was in the hospital with this.' Nate pointed to the mass of bruising.

'What about on the Wednesday?' Dean asked.

'I came home that day. Discharged myself early.'

'So you were here?'

'Yeah. With Carly. She told me I was an idiot then lined up the DVDs and kept me company.' Nate looked at her, beside him on her sofa. 'You worked on an assignment for a while, too.'

'Yes, up at the table, sorting out those notecards.' She smiled, relieved for her friends, for every resident in the warehouse. And for the look in Nate's eyes that said he knew he hadn't let her drown.

When Carly walked Dean out, he'd paused at the door. 'I wanted to ask you a few more questions. On your own.'

She wondered then if he'd figured it out – the break-ins, no finger-prints, a man falling a long way down a ventilation shaft. 'Sure.'

'How are you now? Last time we spoke you weren't so good.'

The humiliating scene in the police station – she knew now the scratches were from Stuart and his drugs had still been in her bloodstream. Carly took a second to look embarrassed. 'Yeah, that day. I'm sorry about that. I took your advice and got myself in to see someone, a psychologist here in Newcastle, and some meds.' She hoped he didn't ask who. 'I'm feeling good and I'm all settled in and life is better now. Thanks for being nice when I was completely weird.'

He nodded, checking her over like he had on dark, scary nights. 'I'm glad you got it sorted. It's a better ending.'

'It is, you're right.'

Carly hadn't been able to bring herself to get back into the ceiling while Stuart's body was there, but a day after the police finished their interviews she climbed the ladder again. For two weeks, before and after classes, while Nate recovered from surgery, she trawled the entire ventilation system, checking every vent opening, removing every trace of Stuart. She'd found a file box above Christina's apartment and a second one above her own, with photos of a woman with tight, dark curls – Talia. Carly emptied the contents of every one she found, prised off the latches and glued down the lids. Then she'd stood on Nate's balcony and burned the photos and notecards in his barbecue.

At Carly's first official meeting as supervisor, the body corporate had approved her suggestion that, in the wake of Stuart's death, the vents be permanently secured down. Who would have guessed the apartments were open to anyone who decided to crawl around up there?

Dakota arrived for dinner first, bringing her new man, Bruno, and a huge bunch of flowers. 'I wasn't sure if these were what you wanted,' she told Carly as she handed them over. 'But they're beautiful, aren't they?'

A few weeks ago, when Carly told her about the supervisor's job, Dakota had laughed. 'Well, that wasn't on the list.' Her kohl-lined eyes widened at Carly's news that she was going back to uni when she'd finished the small business certificate. 'Wow, that's serious.'

'It's not a disease.'

'It's seriously cool, though. So what will you do when you've got a social science degree?'

'I'm still not sure.'

'Excellent. The Big Long List lives on.'

They were all there by seven fifteen. While Bernard poured drinks, Christina glanced warily at Dakota's thigh-high boots and the streaks that were now green, then patted at her own neat hair as Dakota exclaimed how lovely her natural silver was. Dietrich, who it turned out also spoke Italian, shared a foreign-tongued joke with Bruno. Brooke swapped physio stories with Nate.

He wasn't going back to the oil rig, and not because of his knee. It would be fine in time, according to his surgeon, but Nate didn't want to leave now. He'd told Carly, he wanted to spend time with her. It was the closest they'd got to putting a name to what was between them. And that was fine, Carly thought. She was more interested in watching the changes in him, a slow and gradual shedding of his grimness, as though he was making sure the disaster was over, that he was on solid ground and no one had been left behind.

'The lilies are gorgeous on the new table,' Christina said, touching a fingertip to a pink bloom. 'And Elizabeth's vase is the perfect shape for them, isn't it? Lovely her niece insisted you keep it. Lilies are what you bought for Elizabeth before . . . after . . . well, the ones she was so pleased about. She'd be tickled to see them here like this tonight, don't you think?'

'Yes, I think she would be,' Carly said, glad Christina had remembered.

As her guests filled the seats around her table, Carly delivered platters of food and topped up wine glasses, enjoying the sense that they were here for her, knowing what she'd done for them, and that the knowledge was all she needed. Working her way around the table, she wondered again why she'd woken when others hadn't and why Stuart had kept coming back to her loft after she'd reported the break-ins. Questions she'd never have answers for.

Talia, she guessed, had been trying to figure out what had been going on, but Carly wouldn't be asking her – if that memory was something else Talia had lost in the accident, she should be allowed to live without it.

Carly's memories of those long, shadowy tunnels had been transported into her dreams, new images added to her bedtime arsenal. And on nights when she tossed and turned or paced the apartment, she thought about all her years of restless, interrupted, uneasy sleep and whether they had made her respond differently to Stuart.

Or whether fate had just given her a chance to redeem herself.

Had she? Carly couldn't answer that. All she knew was that she'd lain on the edge of another cliff, thrown something poisonous into its depth and waited for remorse and reproach to come back and engulf her – and they hadn't. She'd waited six weeks and all she felt was firmer, stronger and less afraid.

Carly took her place at the head of the table and raised her voice. 'I'd like to make a toast to my second beginning here with some wise words from Elizabeth.' She lifted her glass, waited until the others had joined her. 'Life is a long time.'

Like Elizabeth, Carly had changed her life. She was a friend and a lover now, things she'd denied herself for a long time and which felt like gifts. She was a student again and an employee, although her role as supervisor felt more like a duty of care than a job, one that she was happy to have. Perhaps one she'd always wanted but had failed so badly to fulfil in Burden.

And she was a killer, she'd taken four lives. If she included the three babies that fate had stolen from her, there were seven souls on her account.

Carly understood now that she didn't kill Debs, Jenna and Adam, not in the decisive way she'd ended Stuart's life. The four of them had shared the decisions that took them over that ledge but Carly knew she was responsible for how it finished, as much for the fact that she was alive to bear the burden.

She tried not to lie to herself about Stuart. She killed him and she meant to do it. It helped that he'd intended to murder her, that he'd admitted his part in Elizabeth's death and Talia's accident, that her friends and neighbours were now safe. But she was guilty of taking a life – it didn't cause her a lot of uneasiness though.

She felt bad for that, mostly for what it said about her: that she could kill and walk away.

Would she do it again? She wanted to say no, that she'd seen enough of death, that survival was hard, that she would make better, worthier choices – but she wasn't going to lie about that either. The truth was she would if she had to. The difference now was that she knew she could do it and live with herself.

ACKNOWLEDGMENTS

Some books are more difficult to write than others and this one had more than its share of obstacles. I am massively grateful to Bev Cousins at Penguin Random House for wading through the mountain of words I first sent her, finding the story I was trying to tell and pulling it back on track when I thought it had already fallen off a cliff. Many thanks also to editor Kathryn Knight for a smooth and happy process after the months of problems, and to Virginia Grant for running her eyes over another one of my manuscripts.

Thank you to the rest of the Penguin Random House team for their work in getting the original edition onto bookshelves in Australia and into readers' hands.

Many thanks to my agent Clare Forster for the much appreciated support and advice – and the nice, occasional face-to-face chat when we manage to be in the same city.

Research is always fun, as much for the people whose brains I get to pick. Thanks to Sam Findley who helped out again on this one – always fun cops and murder over coffee. Thanks also to Darren Shepherd for talking me through the job of a patrol officer and letting me run a few of the early crazy ideas past him, some of which made it into the book. Also to Robyn and Jenny for the tour around the fabulous renovated warehouse that became the inspiration for *Darkest Place*.

To my writing friends – a huge thank you to Louise Reynolds for the Friday afternoon emails that started as a plotting experiment and ended up getting me through a rough patch. Big hug to Julia Nalbach for brainstorming ideas in random moments and seeing the best in a messy draft. My writing family – Chris, Isolde, Elizabeth, Melinda, Kandy, Carla, Simone and Carol. Also Fiona McArthur, Cathryn Hein and Monique McDonell for their Indie advice and support. And to the friends I didn't see while I was hunkered down finishing this book – thanks for being patient.

Many thanks to Anne Long for donating her name to *Darkest Place* and in doing so, raising money for the Hunter Westpac Rescue Helicopter Service.

And finally to my family, who had to put up with me during the process to write this story. In particular, to Mark for his engineering help to design the *Darkest Place* warehouse and once again making sure my fictional building won't fall down in a stiff breeze (any mistakes are mine). To Claire for being a sounding board on too many versions of this story and not once rolling her eyes. And to Paul, who has always supported my dream of being a writer and then got stuck with living with an author on deadline. Thanks for reminding me to get out of the office, encouraging me to think of other things, listening and nodding and sometimes just nodding, and for enduring this one without complaint. I couldn't do it without you.

ABOUT THE AUTHOR

Jaye Ford is the author of five chilling suspense novels, *Beyond Fear*, *Scared Yet?*, *Blood Secret*, *Already Dead* and *Darkest Place*. *Beyond Fear* won Best Debut and Reader's Choice at the 2012 Sisters in Crime Davitt Awards. Under the name Janette Paul, she is also the author of two bestselling romantic comedies, *Just Breathe* (ebook only) and *Amber and Alice*.

Jaye is a former news and sport journalist, was the first female presenter of a live national sport show in Australia. She also worked in public relations before turning to crime fiction. She in Newcastle, New South Wales, Australia.

BEYOND FEAR

From the award-winning author of five bestselling Australian psychological thrillers.

At seventeen, Jodie Cramer survived a terrifying assault at the hands of three strangers. Now thirty-five, she is a teacher and mother, her memories of that past horror are buried deep – so when she sets out for a weekend in the country with friends, all she has in mind are a few laughs and a break from routine.

Unknown to the four women, their secluded cabin was once the focus of a police investigation and, like Jodie, it nurtures a dark secret.

As her friends relax, the isolation reawakens Jodie's terrifying memories. When she finds evidence of trespassers, she is convinced they are in danger. But the other women don't believe her and suffering flashbacks that threaten to ruin the weekend for everyone, Jodie begins to doubt herself.

Until two men knock at their door ...

Winner of two Davitt Awards and described by Australia's Sisters in Crime as 'so deliciously scary, it's hard to believe this psychological thriller is a debut novel.'

SCARED YET?

When Livia Prescott rights off a terrifying assault in a deserted car park, the media hails her bravery. After a difficult year – watching her father fade away, her business struggle and her marriage fall apart – it feels good to strike back for once.

But as the police widen their search for her attacker, menacing notes start arriving – and brave is not what she feels any longer.

Someone has decided to rip her life apart, then kick her when she's down. But is it a stranger or someone much closer to home? In fact, is there anyone she can trust now?

When her family and friends are drawn into the stalker's focus – with horrifying consequences – the choice becomes simple. Fight back or lose the people she loves most ...

'The menace dogging Liv's every move creeps into your bones ... Scared Yet is a thriller that's all too terrifyingly believable.' *The Australian Women's Weekly*

BLOOD SECRET

Nothing ever happens in Haven Bay, which is why Rennie Carter – a woman who has been on the run for most of her life – stayed there longer than she should.

But the illusion of security is broken one night when Max Tully, the man she loves and the reason she stayed, vanishes without a trace.

Rennie, however, is the only person who believes Max is in danger. The police are looking in the wrong places, and Max's friends and his business partner keep hinting at another, darker side to him.

Rennie Carter, though, understands about double lives – after all, that's not even her real name ...

And she has a secret too – a big, relentless and violent one that she's terrified has found her again ... and the man she loves.